PIRATES, PRIVATEERS,
AND THE U.S. NAVY

PIRATES, PRIVATEERS,
AND THE U.S. NAVY

Dr. Mark Hopkins

ARPress
45 Dan Road Suite 5
Canton MA 02021
Hotline: 1(888) 821-0229
Fax: 1(508) 545-7580

Ordering Information:
Quantity sales. Special discounts are available on quantity purchases by corporations, associations, and others. For details, contact the publisher at the address above.

Printed in the United States of America.

ISBN-13:	Softcover	979-8-89356-504-1
	eBook	979-8-89356-506-5
	Hardcover	979-8-89356-505-8

Library of Congress Control Number: 2024902546

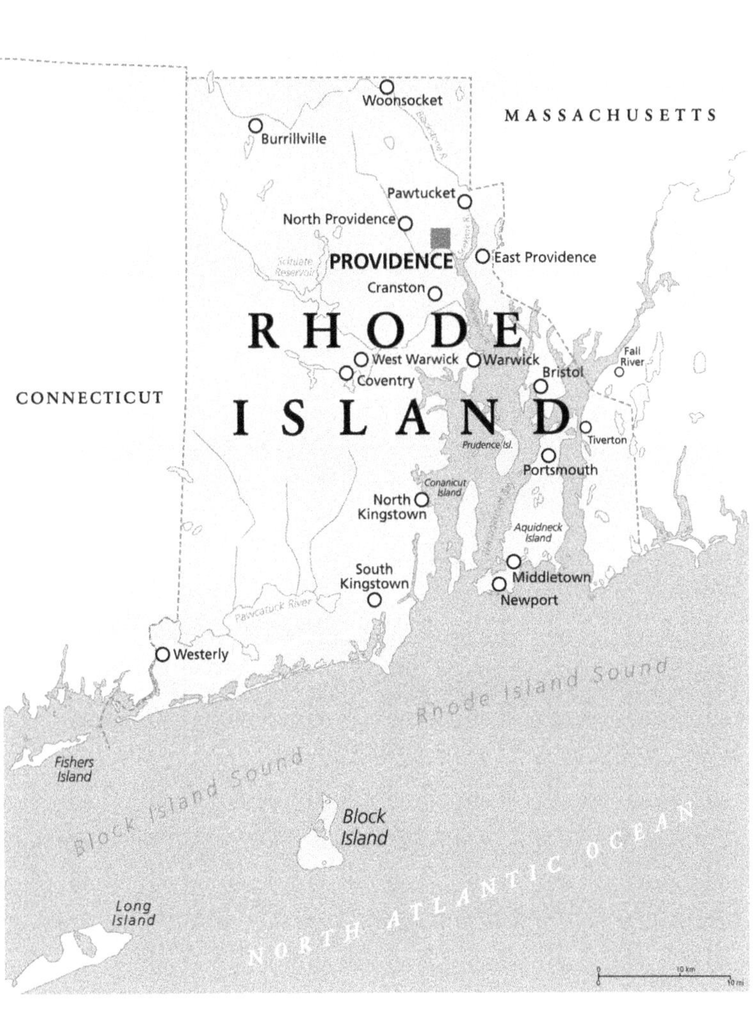

MASSACHUSETTS
CONNECTICUT
Woonsocket
Burrillville
Pawtucket
North Providence
Scituate Reservoir
PROVIDENCE
East Providence
Cranston
RHODE
West Warwick
Warwick
Coventry
Bristol
Fall River
ISLAND
Tiverton
Prudence Isl.
Portsmouth
North Kingstown
Conanicut Island
Aquidneck Island
South Kingstown
Middletown
Newport
Westerly
Pawcatuck River
Rhode Island Sound
Fishers Island
Block Island Sound
Block Island
Long Island
NORTH ATLANTIC OCEAN
10 km
10 mi

CONTENTS

Preface.. ix

Prolouge.. xi

John Paul Jones: Last Will and Testament......................... 2

Growing Conflict in the Colonies 5

The Gaspee Affair 12

Jim-Boy.. 24

The Boston Tea Party.. 36

Pirates and Privateers in Colonial History 51

Meeting of the Second Continental Congress..................... 58

The Navy Commitee Reports to Congress......................... 67

Capturing Powder and Supplies in Nassau........................ 79

Attack of the Glasgow 83

Repair and Recuperation 95

The Ranger... 105

Back Home in Providence 116

Back on the High Seas.. 125

The Flotilla... 134

John Paul Jones and the Ranger Ordered to Europe 142

Back in Providence for Preparations to Sail the Atlantic........ 149

Siling the Atlantic to Europe 162

Facing the British in their Home Waters......................... 171

Whitehaven and the Drake... 181

Benjamin Franklin and John Adams comes to Visit.......... 192

The Bonhomme Richard 203

Once More into the English Channel............................ 212

The British are Coming 221

The Trap... 230

Negotiation 238

New Challenges 244

Once More into the Breach 260

The Bonhomme Richard and the Serapis....................... 265

Epilogue... 275

About the Author... 295

PREFACE

The Hopkins family is similar to many others in that we have a military heritage. Most specifically, we have a family history with the Navy. As you will read in this book, the Hopkins family heritage goes back to the very beginning of the United States Navy and it stretches through ten generations, all the way to the 21st century. Names such as Stephen, Esek, and John Burroughs Hopkins were there at the beginning of the country and of the navy in the 1700s.

In the 1950s my brother and I attempted to join the Navy. They took him and didn't take me; a football injury disqualified me. My brother served for twenty years and traveled the world, including two stints in Viet Nam. I was envious throughout. The point is that the U.S. Navy is a part of the Hopkins heritage just as the Hopkins are a part of the history of the Navy. As you may have surmised by now, doing the research for this book was a labor of love for me.

A number of people have helped write this book. These include my wife, Ruth, always a first editor of my writing, who cautioned me often to slow down and take my time until I could feel the story coming alive. Editor and writing consultant Kathryn Smith cleaned up my writing style and played the role of muse. Each time I seemed to get bogged down, she had a reference to look up or a comment that created the needed motivation. Kathryn continually challenged me to be more descriptive and to paint pictures with words so the reader could not only see what was on the page but could also envision what was in my mind. Al Morin, a friend from Warrick, Rhode Island, became a consultant on sailing in the waters there. A retired business man, he has sailed many miles on the Narragansett and knows its many eccentricities.

In other books I have written, *Journey to Gettysburg, The Wounds of War, Talon's Ridge, Chicago's 9/11, The World as it was when Jesus Came, On the Road with Paul the Apostle* and *Facts & Opinions of the Issues of our Time, Books I,II, & III,* I have cautioned the reader that the characters, though they seem based on real people, are just figments of my imagination. That is not true with this book. The five characters you are introduced to in the early pages, John Brown, the three Hopkins men, and John Paul Jones, were real people from our history books. The incidents in the plot of the story are also taken directly from history, though the links between them are fictional, drawn from the depths of a fertile imagination.

As you read, I hope you are struck by two key elements in the book. First, how the events in history shape lives just as individuals often shape history. Second, relationships with others are what provide the supreme pleasure in life. Life doesn't revolve around money, accomplishments, or things. People we love and who love us make the world go around.

x

PROLOGUE

"Sail ho, sail ho," came the call from the crow's nest at the top of the tallest mast on the *U.S.S. Bonhomme Richard.* "Where about, where about?" came the reply from the sailing master on the bridge of the American ship. "Off the port side at about eleven o'clock," came the response.

The British ship *Serapis* was about ten miles away when it was sighted by the lookout. John Paul Jones, captain of the U.S. Navy ship took his spyglass and moved to the rail of the ship and peered into the distance. It was mid-afternoon on September 23, 1779. A soft wind was blowing from the southwest and the tide was coming in toward Flamborough Head on England's east coast. The two ships had sighted each other at almost the same time and both changed course to move closer to assess the relative fire power of the other. With the light wind, it would take the two ships almost four hours to meet face-to-face there at the edge of the North Sea.

Looking through his telescope behind the British ship, Jones saw a convoy of more than seventy merchant ships in the distance that the British warship was protecting. He could only speculate about the cargos they were carrying, but imagined ship-building materials, commodities such as tea and coffee, and textiles that had made Scandinavian countries famous. *Serapis* approached Jones's ship with confidence. After all, it was a man-of-war class ship built for battle: bigger, stronger, and faster than the *Bonhomme Richard*, which was a converted merchant ship, re-fitted by the French for the Continental Navy barely a year ago.

Three years into the war for independence, no Continental Navy ship had ever captured a British man-of-war. In fact, the Navy Committee of Congress had directed captains of their fledgling navy to stay away from direct confrontation with these fearsome British ships. John Paul Jones was not one to worry about orders from his land-based leadership. They did not know of the challenges faced day-to-day by the ships of the navy, nor of their capability. Jones saw an opportunity to make history and ordered his men to prepare for battle.

By late afternoon, about an hour before the two ships would come together, the upper deck of the *Bonhomme Richard* was cleared for action: everything moveable was stowed in the hold. Anything loose enough to fly around when a cannon ball exploded was taken below to reduce the possibility of injury to the men who would be on the deck manning the sails and the rudder. Sand was sprinkled on the decks to keep them from becoming slick with blood. On the lower decks, below the cannons, carpenters who also served as surgeons put out containers to hold amputated arms and legs should such become necessary.

Marines who were along for the fight when the ships were joined and the engagement became hand-to-hand were below decks until called into action. They were clustered at the gangways leading to the upper deck to be ready to join the fight, but also to prevent sailors who were needed on deck to handle the sails and rudder from disappearing to the safety of the lower decks.

As *Serapis* approached, a second ship that had previously been hidden from sight emerged from the other side of the larger ship. Jones immediately recognized it as a sloop-of-war. The *Serapis* was a heavy frigate, of the size that usually carried sixty or more cannons. The smaller sloop might carry sixteen cannons. Yet Jones was not alone either. The *Bonhomme Richard* was the leader of a small fleet of four ships and it carried forty cannons. The others were the *Alliance*, with thirty-six cannons; the *Pallas*, with thirty-two cannons; and the *Vengeance*, with just twelve. Compared to the two British ships, Captain Jones knew his ships had more fire power. The four American ships could encircle the larger British ship and hammer away at her from all sides, or they could run along in line of battle, discharging broadside after broadside before the enemy could reload.

Jones could envision history in the making. It was as if he had been sailing the oceans for the past decade just for this moment in time. He climbed to the fantail of his ship and looked back at the three ships that were following. Then he turned his full attention to the *Serapis* which was coming ever closer.

He ordered his helmsman to bring his ship about so that he was headed directly toward the bow of the British ship where the only gun was a small swivel single shot. He wanted to avoid a broadside from the larger frigate. They moved ever closer to conflict, ever closer to victory or death, ever closer to history.

So began one of the greatest sea battles in history. It was fought four years into the Revolutionary War off the east coast of England at the edge of the North Sea. Jones's orders, given him by the Commodore of the Continental Navy, Esek Hopkins, four years earlier were to sail British waters and disrupt British shipping. He had proven very adept at doing just that. He had taken more than forty prizes with cargos of much value into French ports and had become something of a local hero to the French. To the colonists back home who read of his exploits in the weekly newspapers of *Providence, Boston,* New York, Philadelphia and Charleston, he was becoming a legend.

John Paul Jones, born in Scotland in 1747, was just thirty-two years of age on the day of this great battle. He had come to the Colonies during his teenage years and served on first one ship and then another. Then, fate put him in charge of a ship when he was only twenty-one, when the captain and first mate were killed. He succeeded in bringing his damaged ship into harbor in *Providence* and a grateful owner, local ship builder John Brown, provided him employment and ships for much of the next decade until the Continental Navy, forerunner of the U.S. Navy, was formed in 1775.

It is hard not to sail directly into the great sea battles of the first American Navy, and there were many, but there is a story to tell before we reach those heroic chapters in American history. In fact, the primary problem of the fledging United States as it entered conflict with Great Britain was not the British Army that had been on the ground in the Colonies for decades but how to deal with the overwhelming might of the British Navy. That they succeeded is a tribute to the leadership of the Navy Committee of the Continental Congress, led by Stephen Hopkins of Rhode Island.

Success could also be attributed to the heroic captains of the ships that constantly harassed British shipping and the Royal Navy from 1775 right through to the end of the war and independence. Those ships were partially the creation of the Continental Congress, but the majority of them were privately built, owned and operated by businesses and private citizens. They called their seamen "privateers." Those from other countries who felt their sting on the high seas called them "pirates."

The story that follows tells some of that history, but not all, not by any stretch of the imagination. Following the exploits of the fledgling navy should give you an understanding of the enormity of the task taken on by the seamen of this newly proclaimed country in its war for independence. It also speaks to the ability of leadership within congress to create both a naval force and a plan capable of meeting the almost impossible challenge they faced from the British Navy on the high seas.

THE PROVIDENCE GAZETTE

PROVIDENCE, Rhode Island, May 1, 1772---The Providence Gazette has promised each month to make note of the fact that the complaints sent to Parliament and King George about the death of seven of our citizens at the hands of British troops in Boston have gone unanswered for yet another month. The date of the Boston Massacre was March 5th, 1770 and there is still no response twenty-four months later.

Now, the British Parliament has created yet another addition to the Navigation Acts. It isn't enough that they have restricted our trade with other nations of Europe, including our most important trading partners, France and Spain. Now they are beginning to restrict what we can and cannot trade with Great Britain itself.

Further, they have now decreed that all trade will be taxed, both coming into the Colonies and going out. To enforce their new taxes, a gun boat has been placed at the mouth of each of the major harbors with orders to board each ship as it comes and goes.

If we didn't know better, we would think war had been declared on us by Great Britain.

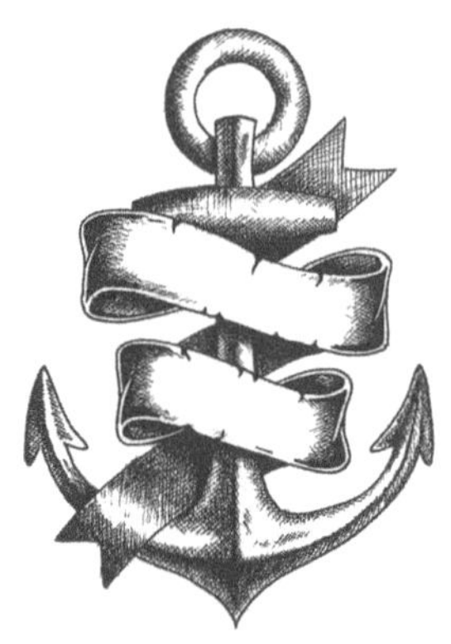

CHAPTER 1

JOHN PAUL JONES: LAST WILL AND TESTAMENT

JUNE, 1792

This is my last will and testament, written by my own hand. I am back in Paris after seven years in Russia. I am suffering with a fever from which the doctors tell me I may not recover. They have suggested that while I have enough strength I should write this last official document. Here are thoughts and feelings I feel inclined to share.

John Paul Jones

I have had enough adventure for at least three lifetimes. Most came because I was a part of the Continental Navy during the war for independence from Great Britain. From the *Boston* Tea Party to the great battle with the British man-of-war, Serapis, and beyond, I was involved in that great war from beginning to end.

I have had three great loves in my life. Two were my wonderful wives, Keziah and Aimee, who gave me five children to love. The third was the love affair I have had with the sea since I ventured onto the deck of the British ship *Friendship* when I was only thirteen years of age. My father apprenticed me to the captain of that ship and I continued to sail on one ship or another for the next thirty-five years.

My father was a gardener on the estate of Arbigland, near Kirkbean, in the Stewarty of Kirkcudbright in Scotland. I was the second child. I had an older brother, William, and two younger sisters, Janet and Mary Ann. After I left to join the *Friendship*, we were never together again. From time to time, word came to me of my family. Today, thirty-five years later, my parents are gone, as is my brother, William, who had migrated to Virginia in the Colonies. Only my sisters remain. With the exception of three bequests, it is to them that I will all my worldly goods in hopes that their lives will be made easier in their declining years.

The three bequests are for Aimee's daughters, Elizabeth and Mary, and their older brother Jim Shelton. The girls I learned to love just like Daniel and Moses. They went back to *Providence* to live with their aunt when Aimee died. They are to have twenty-five hundred English pounds each to use for whatever purpose they decide. Jim was with me from about age twelve until I the war ended. He grew into a fine young man and was like a son to me. He is now back in *Providence* as captain of one of John Brown's ships. He is to have five thousand English pounds.

I have known several great friendships, one that lasted for most of my adult life. Most of these friendships came from my time on shipboard. The first and most important was with John Burroughs Hopkins. He came from a family of great men, including a governor of Rhode Island and the Commodore of the U.S. Navy. John Burroughs was the first mate on the *Katy*, a ship owned by *Providence* ship builder, John Brown. I joined the *Katy* as a lieutenant when I was twenty-five. John Burroughs took me in and became the brother I coveted for much of my life. We sailed together then and, later, in France. He was always there for me in every way. Every day we have been apart, I have missed him.

During my formative years I had two great benefactors, John Brown and Stephen Hopkins. John Brown was the owner and operator of the shipyard in *Providence.* He took me on when I was seventeen and kept a deck under my feet for a decade until the Continental Navy was formed in 1776. Governor Stephen Hopkins was Chairman of the Navy Committee of the Continental Congress and gave me my first commission. Later, he promoted me to captain and gave me command of the *Ranger.*

It would be well to chronicle many of the great battles we fought on the high seas during that great war, but I will leave that to those who write history. I can testify that I never shied away from a battle nor was I ever injured. I remember writing Commodore Esek Hopkins when I was given command of the *Ranger*. He had promised that it would be a sleek, fast, schooner class ship that would have great advantages in ship-to-ship combat. I wrote him back, thanking him, and stated that, "I wish to have no connection with any ship that does not sail fast: for I intend to go in harm's way." He must have smiled at my audacity. The *Ranger* served us well, though not before we had to refit her in John Brown's shipyard in *Providence*. She never really looked like a fighting ship, but that proved to be to our advantage as we pursued British merchant ships both along the Atlantic coast of the Colonies and, later, in British waters.

It pains me to talk about my wives and children. The first great love of my life was Keziah. She gave me two wonderful children, Daniel and Moses. After the birth of Moses, she was never healthy again though she tried valiantly to take care of the boys and do the things necessary for a family whose husband was gone from home much of the time sailing the oceans. She died shortly after the beginning of the great war. The beautiful Aimee entered my life shortly after Keziah passed away. She became my second wife, bringing young Jim, who became my cabin boy, and her two young daughters into my life. Aimee cared for our children, traveled to France with me and then to Russia. I lost her and both boys to the great plague in Russia in 1790. Life was never the same after that.

I understand that someone is standing by to write the story of my life and my involvement in the American revolution. To whatever extent possible, I shall try to share with him the experiences and the excitement of the past thirty-five years. Surely no one could have had a more exciting life. With respect, John Paul Jones

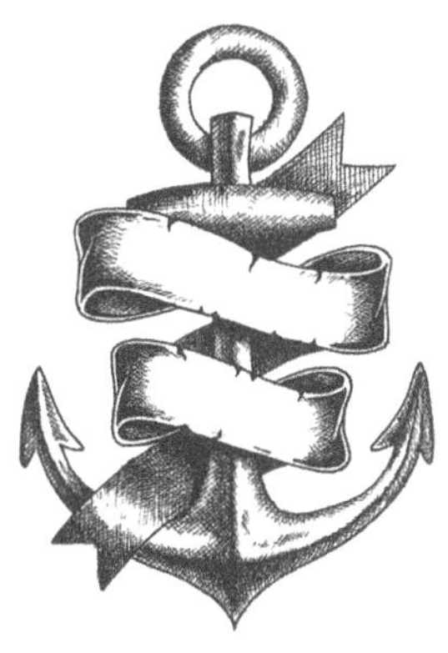

CHAPTER 2
GROWING CONFLICT IN THE COLONIES
SABIN'S TAVERN, PROVIDENCE, RHODE ISLAND

MAY 30, 1772

S abin's Tavern was a popular gathering place for meetings in *Providence*, Rhode Island, primarily because it was located in the center of the city on Towne Street. It was also a place for men of business to meet late in the afternoon before going home to their families. On a day in late May of 1772, it was the scene of a Saturday afternoon gathering of five key leaders of the *Providence* community, called together by a local ship builder, John Brown, and Stephen Hopkins, a former governor of the colony.

"I feel privileged to be included in this elite company, John," said David Howell. "It is not every day I get to break bread with a former governor and three such distinguished men who have been at the heart of the progress in our city over the past two decades."

The speaker was one of the most prosperous merchants in *Providence* and one of the first whose voice was heard when the British moved their troops into the city and began to "house" themselves in the homes of citizens. John Brown was the owner of a variety of businesses in *Providence*, including a shipyard and thirteen ships that traveled the oceans, both in colonial waters and back and forth to Europe.

"We appreciate the compliment, but feel very much that any gathering of the leadership of *Providence* would be incomplete if you were not a part of the group," said Brown. "There are just five of us here today, but when Governor Hopkins and I discussed organizing this group to talk about community concerns, we envisioned at least ten men and maybe more. A part of what should come from this meeting today will be a list of other men to invite to what I hope will become a regular Saturday afternoon discussion."

They were seated in a small meeting room, separated from the tavern's central hall. It had several windows and it was a bright spring Saturday afternoon. Still, the room smelled of stale beer and tobacco smoke. Each of the men had a tankard drink in front of him, and four of the five were smoking pipes. It didn't take long for the smoke to hang in the air above the rough wooden table where the men were seated.

"As I indicated to you when I invited you to this meeting today, Governor Hopkins and I decided to put this discussion group together because of mounting problems in the community," Brown continued. "The British occupancy here, as well as other problems we are experiencing with the new British regulations that have been imposed on us, call out for action on our part. It is our hope that each person we invite to join us will have something of value to contribute."

"If the purpose of this gathering is concerns with the British, I have one to discuss," said Moses Brown, John Brown's brother and business partner.

"Go ahead, Moses," said Brown.

"I can see relationships deteriorating between Rhode Island and King George, and I don't like where it is all heading," Moses said.

"John is right," agreed John Sabin, owner of the tavern where the men were meeting. "We are all loyal subjects of the Crown, but over the last twenty years we have seen several changes in policies and regulations that have created major problems for us. A case in point are the changes made to the Navigation Acts. They were just guidelines when they were written. Now, more and more, they are becoming restrictive. If we are not careful we are going to be strangled by them."

John Brown nodded his head vigorously. "We once had a healthy trade relationship with several European countries," he said. "Now, the new rules say we can't trade with any European country except England. They have restricted the sale of grain to any place outside of the Colonies. That doesn't affect us much right now in Rhode Island, but it certainly does cause problems for the Carolinas. Eventually, it will hit us indirectly because before long they won't have any money to buy the ships we build, nor potash fertilizer, shoes, or any of the household goods we produce."

"I'll tell you a restriction that does affect us directly and could affect employment in *Providence* before too long," said Moses Brown. "Telling us we can no longer make iron or steel products in the Colonies will have a major effect on ship building. We need steel to reinforce the keels of the ships we build, and we need steel to equip those ships with cannons. Waiting for steel to come from London is not an efficient way to run a shipyard."

"Let me bring us back to the real issue at hand," said David Howell. "We can all agree that we are all loyal subjects of King George. But new regulations come with little explanation and some are just unreasonable. How can we get a hearing with King George and Parliament for our concerns? If we don't begin to have some meaningful discussions with the leadership in

London, whatever we say here will avail us nothing."

"It seems that one regulation or another affects every part of our community," agreed James Sabin. "The one I am most concerned about affects everyone in this room and hundreds more on the streets of *Providence*. I run a tavern. The latest addition to the Navigation Acts states that no molasses or sugar can be imported to the Colonies from the West Indies. If we can't trade with the West Indies, where will the necessities for brewing beer and ale and distilling rum come from? Without sugar or molasses, most of what we drink in our taverns cannot be produced."

"James, I am sure you know that King George is trying to put sanctions on Spain and not on you," Stephen Hopkins responded.

"Oh, I know what he is trying to do, but the effect is the same as if he had posted a 'for sale' sign on my front door," James Sabin said sarcastically.

"Much of what King George has done through the Navigation Acts is like cutting off a finger now and another one later until you have no hands left," said John Brown. "Each new regulation hits one part of our community but not others. It is like feeding a bear a little at a time, hoping he will eat you last. We may not be affected directly but we will all be affected eventually."

"You are right, John," said David Howell emphatically. "King George may have been picking on smaller segments of the business community with his many regulations, but this sugar and molasses one is going to hit every man-jack of us. I'd say this was the straw that broke the camel's back."

"If it is enforced, it will sure break my back," muttered James Sabin.

Moses Brown spoke up, "James says, 'if it is enforced,' but that is exactly what is happening with those gun boats they have stationed at the mouth of our harbor and probably every other harbor in the Colonies. I find it intolerable that a Britisher is boarding every ship that goes in and out of Narragansett Bay to levy taxes on our goods. Travel on the oceans has always been free. Next they will station a spy in our bedrooms to regulate what goes on there as well."

That comment drew a few chuckles, but David Howell quickly spoke up. "You may not be far off the mark there, Moses. I have two British soldiers living in my house. Everything we do is watched and judged. My wife, gentle soul that she is, is up to her neck with having to feed and clean up after two strangers who come and go at all hours with hardly a 'hello' or a 'by-your-leave.' If something doesn't change, and quickly, I can envision things getting pretty hostile around my house."

"David is right," said Moses Brown. "We have two living with us as well. Their language is atrocious and demeaning and they put their muddy boots anywhere they take them off. My dear wife is like David's, she says she can't take much more."

"I don't have any Britishers living at my place and I am thankful for that," said James Sabin. "But they come to my tavern by the dozens almost every day and the weekends are terrible. We are averaging about three knock-down-drag-out fights a week and with every fight I lose customers, not to mention furniture."

Stephen Hopkins nodded. "About the best we can say is that we can thank the good Lord that we haven't had a confrontation like they had in *Boston* back in '70 when seven citizens were killed by the king's soldiers."

"The British called that 'The Incident on King Street,'" said John Brown. "Our newspapers called it what it was, 'The *Boston* Massacre.' I understand that protests were lodged in London with both the Parliament and King George."

"That was two years ago, and no one has heard anything back from those complaints," said David Howell.

"And, we are not likely to," added James Sabin.

"I guess I'm back to the soldiers living in our houses and wondering how many of them there are here in *Providence* and throughout the Colonies," said Moses Brown.

"I'm not sure anyone knows how many, but the numbers in *Providence* must be approaching at least a thousand. Perhaps forty to fifty thousand throughout all the Colonies," responded John Brown. "I know there are many more in *Boston* and Philadelphia than here."

The men sat quietly for a few moments, sipping their ale and smoking their pipes. Finally, Stephen Hopkins spoke up. "I'm not sure what we can do about any of the problems we have talked about today," he said. "Perhaps the best we can do is to think about them and try to come up with a solution to each one as we can. When large numbers of soldiers are away from their homes and families, even among men of good will, conflicts are bound to occur. Unfair taxes, restrictions on who we can trade with, having soldiers living in our homes along side of our wives and daughters, being governed by strangers from three thousand miles away, and not being represented in Parliament are all major items of concern. Gentlemen, trouble is coming, and I mean big trouble. It is just a matter of time."

"As distasteful as it is, that is a pretty good summary of where we are today," John Brown agreed, nodding his head. "I'll let that be the benediction for this meeting of what we are going to call the Century Club. Unless you hear differently, we will meet here again next Saturday and each Saturday following at three o'clock. When you come back next week, please bring some suggestions of others who should be a part of these discussions."

There was an undercurrent of comments as the men rose to leave the meeting room.

Two boys came in from the kitchen to clear the tankards and to wipe off the tables for the evening dinner crowd.

Stephen Hopkins moved close to John Brown as they walked out and said quietly, "John, we need to find some good news to focus on next week. Everything that was on the floor today was not only bad news, but things we can't do much about."

"You are right, Governor," John Brown responded. "I hate for everyone to go home on a bad note but lately we have been having nothing but bad notes. We will let it rest a bit and try to come up with something positive for next Saturday."

With those comments, the men left Sabin's Tavern for their homes.

THE PROVIDENCE GAZETTE

PROVIDENCE, Rhode Island June 5, 1772--Relationships between the colonies and Great Britain continue to deteriorate. Several ships from the colonies have been boarded on the high seas by the British Navy and men they believe to be deserters from the British Navy have been taken off and imprisoned at hard labor.

The list of commodities that cannot be traded between the colonies and Great Britain have been increased. Steel is the latest casualty in the marketplace. From this date, steel cannot be manufactured in the colonies. Also, grain cannot be shipped to England and the most recent atrocity is that we are now restricted from importing sugar and molasses from the West Indies. Not being able to manufacture steel will bring our construction of ships to a standstill. Not having sugar and molasses will make the brewing of almost all drinks impossible, and we all know the water supply in many places is not safe.

There is still no word from King George or the British Parliament regarding the death of seven of our citizens at the hands of British troops in Boston in 1770.

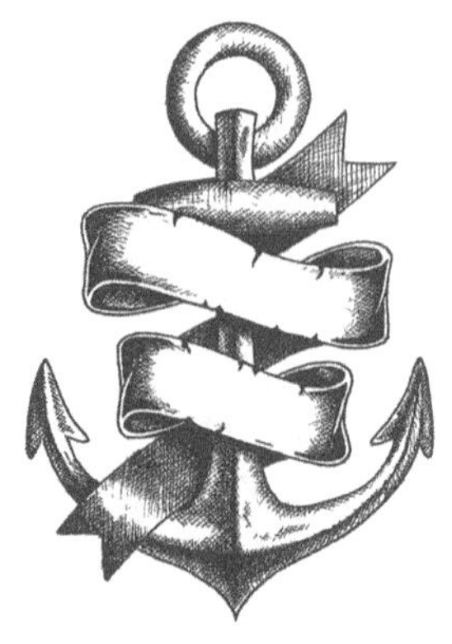

CHAPTER 3

THE GASPEE AFFAIR

PROVIDENCE, RHODE ISLAND

JUNE 9, 1772

By mid-afternoon, the cadence of the drums had been heard all over town. The drums were the best way to get the word out in a hurry in colonial *Providence*. *The Providence Gazette* had been published weekly since 1762, but to spread important information that needed to be heard that day, you alerted the drummers. They could be heard several streets over, and the people would know that there was news being spread. When the drums stopped, crowds would gather to listen to what the drummers had to say.

Today, the big news was that the British ship *Gaspee* was stuck on a sandbar down at Namquid Point about eight miles south of *Providence* in Narragansett Bay.

It was nearing nine o'clock in the evening when the two friends, John Burroughs Hopkins and John Paul, arrived in the street in front of Sabin's Tavern. Earlier in the day, both had heard the drummers marching back and forth through the streets of *Providence* announcing the meeting at the tavern that night and they had come to hear the news first-hand.

Friends seeing John Burroughs and John Paul from a distance could easily tell who they were. They were often together. John Burroughs was tall and thick built, nearly six foot, with dark wavy hair that hung down almost shoulder length. John Paul, by contrast, was short, maybe five foot-five, and looked frail by contrast. His hair was long and tied back in a ponytail. When the two were together they kept up a constant chatter, with John Paul mostly carrying the conversation.

When John Paul spoke it was with a distinctive Scottish accent that set him apart from other local seamen. With that brogue he could never deny where he was from. He had come to *Providence* on the British ship, *Friendship*, when he was just thirteen and had been there ever sense. Both John Burroughs and John Paul worked for local shipyard owner, John Brown, who owned *Katy*. John Burroughs was first mate and John Paul was a lieutenant.

Judging by the number of horses, carriages, and wagons outside of the tavern, the drummers had done their job well. Many horses were tied to hitching posts up and down the street and some were tied to ground anchors that could be carried in the saddle bags. The two friends looked for a free hitching post for the horses, but none was available. Then John Burroughs saw a familiar carriage.

"Let's tie the horses up to the back of this carriage," John Burroughs said. "It belongs to my father, Esek Hopkins."

John Paul replied, "It is hard for me to remember that you are a Hopkins. All of your friends call you John Burroughs. Why is that?"

John Burroughs Hopkins smiled at his younger friend and replied, "I have an uncle and a cousin named John Hopkins, so the name was pretty well taken in the family when I was born. I have always been called John Burroughs to separate me from the others."

The two friends had come together on shipboard just over three years before. They had ridden the thirty minutes into the city from *Providence* Wharf where the *Katy* was tied up to the tavern for the meeting. John Paul's wife was nearing the delivery date of their first child, so he came along more to see what was going on than for any other reason. He told John Burroughs that he couldn't stay late.

John Burroughs smiled at his friend. "I well remember when *Hannah* and I first tried to have children. We lost one, and then a second one. We decided not to risk a third. You are doing just the right thing being there with her to help in any way you can."

They walked in silence the half block to the tavern, being careful where they stepped in the deeply rutted street. There had been a light rain earlier in the day and puddles of water still lingered here and there. It was hard to see in the darkness. There was no moon out and there was just enough cloud cover to mask the stars. At ground level, it was as dark as midnight in a cemetery.

They entered the tavern's dimly lit vestibule and immediately met a man who asked them if they had come for the meeting. They nodded to him and were sent through a double door to the left. They stopped just inside the door to let their eyes adjust to the light. The room was crowded, with virtually every chair taken and men standing around the walls. The tables were loaded with tankards of local beer and almost every man, standing or sitting, held a drink. Tobacco smoke hung over the room and made it hard to see from the front of the room to the back. Light from the fireplace was augmented by whale oil lanterns placed here and there on the tables.

Some of the men were dressed for business with clean white neck cloths and dark cutaway coats, tight knee pants and tall riding boots. However, most were seaman, working men from the ships that came in and out of the harbor. Many of the men were smoking pipes.

The roaring fire was unusual for a June evening in Rhode Island. A closer examination revealed that several men were crowded around the fireplace melting lead for musket balls. As the two friends surveyed the smoke-filled room, they realized that almost every man had a musket by his side.

A man standing at the far end of the room was telling about the confrontation earlier in the day between the *Hannah*, a small trading ship based in Newport, and the British ship *Gaspee*. As John Burroughs scanned the room, he saw his father, Esek Hopkins, waving to him. There was an empty chair next to his father that had, obviously, been saved for him, though there wasn't one for John Paul. He leaned over to his friend and pointed out his father, who was expecting him to join his small group.

John Paul nodded toward Esek Hopkins and whispered, "Who is the man he is sitting with?"

John Burroughs responded, "The man on the left is Stephen Hopkins, my uncle. You know John Brown on the other side. My Uncle Stephen is a silent business partner in many of John Brown's businesses. Together, they own businesses, the shipyard, and the *Katy* and several other smaller ships.

"You go sit with them and I will stand by the wall over here," John Paul suggested. He motioned to the left. John Burroughs nodded and began his slow passage through the crowd to the small grouping of Hopkins men near the front of the room.

The speaker was becoming more animated with every sentence and most of the men gathered around him were listening with much excitement to the tale of the confrontation.

"We was coming up from Newport when this Britisher tried to board us," he said. "Old Bennie was having none of that. He yelled to the crew that if we mind our p's and q's we could out-maneuver and outrun her. We tacked well to the starboard and passed her by. They came around and tried to catch us, but we was headed into a northwestern wind and neither of us could make much headway up the bay. Old Bennie kept them inside of us and tacked back to port."

"Who is this Old Bennie?" someone yelled.

The man stopped for just a second as if to get his breath and responded with feigned amazement that anyone didn't know who Old Bennie was. He raised his voice to an almost shout and said, "Why, that is Captain Benjamin Lindsey of Newport, and there ain't a better captain anywhere sailing the seven seas than Old Bennie!"

His delivery and words drew laughter and shouts of approval.

He composed himself for just a few seconds and continued his story. "It was obvious that the *Gaspee* was trying to get into position to use her guns on us. We didn't have much way to defend ourselves if they caught us in a broadside. But Captain Lindsey watched them carefully and whenever they was just about in position to let us have it, he would tack back to the other side where they couldn't get a good shot at us. Oh, they tried a time or two with their stern guns, but the balls hit the water behind us."

"Old Bennie has been sailing these waters all of his life and he knows them better than anyone," he continued. "We was about halfway up the bay when we all saw the east edge of Namquid Point sticking out into the bay. Everyone knows that there is a sandbar sticking out from the point and anyone sailing this area knows to stay away from there. Course, the Britisher didn't know the bay like Captain Lindsey. We tacked back to port and went wide around the point which left us inside that sandbar. I guess they thought they had us there because they came straight at us. In a jiffy they was hard on the sandbar and stuck solid," he concluded.

By then the entire room of men were laughing at the plight of the *Gaspee* and the mental image of the British gun ship stuck fast to a sandbar in the bay.

The speaker waited for them to settle down, then concluded. "We tacked back to starboard being careful to stay away from their guns. I don't think they could have hit us anyway considering the angle their guns were pointed, perched up on that sandbar."

Having finished his tale, the speaker joined several friends. Someone handed him a tankard of beer and several slapped him on the back and shook his hand.

The commotion in the room grew louder with the conclusion of the tale of the confrontation between the *Hannah* and the *Gaspee*. Everyone was talking while they waited on the next speaker.

They didn't have long to wait. It was John Brown who took the floor. Almost everyone in the city knew John Brown, and if they didn't, they knew of him. His family was one of the oldest in *Providence* and they had prospered significantly because of his ability to see a business opportunity where others might not. John Burroughs had heard him referred to as "the cleverest man in *Providence* town."

Many of the men in the room were sailing on ships made in John Brown's shipyard. When he was a young man, he acquired a ship and then, as the years passed, several more. Then he began building ships for others. He prospered through that effort, but his fortune was made primarily from a triangular trade pattern bringing sugar and molasses from the West Indies to Rhode Island where those commodities were made into rum which was traded for a variety of goods, including slaves from Africa.

A number of ships plying their trade in and out of *Providence* and Newport Harbor made the biggest part of their living raiding British, French, and Spanish shipping up and down the coast between Rhode Island and the Bahamas. Pirates, the French called them. The locals called them privateers. Several of John Brown's ships were involved in such raiding, though it would not have been talked about in polite company.

When John Brown walked to the front of the room, his presence commanded silence. His clothes were those of the typical man of business in *Providence*, including a spotless white neck scarf and black cutaway coat with brass buttons. But his face bore a week of whiskers and his hair looked as if he had been out in the wind all afternoon.

John Brown had a very deep voice with a resonance that could be heard all over the room. He spoke slowly and deliberately when he began addressing the men. "When our neighbors in Newport were faced with such an opportunity in '69, they captured the *Liberty* and set her on fire. We cheered the news of that blow for freedom from British tyranny just three years ago. The question for us is what will we do with our opportunity, what will we do with the *Gaspee*?" he demanded.

Several began shouting support for John Brown, support for action to take the *Gaspee*. Just as things were simmering down, another man raised his voice and shouted, "Let's burn that junker to the water line!" With that, several men stood up and began to shout again. This time they were in a cadence, "Burn it, burn it, burn it," they shouted, until John Brown raised his hands.

When he had their attention again, John Brown continued, his voice rising, "Everything on a ship gets taxed! Farmers can't sell their grain even to the next colony! We can't produce any iron or steel products! We build

British ships in our ship yards but have to send to England for cannons to put on them! Now we have new restrictions on bringing sugar and molasses from the West Indies! Without molasses or sugar, we can't make ale nor beer nor rum! Soon the only drink we will be able to serve in our taverns is sea water!"

There was an explosion of approving shouts, and the chant of "Burn it, burn it, burn it," rose again. The consensus of the men in the room was clear: Something needed to be done to check the unfair Navigation Acts, and the opportunity had arisen to take action against British tyranny.

John Brown waited for the group to settle, and then spoke so softly that many had to strain to hear what he was saying. "As most of you know, the British have taken Canada to the north and the Mississippi River to the west of us. They have had to station hundreds, even thousands of their soldiers here on our shores to protect their new acquisitions. Their presence here has cost the British much money, and they decided last year to tax us to support their efforts. It is another example of our being taxed without representation in the British Parliament."

Heads nodded in agreement around the room.

John Brown continued, "Their new territorial acquisitions have nothing to do with us. We all know about the Brit's Navigation Acts. It tells us that we can't trade with anyone but the British, and that all commerce coming in and out of our harbor is to be taxed at a rate that is intolerable for maintaining profitable commerce. That is what the *Gaspee* is doing down at the entrance to the bay, boarding every ship and placing a tax on whatever we are bringing in. We have objected through all of the normal channels. Those protests have availed us nothing."

John Brown's voice rose to a near shout with those last words. His emotion set the entire room ablaze again with indignant comments. Many jumped to their feet, stomping the floor with their boots to add emphasis to their shouts. There was no doubt that John Brown was speaking for everyone in the room, most of whom made their living either directly or indirectly from sea-going commerce.

Finally, Brown waved them down so he could continue. "When our neighbors in Newport were faced with such an opportunity with the

Liberty in '69, they didn't shy away like a bunch of cowards. They sent her to Davey Jones! We cheered the news of that blow for freedom from British tyranny just three years ago."

The commotion in the room again rose to a fever pitch. Brown let it run for several seconds and then he continued, "I have asked one of my most trusted men, Captain Abraham Whipple, to strike a blow for *Providence* against this unfair tax. He has made preparation to take a number of volunteers down to the point to take the *Gaspee* and send her to an early grave."

With those words, the room full of men erupted with yells of support. Brown now cried, "Who will come along and strike a blow for freedom from British tyranny tonight? I yield the floor to Captain Whipple."

Captain Whipple passed Brown on the way to the front. Their eyes met and both men smiled. With all eyes upon him, Captain Whipple looked around the room and said, "I number about a hundred and twenty men in this room. I think we can carry about seventy men in the long boats we have over at Fener's Wharf. I need one volunteer in each boat to act as captain of that boat and crew."

Several hands were raised and Captain Whipple walked back and forth across the front of the room, choosing men he knew could handle the responsibility. Among those he chose was John Burroughs Hopkins, his first mate on the *Katy*, the ship that was jointly owned by John Brown and Stephen Hopkins.

John Burroughs was delighted to have been chosen as one of the captains. After the meeting adjourned, he made his way back through the crowd to his friend John Paul.

"I'm sorry that I cannot make this trip with you, John, much as I would like to. Keziah is due anytime now, and I need to be home tonight," John Paul apologized.

With that the two friends parted and John Burroughs followed the crowd across the street to Fener's Wharf where Captain Whipple was waiting on him with the others who had been designated as captains of the long boats. Standing with Captain Whipple were several that he knew, including captains Samuel Dunn, Rufus Greene, Sam Potter, Christopher Sheldon, and Joseph Tillinghast. There were a few others in the group that he didn't know; he figured they were probably men from Newport rather than *Providence*, since he knew most of the local seamen.

Captain Whipple gave them their directions. He told them that boats had been rigged for silent running with oars muffled. They were to maintain strict silence in the water. They were to maneuver their long boats so that all could advance southward in a line so that none arrived at the *Gaspee* before another. No shots were to be fired unless they were first fired on by the *Gaspee* crew. He said that his hope was that they could take that ship without bloodshed.

One last direction followed. Captain Whipple said, "If we take the crew of the *Gaspee*, we will bring them back to *Providence* and hold them here. To protect all of our men, no one is to call anyone by name in the presence of the *Gaspee's* crew. When the British come to hunt us down, and they most certainly will, it will not be good if the crew can identify any of us by name."

In a very few minutes, the boats were loaded with about ten men in each and they were paddling out into the black of a moonless night. Namquid Point, their destination, was about eight miles south of Fener's Wharf and they were paddling into the flow of the tide which would make their progress southward slow going. The tide would arrive full force at about three o'clock in the morning. At that point, the bay water would be high enough to float the *Gaspee* off the sandbar. They had a strict time table to meet if they were not to lose their chance to take her.

A light fog hung about three feet thick on the water. Sitting in their boats under the fog, it was difficult to see even the men in the other boats. Finally, after about two hours of rowing, they could make out the fantail lights of the *Gaspee*. Captain Whipple stood up in the lead boat where he could be seen above the low-hanging fog. Using hand signals, he cautioned the men in the other boats to strictest silence.

When they were about twenty-five yards from the marooned ship, they heard a voice from the ship yelling, "Who goes there?" There was no response from the long boats, which began to close in.

The look-out called again, "Who goes there?" Again, there was no response.

The sentry moved quickly to wake the captain of the *Gaspee*, who was asleep below awaiting the time of full tide when he could refloat his ship.

The captain, Lieutenant Dundingston, appeared on the starboard gunwale in his nightshirt, carrying his sword. "Don't come any closer," he shouted, "or we'll open fire!" It was a hollow threat since the boats were approaching the gunboat from the back side where there were no guns.

In response to Dudingston's threat, Captain Whipple shouted back, "I'm the sheriff of the County of Kent. I have a warrant to arrest you, so surrender."

The *Gaspee* captain knew he had only a skeleton crew of men on board but he called to them to break out the weapons and get to their battle stations. Shortly, the British crew opened fire with their small arms. Shots were splashing in the water but none hit any of the *Providence* men. When the first of the long boats reached the stern of the *Gaspee*, the men began climbing up to the deck. Captain Dudingston met the first one with his sword and sent him back over the rail into the water.

A shot rang out from the long boat captained by John Burroughs. He looked around and saw Joseph Bucklin, one of the youngest men in their company, holding a pistol that was still smoking from the barrel. When he looked back to the *Gaspee*, the captain was no longer in sight.

John Burroughs thought about admonishing the young man for shooting but decided against it. After all, the order was that they were not to fire unless they were fired upon by the crew of the *Gaspee*. They had been fired upon. When that order not to fire was given by Captain Whipple, John Burroughs thought it was not one likely to be carried out. What did Captain Whipple think was going to happen when his group of more than seventy armed men began boarding the *Gaspee*?

Within minutes the long boats had emptied their cargo of men onto the deck of the *Gaspee* and the crew, without their leader, lay down their arms and surrendered. Some of the attacking party began loading the captured British seamen into the long boats while others set about taking anything of value off the ship. Long-established rules of the sea were that any abandoned ship was open for the taking and, whatever the reason, the *Gaspee* was now abandoned.

Shortly, all the long boats had cast away except the one led by Captain Whipple. From a short distance out in the bay, the men could see the last of their number moving around on the deck. Almost immediately, flames began to reach for the sky and the last of the boarding party retreated to Whipple's boat and began to row away.

Heading back toward *Providence* was easier because they were rowing with the tide. They were well out into the bay when there was a big explosion and the *Gaspee* filled the sky with debris. Evidently, the fire had reached the powder room in the hold of the ship. The men let out a unified yell of triumph with the explosion, and the chatter in the boats testified to their jubilant feelings as they headed back up the bay. The men busied themselves taking turns rowing the boats back toward home.

A summary of the attack provided by Captain Whipple for John Brown the next day included the information that Captain Dudingston and his men were imprisoned in a house in *Providence*. The gravely wounded captain had a chest wound, which had been ministered to by a *Providence* surgeon, and he was expected to survive. Captain Whipple recommended in his report that the king's men be transported to *Boston* and repatriated to the British.

THE PROVIDENCE GAZETTE

PROVIDENCE, Rhode Island, August 10, 1773--The reverberations from the Gaspee affair are still being felt throughout the Colonies even a year later. The British have taken measures to capture the men involved but as yet have been unsuccessful.

A series of letters written by Thomas Hutchinson, Governor of the Commonwealth of Maryland, have been published in Boston. The essence of these letters is that many of the freedoms currently enjoyed by all British citizens should be curtailed in the Colonies due to the constant agitation against the British military.

We have long experienced a tax on all tea bought or sold in the Colonies. Now, Parliament has exempted The East India Company from such taxes, thus allowing them to undersell other companies involved in the tea commerce. The new action by Parliament constitutes a subsidizing of a particular company in direct conflict with British law.

There appears to be constant conflict between the British military and the Massachusetts Militia, with hostilities breaking out periodically. Boston is becoming an armed camp.

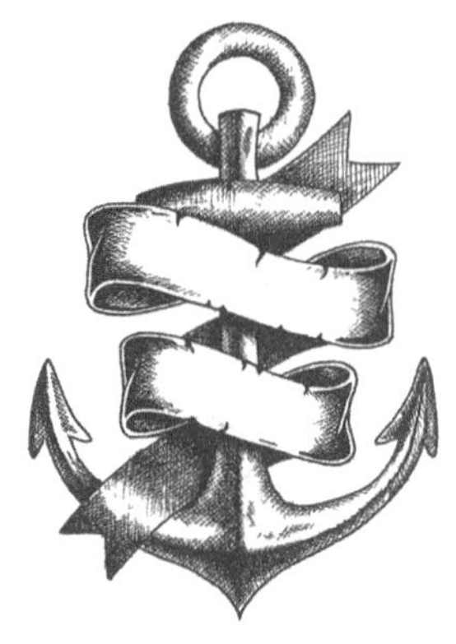

CHAPTER 4

JIM-BOY

PROVIDENCE, RHODE ISLAND
AUGUST 30, 1773

The *Katy* had been in port for about a week getting repairs to the rigging on the second mast. Supervision of that work was left to the first mate, John Burroughs Hopkins, while Captain Whipple was off the ship visiting his home just north of *Providence*.

The repairs were moving along well, with about half of the crew still on board and working in teams to lift the heavy cross-pieces back into place, install the new sails, and repair the old. The retrofitted merchant ship had been at sea for more than a decade and Hopkins knew it needed to be dry-docked and have its hull scrapped. Scraping the hull would clean off the barnacles that had attached to the undersea part of the hull and coming clean would increase the ship's speed, perhaps by as much as five knots. Considering the number of pirates sailing the seas these days, five knots could mean the difference between escape and having to fight if a confrontation should come. Maybe time in the dry dock would come next year.

John Burroughs spent much of his time while they were in port on the fantail, supervising the work from a distance. After an early morning meeting with the sailing master and the boatswain, First Mate Hopkins could back away and let his two veteran leaders direct the other men. The sailing master was responsible for the navigation and sailing of the ship. The boatswain was primarily responsible for the ship's maintenance and seeing that everything needed by the sailing master was in order.

From his vantage point on the fantail, John Burroughs could watch the ships coming into port from Narragansett Bay. He was always fascinated by the variety of countries represented by the ships anchored just off the main wharf and out beyond the Channel. Country flags were flown from the fantail lines so that there was never a doubt which countries had ships in port. On this particular morning, John Burroughs could identify ships from five different countries.

On the other side of the ship, port side, there were always large numbers of people passing by up and down Water Street and people-watching was a pleasant pass-time. Ladies carrying baskets for shopping and merchants plying their products were always on the scene. There was a tavern on the corner just down the street and he wondered if he could spare the time to slip down there for a quick tankard of ale.

He noticed a boy sitting on a crate in front of the tavern. He stood out because he was frail- built with bright yellow hair. John Burroughs could not make out his clothing from this distance but almost anyone walking up and down the street would notice the boy with the bright yellow hair. Several times as he moved back and forth across the fantail, he looked for the boy, and he was still there. From time to time he saw patrons of the tavern stop and hand him a coin, probably a penny or a ha'penny, John Burroughs thought. He didn't appear to be begging for money but with that head of hair he was hard to miss, and several stopped to talk to him as they came out the tavern door.

About mid-afternoon it appeared that the work was going well and that the boatswain had everything well in hand. John Burroughs decided that he could walk down the gangplank onto the wharf, climb the steps to the street and be in and out of the tavern in ten minutes or so. He was about twenty feet from the front door of the tavern when he again noticed the boy. He nodded to him as he went by and the boy stood, took off his cap and bowed to him.

When he came out of the front door of the tavern after having his ale, he reached in his coat pocket for a ha'penny to give the boy and he placed it in his hat. The boy's eyes met his and he said, "Sir, I very much appreciate whatever you have to give me, but what I really need is a job. I have seen you on the fantail of that big ship and was hoping you might have some work for me and, perhaps, a place to sleep."

John Burroughs leaned against the wall next to the boy and looked him over again. His clothes were in tatters and he had no shoes. In contrast to the sorry state of his apparel was his radiant smile and that head of bright yellow hair.

"What is your name, boy?" John Burroughs asked.

"I am called Jim," the boy responded.

"Where are your folks, Jim?" he asked.

"My father went out on one of Mr. Brown's ships a couple of years ago and they never came back. We think he must be dead. My mother lives over on Planet Street with my two little sisters. She sometimes does some work for folks but, mostly, we live off of any odd jobs I can find and what people give me here on the street."

"Jim, how old are you?" John Burroughs asked.

"I am nearly thirteen, sir," Jim responded. "Well, I'll be thirteen in a few months."

John Burroughs looked him over, head to foot, one more time and said, "Let's you and me take a walk, Jim. I think our cook may have some leftovers from the noon meal we can share with you."

"Yes, sir," the boy responded. "Oh, yes sir."

The sound of his last "yes sir," showed significant appreciation and gave John Burroughs a very warm feeling. He couldn't help but smile.

The men were still working on the deck with the sails, with about half of them up on the mast setting the sails and tying the lines. John Burroughs and Jim were careful to walk around the edge of the deck to miss the work area. Jim could not help himself, he looked up to the rigging where the men were hanging from the cross pieces holding the sail in place until it could be tied.

John Burroughs led him down the steps into the hold of the ship and as they entered the narrow hallway, Jim could smell the aroma of food wafting down the hall. John Burroughs led him into a narrow room with a long table flanked by benches. An older man could be seen through a window where steam was coming out, along with that glorious smell.

"Jubal," said John Burroughs, "This is Jim. He is in bad need of one of your delicious ocean meals. Can you fix him up?"

Jubal looked out at them through the window. "Yes sir. Sure as the sun rose in the east this morning. He is just a waif. I can fill him up in a jiffy," said the old sailor.

Jubal stepped out of the little room that was his kitchen and Jim had his first look at a man who he was sure was at least ninety years old. Well, maybe not ninety, but older than any man Jim had ever laid eyes on. Jubal was short and thick with a mustache that seemed to cover the middle part of his face. He had a goatee that, like the mustache, was totally white. The only hair on his head was under his nose and on his chin.

"Sit you down over there by the table and I will see what we have left from our midday meal," said Jubal.

Jim moved quickly to the bench where Jubal had motioned.

John Burroughs smiled at Jubal and said, "Fill him up, Jubal, and then send him up to the fantail to me when he has eaten his fill. All right?"

"Yes sir, Lieutenant Hopkins," Jubal responded. "I should have him fed and watered in about a half hour."

John Burroughs nodded at Jim and exited the room leaving Jim to anticipate whatever was going to come out of Jubal's kitchen. As the boy sat there, he tried to remember the last time he actually had a real meal.

He couldn't remember that far back. He wished his mother and sisters could be here. But, he promised himself, he would find a way to share the bounty with them later in the day.

Jim wasn't sure what was in the bowl that Jubal sat before him, but it appeared to be some kind of chowder. He said the obligatory "Thank you," over and over. He could identify some fish, a part of a potato, and several different kinds of vegetables all mixed together in a thick broth. It was piping hot and it smelled wonderful.

"Where you come from, boy?" Jubal asked.

"I live in *Providence*," the boy responded, savoring his first bite.

Jubal looked at the boy slowly from head to foot and said, "Where your folks?"

Jim looked up at the older man and said, "My Pa's been gone a couple of years on one of Mr. Brown's ships. We think he won't be back. I live with my Ma and two sisters over on Planet Street." It was all he could do to answer the old sailor's questions between mouthfuls of the chowder.

"Boy, do you know anything about cooking?" Jubal asked.

"Some," Jim responded. "I have done some odd jobs over at the tavern. Mostly they have had me serving the tables and washing plates and tankards from time to time."

"Well, you eat your chowder," said Jubal. "When you finish you can wash some plates for me to pay for your fixins."

"I'll be glad to," said Jim. "I'm almost done here. You show me what you want done and I can do most anything."

Jim was amazed at how quickly the bowl emptied. He would gladly have taken a full refill but thought better of asking.

The boy came into the little kitchen carrying his empty tankard and bowl. "Where do you want these?" he asked.

"Just put them on the stack with the others and climb up to the sink," Jubal replied. "Let's see how good a cook's helper you are with those plates and tankards."

There was a short bench which he pulled up to the sink to stand on. The stack of plates seemed endless, but before long Jim was washing the last of them. The tankards were easier to handle and all were finally stacked neatly on the far side of the sink.

"You done that pretty good," said Jubal. "Do you know anything about grill cooking?"

"No sir, but I am a quick learner. If you show me, I'm sure I can do it," Jim replied.

"All right Jim-boy," said Jubal. "I'm going to give you a slab of fish to put on the grill. Now, be careful, the grill is hot. You fry it until you think it is done, and then scoop it off and put it on that plate. I'm going to leave you for a few minutes but I will be back about the time you are done."

Jubal left the room and Jim watched the slab of fish sizzle on the grill. In a few minutes, it looked and smelled just right. He took it off with a big fork and put it on the tin plate just as Jubal had said.

When Jubal came back, the first thing he did was to take a knife and cut a bite from the fish. He put it in his mouth and seemed to roll it around with his tongue. He smiled and said, "Not bad, not bad at all."

Jubal smiled at Jim and told him that Lieutenant Hopkins was waiting for him up on the fantail.

When Jim didn't move from the doorway into the kitchen, Jubal asked him, "What you waiting for boy? Git."

Jim still didn't move. "Sir," Jim said, "I notice that you have some bread and a couple of slabs of fish over on the counter that haven't been cooked yet."

"Yes," Jubal responded.

Jim ducked his head a bit and then said in a low voice, "If you have enough to spare, could I take some to my Ma and sisters, please?"

Jubal turned around to the counter and when he turned back he handed Jim a cloth sack that held several delicious-smelling treasures that would be much appreciated at home.

He said, "Son, you take this and when you come back tomorrow I will have another sack for you just like this one. All right?"

John Burroughs was waiting on him when Jim arrived on the fantail. "Well, boy, are you full?" he asked, smiling.

"Oh yes, sir," he responded. "I never ate so good."

"Jim," said John Burroughs. "I want you to come back to see me again tomorrow about this time. Can you do that?"

"Yes sir," Jim replied. "Do you have some work for me to do?"

"I'm not sure," he responded. "But let's both of us think about it overnight. All right?"

"Yes sir," Jim replied. "You can count on me to be here."

With that final word, the boy was gone down the gangplank, running in a dog-trot. John Burroughs watched him until he was out of sight around the tavern corner carrying his sack of goodies.

True to his word, Jim was back up the gangplank at about mid-afternoon the next day as John Burroughs had requested. The lieutenant was talking to his boatswain. He nodded to Jim as he approached and Jim, knowing his place, stood by the rail until the two men were finished talking.

John Burroughs walked over to Jim and asked, "Are you hungry, Jim?"

"Oh, yes sir," he responded. "These days I seem to always be hungry."

"Well, let's go down to the kitchen and see if Jubal has anything left that might fill up that stomach of yours," said John Burroughs.

When they were sitting at the table outside Jubal's kitchen, John Burroughs smiled at Jim and asked the question Jim was hoping to hear. "Jim, are you free to come on shipboard with us and become a seaman?"

Jim stopped eating. He could feel a heavy lump growing in his throat. "You mean, and work here for you and Mr. Jubal?"

"Yes, that is exactly what I mean," John Burroughs responded.

"Oh yes, I want to do it. What would I do? I'll do anything you want me to," Jim said excitedly.

Those last words had come so fast that John Burroughs and Jubal both laughed. Jim laughed with them too.

"Jim," John Burroughs said, "over a period of time I think you would work in a number of areas of the ship. We have lots of work a boy your age could do. However, in the beginning you should consider yourself a cabin boy and a cook's helper. Jubal will teach you what you need to know to help him with preparing meals for the men and I will tell you what to do around the cabin.

"I started work on a ship when I was sixteen," John Burroughs continued. "My friend John Paul was a cabin boy at thirteen. I am a first mate now and ready to be a captain. John Paul will soon have his own ship too."

"Being a seaman is a way of life," Jubal interjected. "There are easier ways to make a living, and you are away from home a lot. But I've never missed a meal and when we take a big prize there is plenty of money for everyone to share."

Jim sat, wide-eyed, looking from Jubal's face to John Burroughs's.

"So, Jim-boy, are you with us?" exclaimed Jubal.

"Am I ever," said Jim. "What do I have to do to get started?"

"Well, first," John Burroughs said, "I need to talk to your mother. Can you ask her to come to the ship tomorrow so we can have a conversation about you? Because you are just twelve years old, I think we need to hear what she thinks of this idea."

"Yes sir," said Jim. "I know she will think it is a great idea. Shall I bring her around in the mid-afternoon about this time?"

"All right, then I will look forward to meeting her tomorrow," said John Burroughs.

It was right on time the next day when Jim appeared around the corner of the tavern with his mother and two sisters. Jim was carrying the smaller of the girls while his mother held the other little girl's hand.

John Burroughs walked down the gang plank, climbed the stairs and met them at street level. After the introductions were over John Burroughs suggested they go to the tavern where they could escape the August sun and talk in comfort.

There were two small rooms off of the entryway into the tavern and John Burroughs guided the children into one while the adults gathered around a table in the other. In mid-afternoon, there were few people in the tavern, so no one saw them enter. It would not have been seemly for a women to be seen in the main room of the tavern. John Burroughs wanted to speak privately to Jim's mother, and so he asked the bar keep to bring the children some bread and honey and some cider to drink. When they were content, John Burroughs returned to Jim's mother.

"What shall I call you?" John Burroughs asked.

"I am Aimee Shelton," she responded. "I would be pleased if you called me Mistress Aimee."

John Burroughs was immediately impressed with the demeanor of Jim's mother. She was a slight-built lady in her late 20s. She wore a neat white ruffled cap, like most of the women in *Providence*, but he could see a bit of bright yellow hair sticking out the front. He was struck by the fact that Aimee Shelton was a beautiful lady, despite her worn clothes and the fact that she, like Jim, had no shoes. Her little girls had very simple dresses but both babies were obviously clean with that same bright yellow hair hanging down their backs in pig tails, similar white caps on their heads.

"Aimee," John Burroughs said. "We have offered your son a job on the *Katy* as cook's helper and cabin boy. I need to know what you think of giving up your son to the sea and to this kind of work."

"Mr. Burroughs," she responded. "I am a widow lady with three children and no means of support. As much as I hate to give up my son, I see this opportunity for Jim as a God-send." She hesitated a moment, bit her lip, and continued. "I have been living from day to day with my children hardly getting anything at all to eat, only what Jim has been able to bring home, and he is just a boy. Still, I am not sure how I will manage without him."

"Aimee," John Burroughs said. "I would suggest that we create an account for you with Mr. John Brown who owns the *Katy* and several other ships. His book keeper will keep the money that Jim has coming and you can draw on it whenever you have a need. Jim will be paid one pound a month and keep. He will also get a small share of any prizes we win as we sail on the oceans. I am going to open your account with five pounds. It will take him about a year to catch up with the amount I will put in the account, but after that you should have a regular income based on Jim's work with us at sea."

Aimee Shelton looked at her hands before responding, "I don't know what to say. I have mixed emotions about Jim going to sea. I lost his father there about two years ago. We don't know what happened to him, just that his ship and the men on it didn't return when they were supposed to and we assumed they were lost at sea. I don't know what I would do if I lost Jim. But I am going to trust in the good Lord that this is his will for Jim and for us."

"We will do our best to take care of your boy," John Burroughs said. "*Katy* is a fine ship and I have a veteran crew on board. If I move to another ship, I will take Jim with me. In six or eight years, he will be moving up the ladder and taking on more and more responsibility. He may even be captain of his own ship someday."

Just at that moment John Paul walked through the tavern door. He paused for a moment as his eyes adjusted to the dim light, and then he joined John Burroughs in the side room at the table.

John Burroughs stood up and introduced his friend to Jim's mother. "Mistress Aimee, this is my first mate, John Paul. He is a good role model for Jim. He went to sea for the first time when he was just thirteen. He is now twenty-six and is a lieutenant who will soon be captain of his own ship. He and I have been together for several years while both of us have been learning what we need to know to earn a good living at this craft."

Aimee bowed her head to the other man, then the three adults stood and walked to the room where they children were seated. Jim was almost too anxious about the outcome of the conversation to contain himself. "Can I do it, Mother?" he said.

She smiled and nodded.

Jim's delight was almost too great to contain. John Burroughs left some coins on the table to pay for the children's repast, and they all left the tavern together. The older girl clung to Jim, perhaps sensing that he would soon be parted from her for a long time. After they had said their good-byes at the front of the tavern and the Shelton family had walked away, the two friends, John Burroughs and John Paul, walked slowly back to the *Katy*. John Paul was silent but smiling and his friend asked him why. "That is one beautiful woman," he said.

"Yes," John Burroughs agreed. You can certainly see where Jim got his yellow hair. What a dilemma to be in with three children and no husband and no family."

The smile on John Paul's look quickly faded. "John Burroughs," he said quietly, "I need to be gone for a few days."

"Is there trouble at home?" John Burroughs asked.

"Yes, Keziah is sick again," John Paul responded. "She hasn't been right since Daniel was born. We need someone to help her care for Moses and Daniel. Her mother helped some, but she has been sick herself. I'm not sure what we are going to do. This is not a good time to be gone on shipboard, but I don't have many options. That is how I make my living and it is all I know."

"John Paul," John Burroughs said, "you just met a lady, Jim's mother, who needs employment and has been living from hand to mouth. You own a two-story house with several bedrooms and have two children who need care. Have you considered an arrangement with someone who is tied to the home because of the ages of her own children?"

"I have been thinking of little else since we have been off this week, I just didn't have an option to offer Keziah," responded John Paul. "I will talk with her about it this evening. It could be that we can solve several problems at once if we can effect an agreement between Keziah and Jim's mother to care for the children in our home."

John Burroughs put his hand gently on his friend's shoulder. "You go on now and see what you can work out. I won't expect you back until I see you coming."

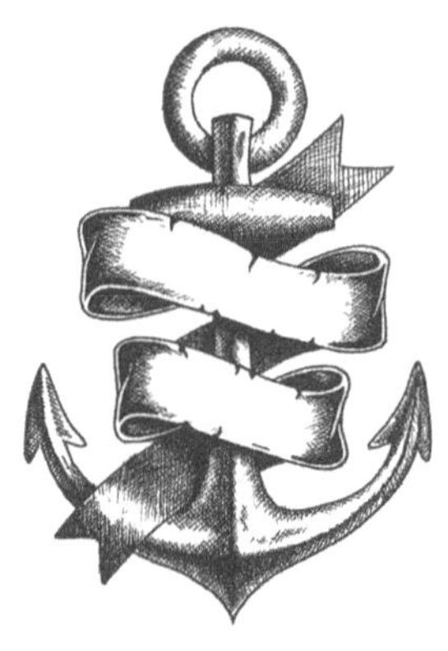

CHAPTER 5

THE BOSTON TEA PARTY

BOSTON, MASSACHUSETTS

DECEMBER 15, 1773

John Burroughs Hopkins was on his first voyage as a ship's captain, appointed temporarily by John Brown, owner of the *Abigale*, to take a cargo of sugar and molasses imported from the West Indies from *Providence* to *Boston*. The new restriction on importing sugar and molasses had not yet caught up with the ships on the high seas headed back to port from the West Indies.

The transition from the *Katy* to the *Abigale* was relatively easy. Several of the crew members of the *Katy* had come along, including young Jim Shelton, the new cook's helper and cabin boy. It was John Burroughs's practice to have a meeting each morning on the fantail to be sure everyone knew what was expected during the work day that would follow. Once everyone knew what was expected, the day generally went very smoothly.

They followed the tide out at the break of dawn and headed for the open seas of Long Island Sound. Normally, with fair winds, it would be a sixteen-hour sail around Cape Cod and up the Massachusetts coast to *Boston* Harbor. Unfortunately, they met a headwind almost as soon as they were clear of Narragansett Bay. The headwind slowed their progress significantly, and in order to make any headway at all, they had to continually tack back and forth to capture the wind with their sails. It took them a full two days to sail around Cape Cod.

They anchored off the shore of the point at the north edge of Cape Cod rather than sail into the harbor of close-by Provincetown, which was a major British Navy stronghold. The plan was to be gone to *Boston* before first light and avoid any contact with the British who controlled the sea lanes into that harbor.

John Burroughs very much enjoyed having the boy, Jim, along for the trip. Several times over the two-day period he saw Jubal with the boy out on the deck talking with him and pointing up into the rigging and watching the movement of the sails as they tacked back and forth. The new captain was pleased that the boy's education as a seaman had begun.

The winds were much more favorable at first light and they made it across open water into *Boston* Harbor by mid-afternoon. There were already five ships at the three wharfs in the harbor at *Boston*, so it was obvious that there was no room for the *Abigale* there. A quick look around the bay that led into the harbor revealed that there were several smaller ships anchored close to the shore across the channel of the bay. John Burroughs maneuvered the *Abigale* to take its place alongside three of those ships. As they set the anchor and dropped the rest of the sails, he could already see a long boat, which served as a water taxi, being rowed out from the largest of the wharfs across the channel.

John Burroughs's best friend, John Paul, had come along on this trip as first mate. The two friends climbed down the rope ladder on the side of the ship and stepped into the long boat. John Burroughs looked back up to the railing and saw the hopeful face of young Jim looking down at him. He knew the boy would have loved to come along with the two men to see the city, but this was not the time for it. Jim would be much better off on board where there was no danger of his getting separated from them.

The man handling the oars asked their names so he could report them and the name of the ship to the harbor master. "I am John Burroughs Hopkins, the captain, and the ship is the *Abigale* from *Providence*, Rhode

Island," he said. When the man finished writing he looked up at John Paul and the younger man said, "I am John Paul Jones, first mate on the Abigail."

John Burroughs knew John Paul had recently changed his name, adding the new last name "Jones." Their eyes met, and both smiled. It was the first time he had heard John Paul give this last name publicly, and certainly it was the first time either had been introduced as a captain or as first mate.

Both took their seats in the stern of the boat and the oarsman began his labors to deposit them on the wharf.

John Burroughs spoke quietly to his younger friend. "I am still getting used to your new name. I like the sound of it but wonder why you added Jones as your family name instead of Paul."

"It was not an easy decision and I thought long and hard about it," he responded. John Paul's voice fell to a whisper. "The fact is that the British are looking for me. John Paul is on their list as a pirate. They never heard of John Jones. They know my family is in *Providence* and that I am there between trips at sea. It was only a matter of time until they caught up with me. Remember, I am a Scot by birth. If I had been born in New England, as you were, they might just put me in jail for a few years. But, if I am caught, as a native of Scotland they will try me in England and I think they will hang me. When I learned of this, I moved Keziah and the children to another part of town, and when we bought the new house we used the Jones name. Hopefully, that other fellow, John Paul, is gone forever."

The long boat docked at the smaller wharf and John Paul climbed up to help secure the line while John Burroughs paid their fare. John Paul heard him ask how much he owed and the man replied that five bob would do it. A bob was slang for a shilling, which meant that the fare cost about a quarter of a pound. John Burroughs hesitated, thinking that was a bit high. But he concluded it was too late to argue over the fare. He reached in his pocket and handed the man five shillings.

As the men were standing on the wharf, a man walked up to them. He introduced himself as Joseph Brantley, owner of one of the *Boston* breweries.

"I have been looking for you since late yesterday," he said. "You must have had some trouble coming in. Is the cargo all right?"

John Burroughs responded, "Everything is fine. We had head winds all day yesterday and it slowed our progress. We had to anchor off Cape Cod last night to wait for fair winds to cross the channel to *Boston*."

"I had hoped to have you unloaded today but it is already too late," said Brantley. "I have the long boats secured for transporting the sugar and molasses, but I have already lost several of the men I had hired to unload you." He shrugged. "We will start first thing in the morning." Joseph Brantley pointed across the street to a pub and suggested that they could get something to eat there, and said lodging for the night was also available.

John Burroughs thanked him, and the two friends headed across the street. It was a dark and musty place filled with the smell of sour beer. He talked to a man at the counter about rooms for the night and with the quick signing of a large book, arrangements were made.

They sat down at a table after ordering from the bar. Before long, their beer arrived, and they began to relax. They were feeling pleased that this place was so close to the wharf and both food and drink were available here, as well as accommodations for the night.

It was hard to ignore the conversation going on at the next table, where several men had gathered. The talk was loud, and they soon learned, among other things, that the speakers were planning walk together to another pub located on King Street, just in front of the Samuel Adams Brewery. Before long they all left, and their section of the room became much quieter.

"Did you get what they were talking about?" John Paul asked.

"I'm not sure, but I think the other meeting has to do with some of the local unrest we have been hearing about," John Burroughs responded.

"I heard them mention an organization called the Sons of *Liberty* several times. I would really like to be in that meeting they are having at the Samuel Adams pub on King Street."

"Well," John Paul said, "let's take a walk. It can't be far if that group was going to walk there."

The sun had disappeared while they had been inside the pub and a cold wind was blowing in off the harbor. Both men pulled their coat collars up around their ears and hoped it didn't take too long to reach their destination. After a short ten minutes of walking, they saw a sign on the wall of one of the buildings identifying King Street. They knew they were close to their destination.

John Paul stopped walking. He turned to John Burroughs and said, "I have heard of King Street going back a-ways. Why would I know of this street in *Boston*?"

John Burroughs responded, "This is the place where the *Boston* Massacre occurred back in '70. I'm not sure exactly where it happened, but a group of British soldiers opened fire on a crowd of local folks and several were killed. Everyone was sure mad about it for a while. The British called it the 'Incident on King Street,' but our people called it what it was, a massacre of unarmed people."

John Burroughs had just finished his last sentence when John Paul said, "There It is, Samuel Adams Tavern."

The two friends went inside and were relieved to find a fireplace roaring in the far corner. It was an atmosphere little different from the one they had left in the pub by the wharf, and they were immediately pleased to be in out of the cold. There were many men in the room and the tables were full of tankards of drink. In a short minute both men had small pewter cups of hot rum in their hands and were looking for a place to sit.

They heard the sound of raised voices coming from a back room and John Burroughs motioned his friend to follow him. He pushed the door open and found another room full of men. Almost immediately the room fell silent.

A man who stood at the front of room spoke to the intruders with a harsh voice, demanding, "Who are you and what are you doing here?" There was a bit of awkward silence as John Burroughs's mind raced for a response to the rather pointed question. *What were they doing here? What had they stumbled into?*

John Burroughs took a few seconds to gather himself, and then responded, "I am John Burroughs Hopkins, captain of the *Abigale*, and this is my first mate, John Paul Jones. We are from *Providence* and we heard there was a meeting of the Sons of *Liberty* tonight. We are curious to know what you are doing in this long-term battle with the British over their outlandish taxes."

Several of the men began talking at once, but they were quieted by the leader. "We did not invite you here and are not sure you belong with us," he said suspiciously. "Tell us more about yourselves."

"Until just a week ago, I was the second officer of the *Katy*, a ship captained by Abraham Whipple, hero of the *Gaspee* Affair. The *Katy* is owned by John Brown. The *Abigale* that we brought into port this afternoon is also owned by John Brown. Surely you have heard of John Brown, who was the mastermind of the destruction of the *Gaspee*."

Several men began nodding their heads and the rumble of voices began to rise again. This time John Burroughs lifted his hands for quiet. "John Paul and I were both in on the planning for the capture and destruction of the *Gaspee*. I was the captain of one of the long boats that captured it and burned it to the waterline." His words met with obvious approval and even some cheers from the men.

The leader of the group was now smiling. He said, "We have heard much about the taking of the *Gaspee* last year, and were cheering your bravery to take on a British gun boat with nothing but long boats. We are pleased you have found us. You are, indeed, in the right place."

A second man stepped up to the front and joined the speaker. He said, "I am Samuel Adams, owner of this pub and the brewery that sits behind it. This is John Hancock, who is the president of the Sons of *Liberty*. We are glad to have you. Come on in and have a seat."

John Burroughs and John Paul made their way further into the room and many of the men stood, shook their hands, and slapped them on their backs as they passed through. They found seats and John Hancock resumed speaking.

"Tomorrow night is the night," he said. "We will meet at the warehouse building just off Water Street, behind the wharf. All of you are to bring a disguise to make yourselves look like Indians. We will dress together in the warehouse. Don't come to the building in groups; come in ones and twos. We don't want to arouse any suspicion. I am going to give you our directions tonight so we won't have to do much talking tomorrow night when we meet. First, what time will we meet at the storage house?"

A chorus of response rose from the men, "Eleven o'clock!"

John Hancock continued, "What are you to bring?"

"Indian disguises!"

"Do you need your muskets?" John Handcock asked.

The response was unanimous and noisy: "Noooooo!"

Samuel Adams now spoke from the front of the room. "We want to caution you one more time. Nothing but the chests of tea are to be taken and thrown overboard. This is a protest against the tax on tea. It is not a raid on British ships. We are not sure of any cargo on the three ships other than tea, but whatever it is should be left alone.

"Our advance men will have the sentries down before you get there. That is why you won't need your muskets. We will pick the locks into the holds of the ships and form a chain from the hold to the side of each ship. There must be about a hundred chests of tea in each ship. They don't weigh very much. We shouldn't have any trouble getting them up on deck. By the time we finish, we should have more than three hundred chests of tea in the bay."

He paused, his eyes sweeping around the room. "Speed is of the upmost importance. We want to be on the ships no more than twenty minutes and then be gone without a trace. The sentries will be the only witnesses and they can only report that the ships were attacked by Indians.

When we finish, anyone who wants tea with their breakfast should be able to scoop it up right out of the bay."

With that last word, a loud cheer came up from the men and, with a signal from the front, they quieted immediately and began to depart. Their excitement was obvious. From the look of them, John Burroughs thought, they were a group of seamen who had never backed down from a fight and they were ready to strike a blow for freedom from British taxes, from British interference from three thousand miles away, from having to house British troops in their homes.

John Burroughs and John Paul waited until the room cleared a bit and then began to make their way to the front. Samuel Adams, John Hancock, and another man were bent over a table, talking in low voices. The *Providence* pair didn't interrupt them and stood silently until Samuel Adams turned to face them.

"Well, what do you think, Captain Hopkins?" he asked.

"It sounds like a protest against taxes and the Navigation Acts, and we would like to be a part of it. Can we join you tomorrow night?" John Burroughs said.

"You most certainly can. We would be honored to have you along," said the third man who was, as yet, unidentified.

John Burroughs smiled at him and said, "I haven't had the pleasure, sir."

The man stood up to his full height, which was not very tall. John Burroughs was a full six feet and the man could not have been more than five-foot-six. He said, "My name is Paul Revere and the three of us, John, Samuel, and I, organized the Sons of *Liberty* three years ago following the Massacre. This is the first major protest event since we organized. We are determined that our planning will be such that it will not be the last."

"I am pleased to make your acquaintance, sir," John Burroughs responded. "My friend and I hope that we can learn some things that we can take home to *Providence*."

"Considering your success with the *Gaspee*, I'm not sure you need any help from us," Mr. Revere said with a broad smile. "It is good that you are here. We need to be in contact with other organizations in the Colonies that are as concerned with the tax situation and the relationship with the British as we are. Excuse us for a moment more." With that comment, Paul Revere turned back to his two companions.

John Burroughs and John Paul stood silently until the three had finished their short discussion. When it appeared they were ready to leave, John Burroughs asked, "We need to know where to meet tomorrow night over by the wharf. We wouldn't want to be left behind."

"Where are you staying tonight, captain?" Samuel Adams asked. John Burroughs told him about the pub just across from the wharf.

"You are in a good location to find us. When you leave the pub through the front door, walk to your left to the corner. Then turn left and walk about half a block. You will see an alley to your right across the street. There is a doorway about thirty yards down that alley. We will be there getting ready at eleven," Samuel Adams said. "I own that warehouse. No one should be on the street at that time of night, but be careful not to let any of the red-coats see you."

Most of the next day was spent supervising the unloading of the cargo of the *Abigale* but there was no denying the growing excitement as both John Burroughs and John Paul anticipated the activities of the night. They went to their room above the pub late in the afternoon with the plan to lie down and get some rest so they would be ready for the raid that evening, but sleep eluded them. Instead, they spent most of the late afternoon talking about what might transpire in the evening to come with the Sons of *Liberty*. A visit to a blacksmith's shop availed them of soot to paint their faces and they also bought two small hatchets to take the place of tomahawks.

It was just before eleven when the two friends stepped inside the warehouse just down the street from the wharf. It was a big room, single story but with a high ceiling to accommodate the many casks of rum and beer that were stacked along the walls. The room was already full of men who were in various stages of undress, putting on their Indian disguises.

Some had turkey feathers in their hair. Many were applying soot to their faces to darken their skin. It was cold in the big facility and once the disguises were in place most of the men pulled rough blankets over their bear chests.

When Samuel Adams walked up to them, John Burroughs had to look at him twice to be sure who it was. He was dressed in a red coat with soot on his face but his deep voice gave him away. "It is good to see you fellows. I had hoped you would be here," he said.

"We wouldn't have missed it. We count ourselves lucky to have arrived here just at the right time," said John Paul.

Samuel Adams sat down on a wine cask next to the wall. He said, "We don't anticipate major trouble on the ships. Our advance group will approach each of them in long boats wearing red coats. They will think it is a part of their company coming back from the taverns. By the time we are on board and they know better, we should have them. We think there may be as few as two sentries on each of the ships but if there are more we are sending eight men in each long boat, so I am sure we can handle them.

"As soon as we see our group of red-coats on board we will cast off from the wharf, and all our people know what to do after that," he continued.

"Do you have anything specific you want us to do?" John Burroughs asked.

"No, you just fill in and do what the others are doing. I have made you a space on the boat commanded by one of our people you haven't yet met. He is Benedict Arnold. Ben is a soldier and is one of our most capable leaders. Come with me and I'll introduce you to him," he said.

They found Benedict Arnold in a back corner putting the finishing touches on his face. "Ben, let me introduce you to the two visitors from *Providence* I told you about. This is Captain John Burroughs Hopkins and his first mate, John Jones," Adams said.

Arnold greeted them in a soft voice. "Welcome to our party, fellows. It is good to have you with us."

"We are glad to be here," responded John Burroughs.

"We won't be ready to go for a while but when we are, stay close to me. Once we are on the ship, you fill in wherever you see the need. Most of the men will be hauling tea chests out of the hold. Once the chests start to move, we have to make sure the only sound anyone hears is them hitting the water," he said. "If guns are fired or it looks as if we are discovered, make quickly for the boats. The boat captains have orders not to return to the wharf but, instead, to row out toward the middle of the channel and circle back down-stream. We will not be meeting back at the warehouse. Instead, everyone is to make their way home and act surprised in the morning when the news of the attack becomes public. When you leave here, you need to tie your clothes in a bundle and carry them with you on to the long boats. When we are back in the boats, you can change out of your Indian gear and dump it in the bay. All of the boats are going to different places. By the time we reach our destination, just south of town, we should look like a group of seamen coming in from a newly anchored ship in the harbor. "

Samuel Adams escorted the two friends back to where they had left their clothes. "I will be leaving in just a minute, so you won't see me again," he said. "I am in one of the advance boats and have to go and get my British Army hat and white nickers on. You come with the others and stay close to Ben. We want you to know how much we admired your bravery with the *Gaspee* attack and are very pleased to have you along for this late-night party." With a quick hand shake, he was gone.

They didn't have long to wait. Several of the men were gathering around the door and the two friends joined them. Before long they were just two in a mass of Indians creeping in the shadows toward the wharf. When they arrived, they could see three long boats in the water headed for the three British merchant ships. They found Benedict Arnold and boarded the boat he was on.

John Burroughs was struck by the silence of that many men headed to battle. Several had knives or hatchets, like the ones he and John Paul wore in their belts, but no one had a gun. All he could hear was the sound of breathing and the steady stroking of oars in the water. He felt the tension of the men close to him and the hair was standing up on the back of his neck. All were straining to hear if a shot was fired or if there was any sound of discovery. None came.

They were about half-way to their assigned target, the farthest British merchant ship out in the harbor, when they saw a red-coated sentry running across the deck of the closest ship. He climbed up the ladder onto the fantail, ran the few steps to the rail, and dove over it into the water below. John Burroughs shivered at the thought of hitting that cold water on this December night. There was an immediate reaction from the men in the boat, but Benedict Arnold said just one word in a whisper and it stopped the noise immediately. "Quiet!"

They kept listening for some sound that would indicate they had been discovered, but they were climbing up the rope ladder on the side of the boat before they heard the first sound from any of the Indians. All of the voices that were heard from that point on were in a whisper.

John Burroughs marveled at the efficiency of the raiders. Everyone seemed to know exactly what to do. Some were in the hold already and chests of tea were coming up to be pitched over the side into the bay. The two friends from *Providence* took a position at the side rail and together they grabbed chests of tea from the chain of men and lifted them over the rail. The first time they heard the splash of a chest hitting the water, it sounded like an explosion. *Surely someone on shore could hear the noises that were coming from the British ships,* John Burroughs thought but, surprisingly, there was no sound from shore that indicated anyone was aware of what was happening out in the bay.

Soon the hold of their ship was empty. It was evidently the same on the other two ships as well, since the sounds of chests splashing into the bay stopped and, instead, they could hear the sounds of men climbing over the rail to the rope ladders and into the long boats. The boat led by Benedict Arnold was the last to leave the side of the British ship. One man was carried to the rail and hoisted over the side into their boat. He appeared to be lifeless.

"What happened to him?" John Burroughs whispered.

"He was down in the hold and someone dropped a chest. It hit him in the head. I think he is dead," a man responded.

"Who is he?" another man asked.

"His name is John Crane. He is a carpenter and lives just south of the down town. We are going to take him home to his wife," the other man replied. "Poor lady."

Within minutes the channel of the bay was filled with long boats making their way southward toward a landing well below the main wharf. It was the first time John Burroughs had been able to count how many long boats had been involved. He could see four in the channel but knew there were more in the shadows along the shore.

It was as Benedict Arnold had said. By the time the long boats reached their destination well south of the wharf area, all were out of their Indian gear and dressed like seamen again. The only evidence they had been in the raiding party was the soot still on the faces of several of the men. They were dipping water from over the side of the boat to wash off the last remnants of the tell-tale soot.

John Burroughs and John Paul stopped for just a few seconds and shook hands with their leader, Benedict Arnold, before heading into the shadows to make their way back to the tavern and their room upstairs.

There would be no sleep that night. Back in their room, they gathered their things and quietly made their way downstairs. The night clerk signed them out and seemed pleased to put their money in his cash box. John Burroughs thought to himself as they made their way back to the wharf and the water taxi, *There is a maid who will be pleased that she doesn't have to make up any beds in our room. They ought to give us a refund for what we didn't use.* Before many minutes had passed they were on a water taxi headed toward the *Abigale*. It was their plan to make ready to sail and to be out of the harbor at first light. They were a bit disappointed to miss the excitement of the morning when the word began to spread about the events of the night before, but it was much safer to be gone.

It was about mid-morning and they were well out in the Atlantic headed toward Cape Cod before the two friends met on the fantail of the ship to talk about their adventure with the Sons of *Liberty*. Who could have thought when they accepted the assignment to take a cargo of sugar and molasses up to *Boston* they would be walking into such an opportunity? Who could have known they would meet four stalwarts of the fight against the evils of the Navigation Acts in the persons of John Hancock, Samuel Adams, Paul Revere, and Benedict Arnold?

Twice young Jim had come up on the fantail where John Burroughs was standing as the ship made its way across Cape Cod Bay to the point just above Provincetown. He was anxious to hear about their visit to *Boston.* John Burroughs was not sure how much to tell him about the so-called Indian attack on the three British ships in the harbor. He finally settled on a more limited story that included their meeting with the Sons of *Liberty* and the determination of that group to be free of British rule. He knew the newspapers would be full of the Indian raid and expected that young Jim would put two and two together and realize there was more stories to tell.

The two friends did not talk much about the attack of the three British ships in *Boston* harbor when they returned to *Providence.* They didn't have to. The newspaper in *Providence* and those all up and down the coast of the Colonies were full of the story of the Indians who threw more than three hundred chests of tea into *Boston* Harbor. Humorist Benjamin Franklin of Philadelphia, writing in his magazine, *Poor Richard's Almanac,* speculated it was because Indians actually preferred coffee over tea. He said they obviously had come to pillage the ships but, finding nothing of value on board, had thrown the tea overboard in frustration.

John Burroughs Hopkins and John Paul Jones knew better.

THE PROVIDENCE GAZETTE

PROVIDENCE, Rhode Island, September 1, 1774--The history of relationships between Great Britain and the thirteen colonies in the new world has always been mutually supportive. The British have provided protection from hostile Indians and from the French and Spanish when such protection was needed. In return, we have sent the great majority of our products to England for their use. One might expect, from time to time, that conflict would materialize.

Finally, the other shoe has dropped in Boston. Reacting to the dumping of 300 chests of tea into Boston Harbor, the British Parliament has passed four measures that have effectively stripped the state of Massachusetts of self-government and judicial independence. In addition, the Boston port has been closed while Massachusetts is brought under Crown control and additional British troops are brought in.

The colonies all up and down the Atlantic coast have responded in an unusual show of solidarity against such heavy- handed measures. All have declared a general boycott of British goods. In addition, in reaction to the British Parliament's actions, each colony is sending delegates to meet in Philadelphia to organize opposition to these intolerable acts.

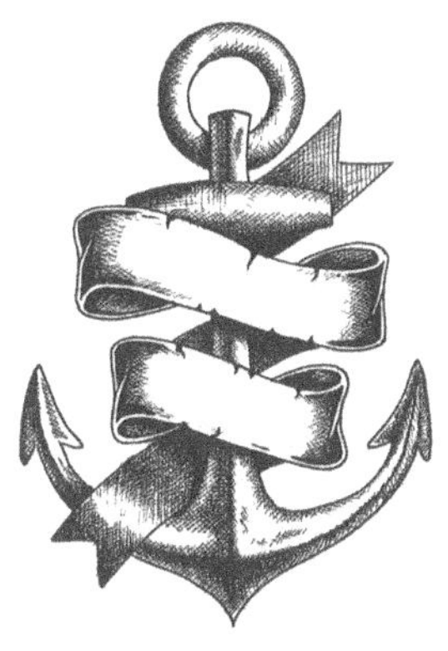

CHAPTER 6
PIRATES AND PRIVATEERS IN COLONIAL HISTORY
PROVIDENCE, RHODE ISLAND
SEPTEMBER 30, 1774

"I don't care how many ships you have involved in the slave trade or how much money you are making, John, it is just wrong," said Moses Brown to his brother John.

"That is not the way you felt about it before you moved your family into the Quaker fold," responded John. "Brothers Nicholas and Joseph don't feel that way about it at all."

The two brothers stared at each other across the table in the kitchen of John Brown's house on Planet Street near the center of *Providence* where they had been sitting with mugs of coffee. Coffee had become the preferred beverage of the Colonies after the *Boston* Tea Party, but their discussion was not new. In fact, it had recurred over and over during their business partnership. John Brown was a devoted Baptist, while brother Moses was a Quaker.

"I either own or have invested in thirteen ships that make money in a variety of ways on the ocean," John Brown continued. "And I have built a good many more which I sold to others who do the same thing. It just makes sense to keep the hold of a ship filled with saleable commodities wherever they are traveling. The Caribbean Islands and the southern Colonies are hungry for slaves. The rum we make here from Caribbean molasses and sugar is legal tender in Africa. By the time we bring the makings of rum from the Caribbean, haul the rum to Africa, and take slaves to the south, we have made money on all three corners of the triangle."

"John, just how rich do you need to be? Surely there is another way," Moses protested. "Selling a man into permanent servitude is just wrong."

"Little brother, slavery has existed since the beginning of time and it will outlast all of us," said John. "Read your Bible."

"John, the slavery isn't the only thing that bothers me," said Moses.

"So, what else?" John responded with a sigh, lighting his pipe.

"How many of your ships are involved in piracy?" he asked, staring at his brother with sober eyes.

John paused for a few seconds, gathering his thoughts and smoking, and then replied, "Moses, it isn't piracy. We call it 'privateering.' We are loyal British subjects and our mother country has just finished a decade-long war with France. In other years, they have been at war with Spain. You know as well as I do that the King has encouraged us to do whatever we can to help their war effort by raiding French and Spanish shipping. How many of my ships are involved, you ask? Well, pretty nearly all of them. We send them to other ports to acquire or sell merchandise but if they happen to run across a French or Spanish ship on the way, then we run up our British flag and take them for the good of the Crown. It is good business and if we take a French ship on the high seas, both the ship and anything it is carrying become ours. We can sell the merchandise and refit the ship for our purpose."

"You can call it privateering if you want to, but it sounds a lot like stealing to me," Moses responded. "The Bible says, 'Thou shalt not steal.'"

"That may be true," John said, "but someone smarter than me said, 'All is fair in love and war,' and we have been at war."

Moses took a long sip of his own coffee and continued his interrogation.

"John, I know you have been doing this for months, if not years," he said. "Are there others like you who have ships on the high seas involved in piracy?"

"Moses, *privateering* has been here as long as ships have sailed the seven seas," John replied patiently. "For every harbor up and down the Atlantic coast, there are dozens of ships devoted to the privateering trade. That is true from *Boston* to Charleston and south into the Caribbean. In fact, it is in the Caribbean where privateering thrives most. That is due to the amount of Spanish and French ship traffic in that region throughout the year. King George encouraged us to do whatever damage we could to French merchant traffic as long as the war was going on. The Spanish control that area so their ships are numerous there and easy to take."

"Why the Caribbean? It seems that there should be more traffic in this area, with *Boston* and New York harbors being the most active in the Colonies," asked Moses.

"It has mostly to do with the weather, Moses," John responded. "For much of the year the north Atlantic is a difficult sea to travel. Not so with the more southern climate of the Caribbean. Ships from Europe could travel the north Atlantic and find a shorter trip, but they are fighting a headwind most of the way because of the prevailing winds and they are likely to meet one or more storms coming across without the advantage of the wind to outrun them. Traveling the southern route, they can travel south from Europe to the Canary Islands and head due west with tail winds all the way into warmer and calmer seas. They do have to worry about the occasional hurricane."

"Just how many pirate ships do you sponsor, John?" asked Moses.

John frowned at the use of the word "pirate" and re-lit his pipe, which had gone out. "We have thirteen right now, but we have built many more in our shipyard over the years that are now used as privateers," he said. "Moses, my thirteen ships are just a drop in the bucket. I am sure we could count more than fifty ships that make their living as privateers that call *Providence* Harbor home."

"I had no idea," said Moses. "Does that hold true for the other major ports in the Colonies?"

"Oh, yes," John replied. "Fifty seems like a large number for *Providence*, but I would wager that *Boston* and Charleston both have many more than we do."

"How many altogether, John?" asked Moses. "How many would you guess?"

"I'm sure no one knows for sure, but I'm sure there are more than one thousand," John replied. "My ship captains tell me they are forever running into competition when they find a prize worth taking. There are usually two or three other privateers staking out the same target. The problem has become so great for the European countries that they have begun to travel with guard ships and in convoys for protection."

"There must be hundreds of men killed with each fight," said Moses, shaking his head and shuddering a little.

"Actually, a surprising few are killed. Most of the merchant ships are not equipped to fight a privateer and so they surrender without a fight," said John. "Of course, if there is resistance, then someone is bound to get hurt. If there is no resistance, then the captain and crew of the captured ship are released when we get to port."

John continued, "Moses, my ships and most of the others carry soldiers on board with them to handle the heavy fighting if it should occur. Each ship also has a group of extra seamen to handle the prizes when we take them, so we can be sure to get them back to port where we can unload the cargo and auction off the ships.

"One of the problems we struggle with is that we may start a voyage with an empty hold and a larger than necessary crew, but by the time we are well into our trip, if we have been successful, our ships are dangerously undermanned. The extra crewmen and soldiers will be used to man the captured ships and will be headed back to port leaving my ships vulnerable. I have lost a number of ships due to that problem."

He stretched his long legs. "In recent months, the French and British have gotten smart and we find their hostile man-of-war class ships waiting for us when we get back close to home," John concluded.

"Well, if there is such risk of losses, why do you continue to do it?" asked Moses grumpily.

"There is a risk of loss. It is the chance you take as a man of business," replied John. "The risk is great but so are the rewards. On the ledger of profit and loss, we are running way ahead on the profit side."

"John, it still sounds like stealing to me," replied Moses, draining his coffee mug.

"You can call it whatever you want," John responded. "But we owe much of our wealth to the success of our ships and captains. If we were dependent only on the sugar and molasses trade from the West Indies, we would already be in the poor house. For that matter, so would the majority of merchants and traders in *Providence*. We are not by ourselves taking advantage of this challenge King George gave us to help him with the conflict he had with France and Spain."

The brothers sat quietly for a moment, John continuing to enjoy his pipe. Finally, Moses spoke up. "Let me get this straight," he said. "You are telling me that the pirate enterprise going on now from our shores is primarily a product of the wars with Spain and France and King George's call for colonial ships and captains to help him with the war effort."

John nodded. "There you have it. There were pirates before the wars, all the way back to 1650, plying their trade up and down the Atlantic coast, but there were just a few truly bloodthirsty ones, like Blackbeard and Captain Kidd, back in our grandfather's day. After the latest challenge from King George and Parliament, these Intolerable Acts, we have filled the oceans with them. I said earlier I thought there were maybe one thousand or more. Actually, I think that number may be way low, maybe by fifty percent or more."

Moses still wasn't satisfied with his brother's answers. "You and our brothers may all agree that this is good business and is legitimate enterprise, but I don't think so. Slavery and stealing, no matter how you label them, are both a violation of what we have been taught in the Holy Scriptures."

"I don't think we are going to agree on this subject, Moses. Let's let it rest and agree to disagree," responded John. "Let me see what my lovely wife has planned for supper. Will you stay and take a meal with us?"

THE PROVIDENCE GAZETTE

PROVIDENCE, Rhode Island, September 30, 1775--We are at war! The Massachusetts Militia has formed a ring around Boston in reaction to the closing of Boston Harbor and the removal of self-determination rights. General George Washington has been sent to command the troops that seem to grow in number each day.

In April, a battle between the British Army and a group of militiamen occurred on the green at Lexington and resulted in eight patriots lost. It is reported that the British tallied 73 dead and 174 wounded. The militia was made up primarily of local farmers and shop keepers from Lexington and Concord. They were protecting a store of arms and powder stored in Concord.

In June, General Washington fortified Breeds Hill and Bunker Hill on the outskirts of Boston and the British attacked. The colonial militia had to withdraw but not before creating havoc among the British troops and causing a high number of causalities.

Delegates from the thirteen Colonies continue to meet in Philadelphia regarding the Intolerable Acts and the hostilities that have broken out around Boston.

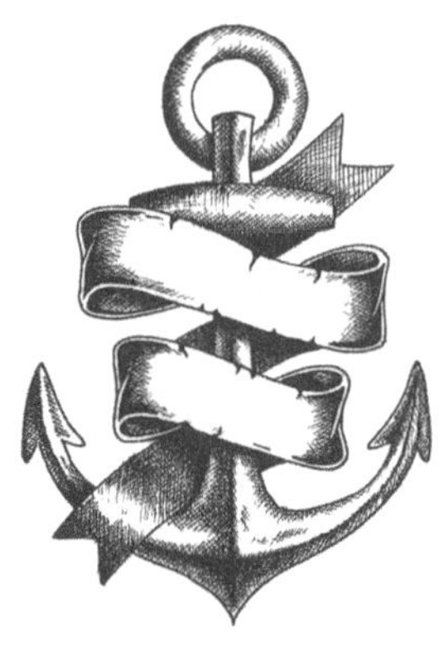

CHAPTER 7
MEETING OF THE SECOND CONTINENTAL CONGRESS

PHILADELPHIA, PENNSYLVANIA

OCTOBER 30, 1775

It was approaching nine o'clock in the morning when the gavel struck the chairman's table at the front of the Continental Congress's meeting room in the Pennsylvania State House. Delegates from the thirteen Colonies were still arriving, placing their great coats on the hooks around the wall and taking their places at the various tables in the room.

The total membership of the Second Continental Congress, which had begun meeting in May, was fifty-six men, at least three from each colony and four from several with larger populations. Not every delegate was at every meeting, but a quorum of thirty-three was needed for the group to take action. A murmur of voices could be heard from across the room as the delegates reluctantly came to order.

Chairman John Hancock was on his feet in front of the group and his voice dominated the room as he moderated the latest debate between the delegates.

"A statement is in order before we begin our business of the day, which is to be a discussion on creating a navy," he said. "We have held many discussions about the possibility of war with Great Britain over the past several months. We need to recognize that hostilities have broken out in a number of locations going back as far as 1769 in Newport, Rhode Island. It happened again with the *Gaspee* Affair in 1772. *Boston* Harbor witnessed the 'Indian' attack in December of 1773."

His words were met with nods and muttering, as these events were well known to them all. Hancock continued, "This past spring, twenty-five of our young men were killed by the British at Lexington, Massachusetts. Since then, the Massachusetts Militia has pretty well declared war on the British occupying forces in *Boston*. The militia are poised at the outskirts of the city and stand ready to attack as soon as the winter weather breaks. Some would say we are already at war with Great Britain. At the very least, the hostilities that are apparent in our northern Colonies lend a seriousness to these discussions."

He paused to survey the room of men, all of whom were giving him keen attention. "Now, let us focus our attention on the issue of creating a navy," said Chairman Hancock. "The chair recognizes the honorable Silas Deane of Connecticut, who requested an opportunity to address you this morning."

Silas Dean was a slightly built man who was well known to the Congress as both a lawyer and merchant. He said, "Honored gentlemen, if hostilitics come, the major challenge we have is how to keep the British from supplying their troops here on our shores. Right now, they have complete freedom of the seas, as well as ships that number with the grains of sand on our beaches. They can bring both reinforcements and supplies in and out of our ports with impunity. We need a plan to cut off their supply lines. If we can do that, we can starve them out of action."

It was customary to approve of a statement by stomping feet, slapping hands on a table or raising voices. When Silas Deane sat down, the men of the Congress were doing all three.

Immediately, two others stood, seeking attention from the chair: *Richard* Henry Lee of Virginia and John Adams of Massachusetts. "The chair recognizes the honorable *Richard* Henry Lee of Virginia," John Hancock said. John Adams resumed his front row seat and listened while Delegate Lee addressed the group.

"The honorable Silas Deane of Connecticut is right," Lee said. "We have to do something that affects the shipping of goods to the British Army on our shores. We also have a second problem that relates to shipping. Should hostilities come, it is obvious that the British marketplace will be cut off to us. But we won't be able ship any of our goods to France or Spain either. The British can easily blockade our ports so that nothing goes in or out. Spain and France can be a major market for our goods and put money in our coffers. We need a navy that can cut through the blockade that is surely coming."

Again, the men of the Congress made their sounds of approval. Again, there were two men standing for an opportunity to speak: John Adams of Massachusetts and Joseph Hewes of North Carolina. John Handcock boomed, "The chair recognizes the honorable Joseph Hewes of North Carolina."

As Hewes rose to speak, John Adams moved quietly from his seat and approached Chairman Hancock at the front of the room.

"Honored gentlemen," Hewes said, "I can second the position of Delegate Lee from Virginia. We have three viable ports in North Carolina, at Elizabeth City, New Bern, and Wilmington. All three appear to be bottled up by British war ships. If we can't find a way to break free, we have no choice but to haul our goods north to Portsmouth or south to Charleston. Both of those will most likely be blockaded with the firing of the first musket."

While Joseph Hewes was speaking, a whispered conversation had been going on next to the chairman's desk at the front of the room. Chairman Hancock's voice carried a bit better than that of John Adams. Those on the front row heard him say, "I don't care, John. I'm not letting you on the floor to speak to this issue. I will let you speak in front of the group when the issue comes to a head. Right now, I intend to let everyone have their say before we move on to creating a committee to form a navy."

John Adams spoke again to the chairman, his voice too soft to hear. Then the close listeners on the front row heard Chairman Hancock say, "John, no one wants to hear you pontificate on the subject of trade difficulties." In exasperation, he added, "John, as difficult as it is to hear, no one likes you. Your presence at the front of the room right now will simply slow down our progress."

Again, John Adams's soft reply could not be heard, but Hancock's words showed he had made his point. "All right, John," the chairman said, "I'll appoint you to the committee." Satisfied, Adams returned to his front row seat.

Chairman Hancock reclaimed the floor. "About three weeks ago," he said, "this Congress authorized the construction and arming of ships to become the first navy of these united Colonies. What we need today is a committee made up of capable leaders who can provide guidance for the staffing of our new navy and planning for additional ships to join these first twelve that should be ready to put to sea sometime in January of 1776. With that in mind, I would like to appoint the following people to the Congressional Navy Committee. Those who are present and will accept the challenge, please answer 'Yea' as I call your name."

Hancock looked about the room, making eye contact with his appointees.

"John Adams of Massachusetts."

"Yea."

"Joseph Hewes of North Carolina."

"Yea."

"John Langdon of New Hampshire"

"Yea."

"*Richard* Henry Lee of Virginia."

"Yea."

"Silas Deane of Connecticut."

"Yea."

"And, as chairman of the committee," Hancock concluded, "I appoint Stephen Hopkins of Rhode Island."

Stephen Hopkins said, "Yea."

"I would like a vote of confidence from the Congress for the work of this committee," Chairman Handcock said.

As if in one voice, the men shouted, "Yea!"

"Now," Chairman Handcock said, "I declare this meeting adjourned. I would suggest to Mr. Hopkins that the Navy Committee convene for a few minutes before you leave to set a time for your first full meeting. I'm sure you can use this room for your meetings."

The body of fifty-six men filed slowly out of the room, many of them to meet at Johnson's Pub that was located just across the back street behind the State House in Philadelphia. The new committee gathered in the back corner of the meeting room, where Stephen Hopkins addressed them quietly. "It is already late in the day, gentlemen. I suggest that we meet informally over at Johnson's and get better acquainted. Then we can set a time and place that is convenient for all for our first official meeting."

About twenty minutes later, all six of the new appointees had gathered around a table near the fireplace at the pub. "Gentlemen, let's take a few minutes and introduce ourselves," Stephen Hopkins said. "We all know each other by face and reputation, but I would like each of you to tell why you think you were appointed to this committee and what you can contribute to our efforts. With your kind permission, I will go first.

"I am Stephen Hopkins, and I began working on ships when I was just a boy. In *Providence*, we have the sea and what comes from the sea. There isn't anything else. I have also been governor of Rhode Island and, until I came down here, I was the chief justice of the supreme court of that colony. With my business partner, John Brown, I build ships and own several ships including our flagship, the *Katy*. My brother, Esek, is a ship's captain, as is my nephew, John Burroughs Hopkins. I suspect I was named chairman of this group because I have served on ships, built ships, and own ships."

When Stephen Hopkins finished he nodded at John Langdon.

John Langdon shook his head, saying, "I'm not sure any of us can match the background of Mr. Hopkins. As you know, I am from New Hampshire. My family made their living farming, and I did that, too, for a while. Then I got into ship building and then became captain of a cargo ship. I have no experience being a soldier or doing battle, but I do know ships and I know about trade and the necessities of trade on the high seas."

Steven Hopkins then nodded at Joseph Hewes.

Joseph Hewes spoke slowly and in a low voice. "As you know, I am from North Carolina. My people are all farmers. We know about getting a crop up and getting it to market, both in our colony and to the next one. We have been trading with France now for several years despite the Navigation Acts and the many restrictions they impose.

John Adams spoke next. "I am an attorney from *Boston*. Most of my legal practice has been with merchants and seaman. We are the biggest port city in the Colonies, and I am certainly aware of the strength of the British Navy, which has been using *Boston* Harbor as its home base for the past two decades."

Next up was *Richard* Henry Lee. "Like Mr. Hewes, we are farmers. However, I have been in the Virginia legislature for the past decade when we have had no small amount of trouble with the British. I believe we have to find a way to break out of being landlocked by the British and we need to use our best thinking to trade with the French and the Spanish. Neither have any love for the British and will help us if they can." *Richard* Henry Lee looked over at Silas Deane and smiled.

"I guess that leaves me," Silas Deane said. "I am a merchant who has been trading on the high seas for many years. I am also a lawyer who has served both merchants and ship owners. Connecticut has several ports, but all are tied up now with British ships of various sizes and descriptions. In recent times, I have seen more man-of-war ships than I have in my lifetime. Gentlemen, we have our work cut out for us."

"I appreciate all of you coming and sharing with us," said Chairman Hopkins. "Let's close this off now and meet again in the morning at nine o'clock in the meeting room of the State House. In the meantime, I will do some homework and see if I can find a place for us to start our deliberations."

It was just after nine the next morning when the committee of six reconvened. Chairman Hopkins addressed the group. "Gentlemen, we have several serious issues to discuss. Let's start with what the primary goal of our navy should be as we enter conflict with Great Britain. Who would like to speak first?"

Several hands were raised, but the chairman called on John Adams.

"The largest ship in our navy is the *Katy* from *Providence*," the *Boston* lawyer said. "I understand it has recently been renamed the *Providence*. It carries sixteen cannons and two swivel guns. It is outfitted for a crew of sixty men, including soldiers. That is no match for most of the British ships we have seen near our ports in recent months. A British man-of-war is a fearsome weapon with more than a hundred cannons and a crew of three hundred or more. If we try to match up with the British ship-on-ship, our navy will disappear with the first engagement. It won't be like the *Gaspee* Affair, where the British gun boat was marooned on a sandbar and men in long boats with nothing but muskets could take it."

Several men nodded and voiced approval of John Adams's comments. He continued, "We have to do our best not to face off directly with the British Navy. Instead, we need to concentrate on the words shared by Silas Deane yesterday. We must focus on British shipping. We must do whatever is necessary to keep the British from resupplying their troops here on our soil."

Again, several men voiced their approval of John Adams's comments. Then Joseph Hewes from North Carolina spoke up. "If it is allowed, I would like to ask the learned gentleman a question."

Chairman Hopkins nodded in the direction of Joseph Hewes. He faced John Adams directly and said, "How, sir, do you intend to get our ships out of the ports where the British Navy has them blockaded, so they can do some damage to British shipping?" His voice took on a hostile tone toward the end and it was obvious that he intended a confrontation.

Chairman Hopkins interrupted to respond to the question knowing that John Adams was not popular with the group. He felt he needed to prevent a possible confrontation between the delegates. "It's a good question," responded Hopkins. "If we have to rely only on the twelve ships currently being prepared by our Congress, we don't have a chance to do any real damage."

"So, what do you propose, Mr.. Hopkins?" said Hewes.

Chairman Hopkins smiled to himself, pleased that he had shifted the conversation to himself instead of to John Adams. He replied. "I would like to point out that every port along the Atlantic Ocean, every port from every colony, has ships of various sizes as well as seamen to man them. They may not be strong enough to do damage to the British Navy, but they most certainly can do damage to British shipping. In fact, they have been doing damage to British, French, and Spanish shipping for close to a hundred years now. Some call them pirates and others call them privateers. Whatever you call them, they have the experience and the fire power to do much damage to those who are bringing supplies to the British Army. We just have to rally them to our cause, instead of their own," said Hopkins.

"You are begging the question, Mr. Hopkins," Joseph Hewes said. "Whether it is our small navy or these pirates you talk about, how can they beat a British blockade?"

"It is a matter of numbers, Mr. Hewes," responded Hopkins patiently. "You are focused on the small number of twelve, twelve ships in our navy. However, if our navy had several hundred ships, maybe even a thousand coming out of our ports in the dark of night, how would two or three man-of-war ships cope with them?"

"I'm beginning to see the seeds of a plan," said *Richard* Henry Lee of Virginia. "We have no hope whatsoever of building a navy to cope with the British three-masters, but if we can enlist the pirates from up and down the coast to join our cause, we have a chance to counter British power with numbers."

"I can't believe we are honestly talking about incorporating pirates into our navy," sputtered Silas Deane. "They have been the scourge of the seas as long as the colonies have been here. We have tried to exterminate them every way we know how and now we are talking about making peace with them and giving them the legitimacy of becoming a part of our navy!"

John Langdon countered, "There is another problem bigger than whether to have them as a part of our navy or not, and that is whether or not they would consent to join us. Why should they leave their very lucrative business of thievery on the high seas and become subject to colonial authority as a part of our navy?"

The comments of Deane and Langdon led to a lively discussion but, as several men began to speak at once Chairman Hopkins raised his hand, asking for silence. He said, "Let's agree on three things from this meeting. If anyone disagrees with anything I list, please make it known now. I don't want to present anything to the Congress that is not unanimous among us. First, we should ask Congress for the money to outfit more ships. We don't need twelve ships, we need dozens. Second, we need all of us to return home and find leadership not only for the twelve ships we will have shortly, but also for those we intend to have down the road. It is not too soon to begin identifying our new navy's leadership. Third, we need to begin identifying the pirate ships in our harbors that may become the focus as we set up our auxiliary navy."

The men around the table nodded, though Silas Deane was the last to agree.

"Could I add one more thing?" said John Adams, glancing at Deane. "We need to stop calling them pirates. Let's call them privateers. We have a better chance of getting approval for our new approach to solving the navy problem if we are dealing with private businessmen as opposed to outlaw pirates."

Chairman Hopkins responded, "Mr. Adams is right. From this point on, every reference to the auxiliary navy will use the word 'privateer' as opposed to that much more offensive word. Gentlemen, we are adjourned."

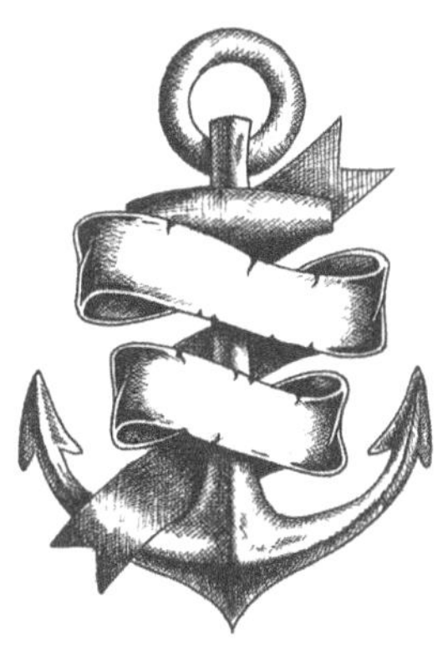

CHAPTER 8
THE NAVY COMMITTEE REPORTS TO CONGRESS

PHILADELPHIA, PENNSYLVANIA

DECEMBER 22, 1775

December in Philadelphia is both wet and cold. Frost is on the ground almost every morning when it isn't snowingThe room in the Pennsylvania State House where the Second Continental Congress was meeting was heated by a fireplace, but that caused the group to cluster at one end of the room close to the fireplace for warmth. Most of the men in the room keep their over coats on, and were glad they wore wigs. Although wigs were a practical response to the problems of head lice—a gentleman could shave his head and still have a head of hairthey also kept the heads warm. In addition, some men continued to wear their tri-corner hats as well.

Fortunately, the Congress was beginning its last day of discussion prior to taking a four-week recess for the Christmas season.

John Hancock banged his gavel on the old wooden table at the front of the room. "The Continental Congress will come to order," he said formally. "The first order of business is a report from the Congressional Navy Committee. The chair recognizes the Honorable Stephen Hopkins of Rhode Island, chairman of the committee."

"Thank you, Mr. Chairman," responded Stephen Hopkins. "The committee has been working diligently for the past month on the task assigned and will make a report to this body in two parts. First, we want to nominate to you the first leadership of our navy and to tell you a bit about the ships that have been prepared to meet our opposition on the high seas. Second, we want to share a plan of defense of our shores and our ports. We would appreciate action by this body to endorse the leadership, the ships, and the plan we are presenting. As is always our practice, we would invite any of the best thoughts and advice from the membership."

He looked around the room, gratified by the nodding heads and attentive postures of the men. "First, I would like to reintroduce the members of our committee. Gentlemen, please stand as I call your name," Hopkins said. "From Massachusetts, Mr. John Adams, *Richard* Henry Lee from Virginia, John Langdon of New Hampshire, Silas Deane from Connecticut, and John Hewes of North Carolina."

Several men began to show their approval by clapping their hands and slapping them on the tables. However, one voice of dissent rose from the floor. It was John Rutledge of South Carolina, who asked querulously, "I can see why most of these men were placed on the committee. But when has John Adams ever gone to sea?"

Muffled laughter arose. John Rutledge's was a voice they heard often in the Continental Congress. He was not a popular speaker, given to making wild gestures with his hands as he talked, and with an extreme nasal quality to his voice. He was, as some called him, a bit of an agitator, and there was no mistaking his disdain for John Adams. They had clashed many times in discussions before during meetings of the Congress.

"John Adams is a man known to us all," Hopkins responded evenly. "He has lived near *Boston* Harbor most of his life and has much experience dealing with the issues of the British Navy."

"Yes, and he was the one who defended those murderers from the *Boston* Massacre," Rutledge responded acidly.

John Adams was on his feet immediately, ready to defend himself, but Chairman Hopkins intervened. "He was, indeed, and they were found innocent of all charges by a jury of men from *Boston*," Hopkins responded.

"Gentlemen," Chairman Hancock said, "There have been times when open discussion is very much in order. This isn't one of them. We have serious issues on the floor from our navy committee that we need to hear. Let's concentrate on the report that is before us. Chairman Hopkins, please proceed."

Rutledge resumed his seat, looking grumpy. Hopkins resumed with his presentation. "First, we would like to recommend to you four captains to provide leadership to our ships. They are Abraham Whipple, the hero of the *Gaspee* Affair; Nicholas Biddle from Pennsylvania; John Burroughs Hopkins of Rhode Island; and Dudley Saltonstall of Connecticut. As the commander- in-chief with the title of commodore, we recommend Esek Hopkins of Rhode Island."

There were approving nods around the room. "In addition, we recommend the commissioning of five first lieutenants and seven other officers. Several sheets of paper with their names have been circulating in the room since the meeting began. I hope everyone has gotten a chance to read them," Hopkins concluded.

Turning to Hancock, he said, "Mr. Chairman, we would appreciate action on the part of the Congress to commission these various officers as listed."

"Thank you, Mr. Hopkins," Chairman Handcock said. "Gentlemen, you have heard the recommendation of the Navy Committee and we will take their recommendation as a motion. Do I hear a second?"

"I second the motion," said a man at the front of the room.

"We have a motion on the floor that has been seconded, do I hear any discussion?" Hancock asked.

One hand was lifted. Again, it was John Rutledge of South Carolina, and in it he held a sheet of paper. "Mr. Chairman and Mr. Hopkins, I commend you on the choices of veteran seaman like Captains Sultonstall and Hopkins. But other names on your list raise questions. I see that as a captain you have Nicholas Biddle, who is only twenty-five years of age, and as a first lieutenant John Paul Jones, who is just twenty-eight. Could we not find anyone with more experience to lead our ships into battle against the most formidable navy in history?"

Responding to a nod from Chairman Hancock, Stephen Hopkins rose from his front row seat and faced the group. "Gentlemen, we have had much discussion on the names we are recommending to you. Captain Biddle and Lieutenant Jones are both veteran seaman.Both have been on shipboard since they were young men and both have been captaining ships since they were just twenty-one. You don't know these young men as I do but let me assure you, we have chosen well."

There was a rustle of movement and someone said, "Let's get on with it."

Chairman Hancock said, "Hearing no further discussion, I call for the vote to commission these officers of the first Continental Navy as recommended by the Navy Committee. All in favor say 'yea.'" The response was overwhelming in favor of the action. "Hearing such overwhelming vocal support, there is no need to call for a 'nay' vote. Mr. Hopkins, will you take the floor for your additional business?"

"Thank you, Mr. Chairman," Hopkins responded. "We would like for you to know that we have made the following assignments thus far. Abraham Whipple will command the *Providence*, our largest and strongest ship. It has thirty-four cannons and two swivel guns. He has actually been the captain of that ship for the past three years, working for John Brown in *Providence*. Dudley Sultonstall will command the *Alfred*, which will serve as the flag ship for Commodore Hopkins. Nicholas Biddle will be captain of the *Andrew Doria*, and Captain John Burroughs will command the *Cabot*.

"We have three other schooners ready to sail," Hopkins continued. "They are the *Hornet*, the *Wasp*, and the *Fly*. Officer assignments will be made for those ships in the next few weeks."

Dr. Josiah Barlett of New Hampshire posed a question. "So, Mr. Hopkins, when can we hope to have ships ready to rid our harbors of these British man-of-war ships that have us blockaded? We have much need of the medical supplies that come to us only by ship from Europe."

Stephen Crane of New Jersey agreed. "I am as concerned as Dr. Bartlett is with how we are going to be able to treat the wounded should war come to us. Virtually all our medical supplies come to us from England and France, and if we can't be supplied from there, I am not sure where such supplies will come from."

"Gentlemen, you raise a serious question," Hopkins said. "One that I hope will be partially answered with this next report. Mr. Chairman, if I may continue?"

"By all means, Mr. Hopkins," said Chairman Hancock.

"As much as it pains me to say it, we do not have the firepower to rid our harbors of these man-of-war ships the British seem to have in such abundance. It is likely that if we fight them for the next decade, they will still have superiority on the seas. Because fighting them ship-to- ship appears to be well beyond our capabilities, both now and in the future, we need yet another strategy to deal with the problem."

"What, pray tell, is that?" came a voice from the back of the room.

"It is our intent to attack the British on the seas in a different way. Most of you are aware of the number of ships currently working the oceans from your own home colonies as privateers. You may not be aware of the number of ships we have all up and down the Atlantic coast. In Rhode Island alone, we have more than fifty ships that make their living privateering. We estimate that from *Boston* to Savannah we may have as many as fifteen hundred. Our plan is to utilize these privateers to prey on British shipping, especially those merchant ships that are carrying support materials for British troops on our shores."

Even as Hopkins spoke, John Rutledge rose from his seat near the back of the room and walked slowly and dramatically to the front. As he reached the front of the room, Hopkins slowed his speech and finally deferred to the delegate from South Carolina.

"It is as I feared, gentlemen," Rutledge said in his unpleasant nasal voice. "These men intend to trust our safety and our merchandise to a bunch of pirates."

His words were met with the sound of feet stomping and hands slapping. Many of the men were, quite obviously, concerned with where this discussion was going.

John Rutledge continued, his hands gesticulating in an animated fashion and his speech growing louder with each word. "Many of us have spent much time and money trying to eliminate these despicable pirates from our shores. They have cost us dearly in both lives and money in past years." He gave Hopkins an accusing look. "I cannot believe we are going to now embrace them and join with them in this holy war we are preparing to fight. Believe me, nothing good under God's heaven can come from this."

Again, his words drew approval from the hand-slappers and foot-stompers. Rutledge turned on his heel and walked slowly back to his seat, receiving hand-shakes and pats of approval as he moved down the aisle.

"Mr. Chairman, if I may," said Stephen Hopkins.

"The chair recognizes Mr. Hopkins to finish his report and expects quiet and decorum to reign in this room," Chairman Handcock said sternly.

"Gentlemen, our research has revealed that not only do we have many more ships we can put to sea should war come," Mr. Hopkins said, "but these ships are manned by skilled seamen. All are experienced blockade runners. Even if we have three man-of-war ships holding forth at a harbor just off shore, what will they do with twenty schooners that are both faster and more maneuverable than they? We may lose some ships to their superior fire power, but many others will get through that can lay in wait just off shore for the supply ships that are coming from England."

He paused, eyes sweeping the room. "If we need medical supplies, won't we find them on the British supply ships? The British soldiers need those supplies as much as we do. If we need powder and muskets, don't the British need those as much as we do? Our success may well depend on two factors. First, how well we can supply our own troops with British cargo, and second, how successfully we can take their supplies and starve their troops of the materials they need to fight us."

As Stephen Hopkins finished, many in the room were again stomping their feet and slapping their hands on the tables. This time, however, they were showing their favor to the plan that was being presented to the group.

Thomas Cushing of Massachusetts was next on his feet to address the Congress. He said, "Gentlemen, most of you are aware that I am cool toward this idea of independence from Great Britain. The primary reason I am not pleased with the direction this body is headed is because I see great benefit with being allied with the greatest power on the globe. The second reason is that I don't think we can win."

Many in the room showed their displeasure vocally with what Mr. Cushing was saying.

Chairman Hancock rose to his feet and intervened. "Gentlemen, we will have quiet in the room. Every opinion will be heard here, whether we like hearing it or not. Please continue, Mr. Cushing."

"Thank you, Mr. Chairman," Cushing said. "The idea of using the pirates is interesting. However, I don't think you can rally them to your cause. They are an independent lot, given to thievery and barbarism. There is no honor among them. Why would they leave their profitable ways to join in this almost impossible venture?"

"I have an answer for you, Mr. Cushing," said Stephen Hopkins. "We intend to make them an offer that any sane man would accept. There are three parts to this offer and each has a potential for attracting them, along with a sacrifice on our part."

Mr. Cushing words were laced with acid. "I am skeptical of this idea but can't wait to hear what scheme you have cooked up to lure these pirates into your navy."

"Before I tell you what we will offer them, I want to tell you what we will require of them," said Hopkins. "First, we will require them to leave our merchant ships alone to sail to whatever countries they choose, other than Great Britain. Second, we will require that they leave all ships alone if they are coming to trade with the Colonies, except for those coming from Great Britain."

Heads began to nod around the room, though Cushing appeared unmoved.

Hopkins continued, "This means that those ships capable of running the blockades will be able to sail with security to any destination other than Great Britain, so we can continue to benefit from trade with those countries. Second, ships from those countries will be able to continue to trade with us. Those foreign merchants who doubt their ability to penetrate the blockades at our ports can meet our ships at ports in the Caribbean. We can unload their cargos onto our ships there and bring them north in our ships."

He paused and surveyed the room. "Are there any questions so far?"

Richard Bland of Virginia raised his hand and stood to face the Congress from his front row seat. "Most of you know that I am a farmer with land on the James River in Virginia. We use the river as a means to get our produce to Richmond and to the port at Norfolk. From there it is put on shipboard to sail into the Chesapeake and across the Atlantic to France.Mr. Hopkins has indicated that the Navy Committee envisions using what he is calling 'privateers' to help us get our goods to European markets. I am for any means to break out of our landlocked situation and to be able to continue to trade with countries of our choosing across the Atlantic."

He directed his final remark to Hopkins. "What is not yet clear is what we have to give to these privateers to get them to leave our shipping alone and to concentrate on British merchants sending supplies here. I would appreciate knowing what we must give to get compliance on their part."

"Thank you, Mr. Bland," Hopkins said. "What we plan to give are just three things. First, we will guarantee to the privateers that we will forgive any past crimes against either the individual Colonies or businesses within the Colonies. Second, we want them to focus on British supply ships and, thus, we guarantee them ownership of any supplies they take from the British. Those supplies will, in turn, be sold at a fair price to the Colonies and used by our troops in the field against the British.Third, if our efforts against the British are successful, they will be offered a continuing involvement with the newly formed Continental Navy following the war.

Obviously, if we are not successful, we will have no obligation following the war."

For a few seconds, there was dead silence in the room, then one by one voices were raised, some for the proposal and some against. Many of the men seemed upset with the idea of granting forgiveness for past crimes. Others were concerned about how the process would work to get the supplies from the privateers to the places where they were needed.

When the bluster had quieted, Chairman Hancock again took the floor. He said, "Gentlemen, you have heard the proposal of the Navy Committee. Because of the seriousness of what has been proposed, I suggest that we sleep on it and gather here for one more meeting in the morning before we recess for the Christmas holidays.If I hear no disagreement, this meeting will be adjourned."

The room emptied slowly, and many men stayed to talk to members of the Navy Committee about the details of the proposal. Some were, obviously, unhappy that they could not leave the meeting and immediately head toward home--especially considering that home for some was a great distance away. However, there was no mistaking the feeling of optimism on the part of some of the delegates, who were beginning to see a plan take shape, one that had real possibilities of success.

At exactly 9 a.m. on the twenty-third of December, Chairman Hancock stepped to the podium and called the meeting to order. He said, "Gentlemen, I am a bit disappointed in the attendance this morning. I realize that several of our number have a long way to go to make it home by Christmas. However, the business we transact here is highly important, a matter even of life and death. I have counted the house and know that we have quorum for action. We need thirty-seven members to conduct business and we have forty present. So, I call this meeting to order for the purpose of completing the business placed before us by the Navy Committee."

He made eye contact with Stephen Hopkins. "Mr. Hopkins, would you take the floor, please," said John Handcock.

"Thank you, sir," replied Hopkins. "Yesterday you heard our report and several questions were raised regarding what was presented. Are there more questions that need attention this morning?"

The first hand in the air belonged to John Asop of New York. "As most of you realize, I came late to this Congress and this is my first time to address the group," he said. "My brother and I are merchants in the city of New York. Much of our business is in trade with the European nations. We own several ships and we contract with several others to carry our merchandise. I tell you this so you will know how seriously I take the report and the efforts of the Navy Committee."

John Asop continued, "*Richard* and I are very much in support of anything we can do to break the blockade and get our goods to market. We realize that our ships are not a match for the British man-of-war ships that sit at the mouth of our harbors. I was deeply depressed over the situation until I heard of this new plan to use the privateers to help break the blockade with numbers, using speed and deception to get our ships free on the high seas to carry our goods to France and Spain. Many of you voiced your approval of the plan presented yesterday by Mr. Hopkins. Let me add my voice to that number and offer any service we can to help make the effort successful."

Asop's words were met with the familiar positive sounds of hands clapping and slapping the tables.

John Hancock then asked, "Are there other comments or questions from the Congress?"

There was silence except for a familiar voice from the back, who said, "Let's get on with it."

"Hearing nothing else, could I hear a motion and a second to accept the report?" Chairman Hancock asked.

The same voice came from the back of the room: "I move that we accept the report and express confidence in the work of the Navy Committee." The motion quickly drew a second.

"Gentlemen, we have a motion and a second on the floor," John Hancock said. "Is there any further discussion?" Silence followed his question.

"Hearing none, could I hear a voice vote for the motion." The delegates responded with an almost unanimous "yea."

"No nay vote is needed," Hancock said. "Gentlemen, I declare this meeting of the Continental Congress in recess until four weeks from yesterday." With that comment, he lifted the gavel that was on the table in front of him and struck it on the table twice.

Stephen Hopkins and the Navy Committee gathered for just a few minutes following the meeting. They had succeeded in getting their vote of support from the Congress. However, most were painfully aware that many who were not for the plan had left the meeting the day before and departed Philadelphia for home.

"I am gratified that the actions of the Navy Committee have been ratified by the Continental Congress," he told his fellow committee members, "and I thank you for your hard work. We must remember though, that opposition to our path to independence may well reappear when the Congress reconvenes in the new year."

As he left the room, Stephen Hopkins's mind continued to be troubled.

THE PROVIDENCE GAZETTE

PROVIDENCE, Rhode Island, February 1, 1776--Our delegates meeting in Philadelphia have appointed Silas Deane of New Hampshire as diplomatic representative to France. His primary task is to convince the French to provide military aid to the colonies as they battle Great Britain.

The Massachusetts militia continues to hold the high ground just north of Boston Harbor and the British have remained camped just to the west of the city. We have learned that the cannons placed on that hill overlooking the harbor were brought from Fort Ticonderoga by militia artillery chief, Henry Knox. There are no reports of British reinforcements arriving from Canada or New York.

North Carolina Militia has defeated a British loyalist force at the Battle of Moore's Creek Bridge near Wilmington, North Carolina.

The Continental Navy has sailed from Dorchester Harbor. Their first great success is in the taking of two British ships and a great store of war material from Nassau in the Bahamas. The captured supplies, cannons, powder, and various other items were returned to Delaware Bay and sent to General Washington.

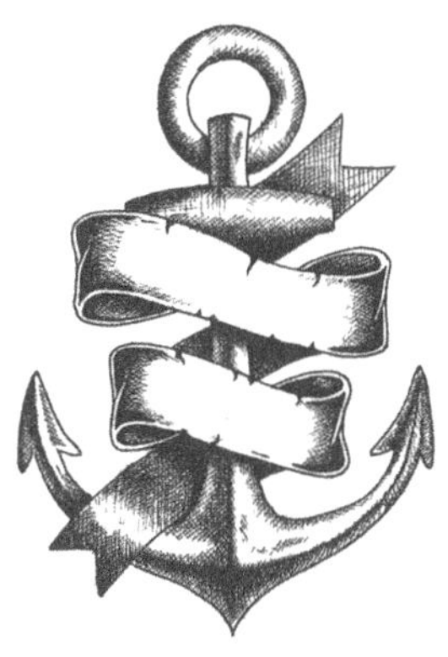

CHAPTER 9
CAPTURING POWDER AND SUPPLIES IN NASSAU
FEBRUARY 1776

The Continental Navy was now in place. It was composed of a small fleet of eight ships in Delaware Bay that was awaiting the arrival of five more ships that were being outfitted in other locations. In late February, the *Hornet* and the *Wasp* joined the navy and the weather broke so that they could set sail. Orders had been given by the Navy Committee to avoid engaging the British fleet directly.

A letter from General George Washington to Commodore Hopkins on the *Alfred* warned that the British spies had done their work well and knew that Hopkins was making ready to sail. Thus, a formidable fleet under British Admiral Snape Hammond was waiting for him at the mouth of the Chesapeake, less than a hundred miles south of Delaware Bay. With the firepower of the British ships awaiting the new American fleet, it was obvious any confrontation would have been a slaughter.

Commodore Hopkins, mindful of his orders to avoid confronting the British fleet directly, sailed by the British ships at night and headed southeast toward Nassau. There, his men were able to capture two British ships. Intelligence gained from those ships revealed there was a store of arms in Nassau that was unprotected by the British. When the small fleet arrived at the warehouse in Nassau, they found cannons, mortars, thousands of shells, cannon balls, and fuses, as well as gun carriages, ordnance tools, and twenty-four casks of gun power. These were exactly what General Washington needed for his troops.

It took several days to load everything into the ships, and every ship was carrying all the weight it could manage and stay sea-worthy. The fleet retraced its route to Delaware Bay where the captured munitions could be unloaded and transported overland to General Washington. The closer the ships came to American soil, the more danger they were in from the British fleet. Being isolated on the high seas for more than a month, they did not have intelligence about where the British fleet might be waiting for them, thus they were careful to sail mostly at night and to stay well out of sight of land. Finally, they reached their destination in Delaware Bay and began the task of unloading their heavy cargo.

General Washington was overjoyed with the efforts of the new navy and the arrival of much needed supplies. He wrote a letter to Commodore Hopkins thanking him for the "unexpected bounty."

While the *Alfred* was in port, John Paul Jones received a troubling letter from *Providence* which had been sent to the harbor master's office. It was from Aimee Shelton.

February 22, 1776

Mr. John Paul Jones
The Alfred

Dear Mr. Jones,

I take pen in hand to write you of your children and your beloved wife. The boys are fine, eating well and growing every day. They treat my girls well... most of the time.

Mr. John Brown helped me acquire a map of the world and I spread it out on the table each day to show the boys where their father is. Of course, we don't know exactly, but it is a good exercise both in keeping close touch with their father and also to learn geography.

The girls and I have missed Jim every day but I thank God that he is there with you and learning a new trade for his future. John Burroughs suggested that he might even be a Captain someday. That is certainly my hope. I know you and John will take good care of him and that we will get to see him from time to time when your ship is in port.

I wish I had good news about poor Mrs. Jones. She seems to grow weaker every day. Some days she cannot get out of bed and when she does she mostly sits by the second-floor window where she can see the ocean and look for your ship coming into port. The doctor says there is little that can be done, and she is in God's hands for recovery or not. I know that is not encouraging to you but believe you desire the truth in all things and keeping this from you would not be in your best interest or hers.

Rest assured that all is well in hand here. I shall endeavor to take care of your wife and your boys to the very best of my abilities. And we anticipate your return at the earliest.

Your Devoted Servant,

Aimee Shelton

Shortly after unloading the munitions, the American fleet sailed north from Delaware Bay to Montauk Point on the east end of Long Island. There, they captured two British ships, the *Hawk* and the *Belton*. Through intelligence gathered from the crew of the *Belton*, they learned that a strong British squadron was anchored at Newport, Rhode Island under British Captain James Wallace. As several of the seamen, including Captain John Burroughs Hopkins and Commodore Esek Hopkins, were from *Providence*, they had hoped to find port at the north end of Narragansett Bay. However, the possibility of being able to bypass the British fleet at Newport was small and they did not want a confrontation that would cost them ships after just having had their first great success for the Continental Army. Thus, they stayed anchored at Montauk Point, awaiting word that the British fleet had moved on.

THE PROVIDENCE GAZETTE

PROVIDENCE, Rhode Island, March 15, 1776--With the rejection of the peace initiative advanced by our delegates in Philadelphia, the primary focus of our Congress is preparing to deal with all aspects of a war with Great Britain. There is no longer any illusion that peace can be achieved.

The Massachusetts militia continues to hold the high ground above Boston Harbor while the British languish in camps just west of Boston. No British reinforcements have arrived from either Canada or New York.

Abigail Adams has issued an historic plea for women's rights, urging her husband, John Adams, a delegate to the Congress in Philadelphia to, "remember the ladies," as Congress drafts new laws for a new country.

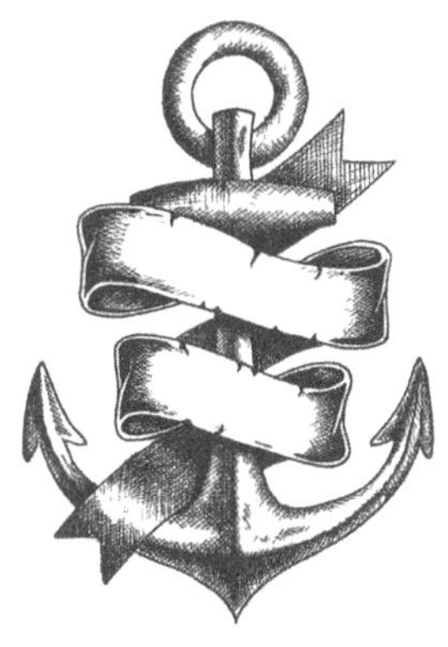

CHAPTER 10

ATTACK OF THE GLASGOW

MARCH 3, 1776

Knowing that the British fleet was anchored at Newport, Rhode Island at the mouth of Narragansett Bay, the new Continental Navy remained anchored at Montauk at the eastern edge of Long Island.

On the second day, just at dawn, the American ships were attacked by the HMS *Glasgow*. The *Cabot* under Captain John Burroughs Hopkins was the first to feel the brunt of the attack. Captain Hopkins was standing on the fantail with young Jim Shelton when the *Glasgow* came at them out of the morning mist. There was barely time to make any preparation for fighting back.

"Jim, you get below and call the crew to battle stations. Then you stay there and help the surgeons handle the injuries," said Captain Hopkins. Within seconds the *Cabot* felt the first cannon ball fired across its bow. The *Glasgow*'s nine-pounders proved to be devastating to the smaller ship.

The *Glasgow* was not only much larger than the *Cabot*, but it also had the wind behind it as it approached the small American fleet. The British ship maneuvered across the bow of the *Cabot* and raked it mercilessly, fore and aft. Almost immediately, Captain Hopkins was felled by a part of the aft mast that collapsed with the onslaught.

Dazed and trapped under the mast, Captain Hopkins felt hands pulling the weight off him. Blood was flowing from a gash on his head and he looked through the blood to see the face of young Jim straining against the weight of the cross spar.

"I told you to get below," Hopkins said through teeth gritted in pain.

"Yes sir. I will go below as soon as I get this mess off of you," the boy responded.

Within seconds Hopkins felt the weight of the mast gone, then other hands were lifting him up and carrying him. He tried to move his legs, but the feeling was gone. Then he knew nothing.

At that crucial moment, the Continental Navy's ship the *Providence* had appeared and sailed between the *Glasgow* and the *Cabot*, interrupting the British ship's attack on the *Cabot*. Captain Hopkins's good friend, John Paul Jones, had been assigned to be first mate on the *Providence* but happened to be at the helm since Captain Whipple had taken sick and was below deck with the surgeon. The *Glasgow* used the wind to its advantage and sailed away from the small Continental Navy that had begun to follow the *Providence* into battle. By the time the *Providence* had turned about, the *Glasgow* had a several hundred-yard advantage. The *Providence* was not known for its speed and after an hour of futile chase, it turned about and arrived back at the side of the badly damaged *Cabot*, which was drifting windward into Long Island Sound.

The *Glasgow*'s nine-pounders had not only devastated the masts, but also had cut the lines to the rudder, making it inoperable and leaving the *Cabot* to the mercy of the seas. She was drifting aimlessly when the *Providence* arrived back at her side. The much smaller *Wasp* had already tied up to the starboard side of the *Cabot*. The *Providence* cut sail to tie up along-side the *Cabot* on the port side. Both ships provided stability for the ailing *Cabot*.

John Paul Jones had been in charge of the chase after the *Glasgow*, but had been anxious to get back to the *Cabot*, knowing that his long-time friend John Burroughs Hopkins was its captain. Much of the crew of the *Cabot* was looking over the rail as the *Providence* moved into position. John Paul Jones yelled to them, "What of your captain?"

Word came back from a voice on the deck of *Cabot*, "He is gravely injured and is below with the surgeons."

Jones yelled back again, "Can he be moved?"

The voice responded, "We don't know. He was carried below early in the battle with the *Glasgow* and hasn't been topside since."

John Paul Jones ordered the mid-ship gangplank of the *Providence* put out to connect the two ships and, using one of the grappling iron lines to steady himself, he walked across the gangplank and jumped down onto the deck of the *Cabot*. In a moment, he was below deck looking for his friend.

When he found John Burroughs, it was hard to be optimistic. The unconscious captain had a nasty gash on his head and his left arm and shoulder were wrapped up tightly, indicating either a broken arm or shoulder.

A quiet conversation with the surgeon confirmed John Paul's worst thoughts. When the aft mast fell, John Burroughs had been hit on the head and had sustained a serious head wound. He had not regained consciousness since he had been brought down to the surgeon. His arm was not broken but it was obvious that the shoulder had been dislocated and the collar bone was broken. Other possible damage would require further examination. The surgeon had taken advantage of the captain's unconscious state to put the shoulder back in place, a very painful process, and to wrap him in such a way as to avoid further injury when he was moved.

The surgeon was sure John Burroughs needed more medical attention than he could give aboard the *Cabot* and recommended that he be transported back to port to other doctors more experienced in dealing with head injuries.

While Captain Jones talked with the surgeons, young Jim, the cabin boy, stood at his side. Their faces were creased with concern as they heard the surgeon say there was nothing more that could be done for Captain Hopkins on shipboard.

John Paul Jones resolved in his mind to get his friend to a doctor in *Providence* or New York as quickly as possible. It would mean leaving the fleet and taking the *Providence* off on its own into dangerous waters regularly patrolled by the British. He reasoned that the *Providence* had been home-based in *Providence* while it was still called the *Katy* and many of the seaman on board called *Providence* their home port. It would be a popular destination for the crew and he knew of experienced surgeons there who could give his friend proper medical care. New York was the next closest port where medical services were available. Unfortunately, the British fleet was known to come in and out of New York harbor on a regular basis, just as it did Newport in Rhode Island. It seemed there were no good choices.

He quickly settled on making for *Providence*, reasoning that one ship might be able to sneak by the British fleet in Newport harbor where the entire American fleet could not. And Captain Jones had the advantage of being on his home turf and knowing Narragansett Bay like the back of his hand.

After moving Captain Hopkins and young Jim on board the *Providence*, John Paul Jones stayed in the harbor at Montauk Bay until nearly night fall. He made sure that the carpenters and crew had made enough repairs to the *Cabot* to stabilize it before heading north across Long Island Sound toward Newport and *Providence*. It was his plan to enter the bay in the dead of night. The British would never expect anyone to try to negotiate Narragansett Bay at night, but Captain Jones was confident he could avoid the reefs and sandbars and stay near the channel of the bay.

It was just after midnight when the *Providence* arrived at the mouth of the bay. Captain Jones and young Jim were standing on the fantail of the ship where they could see danger coming from any direction. The ship was sailing in total darkness with both fore and aft lights doused. There was no moon and drifting clouds hid most of the stars. The lookouts were high on the masts with orders to signal any sightings rather than to yell them down to the captain. Mercifully, the wind had waned and the ship was moving at about half its usual speed. Jones ordered the main sails to be dropped so there was less danger of being sighted, knowing their progress forward would be slower yet. The wind was light but steady, coming from the southwest.

All hands were on deck and maintaining absolute silence. The lookouts, high on the masts, were keeping their eyes peeled for hostile sails or lights that would indicate a British ship was on the move. They could see the lights from Newport harbor just a short three miles away across the channel of the bay.

Just inside the entrance to the bay they were at the most dangerous point. Whale Rock, so called because of its shape and the way it stuck up above the water line, dominated the channel just inside the entry to the bay. Sailing west of it took them dangerously close to sand bars. East of it, sailing into the channel of the bay, brought them closest to the harbor at Newport and within sight of the British ships, if anyone on board was looking.

They swung silently out into the channel of the bay. Minutes passed and those standing quietly on the deck of the *Providence* began to breathe easier. Not a sound was heard from the British fleet and soon John Paul ordered deployment of the main sails which would speed them along their way toward *Providence* and their home base.

It was another two hours before they arrived and yet another before they could get Captain John Burroughs Hopkins loaded into a long boat and headed for the wharf. From there it was a three-block wagon ride to Esek Hopkins's home, where a local doctor could attend him.

John Paul Jones and Jim rode in the wagon with John Burroughs to the family home and turned him over to his mother and older sister.

"Jim, I want you to stay here with John Burroughs," said Jones.

"Yes sir," the boy responded. "Is there anything else I can do for you?"

"No," said Jones. "You stay here with him and do anything the doctor or these ladies want you to do. If there is a change in his status, if he wakes up or, worse, if he doesn't, you come and find me. I am going to his house to tell his wife where he is and I'm sure she will be here as quickly as she can. I will also get word to your mother that we are in port and that you are at Esek Hopkins's home."

"Where will you be, sir?" asked Jim.

"I'm going back to the ship and you can find me there if you need me," responded Jones.

Jim sat in the hallway outside of John Burroughs' room for about an hour before the light began to come in through the window. He must have dozed off because he felt a gentle shaking that brought him back to reality. The face he looked into was that of the doctor who had been called to minister to John Burroughs.

"Who are you, boy?" the doctor asked.

Jim was startled awake and his answer to the doctor came in a rush. "I am Jim Shelton, cabin boy on the *Cabot*, which was about blown out of the water over at Montauk Bay yesterday. They brought me here with Captain Hopkins on the ship *Providence*. Captain Hopkins is captain of the *Cabot*. It was Lieutenant John Paul Jones who brought us here. He is first mate of the *Providence*. We came here because it was the closest port where we were sure we could get help for Captain Hopkins."

"Well, I have examined him, and he has had a nasty blow to his head and several other injuries,' the doctor said. "He is going to be with us for some time before he is ready to go back to sea."

"Is he awake?" asked Jim.

"No, son, he is still out," the doctor responded. "There is nothing we can do for him until nature takes its course. He will wake up in due time if he is to wake up at all. Much depends on how hard the blow was to his head. How did it happen?"

"I was below deck so I didn't see it, but I felt a major jolt when the first cannon balls hit us," Jim said. "I rushed up the stairs and saw that the aft mast was down across the fantail. I knew that is where Captain Hopkins had been just a few minutes before. When I got up to the fantail it was obvious that the mast had fallen on Captain Hopkins. He was lying under a part of the mast and blood was everywhere. I thought he was dead. When I got to him he was still breathing but he wasn't moving. It was all I could do to get the cross spar off of him. Several of the men carried him down to the lower deck. Then the *Glasgow* came back for another pass at us and we all ran for the lower decks."

"Well, your captain is lucky to be alive," said the doctor. "I haven't been able to examine his arm and shoulder and won't until he wakes up. I think you can go back to your ship. It is going to be a very long day for your captain."

"No sir, I am to stay here," said Jim. "Lieutenant Jones told me to stay by his side and to report back when he wakes up or when any change occurs."

"Well, all right," said the doctor. "You rest here, and I will have the ladies bring you some breakfast when it is ready."

It did not take long for word of the return of the *Providence* to be spread around the community. No local ships had come into the harbor since the British had set up camp at Newport. Any ship was welcome, but the *Providence* was a John Brown ship before he sold it to the Continental Navy, and many of the men on board were from *Providence*. The word spread rapidly to the families of the men on board and they began to show up at the wharf to welcome them.

When he arrived back on the *Providence*, John Paul Jones looked first for Captain Whipple. He was no longer on the ship, having been taken to his home just north of *Providence*. John Paul took charge just as he had when Captain Whipple took sick over at Montauk Bay. He called a meeting of the ship's leadership. He wanted to make sure that the *Providence* was unloaded of its provisions and stores and that the men were released for port time when the work was done. During the meeting, a messenger came on board the boat from John Brown's office.

He took just a minute in the middle of his meeting and walked over to the messenger, who handed him a letter. He glanced at it long enough to know it was from Aimee Shelton, the second letter he had received from her. He stuck it in his coat pocket and continued speaking to the men.

A little later, when he was alone, he took out the letter and opened it. Before he had read the first short paragraph, the tears were rolling down his cheeks.

May 30, 1776

Mr. John Paul Jones
The Providence

Dear Mr. Jones,

I wish there was a better way to share this terrible news but here it is in one tragic sentence. Your wife died last week. I walked into her room to wake her one morning and she was gone. Before we could handle the formalities of her funeral and burial, her mother died also. So, we have experienced a double tragedy.

It is my greatest hope that you can come home to us as soon as possible. Your boys, Moses and Daniel, need you now. Your presence would provide security and comfort for them and you could help them understand the cycle of life and death that we all know about but find so difficult to accept. I do not know how long it will take for this letter to find you, but wherever you are I hope you are well. Perhaps someone can take your place on the ship and you can make your way home as soon as possible. We need you.

Until I hear from you I will continue to care for your boys here in the wonderful house you have provided. Hearts are heavy here in Providence. Please hurry home.

Your Devoted Servant,

Aimee Shelton

John Paul Jones had been thinking of little other than the grave injuries to his long-time friend, John Burroughs Hopkins, since the run-in with the *Glasgow.*

Now his mind was turned in a very different direction. His beautiful Keziah was gone, the lady he had met a decade ago, who had become his wife and given him his two boys. She was gone. He had known she was ill, but thought it to be an illness that would pass. Instead, she died while he was at sea and a stranger had to handle the arrangements for her funeral and burial.

There was no time to feel sorry for himself; he had Moses and Daniel to think of. Neither boy was old enough to take responsibility for a home and would not be for several years. His mind was moving too fast and before he knew it he was on the street where he and Keziah had bought their house just three years earlier.

As soon as he began to mount the steps into the house, he heard Daniel's voice, and then both boys were on him almost before he was in the door. As he stood in the front room with his arms around the boys, Aimee came in and watched the three of them from a few feet away. Daniel and Moses were both obviously delighted at the presence of their father, but it was a time of mixed emotions. The boys began to cry, and John Paul joined them. Soon Aimee was crying too. One of Aimee's daughters arrived and began to pull on her mother's dress. She asked, "Why are you crying, Mother?"

There was no answer for that question that would satisfy a four-year-old. Aimee picked her daughter up and carried her back into the kitchen where some cookies were still warm from the oven, built into the wall beside the fireplace where she did her cooking. John Paul and the boys followed Aimee and her daughter into the kitchen. The boys were still clinging tightly to their father. No words passed between John Paul and Aimee. It seemed no words were necessary.

Quickly, Aimee set a pewter plate full of hot-baked cookies in the middle of the table. Soon there were three children sitting with a warm cookie in hand. Aimee's smallest child appeared at the door and ran the last few steps to her mother, who picked her up and gave a cookie to her. Now, the whole family was at the table, John Paul and his two boys, Daniel and Moses, and Aimee and her girls, Mary and Elizabeth. For just a few minutes there was silence as the cookies disappeared, just as you would expect with four children at the table.

Then, Aimee spoke softly, "We are so pleased you are home, Lieutenant Jones. We have needed you, and the boys have missed you terribly."

"I'm sorry, I'm not over the shock of your letter yet. I just got it about an hour ago. I came as soon as I could," responded John Paul. "I know the last couple of weeks have been very trying for you, handling all of the necessities, the details, as well as dealing with the loss of my wife and her mother. Coping with one was bad enough, but two at the same time must have been terrible."

"Let's get the children settled down and then we can talk privately," said Aimee. "There are several details you need to know and a list of things to take care of that I have left undone because of responsibilities with the children."

Twenty minutes later one of the children was down for a nap and the other three were playing in the parlor. John Paul walked back into the kitchen to find Aimee removing a kettle from the fireplace.

"I hope that is a cup of coffee you are brewing," he said.

Aimee turned and smiled at him and said, "I have supper almost ready and would you settle for a cup of tea instead?"

"Tea will do nicely," he responded, and sat down at the table. Shortly, there were steaming cups on the table, and Aimee joined him there. Both had their first sip of tea before either spoke again.

"I can't tell you how much I appreciate your taking over and dealing with all that has happened the past two weeks," John Paul said. The boys seem fine and are adjusting to their mother being gone. They obviously looked to you for comfort and you gave them exactly what they needed."

"I think the adjustment will come easily because of their age. It could be that they will miss her more and more as the years pass," responded Aimee softly.

"You mentioned things I needed to do, Aimee," said John Paul.

"Yes," she responded. "The minister at the First Baptist Church was a bastion of strength, and several ladies of the church helped us lay out Keziah and her mother for the receiving of friends in the parlor. They are buried side by side in the church cemetery. I didn't know where you would want them but that seemed the best alternative at the time. You will want to pay the minister something for his services."

Their conversation went on into the evening, with many questions asked and answered. John Paul told her he had asked young Jim to stay at the Esek Hopkins's house with John Burroughs and to report any change in his situation. The primary topic of conversation, however, related to Aimee and the girls staying on to live in the house and her commitment to take care of the boys.

"I am pleased to stay with the boys, Captain Jones," she said. "They take a little care around mealtimes and at bed time in the evenings. That is when they miss you most. During the day they mostly entertain themselves and Daniel even helps me some with the girls."

"They have their mother's gentle spirit, and we can be thankful for that," replied John Paul.

"I do have two concerns that only you can answer," she said. "I need to know how long you think you will be away with your responsibilities with the ship."

"And the second concern?" asked John Paul.

She began her response very slowly and by the end you could hardly hear her words. "I want to know what to do with the boys if, like my husband, someday you don't return?"

John Paul looked over at her and found her eyes staring down at her hands. He took a deep breath and responded, "When we go out we never know when we are coming back. It depends on the prizes we take and where the navy responsibilities take us. Usually, we are in port about every three months, but it could be less or more depending on a number of factors that are not in my control. About what to do with the boys should I have an untimely demise, I am not sure," he said.

He thought a moment. "I have a brother down in North Carolina. He is the only relative I have on this side of the Atlantic. He would take the boys, but I'm not sure how you get word to him or how long it would take for him to come and get them. I will write down how to reach him, should you need him. I would add, unless you get word otherwise from John Brown, even if I don't make it home for six months, don't count me out. I am a pretty tough Scott. Sometimes if we are captured we are put in jail. Unfortunately, if the British caught me on the high seas, they would probably hang me. Whatever happened, I think you would hear from the office here before long."

"Oh, Captain Jones," she responded, "That doesn't ease my mind much. The very idea of you being killed or finding your destiny at the end of a rope leaves me without the right words to say to the boys about their father."

Later that night, after the supper dishes had been put away, the children were in bed, John Paul and Aimee met at their regular place by the fireplace in the parlor. When the conversation slowed Aimee went up the stairs to check on the children and then to her room on the second floor of the house. Later that night, Aimee heard sounds she had never heard before coming from the downstairs. She slipped her housecoat over her gown, took her bedside candle and walked slowly down the hall to investigate. She paused at the stairs to listen again and found the sound coming from the parlor.

From the third step down, she could see into the parlor where John Paul still sitting in front of the fireplace with his face in his hands. She slowly retraced her steps back to the bedroom.

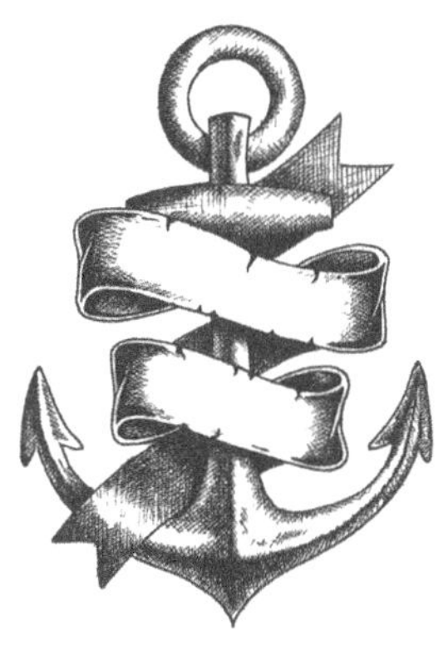

CHAPTER 11
REPAIR AND RECUPERATION

MARCH 15, 1776

The next day, a knock on the door at the Jones house on Planet Street found Aimee in the kitchen. Wiping her hands on her apron, she hurried to the front door and peeped out the curtains. It was Jim. She threw open the door and grabbed him in a bear hug.

She said, "Oh, darling Jim, it is so good to see you. I was coming to find you this morning as soon as I had breakfast made for the children." Aimee escorted her son into the kitchen and sat him down at the big table. She placed fresh, hot bread and a pot of jam in front of him and watched him take the first couple of bites.

Jim said, "Mother, I came to find Lieutenant Jones. Captain Hopkins is awake. Lieutenant Jones told me to tell him of any change, and he is not only awake, he seems to have his wits about him! He told me to go and find Lieutenant Jones and to tell him everything is going to be all right."

"What's that?" came John Paul's voice from the doorway. "Is John Burroughs awake?" he asked.

"Yes sir," responded Jim. "He woke up first thing this morning even before the doctor came. I heard him talking with his sister in the bedroom and I stuck my head in the door. He asked me right away, 'What are you doing here?' I told him that you asked me to stay with him until he woke up and then to come and tell you," Jim continued. "So, Captain Hopkins told me, 'Well, what are you waiting for? I'm awake and I'm getting up in a few minutes. *Hannah* tells me I have already lost two days since that rigging fell on me. I have a ship in bad shape at the shipyard. I have to see about it."

Both John Paul and Aimee were laughing when Jim finished.

"That is just like him," John Paul said. "He can't stay down and let himself get well. He has to get involved in everything."

"Well, he won't be at the shipyard when you go to see him," Jim said. "I heard his sister tell him that the doctor said he was to stay in bed until he came and checked his shoulder and arm. Evidently, if his head is all right, and it certainly seems all right, there is still serous concern about his arm and shoulder which is still wrapped up tight. The doctor didn't want to examine it until Captain Hopkins was awake."

"Jim," said John Paul, "You eat your breakfast and talk to your Ma. Then you go back to the Hopkins's house and tell Captain Hopkins that I will be over after I look after some personal matters. I should be there by early afternoon. Surely, the doctor won't release him before then."

John Paul was at the door ready to leave for his short list of family responsibilities when Aimee joined him. "How long do you think you will be gone? I want to tell the boys when they wake up," she said.

"I am going to see the pastor and the women who helped with the funeral," said John Paul. "I will pay them for helping us and then I will come back here. My ship is in good hands and I won't go to the wharf until later in the afternoon after I have seen John Burroughs."

Aimee's hand reached out and caught his arm. Her voice was low and filled with emotion. She said, "Captain Jones…John Paul, I am so glad you are home. We needed you. The boys needed you, but so did I. We still have so much to talk about. Set aside some time for me later in the evening when you have your other responsibilities taken care of."

John Paul was more than a little surprised at her boldness but, nevertheless, put his hand on top of hers. "I'm sorry you have had to handle this difficult time by yourself, Aimee. We will talk after supper."

With that John Paul was out the door and down the steps. His mind came back to her and the comment, as well as their physical contact, many times over the course of the day.

Later that day when he approached the home of Esek Hopkins, where John Burroughs was staying, he could feel his excitement building. He had not seen his friend since the two had drawn different assignments with the fledgling Continental Navy. After being together for most of the past ten years, they had now been apart for several months except for a few greetings exchanged in passing.

The wait at the door seemed interminable after the knock but shortly the door moved and a female face, that of John's sister, appeared. John Paul introduced himself and was ushered into the parlor just inside the door to the left.

"It was my hope to see John Burroughs, ma'am, if he is up to having visitors," he said.

"I don't know if he is up to it, but he would never forgive me if I didn't escort you right to his room," she responded.

In a few seconds, they were up the stairs and down the hall to where young Jim was sitting dutifully on a chair just outside the bedroom door. John Paul leaned down and whispered to Jim. "You go back to the house and be of help to your Ma."

A look inside the room revealed John Burroughs lying restlessly on the bed. He had heard the footsteps coming down the hall and was looking expectantly at the door when John Paul appeared.

"Come on in here, friend. It has been way too long," John Burroughs said.

John Paul entered the room to find *Hannah*, John Burroughs's wife, standing next to his bed.

John Burroughs extended his good hand and John Paul took it and held it. "You look hale and hearty, friend. I am so pleased you are doing so well. You gave us a real scare."

"I may get a few bumps and bruises but I'm not that easy to kill," said John Burroughs. "It will take more than a few shots from the likes of the *Glasgow* to put me under. I do have one killer of a headache, though."

"Well, you took quite a blow on the head and shoulder," said John Paul. "Obviously, your head is coming along. What does the doctor say about your arm and shoulder?"

"It is evidently a bit complicated," said John Burroughs. "The arm seems all right. The problem is in the shoulder. It was dislocated, and the collar bone was broken. There is something else he calls a shoulder separation that I don't quite understand. It is right on top of the shoulder. He tells me several bones are held together there by some ligaments and they have come apart. Mercifully, it is my left shoulder and it will all heal in time."

"Has he told you how long you will be laid up?" asked John Paul.

"No, but I will guarantee you it won't be as long as he says. I am a quick healer and I will be back on shipboard before they get the *Cabot* refitted and seaworthy," said John Burroughs.

As John Burroughs was talking, John Paul noticed his wife, *Hannah*, on the other side of the bed shaking her head. She didn't say anything but the resolve in her face spoke volumes about how soon he might be back on his feet and ready to go back to the *Cabot*.

"How are Keziah and the boys?" John Burroughs asked.

With that question John Paul's eyes met *Hannah*'s. He knew from her look that she had kept the sad news about Keziah and her mother from her husband.

John Paul didn't answer right away. He felt emotion well up in him and his eyes filled with tears. "That is a sad story, my friend. Keziah died about a week before we arrived home. I got word just yesterday after we had docked and brought you here."

John Burroughs responded in a very low voice. "I am so sorry, friend. How are the boys and Keziah's mother handling it?"

John Paul again looked at *Hannah*? She had ducked her head and backed away from the side of John Burroughs' bed.

"That is also a part of the sad story," John Paul replied. "Keziah's mother passed away just a few days after Keziah's death. The boys seem fine, but they have had a double blow. I was lucky to have Aimee Shelton taking care of them. She is so good with the boys."

"What are you going to do about them?" asked John Burroughs.

"Honestly, I don't know," responded John Paul. "It is a difficult problem. We don't have any relatives here. The closest I have is my brother in North Carolina I have talked with Aimee about staying on with the boys in the house. That conversation will continue this evening after supper. If she can do it, that will solve one problem, at least temporarily. If not, I don't know. I can't go back to sea and leave this unresolved and if everything goes as usual, Commodore Hopkins will have us back on the ocean within a week or so."

"John Paul," said, *Hannah*. "Please consider us as your family here and whatever you or the boys need, we will be pleased to provide. We have a big house and you and the boys are welcome anytime."

"Thank you, *Hannah*," responded John Paul. "I am not sure what to do right now. It is constantly on my mind and I know I have responsibilities to our new country, but the boys are my top priority. I hope I can work it all out without having to resign my commission."

The two friends continued to talk into the afternoon and both *Hannah* and John Burroughs's sister came and went several times. It was obvious that John Burroughs was in a great deal of discomfort with this arm and shoulder. He did his best to mask the pain but was not always successful.

Young Jim had returned to the Hopkins's house and resumed his seat in the chair just outside the door to John Burroughs's room. They called for Jim to come in and talk with them.

"Sit down and join us, Jim," John Burroughs said. "We have talked about several things and have now reached a point where you are the subject of the next conversation."

Jim sat down and looked at the two of them expectantly.

"I want you to know that I very much appreciate your efforts to save my life when we were under fire," said John Burroughs. "I know I had told you to go below and the next thing I knew I saw your face when I was under all of that rigging. My immediate response was to chew you out for not following orders because you were on the deck in jeopardy when you shouldn't have been.

"However," John Burroughs continued, "I have rethought that perspective and think you were showing initiative way beyond your years. I owe my life to that initiative."

John Paul took over the conversation at that point. "Jim, it looks as if it is going to be several weeks, even a month or more, before the Brown shipyard can get the *Cabot* back up to speed."

John Burroughs broke in, "All reports tell me that she is very badly damaged. I have tried to get the doctor to let me go to the shipyard, but that visit is still more than a week away."

"The *Cabot* is a mess," John Paul responded. "It is a miracle it made it back to port at all. The sailing master tells me that it could be three months before it is back in shape. And, from the looks of your shoulder, you may not be about ready to take her back to sea until about then."

"The point of this conversation, Jim," said John Burroughs, "is that we think you should move your duff to the *Providence* and be whatever help you can to Captain Jones when he is called back to duty."

"Yes sir," said Jim. "I'll do whatever you think best." He looked over at John Paul and said, "If it is all right with you I will stay at your house while we are in port and I will do whatever I can to help Mother with the children. When you want me to board the *Providence*, I will be ready."

A few minutes later John Paul and Jim were standing on the front steps of the Hopkins' house. John Paul said, "Jim, you go on back to the house. I am going to the shipyard and then to the wharf. Tell your mother I will be home for supper at around seven or so."

"Yes sir, Lieutenant Jones," responded Jim. "I will see you in the early evening."

John Paul made his calls on the minister and the women who had helped with the funeral before heading to the wharf. He was treated to much sympathy, as well as coffee and cakes.

When he arrived back at the *Providence*, John Paul found yet another surprise. He had a letter there from Commodore Hopkins that had come for him through John Brown's office.

March 1, 1776

TO: The Honorable John Paul Jones

FROM: Esek Hopkins, Commodore, Continental Navy

Dear Mr. Jones,

Word continues to come to us of the good work you have provided aboard the Providence. The reports from Captain Whipple indicate that you are ready for your own command. The Continental Congress voted for your promotion on February 28, 1776. We currently have a new ship, the Ranger, being refitted in the shipyard at Portsmouth, New Hampshire. The Ranger is a schooner that will carry sixteen cannons. It should be faster than virtually any other ship on the seas, which should be much to your advantage as you work to harass British shipping. It should be ready for you to retrieve by April 15th.

Please use this letter as your authorization to take charge of the Ranger and to recruit a suitable crew.

We are considering a new strategy for future operations upon which we would appreciate your advice. At this time, we have more than fifteen hundred ships harassing British supply ships in American waters. We are considering sending a number of ships to Europe to pursue the same efforts in the waters around the British Isles. For every ship that comes to our shores with supplies for the British Army, we know there are at least five traveling the waters of the English Channel and both east and west of the British Isles. Please share your thoughts about such a strategy and whether or not you would consent to being sent on such a mission.

My brother, Stephen Hopkins, Chairman of the Navy Committee of the Continental Congress, joins me in congratulating you on your good work and your advancement to the rank of Captain. Good luck to you in your future efforts as you pursue British shipping wherever the battles take you.

With my personal compliments,

Esek Hopkins

Commodore, Continental Navy

John Paul read the letter again, and then read it a third time. The emotion he felt was almost overwhelming. He was getting his own command! The *Ranger* sounded like his type of ship, faster and more mobile. He would be able to pursue British shipping almost anywhere and to avoid the man-of-war ships that were larger and carried more fire power. He couldn't think of anything more wonderful. The thought came back in his mind over and over, *I am getting my own command.*

His first thought was to tell John Burroughs of his good fortune. His second was to tell Aimee. He knew his long-time friend would be happy for him. He wondered how Aimee would take the news. He hoped she would be happy for him, but knew she would be concerned about his leaving and its effects on the boys. He thought for a few minutes about how he felt about leaving his sons, and of the growing warmth he felt for her. He decided he would think more about that later.

For now, it was enough to know that he had a date for leaving *Providence*. He was to take command of the *Ranger* by the fifteenth of April. He had more than a full month before he needed to leave for Portsmouth.

In the weeks that followed, John Paul found his days full of activities. Captain Whipple was still ill and staying at this home north of *Providence*. His responsibilities as first mate took him back to the *Providence* each day to be sure the ship was being cared for properly. He also visited the shipyard every couple of days, so he could tell John Burroughs of the progress in refitting his ship, the *Cabot*. He set aside several hours in the middle of the day and in the early evenings to spend with Daniel and Moses. They required constant attention when he was in the house. Several times he took them on walks to the wharf where they could watch the ships come in and the sea gulls flying around looking for dinner.

Twice he took along some fishing line and they put bait in the water to attract the fish that swam under the wharf. Both times the boys caught several fish. You could not mistake the excitement in their voices when they arrived back at the house to tell Aimee and the girls about their big catch. Each time, Aimee would shake her head. She was not at all pleased with the prospect of having fish cleaned in the kitchen where she would have to smell them for the next couple of days. So, it was out to the back yard to clean the fish. To all three, John Paul, Daniel, and Moses, catching the fish was more fun than cleaning them. Finding out that there is always some bad that comes with every good. was an early life lesson.

More and more John Paul began to look forward to the quiet times in the evenings when his boys and Aimee's girls were in bed. They would retreat to the parlor to sit in the two comfortable chairs there in front of the fireplace. The talk was soft and easy between the two of them. Aimee always seemed to have some hand work on her lap, mending that needed to be done, a dress or shirt for one of the children she was making, something. They talked about the children, the future, and whatever else came to mind. More than once, when the hour grew late and they started up the stairs to their bedrooms, they would find the two oldest children, Daniel and Mary, asleep on the steps. Obviously, they had heard the familiar voices talking quietly by the downstairs fire and had come to the steps to hear what they could of the conversation.

One night, toward the end of the first week in April, that familiar evening pattern again had been followed. As John Paul and Aimee climbed the stairs, they again found the two older children asleep on the steps. Aimee took Mary and John Paul picked up Daniel. A few minutes later when both children were in bed and fast asleep, the adults both came out of their children's rooms at the same time and met face-to-face in the hall. It seemed the natural thing to do to come together in a gentle hug except, when decorum would have required them to part, neither seemed to be ready to move on into their separate bedrooms. They stood that way for several seconds, maybe minutes. Then Aimee backed away and without a word she turned and entered her room. John Paul stood in the middle of the hall for a full minute before he, too, retreated into his bedroom. Neither slept well that night.

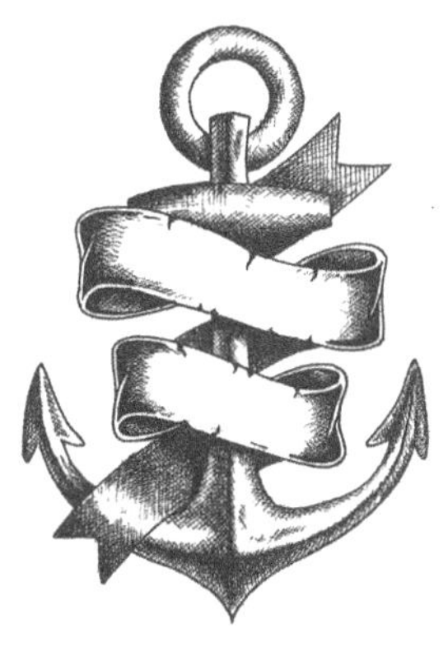

CHAPTER 12

THE RANGER

APRIL 13, 1776

John Paul looked for passage on a ship headed for New Hampshire but couldn't find one. Finally, he bought a horse for his trip north. Although he had ridden horses since boyhood, this was the first horse he had ever owned. It was not a "noble" steed, as he had often imagined in his boyhood dreams. In fact, when he made the purchase he wondered if the little mare would make the trip all the way to Portsmouth. When he brought her home, his boys and little Mary were excited that the family now owned a horse. John Paul was not one who had been a horse more than once or twice. He asked young Jim if he could rid and he told him he had worked part time at the livery stable and had ridden horses many time. John Paul sat on the steps and watched Jim take the children for rides up and down the street until Aimee called them all for supper.

He was up early the next morning to begin his journey north. He was full of excitement and ready for his first venture as captain of a newly commissioned Continental Navy ship. To reach shipboard, he had to first negotiate the road north through *Boston*, avoiding both the British Army and Massachusetts Militia campsites on the way. Word had come via the *Providence Gazette* of the siege of *Boston* by the militia. The Continental Congress had sent General Washington to take charge of the militia to insure the best possibility of success in *Boston*. They had succeeded in running the British occupiers out of the city on the fifteenth of March. That news was met with much celebration on the streets of *Providence*.

Unfortunately, John Paul anticipated that it probably left the British with a bad taste in their mouths and they were sure to deal harshly with anyone associated with the Continental military. Being a Scot by birth meant to the British that John Paul was a traitor to the Crown, and that was grounds for being shot or hanged. For the week prior to his departure, he had talked to every traveler who came into the three main taverns in *Providence*, hoping to get information about where the British were camped as well as where the Massachusetts Militia's troops were. He didn't want to find himself in either camp, but he especially wanted to avoid the British.

John Paul hoped to travel right through the middle of *Boston* and stop over for the night at the inn on the harbor where he and John Burroughs had stayed when they were last in *Boston* in 1773. That was the night when they had their adventure with the so-called Indian raid on the three British ships. Just heading north toward *Boston* brought back a flood of memories of that night more than two years before.

He also wanted to visit the Samuel Adams Tavern on King Street, hoping to meet with Adams himself and learn what the Sons of *Liberty* were up to.

Aimee had a full breakfast ready for him when he came downstairs. They sat and talked for a few minutes before he felt the urgency to get on his way. Before he opened the front door, he gave her a hug that seemed just right. But this time, he held her close and just as she began to pull away, he kissed her. Later, when he thought about it, he noted that she didn't resist and seemed willing enough accept his kiss, even kissed him back just enough so as to not appear overly aggressive. That kiss was much on his mind as he rode north out of *Providence*. It was a good thought and a good memory.

John Paul rode north on his little mare, following the river above the falls, and proceeded north toward *Boston*. His plan was to find a place to stay that night in Dedham, a small city just south of *Boston*. He made pretty good progress early in the day but found riding a horse over long distances nothing like he imagined. He had to get off the horse several times and just walk a bit. He had heard of saddle sores but had never taken a long enough journey to experience such. Now, he knew exactly what people were talking about. Riding was better than walking but nowhere near as comfortable as he had hoped.

By the time he reached Dedham, it was well into the night. So far, his information on troop encampments had been correct. He had been told that the British were camped west of *Boston* and so he thought he was probably clear riding into the city. General Washington's troops were in the city itself and he hoped he would have no difficulty moving through *Boston* the next day and on north toward Portsmouth the day following.

He found a tavern with rooms upstairs where he could stay the night and left his horse at a livery stable. During supper he listened to several of the men talk about the hostilities that were growing between the colonists and the British. It had been just a few weeks since George Washington and the militia had pushed into *Boston* from the north and forced the occupying British forces to withdraw. The consensus of the group in the tavern was that the British would retake *Boston* as soon as reinforcements arrived, either by ship or overland from Canada.

When the conversation subsided, he asked one of the participants, who seemed to know much about troop movements and the relative strength of the two armies, if any armed conflict was anticipated in the next few days. The man told John Paul that everything was quiet in *Boston*, at least for the present.

John Paul was up at the break of day, had a light breakfast in the tavern, and was on his way before he heard the first rooster crow. He felt the effects of yesterday's travel as soon as he put his foot in the stirrup. It seemed that everything hurt, especially his sitter. He smiled to himself and thought, *If I survive these four days on horseback, I resolve to never again attempt to travel anywhere on a horse.*

Three hours of riding brought him into the edge of the city. He made his way down to the wharf. From there, finding the tavern where he and John Burroughs had spent that half-a- night two years ago was easy. After registering and seeing the horse settled into a livery stable down the street behind the tavern, he lay down for an hour to rest. Sleep captured him, and it was late in the afternoon before he woke up. He dressed quickly and made the short walk to King Street and the Samuel Adams Tavern.

John Paul ordered a tankard of ale at the bar and asked the barkeep if Samuel Adams was close by. The barkeep said he would get word to Mr. Adams that a visitor was there to see him. "I'm sure he will be out shortly," the man said.

In a few minutes, John Paul saw Samuel Adams come through the kitchen door, stop, and survey the tables. He then made his way across the room to where John Paul was sitting. "Sir, I remember your face but not your name," Samuel Adams said.

"I am John Paul Jones from *Providence*," replied John Paul.

Recognition broke across Adams's face. "Now I remember you, from that little bit of fireworks in the harbor a couple of years back," he said smiling.

"You are right. Captain John Burroughs Hopkins and I were both here on a different errand and were lucky enough to become involved in your evening's entertainment," responded John Paul with an answering grin.

"What brings you here this time?" asked Samuel.

"I am on my way to Portsmouth to take command of a new Continental Navy ship," replied John Paul.

"So, you and your friend are both in the new navy?" asked Samuel.

"Yes sir. John Burroughs is captain of the *Cabot* and I am now captain of the *Ranger*," he said, perhaps with a bit too much pride in his voice.

John Paul leaned over toward Samuel Adams and lowered his voice to a whisper. He said, "Samuel, can you get me up to date on what you and your organization are doing now to help General Washington and his militia effort?"

Samuel lowered his voice as well. "Actually," he replied, "we were very involved with the effort to get the British out of our city. They have been gone a little over a month now and we have a meeting scheduled for tomorrow night. There is a real fear that the British will come back stronger than ever. They can't let us control the harbor where their ships and supplies come in and out. They have to hold *Boston*, or the entire New England region will fall."

"So, you feel that we are already at war with Great Britain here in Massachusetts?" asked John Paul.

Samuel's voice rose so that people at other tables could hear. "Of course, we are at war," said Samuel. "We have been at war ever since the massacre on our streets in 1770. Our representatives are in Philadelphia talking the issue to death right now. John Adams and John Hancock are both there. Maybe there are some Colonies that believe our relationship with the Crown can be saved, but you won't find many of them in *Boston*. We are for kicking the red coats out right now. If the rest of the Colonies don't want to help us, we will do it by ourselves."

"Samuel, what about that man we rode with that night into the harbor, Benedict Arnold? Is he with them in Philadelphia too?" John Paul asked.

"No," Samuel responded. "He is here in *Boston* right now. He is on the staff of General Washington and has been promoted to the rank of general. When he was here last night, he told me he was being sent over to the Hudson River to set up defenses against a possible British invasion down the river from Canada."

"So, you think all-out war with Great Britain is inevitable?" asked John Paul.

"We are already in it," responded Samuel Adams. "The British have long overstayed their welcome on our shores. General Washington has several militias under his control now and the numbers are growing by the day. Now it is only smaller militia groups, but soon it will be an army. Washington can only get stronger with successes like pushing the British out of *Boston*. I think the British will retake *Boston* before long, but I don't think it will stave off the inevitable. We are going to have war and we are going to have our new nation. I'd bet the family jewels."

The two men fell silent, John Paul digesting this news as he sipped his ale. Finally, Samuel Adams stood. "John Paul, I have to leave you now," he said. "I have a meeting with several of our people and I don't want to keep them waiting."

John Paul stood up to shake hands with his genial host and said, "I do sincerely appreciate your time and the information. I believe you are right on every count. The Navy Committee of the Continental Congress already has us out harassing British shipping in these waters. It may be an undeclared war, but it is war, nevertheless."

"Good night to you, John Paul, and good luck to you with your new ship," responded Samuel Adams.

Sleep came slowly that night. The conversation with Samuel Adams was on his mind but, also, the pain in his back and legs, the effects of two days riding on a horse. He could feel the soreness with every movement.

John Paul took his time getting back on the road the next morning. He was more stiff and sore than he had been the day before. Riding horseback did not agree with him at all. He knew he had two more days of riding north to reach Portsmouth, New Hampshire which he didn't relish. But at the end of his torture, he knew he would see his new ship, the *Ranger*. That, he thought, at least made it all tolerable.

He spent the next night at an inn in Marlboro, Massachusetts. This time there was no conversation in the evening in a local tavern. By the time he arrived in Marlboro he was totally exhausted and was sure he never wanted to see a horse again. He had a quick supper and went straight to bed. Tomorrow would be a most eventful day. He would arrive in Portsmouth and would see his ship for the first time. If he had not been so weary and sore, he would have been too excited to sleep. However, weariness won out and he was asleep as soon as his head hit the pillow.

It was with great reluctance that he mounted his horse one more time. The only reason he was able to do it was because he knew it would be the last time. He arrived in Portsmouth just after dark and found an inn close to the shipyard. He fought the urge to go to the shipyard to try to see the *Ranger* at night. Instead, he found a local livery stable and bedded down his horse. He had a short conversation with the attendant at the stable about selling the horse and was assured that a deal could be struck for both the horse and the saddle. Looking at the tired little mare, the attendant volunteered that John Paul might get more for the saddle than the horse.

When John Paul left the horse, he felt like celebrating. If he ever climbed on a horse again it would be too soon. He went back to the inn and had a leisurely supper. Despite weariness, sleep just would not come this night. Tomorrow held too much excitement for him. He stared at the ceiling of his room most of the night and watched the sun come in through windows that faced east toward the wharf.

He was the first one up for breakfast that morning. His back and legs were stiff from riding horseback for four days, but even those pains couldn't dull his enthusiasm to get this day started.

He made his way toward the shipyard to get his first look at his new ship. There it was, the *Ranger*. Immediately, he was totally deflated. He knew right away that the *Ranger* was not as it had been advertised, not at all what Commodore Hopkins had told him. He was anticipating a sleek sloop with low sails and a low draft keel that could pass over sand bars that would snare a larger ship. He could see immediately that the ship builder had put two masts on the ship that were too large for her frame. Such height would catch more air than the narrow draft bottom could handle. Any significant wind would turn her over and cause her to flounder. In short, the builder was no John Brown.

Over the years John Paul had grown used to the quality engineering of a John Brown-built ship in the ship yard at *Providence*. This builder had evidently reasoned out that if two thirty-foot masts were good, then a forty-foot mast was better. He obviously had never been to sea in one of his own ships. He had no understanding of the necessity of matching the right size masts and sails with the right size frame.

The ship was a mess. What to do to salvage it was the problem. He went to look for the builder and found him in a small office near the wharf, looking over plans for another ship. His name was James Langdon.

When John Paul identified himself as the captain of the *Ranger*, a broad smile broke out on Langdon's face. "Have you seen the ship?" he asked proudly. "Did you see what I have done for you at no additional expense to the Continental Congress?"

"I think you are talking about the size of the main and aft masts," responded John Paul.

"You are right. I put another ten feet of mast on her, so she would catch the wind better than anything on the ocean. They said they wanted it to be fast and this should be the fasted sloop afloat," boasted the builder.

"Perhaps you are right," replied John Paul. "She might be fast with the wind behind her when sailing in a straight line in calm seas. How do you think she will do with a stiff cross-wind? With all that extra weight, will she heel over? Can a ship with such masts be as maneuverable as she needs to be during battle? With all that weight topside, what is to keep her from just laying over on her side? Have you tested your theory about higher masts on a sloop frame of this size?"

"Hmmm," responded the builder, his smile fading. "No. It just made sense to me that if you wanted it to be fast you needed to catch as much wind as possible."

"Sir," said John Paul. "The *Ranger* has the potential to be a serviceable ship for the navy but not with those masts on her. We need for you to take them down and replace them with two that are the proper height for her frame."

"That could be a problem," said the builder. "I don't have any masts on hand that are the size you want. To replace these, we will have to go back to the north woods and cut some trees. It will take us at least a month to get the timber back here and another two weeks to mount them on the ship."

John Paul walked over and sat down in a chair near the door to the small building. He said, "Sir, I came to fetch the *Ranger*, but I am not accepting this ship, nor authorizing payment from the Continental Congress, until it is right."

The builder looked at him with great frustration. He said, "Captain Jones, I suggest that you go look at the ship and see the workmanship and quality we have put into it. Then come back. By then, I will have had time to think of possible alternatives to solve the problem with the masts."

Jones was skeptical but agreed to do a walk-through of the *Ranger*. He was gone from the office for just over an hour. When he returned, Mr. Langdon was working on some drawings on the big table in the middle of the room.

The shipbuilder looked up at John Paul and said, somewhat warily, "Well, Captain Jones, how did you find the rest of the *Ranger*?"

"Your carpenters have done well," John Paul responded. "Of course, anything can look good sitting by the dock. The proof will be known when we get her out to sea and test her out."

"Have a seat, Captain Jones," Langdon said. "Let me suggest an alternative that may solve our problem with the masts."

John Paul retreated to the chair by the door and sat down. He looked expectantly at Mr. Langdon.

"As I see it, we have a height problem. I thought I could enhance the speed of the ship by adding about ten feet to the height of the masts and by adding two top-mast sails to better catch the wind. You make a good point with the weight problem, which I should have thought about before I put the masts up. I suggest that instead of going to the north woods to find appropriate replacements, we simply cut off the top ten feet of the fore and aft masts. We could then re-fit the spars for the smaller masts and it should be good to go."

"Mr. Langdon," said John Paul, "I don't know if that will work since the trunks of both masts are larger than needed and both weigh significantly more than shorter masts would weigh. What it may gain in catching the wind it will lose in extra weight and deeper draft. Without the right weight masts, the balance is still likely to be off enough to affect the handling of the ship in wind and high surf."

"How would we know whether or not it will work unless we try it?" asked Langdon. I think the frame is strong enough to handle the extra weight."

When John Paul left the office, he was not sure the solution presented by James Langdon would work, but he had agreed to try it. If it could work, it would get him back on the ocean again well before the six weeks to two months Langdon was projecting.

What became obvious with the first two days at the ship yard was that the *Ranger* was not ready and wouldn't be for a week or two, even if the alternative with the masts worked. If not, he was destined to be in Portsmouth for six weeks to two months. He knew that Aimee and the boys were expecting him back in another week, two at the most. The third night in Portsmouth John Paul wrote them a letter detailing the problems he was facing. He knew that transporting a letter all the way from New Hampshire to Rhode Island overland would take a week or more but, perhaps, if it arrived in a timely fashion it would ease their anxiety of not knowing where he was or what he was doing.

April 22, 1776
Mrs. Aimee Shelton
Planet Street
Providence, Rhode Island

Dear Aimee and boys,

The Ranger, my first command, is not at all as advertised. Some important aspects of the ship must be remedied before it can go to sea. So, I am stuck here in Portsmouth until the work is completed.

The primary problem is that the builder put two masts up that are suitable for a much larger ship. The result is a ship that is top heavy and, in a gale, is most likely to heel over. He says he thought the taller masts were a good improvement in the building plan allowing the sail to catch more wind. I suspect he was just using materials on hand rather than the reason he gave me.

I believe I will be here at least until the end of the first week in May and maybe longer. Don't look for me until you see me coming up the street. If I get more current information about when I might be home, I will write again.

Your Humble Servant,

John Paul Jones, Captain

John Paul came to the ship yard each day to watch the progress on the *Ranger*. It was slow going, and he realized after watching the progress on two other ships John Langdon was working on, that the *Ranger* was third choice on all materials. Sails were a good example. When it came time to equip the ship with sails, there was no proper material on hand. The other two ships had sails, but the *Ranger* sat for two days waiting on new supplies. Finally, sail material arrived. Any seasoned sailor would say it looked more like old gunny-sacks that the pure white material from which most sails are made.

He said nothing to John Langdon. John Paul's plan was to get the ship on the water as soon as possible and to John Brown's ship yard in *Providence*. There he could re-fit the ship as necessary with quality materials and workmanship.

Finally, the ship was ready for a trial run. James Langdon had provided him with a make-shift crew and they guided the *Ranger* out of the small harbor to the open seas. It didn't take long for John Paul to realize that his crew was as lacking as his ship. Still, he was on the ocean and closer to his goal to arrive back in *Providence* where he could shape up his first command with proper equipment and a crew worthy of the name. These New Hampshire boys acted like total first-timers. A short conversation with several revealed exactly that; most had never been to sea at all.

They tested out the maneuverability of the ship. It was sluggish in the turns when he tried to tack back and forth, but its forward speed was better than he expected. He thought, *Of course, when the seas are calm and the winds fair, all ships can sail. It is when the weather turns fierce and the seas come at you with twenty-foot waves that you really test the capability of a ship.*

One thing surprised him about the ship. Though he didn't like the look of the sails with their ugly gray cloth, he realized that at one hundred yards the *Ranger* looked like anything but what it was, a new ship with a sleek bottom and sixteen cannons. At a distance, the sails were harder to see than the pure white sails on most ships, which could be seen at a distance of ten miles or more. He liked the idea of having gray sails and getting closer to his targets before they knew he was closing in on them.

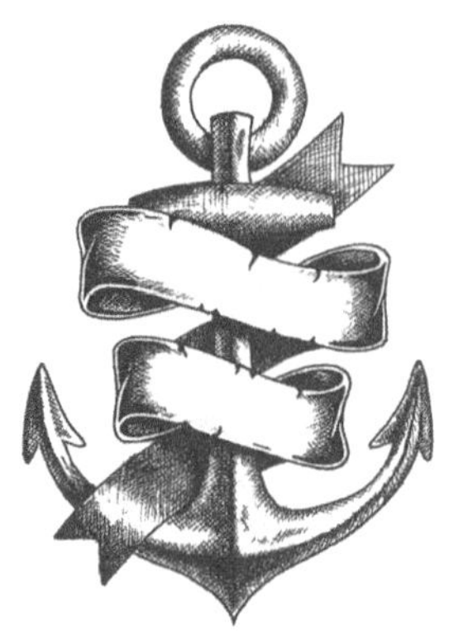

CHAPTER 13

BACK HOME IN PROVIDENCE

MAY 3, 1776

Finally, John Paul and the *Ranger* were fully equipped and had a crew, such as it was, and were headed home. They had skirted the edge of Cape Ann, Massachusetts on the way south from Portsmouth and had sailed directly for Race Point at the tip of Cape Cod. John Paul's primary goal was to stay away from *Boston* Harbor and any British ships that might be sitting just out to sea east of the city. Provincetown, at the upper end of Cape Cod, was a British Harbor too, and he wanted to stay clear of it as well. That meant he had to put his navigation skills to work in order to stay well away from danger on the way back to *Providence*. Normally his navigator would have been making the necessary calculations and governing the course, but he had no trust in any of the crew members James Langdon had provided. Better to trust himself than to find his ship in British hands at the end of its maiden voyage.

It took a full three days to negotiate the wind and the currents off Cape Cod and through the Vineyard Sound to the mouth of Narragansett Bay. John Paul maneuvered the *Ranger* to a position just south of the bay by just after dusk on the fourth day. He kept the *Ranger* out of sight of land and intended to make his move as the tide came in at around three in the morning. He knew he could ride her into the bay and past the harbor at Newport before anyone learned she was there.

He had learned enough about *Ranger* after four days on the ocean that he knew under full sail and with the wind at their back, they could make fifteen knots and maybe a little more. With the tide pushing them, they might reach a full twenty knots. If they could get even with Newport Harbor before any of the British ships spotted them, he had confidence they could make it to *Providence* before anyone could catch them. Though he would never have admitted it to James Langdon, his plan was aided by the fact that his sails were made out of the dark gray gunny-sack material. They would not stand out at night even if the moon was bright.

John Paul stood on the deck in the darkest of night. The lanterns usually displayed on the front and back of the ship had not been lit, and there was no moon. He noted that there was a fair wind blowing from the southwest that would fill his sails when they were ready to make their run. He waited until he felt the tide begin to move toward the mouth of the bay before he gave the order to drop the sails. Within minutes they were moving at maximum speed.

The point of greatest danger was just inside the bay at a place the seamen called Whale Rock. The Newport people had tried with no luck to get a permanent lantern attached to the rock, which stuck out of the water like the back of a whale. At night, with no light on it, you had to know exactly where it was, so you could miss it to the east. It would have been a safer route passing Whale Rock to the west farther away from the British ships in Newport Harbor, but there were several sandbars extending out from the shore on that side so the only reasonable route was to ease by the rock on the east side which carried them out into the channel of the bay. That was good sailing water but was dangerously close to the harbor at Newport where the British ships were anchored.

It was as if everyone stopped breathing when they entered the mouth of the bay. John Paul did not hear a sound from the crew, most of whom were frozen with fear to be sailing in such dangerous waters with no lights and just the educated judgement of their captain to keep them off the rocks. Luck was with them, though, and no-one from Newport Harbor saw them. At least no one gave chase. They arrived at the wharf in

Providence and sailed right by it to the shipyards. John Paul wanted to be first in line the next morning when the shipyard opened to get the *Ranger* on the work schedule.

He gave instruction to the crew to stay on board that night but to plan a move to more permanent lodging in the city the next day. He had thirty men on board and each would need housing for the night. Some would need to have a place to stay for a month until the *Ranger* was ready for service, but more than half of the men he intended to let go to return to Portsmouth. Not only did they not know the difference between a slip knot and a bowline, they did not know what they were getting into with a life at sea. After the past night's experience, he imagined they would not mind being sent home by land. They might even bless him for it.

He wanted to pick his own crew from *Providence* men he knew to be capable seamen. Most specifically, he was concerned about the leadership he would hire: the sailing master, the boatswain, the carpenter, a surgeon, and more.

John Paul stayed on board with his men through the night and then saw all but a skeleton crew off of the ship the next morning. Then he felt secure enough to leave the ship for his home on Planet Street. The sun was coming up as he made his way to his house. When he pushed the door open, he could smell breakfast cooking in the kitchen. Aimee heard the door open and came to see who was there. When she saw him, she flew across the room and into his arms.

They stood that way for several seconds before he held her back at arm's length and said, "Surprise."

She laughed and replied, "Surprise, indeed. I got your letter and we weren't expecting you for another week or two. The boys will be delighted."

"How about you?" he asked. "Are you delighted?"

He could see just a touch of blush on her cheeks and she thought for just a few seconds before responding. "Yes, of course, I am delighted too. Having you home makes everything seem like all is right with the world. When you aren't here we get into a pattern of eating, sleeping, marketing, lessons, and doing all the humdrum things. With you here the world is very different for the boys. They are going to be so pleased you are home. I hesitate to ask, but how long can you stay home with us?"

"Aimee, I never know for sure, but I should here for at least a month," said John Paul. "The *Ranger* needs some major work before she is sea worthy. I told you about that in the letter. It is some better now but there is still much to be done. I did not want them to work on her further in Portsmouth because, looking at what I saw the first day I was there, I could not trust the quality of the builder's work. I will feel much better with the people at the *Providence* shipyard taking her apart and putting her back together as she should be."

It didn't take long for John Paul to slip back into his pattern of visiting the shipyard in the morning to see the progress on both the *Cabot* and the *Ranger*, dropping by to see John Burroughs in the early afternoon, arriving home in time to play with the boys before supper. The boys were always such fun to be with, but the highlight of each day was the quiet time he spent with Aimee each evening sitting by the fire in the parlor.

The late-night conversations were moving well beyond the welfare of the children and the needs of the house. He and Aimee were talking more and more about the future and her role with the boys until they were grown. Each night the hug in the hallway at the top of the stairs grew longer and longer, and he had added a kiss to their ritual.

Each night they parted, though each night the partings were slower and slower. Then, one night, they didn't part.

The next morning, John Paul was up earlier than usual. He made his usual rounds and found himself talking to his close friend, John Burroughs Hopkins, late in the morning.

"You seem troubled this morning, my friend," said John Burroughs. "What is it?"

"You are pretty perceptive," John Paul responded. "I am more than troubled, I am confused. The last several months have been very difficult and filled with some very high points and some not so high. As you know, my beloved Keziah died and left me with Daniel and Moses to raise by myself. And me with a job that requires being gone more than at home.

I got my first command, then found out the ship was not as advertised. John Brown's shipyard is trying to straighten out the problems and I have hopes they will succeed. The crew of the *Ranger* has been no small problem and I have sent most of them back to Portsmouth. Finding a competent crew when the privateers pay so much better than the Continental Navy has been a real challenge. And, my friend, your injury and slow recovery have been a burden on my mind. Of course, you haven't missed anything on the ocean because the *Cabot* was in such bad shape that it wasn't going anyplace anyway."

"All of these seem pretty typical problems, except for the challenge of raising children and being captain of a ship at the same time," said John Burroughs. "It appears to me you are handling each one in turn as you always have. So, what is the heavy burden that I detect just under the surface, John Paul?"

John Paul started his response slowly and his voice dropped so low that John Burroughs had to lean forward to hear what he was saying. "John Burroughs, Keziah has been gone less than three months now and she was the mother of my children and the love of my life. In the time I have been home I have gotten much better acquainted with Daniel and Moses, enough so that I will really hate to leave them when the *Ranger* is ready and I have to go back to sea."

"I can understand that," said John Burroughs. "I don't have children, so I don't know what that feels like, but leaving *Hannah* for months at a time takes a bit of my heart every time I sail away. I have to remind myself that the sea is how I make our living. I know you have had these thoughts before when you had to leave Keziah and the boys. So, what is the new problem you are struggling with?"

Again, John Burroughs had to lean forward to hear John Paul's voice. "I have fallen in love with Aimee Shelton," his friend said, staring at his hands. "There, I said it. That is the first time I have said it out loud and I feel like a traitor to Keziah's memory."

John Burroughs leaned back and did his best to stifle his smile. His mind was racing to think of how best to respond to his friend. Finally, he said, "John Paul, I think that is wonderful."

John Paul raised he head and looked directly at this friend. "You do?" he asked.

"Of course, I do," said John Burroughs with a chuckle. "As you have told me before, the boys love her, and she is a wonderful mother to all four of the children. What could be better than falling in love with such a beautiful woman, who has all of the traits you came to appreciate in Keziah? I think Keziah would want you to find such a person who was very much like her, and to create a new home for the boys."

John Paul's demeanor changed immediately, a broad smile on his razor-thin face. "Oh, my friend, I have told no one else of my dilemma, but your response makes it all right. Before the week is over, Aimee and I will tell the whole city. I am going to leave you and go straight home. If Aimee approves, I will visit with the pastor of the First Baptist Church this afternoon and we will arrange a wedding as quickly as he can find a time on his schedule."

When John Paul left the Hopkins house, he was whistling softly to himself. John Burroughs stood in the doorway and watched his friend walk down the street. When he made the turn, and was out of sight, John Burroughs leaned back and laughed his loudest laugh. His friend was happy, and all seemed right with the world again.

Yes, everything was right except his arm and shoulder, which seemed to be healing in slow motion.

The wedding of John Paul Jones and Aimee Shelton was held that Friday. It was a small group that gathered at the church that Roger Williams had founded at about the time he was helping to create the city of *Providence*. The pastor paused at the appointed time and asked, "Is this the entire group?"

John Paul responded, "It is."

They had had three days to invite anyone who would have been interested in being a part of the wedding party. In truth, beside John Burroughs, *Hannah*, and the children, there were no more. Neither John Paul nor Aimee had any family left.

The pastor was about to begin the service when they heard a noise at the door. The light was bright when the door opened, and when it closed there were three new members of the wedding party. John Brown and his brother, Moses, came walking down the aisle while former Governor Stephen Hopkins followed just a few steps behind.

The pastor began the marriage ceremony with the traditional Baptist words, "Dearly Beloved, we are gathered here today to join these two in Holy Matrimony..."

The rest of the words were lost on John Paul. He was smiling inwardly to himself. His wedding was a small one, but in the company was the richest man in town and a former governor. That was far more than he could have hoped.

Later, when they were all having dinner together at Sabin's Tavern, John and Moses Brown and Stephen Hopkins held a whispered conversation. "Yes, John it was a very nice Baptist wedding," said Moses. "I remember well when Anna and I got married in that very building back in 1764, with both of our families present. We were about half-way through the service when a mule started braying, right under our feet. Do they still keep mules and horses under the church building?"

John Brown and Stephen Hopkins both laughed at the mental picture of the mule disrupting the wedding service. "Moses, that just made it all the more memorable," said John Brown. "I'll bet that mule was the talk of the town and made for family folklore conversations for you and Anna for years."

"You are right about that," replied Moses.

Later, when they were home together, and the children were playing in the parlor, John Paul and Aimee had a moment of quiet time. Aimee said, "John Paul, I hope this wasn't all too sudden for you. I have a confession to make."

John Paul set his hot coffee down and looked closely at his new wife. "What is it?"

"You may not have thought of us together until just last week, but I have been thinking about it ever since Keziah died," she replied. "Was that too bad of me, to be thinking of that so soon after your wife died?"

John Paul considered for a moment. "I don't think so," he said. "In fact, considering the children and an absentee father, it was a logical thing to think."

"John Paul, that makes me feel so much better. You have been on my mind almost constantly for three months now," she said.

"Aimee, you didn't let on at all you were thinking of marriage," said John Paul.

"I was afraid to. I didn't know what you might think. If I had said anything, it might not have been at all what was on your mind," she replied.

"We won't mention it again, but after the other night when I just didn't let go of you in the upstairs hall, it should have been obvious what was on my mind," he said.

"Well, at that moment it was surely obvious what was on your mind, but it wasn't marriage," she responded.

They both laughed, and he leaned over and kissed her, their first kiss since the wedding ceremony. This one wasn't a peck on the lips like the one done for the company at church. This one was for keeps.

THE PROVIDENCE GAZETTE

PROVIDENCE, Rhode Island, May 25, 1776--Our delegates to the Continental Congress continue to work on the war effort. There was great celebration when the new fleet came back from Nassau with gun powder, cannons, and a variety of other war materials taken from British stores for General Washington.

The privateers continue to harass the British supply boats and have had great success not only limiting supplies to the British Army but, also, in providing everything from medical supplies to muskets and cannonballs to General Washington and our troops.

We lament that a number of privateer ships appear to have disappeared while operating in the service of their country. The British man-of-war continues to be the most fearsome ship on the seas and they, evidently, have sunk a number of the privateers' ships.

A new Continental Navy ship has been taken into the Providence shipyard to be refitted. It is the Ranger. Its captain is John Paul Jones, one of local seamen who was once an officer on the Katy when it was based in Providence.

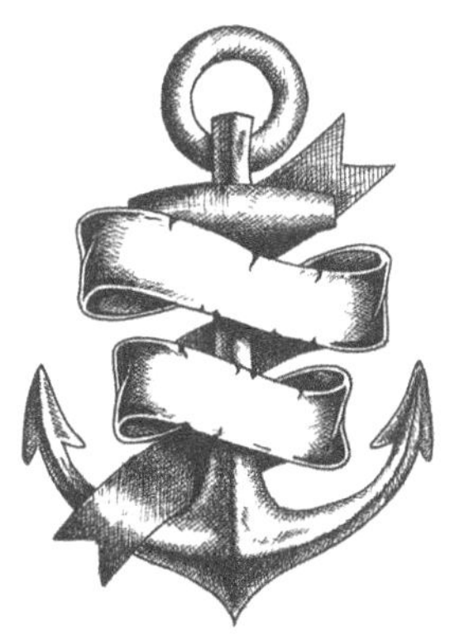

CHAPTER 14

BACK ON THE HIGH SEAS

MAY 25, 1776

Once again, the cadence of drums was heard on the streets of *Providence*, this time to announce a meeting of ship owners and captains at Sabin's Tavern. Many of the men of *Providence* remembered the meeting four years before when they had plotted the demise of the *Gaspee*, the gun boat that was harassing shipping at the mouth of the Narragansett Bay. John Brown and Stephen Hopkins, well known and well-respected leaders, had called that earlier meeting, which had filled the tavern meeting room to overflowing. This one was called by John Paul Jones.

While Jones was well known among the seafaring population in *Providence*, it remained to be seen whether he had the "draw" to fill the meeting room at Sabin's. The situation with the British was noticeably worse now. Instead of a schooner impeding trade and commerce at the edge of the ocean, it was two man-of-war class ships. A single ship leaving *Providence* port had little chance of making it to the open seas without being boarded and losing their cargo and maybe even their ship. All agreed something had to be done. The question was what?

He needn't have worried. There were already several men at the tavern when he and young Jim Shelton arrived to set up the room. Before long the room was filled to overflowing, with some men standing along the walls. As the appointed time approached ,the room took on an almost eerie look. Pipe smoke drifted above the tables, and the smell was of tobacco, ale, beer, and working men who had come directly from the job.

Among the best known of the participants were John and Moses Brown, the ship builders and owners who had instigated the attack on the *Gaspee*. However, their partner, former Governor Stephen Hopkins, who had attended the earlier meeting about the *Gaspee*, was in Philadelphia serving In the Continental Congress.

John Brown offered his help to John Paul as soon as he arrived, and it was gratefully accepted. John Brown said he would be happy to the meeting and introduce John Paul. As John Brown walked to the front of the room, almost immediately the chatter and noise subsided.

"We are here for a very serious discussion," he said. "You all know the serious dilemma we are in with those two man-of-war ships sitting at the mouth of Narragansett Bay. We can't get in or out without losing our merchandise and maybe even our ships to the British. They hold the port at Newport and, because of that, they command our opening to the sea," he said.

There was an immediate reaction from the men. One shouted from the back of the room, "What can we do against two of their high masters?"

John Brown signaled for quiet. He continued. "The last time I stood in front of you was in 1772 when the *Gaspee* was causing havoc with our shipping. We took care of the situation under the leadership of Captain Abraham Whipple. When we left the wharf that night, we rowed our long boats not knowing how the evening would end. The risk was great but because we came together to solve the problem, not a man was injured, and the problem was solved, at least for that time. Today, we have a greater challenge. There are two man-of-war ships sailing patrol at the mouth of Narragansett Bay, not just a single gunboat as was true in 1772."

At this point John Brown's voice lifted in volume and he almost yelled his last sentence. "They won't let us in or out without paying a toll that makes commerce on the ocean near impossible!"

In response, the room erupted. Several of the men stood and yelled comments and others raised their muskets showing their willingness to go to war.

It took a few minutes to get the group quieted down again. Then John Brown said, "When the Continental Navy was formed by the Congress last year, they created a plan for dealing with just such circumstances as we find ourselves in today, landlocked by a couple of British enforcers. I am sure you know that we have two Continental Navy ships in our shipyard being made seaworthy, the *Cabot* and *Ranger*. The *Cabot* is still a few weeks away from heading back to the open sea, but the *Ranger* is almost ready. The man who called this meeting is Captain John Paul Jones of the *Ranger*. He has a plan which is being used all up and down the Atlantic coast. He will share that plan with you and give you the opportunity to ask your questions and raise your concerns."

As John Paul passed John Brown on the way to the front of the room, he nodded his appreciation to him for powerful introduction. The men listened intently as John Paul spoke. "Men, none of us have a chance to make it to the open sea by ourselves. In fact, with a war looming with Great Britain, we have little choice but to work together if we are to be successful. With that in mind, I need your help. The *Ranger* is almost seaworthy again. The job of the *Ranger* and all the ships of the new Continental Navy is to disrupt British supply lines to their army and to take what we can for the benefit of our own army. The *Ranger* needs to be back on the open sea."

There was instant disruption. Many voices were heard but one stood out, "How are you going to do that with a ship which is less than half the size of a man-of-war?"

"That is where I need your help," said John Paul. "One ship sailing by itself is bound to be attacked by the British at the mouth of the Narragansett. But if we can sail fifteen to twenty ships down to the mouth of the bay at the same time and all go in different directions when we get there, the British will have to choose who to chase down. If we have twenty ships, eighteen of them should break free of the blockade into the open sea. I know it is a sacrifice and a risk for each of us, but we are at war and I see no other way to break out of this blockade."

Again, many voices were raised. Finally, as the group quieted, one man stood up. He said, "I am Phillip Cambridge from North *Providence*, sir. If I have this straight, you would like fifteen or twenty of us who have ships that are seaworthy to join together and form a flotilla that will travel down the Narragansett together."

"You have that right, sir," responded John Paul.

"What then do you expect the man-of-war ships to do with such a mass of ships all at the same time?" Cambridge asked.

"The only thing I think they can do is pick out two of us and attempt to run us down and board us," John Paul responded. "If we are lucky, they will be so surprised and confused they won't know what to do with us. If worse comes to worse and they run down one or two of us, I am not sure what they will do, but I anticipate the ship and crew are in for some hard time in the jail at Newport."

"Sir, do you think they might try to sink us?" asked Cambridge.

"I don't think it makes sense to attempt to match cannon fire with a British man-of-war and I would recommend that anyone who is pursued pull sails and let them board," responded John Paul. "While they are occupied the rest of us will be long gone. If they are drawn away from the mouth of the Narragansett the rest can simply retrace their route back to *Providence* Harbor."

Another man stood. "Captain Jones, as you know, I am Brace Pontiac, harbor master here at *Providence*," he said. "Can you tell me when you anticipate putting together the flotilla to challenge the British at the mouth of the bay? I need to be ready to accommodate everyone who anticipates participating."

"That is a very good question, Mr. Pontiac," said John Paul. "The date I have set is two weeks from tonight. We would plan on leaving the harbor area at around eleven o'clock in the evening. That will give us about five hours to get to the mouth of the bay before dawn. We will be fighting the incoming tide for a part of the trip down, and having a fair wind is important. This time of year, we get mostly winds out of the northwest, so we can be hopeful. If it rains, that will be better for the surprise and confusion, even though it will make sailing conditions more difficult. We are all veterans of these waters and are used to dealing with the tides, winds, rain, and whatever old Neptune throws at us. So, the date is set."

He looked about the room where all eyes were focused on him. "I will ask those of you who intend to be a part of this flotilla to make contact with Mr. Pontiac at the harbor master's office so we know how many to expect," said John Paul. "We need at least fifteen ships, but I would like twenty. If we get more, we will use the overage next time. This will not be our only time. We will also have to get the *Cabot* back onto the high seas in three to four weeks."

"One more question, Captain Jones," said a distinguished looking gentleman from about half way back in the room. "The British are continually looking for seamen that they believe have deserted from their ships. When they find them, the punishment is severe, and they generally end up either hanged or in jail. Could I suggest that if a captain knows he has a Brit on his crew that he leave them behind this trip?"

"A very good thought sir," responded John Paul. "Any Brit who has left them is now one of us, but we don't want to create any more hardship that necessary for any of our seamen."

With that, the men slowly began to leave the room, talking among themselves. Then John Paul felt a familiar presence at his side. Both John Burroughs and young Jim had joined him at the front of the room.

"John Paul, this was a great meeting," said John Burroughs. "Not only are you beginning to pull together the leadership of the port, but there is a real spirit of comradery in this group. I never knew it before, but it should have been obvious. You, my young friend, have a real knack for speaking to groups. You had them in the palm of your hand."

John Paul looked down and winked at young Jim, who smiled back at him.

The next two weeks flew by with preparations for the escape into the north Atlantic. John Paul used every waking minute to get his ship ready with a new crew and provisions for a two-month journey. Each day he came home for a mid-day meal and to spend some time with the boys and Aimee. Each evening he enjoyed the company of his new wife in front of the fireplace. As the evening waned, they would go up the stairs and, generally, pick up Mary and Daniel at the top of the stairs, carry them into their rooms and then meet in the dark of their bedroom at the end of the hall. John Paul could not remember being so happy.

Every morning John Paul would go to the shipyard to check on the progress of the *Ranger* and, while there, he would climb on board the *Cabot* and make a complete inspection, so he could report later in the day to John Burroughs. Young Jim was with John Paul everywhere he went. There was no accounting for the number of questions he could ask, and he seemed to absorb information like a sponge. He was a delightful young man, one John Paul hoped he had been like at the same age. For sure, Aimee had every reason to be very proud of him.

Finally, he had a crew, all except a cook. He had advertised through the harbor master's office where many out-of-work seamen checked in on a daily basis. Late one morning when he was on board the *Ranger*, a familiar figure came walking up the gangplank. It was Jubal, the cook who had been on the *Katy* with John Paul, then switched to the *Cabot* when John Burroughs had become captain of that smaller ship. John Paul and Jubal greeted each other like old friends.

"Jubal, it is good to see you," said John Paul.

"You too, Captain Jones," responded Jubal.

"What brings you aboard the *Ranger*?" asked John Paul.

"Sir, I'm looking for a job," replied Jubal. "I have had no work since we arrived here with the *Cabot* and I am down to my last shilling. The man at the shipyard office says you are looking for a cook. Will I do?"

"Will you do? Jubal, you are an answer to prayer! I will be glad to have you and count myself lucky to have hired the best," said John Paul.

"I had hoped you would say that," said Jubal. "So, where is my galley? If we are sailing in three days, I have a lot of work to do."

"Jim, you show Jubal the galley. I am going to the harbor master's office and will meet you at home for dinner in an hour or so," John Paul said.

"Yes sir, Captain Jones," said Jim.

John Paul watched Jubal and Jim walk toward the stairs to the lower deck and noted Jubal's hand on Jim's shoulder. He thought to himself, *Jubal will, indeed, be a nice addition to the crew, and one that will add some security for young Jim.*

He was walking toward the harbor master's office feeling good about Jubal joining his crew when he felt a stab of conscience. Jubal, after all, had been John Burroughs's cook and now he was taking him away from his friend. He resolved to talk to John Burroughs at his first opportunity.

When he checked with the harbor master, he noted that he had fifteen volunteers for his flotilla. The major exodus was scheduled for three nights away and he was hopeful that he would get two or three more ships to join them. Every addition made the odds better for whichever ships the man-of-war ships chose to chase.

The last day before their departure was hectic. John Paul met early with the sailing master, boatswain, master gunner, and the carpenter. He asked Jubal to sit in on this meeting because of the issue of provisions for the crew. John Paul was concerned that they would not have any time to practice their gunnery before possible conflict at the mouth of the Narragansett. Still, if everything went as planned, perhaps they wouldn't need the cannons.

The *Ranger* had been outfitted exactly to John Paul's specifications. Well-disguised cannon covers had been created so that at a distance you could not tell if the ship had cannons, much less how many it had. It appeared to be a merchant ship carrying a cargo. High in the rigging, well disguised, they had built a series of wooden platforms designed to allow the marines to climb the rope ladders into the highest vantage point on the ship to give them full coverage of the top deck of any ship they encountered. Because of the extra-large and heavy masts that had been put on the *Ranger* in Portsmouth, John Paul still was not sure of the speed of the ship nor of its maneuverability. If he made it out of the mouth of the bay his first order of business would be to test out both speed and maneuverability as well as to give the gunnery crew an opportunity to practice.

Finally, the appointed day moved into evening and John Paul made preparation to leave the house. He found his children on the floor of the parlor playing and he sat down on the floor with them. It was just a few seconds before the two youngest, Moses and Elizabeth, climbed on his lap, and the others came over close to him.

"I am going to be gone for a while," he said.

"Where are you going?" Daniel responded. "Can we go with you?"

"No, I am going to be on the ship for several weeks and it isn't a good place for children," said John Paul.

Daniel's voice broke into a whine and he said, "We never get to go anyplace with you."

"Someday I will take you, but not now," John Paul responded.

"I want you to promise me that you will mind Mother Aimee in everything she asks you to do. That is very important," added John Paul.

"We will, Father," said little Moses.

John Paul was immediately surprised to hear from Moses. He was the one of the four children whose voice he heard the least. "Thank you, Moses, I am sure you will."

John Paul stood up and walked to the door where Aimee was waiting. She gave him his bag and said, "John Paul, I know you don't know when you will be back to *Providence*, but I want you to know you will be missed every minute you are gone."

Before she said another word, John Paul took her in his arms and their lips met in one last kiss. When they parted, John Paul said, "I will be back as soon as I can. You take care of yourself and the children. If there is anything you need, ask at John Brown's office. They have whatever money you may need, and they will have word of us wherever we are."

Jim had been sitting on the front steps watching John Paul and his mother at the door. Once John Paul was outside, he gave his mother a quick hug and joined John Paul on the sidewalk. Together they walked down the street toward the shipyard where the *Ranger* would be launched. Aimee stood at the door watching them until they were out of sight. Then the tears came.

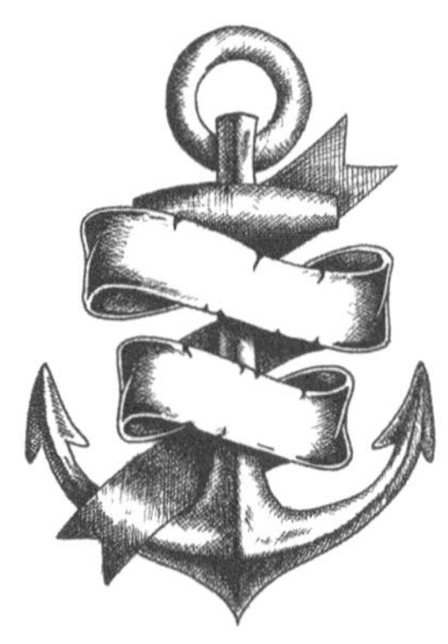

CHAPTER 15

THE FLOTILLA

JUNE 20, 1776

John Paul had been right earlier: two additional ships had joined their flotilla, bringing the number to seventeen. It wasn't the twenty he had hoped for, but seventeen was a pretty good number. As he left the port late that night and brought the *Ranger* into the channel of the bay, he watched as one by one the other ships lifted their anchors and began to drop sails. Slowly the group of ships began to make their way southward down the bay. He noted with some disappointment that his was the largest ship in the group. That might be something of a handicap when they faced the man-of-war ships at the mouth of the Narragansett. Being the largest of the ships might entice the British to give chase to the *Ranger* because it might hold the most promise for cargo.

Traveling by darkness, all of the ships moved slowly down the bay, passing the site of the *Gaspee* affar from 1772, and then into the larger bay channel. The breeze was carrying them easily southward and he had not felt the tide change yet. He knew it would be necessary to carry more sails when the tide changed, which he expected at about 3 a.m. But the breeze would overpower the tide. He calculated that they would reach the mouth of the bay at around five in the morning.

He had heard that Admiral *Richard* Howe was captain of one of the British ships that was stationed at Newport and took a regular turn patrolling the mouth of the bay. Admiral Howe was the younger brother of General Howe of British Army fame, who had been killed at Ticonderoga earlier in the conflict. He had many reasons to want to fight the Colonies and was known to be more inclined to use his cannons rather than to persuade his quarry to stop and be boarded.

All the way down the bay channel, *Ranger* had been leading the flotilla. John Paul could see Whale Rock protruding out of the water to his starboard side. It was at this point the flotilla was to pull up alongside of him and make a long double line of ships. He lifted his sails to let the others form on him on both sides and then, as if on a signal, all the ships put out all of their sails in order to take advantage of the breeze. They had been moving at about four knots up to now, but he could feel his ship respond to the additional sails and the entire flotilla picked up speed.

As if on signal he heard sounds of activity on board the two man-of-war class ships, one stationed on each side of the mouth of the bay. He could see men scurrying on the decks as they dropped sail and began to give chase. He couldn't quite make out the side of the ship on the left but the closer one on the right opened her gun doors to show her teeth and ran several cannons out demonstrating their willingness to open fire.

All the ships in the flotilla were even with the man-of-war ships by this time and were beginning to break in different directions. He knew several would head down cast toward New York. Others might head across Long Island Sound to Montauk Bay. Still others would head for Block Island and hope to turn around and head back up the bay toward *Providence* when the British ships had chosen their prey.

John Paul had previously ordered the sailing master to chart a course for Cape Cod. He knew that the southeaster breeze would keep his sails full and that once he was past the man-of-war on the eastern side of the bay, he would be hard to catch.

As he passed the nearest British ship, it was obvious they were turning to give chase and evidently, they had chosen to run down the *Ranger*. John Paul ordered full sails and the *Ranger* jumped forward, just as he had hoped. John Paul knew well the capabilities of a man-of-war class British ship. They were larger than the *Ranger*, with much more fire power. They also were surprisingly maneuverable and could travel at a good clip, maybe faster than the *Ranger*, though, hopefully, not by much. They were going to find out soon enough.

The route John Paul had chosen would take him around Cuttyhunk Island and into the Vineyard Sound. It would take most of the day to clear the sound and the next port was Hyannisport, on the southern coast of Cape Cod. That was a British base like Newport and he needed to pass that port well out to sea. Once clear of the sound, he would chart a course dead east to Monomoy Point at the southern end of the sandbar that bordered Cape Cod on the east. There was no cover, no place to hide along that coast where the man-of-war wouldn't find them. He had to count on the speed of the *Ranger* to get him out of trouble.

It was mid-afternoon when the *Ranger* broke out of the Vineyard Sound into open water south of Cape Cod. The man-of-war was still giving chase and was slowly catching up. He estimated the speed of the *Ranger* to be around fourteen knots but assumed the man-of-war was moving at about two knots faster. If everything remained as it had been all day while the British ship chased the *Ranger*, it would come alongside sometime in the night.

John Paul was thankful for the steady breeze that filled his sails. He had given thought to their fate if the *Ranger* was caught. The flag on the front of the man-of-war told him that the captain was, indeed, Admiral *Richard* Howe. He knew he could expect no quarter from Admiral Howe and his reputation was to fire first and ask questions later. He was sure that as a Scot fighting for the Colonies, he would be judged a traitor and hanged. He needed a plan.

John Paul sent Jim to ask the carpenter to meet with him on the fantail. By the time he arrived John Paul had drawn a diagram on a piece of parchment. The carpenter, who doubled as ship's surgeon, climbed the ladder and approach him as if he had way too many things to do to get ready for a face-off with a British man-of-war than to be coming to a meeting on the fantail.

"Sir, we are not ready below. We have some medical supplies but, I'm afraid, not nearly enough if we have some serious injuries. Are we not better off dropping sails and letting them catch us to see if we can avoid needless bloodshed?" he asked.

"Indeed, you are right, sir," John Paul responded. "However, I intend to avoid a fight if we can effect a bit of subterfuge. I have drawn out a design which I would appreciate your pulling together over the next couple of hours. I will keep us ahead of the enemy as long as possible and, hopefully, until dark. Then we will see if we can find a way out of this hound-and-rabbit chase."

John Paul watched the carpenter descend the ladder and make his way back down to the lower deck. He then called for his first mate and asked him to hoist one of the life boats over the ledge and onto the main deck.

They continued to sail due east toward Monomoy Point. He watched the sky intently as the clouds gathered and the darkness began to close in. It was going to be a night with cloud cover, no stars or moon, perfect for the plan he had in mind.

John Paul knew it was traditional for British ships to have lights on both the front and back when they sailed at night. The same was true for most ships that sailed the oceans, though the pattern of lights was different with each country. The front of the *Ranger* was lit by a single light while the back had a triangle of lights in a reverse "V" shape, just like the British ships. John Paul ordered the three lanterns on the back of the *Ranger* to be lit so that the following man-of-war could clearly see them in the distance as the darkness covered the ship.

It was just past dusk when the carpenter hauled the apparatus John Paul had designed up on deck and began to erect it on the life boat. Using a cross spar, he and his assistants had created what looked to be a mast in the middle of the life boat. Then they put a cross-piece on it with a lantern on top, and one each on the ends of the cross-piece. Below the cross-pieces they dropped a small sail. John Paul thought that a small sail would keep the life boat sailing in front of the wind and the incoming tide would take the small boat and its apparatus in toward the shore.

John Paul ordered the sailing master to turn the ship just slightly southward, so the British lookouts could see the starboard side of the ship from the back through the gloom of early night, if they happened to be looking through their spyglasses. They could not see what was happening on the port side of the ship.

When they were ready, they called all the deck hands together and they lifted the life boat and its apparatus over the port side of the ship and lowered it into the water.

"How does it look, men?" John Paul asked.

"We have it securely tied to the side of the ship, but the water line is right to the edge, the life boat is barely afloat. If we had even a little heavy sea it would flounder," said the carpenter.

"Well, we don't need much above water level, but we do need our smallest sailor to go aboard to make sure it is headed northeast with the wind and the tide. Who is that?" asked John Paul.

"Sir," said a voice just behind John Paul. "I'm the smallest one on board. What do you want me to do?" It was young Jim. Jim had grown taller during his years on shipboard but, even with Jubal's hearty meals, he had gained little weight.

"Jim, this isn't a job for you," said John Paul. "We need one of the men who swims very well and isn't afraid to be adrift in the ocean."

"Sir," responded Jim. "I swim very well. You have seen for yourself when you were watching us swim down at Nassau. I can swim like a fish, and I'm not afraid."

John Paul turned to the sailing master and asked, "Do we have anyone else we can assign this task?"

"Captain, the margin in the life boat with all of that weight in it is very small," he said. "If the boy can do it, he is the right choice."

"All right, Jim," he replied. "You have the job." As soon as he said it, he saw Jubal coming across the deck. He felt his presence just to his back but heard his voice softly, as if he did not want anyone but John Paul to hear what he was saying.

"Sir, I can't help but question this choice of Jim to carry out this all-important job," Jubal said. "He is just a boy, and if this fails we may all be in a British prison by tomorrow."

"Jubal, you are right," John Paul responded. "But the decision is made. Jim is almost sixteen now. He is going to handle this responsibility, and he will do it well. Help me get this rope around his waist."

"Sir," Jubal said, "can he swim well enough to be safe?"

"Jubal, he is young and he is small but he can swim like a fish," said John Paul. "I watched him off the fantail while the men were swimming in the bay at Nassau. He can swim as well as any of the men and better than most."

Jubal nodded but seemed unconvinced. Soon the rope was fixed around Jim's waist.

"All right, son, over the side with you," said John Paul. "We can light the lanterns from the deck. Your job is to ride the life boat until it is in behind us and to make sure it is headed with the wind and tide. Then, we will haul you in."

As soon as the life boat with its mast and cross rigging was clear of the ship, John Paul ordered the *Ranger*'s lights to be put out. To the trailing man-of-war, the only sight in the distance were the three lanterns on the life boat that in the dark looked like the back of the *Ranger*.

John Paul checked the life boat floating slowly after the larger ship. Everything seemed just as he had envisioned it. He waved at Jim who moved carefully to the side of the life boat and slipped into the water. Several men began to pull on the rope that was tied around Jim's waist. Before long he was along-side the *Ranger* and the men were pulling him up the side to the deck. Jim was wet from head to toe but he had a big smile on his face.

John Paul picked him up in a bear hug, wet clothes and all. "You did just fine, Jim," he said. "I'm proud of you."

Several of the men began slapping him on the back and Jubal stepped in and took Jim off toward the stairs to the lower deck to change into dry clothes.

John Paul turned to the sailing master and said, "Sir, set a course south-southeast for Nantucket. When the Brits catch up with our lifeboat, we will be long gone into the open sea."

It was much later that John Paul allowed himself a soft chuckle, thinking about what Admiral Howe would think when he found he had been chasing a lifeboat for most of the night.

When dawn broke there was not a ship in sight in any direction. John Paul imagined that the flotilla had dispersed to their own destinations and hoped that the confusion of the seventeen ships had made it impossible for any of them to be caught. He wouldn't know how successful the ruse had been until he was able to return to *Providence* in several weeks. He did imagine that several of the ships had waited until the two British ships had chosen their targets and then took their best opportunity to slip back into the bay and return to *Providence*.

John Paul had heard that the British had blockaded virtually all of the ports from *Boston* south to Charleston. That meant any prizes they were able to capture would have to be taken north to a port in Maine. There were four major ports in Maine but the best of those was Bar Harbor. That meant slow going for him and the *Ranger*. Before now, if they took a prize in Long Island Sound, it was a short haul to get it to port in *Providence*, Newport, or Montauk. Now, any prize would require a voyage several hundred miles north.

THE PROVIDENCE GAZETTE

PROVIDENCE, Rhode Island, October 14, 1776--Freedom! Freedom! Freedom! The news of the adoption of the Declaration of Independence from Great Britain has spread across the land. Celebrations occurred in virtually all of the cities across the former thirteen colonies. Instead of referring to ourselves as thirteen colonies belonging to Great Britain, we will now be called the United States Of America.

Of great importance is the realization that we are now not just embroiled in several separate rebellions against the tyranny of Great Britain but, instead, are fighting to become a new nation. As a result, General Washington's army is growing by more than a hundred fighting men each day.

On the negative side, General Sir William Howe has brought an additional 32,000 troops, including 9,000 German mercenaries to our shores to join the fight.

In very late August General Howe attacked the patriot positions in Brooklyn Heights and General Washington had to withdraw to the river. The army was saved by a fleet of boats from New Jersey and Long island that came across the river to ferry our battered army to safety. Thus, all of New York is now in the hands of the British.

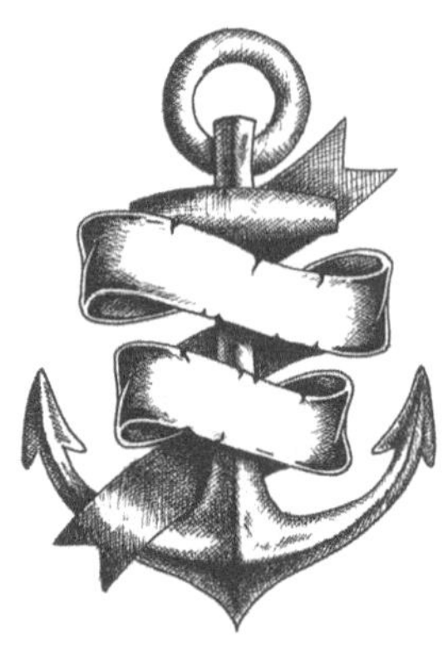

CHAPTER 16

JOHN PAUL JONES AND THE RANGER ORDERED TO EUROPE

JULY 1, 1776

John Paul used much of the time at sea between Cape Cod and Nantucket drilling his new crew, especially the gunnery group working with the cannons. Timing was crucial. If they could fire their cannons twice as fast as a British ship, their twenty-six cannons could become like fifty-two. It would neutralize their major deficiency in comparison to a British gun boat. At first, it took them about two and a half minutes to reload the cannons after firing and to run them out ready to fire again. By the time they had practiced the better part of two days, that time was just over a minute. Finally, John Paul was satisfied with the cannons.

While he had the *Ranger* in the shipyard at *Providence*, he had directed that a platform be built up in the rigging of the two major masts. His plan was to put a troop of marines up on those platforms to fire down on anyone moving on the deck of another ship. British ships were prohibited from firing muskets from the masts because of the danger of catching the sails on fire. John Paul planned to use that British rule to his advantage. Like the British, he was concerned about fire, but he liked the idea of having a firepower advantage over any British ship he met in combat. If he couldn't do it with cannons, he would do it with muskets and sharp shooters.

John Paul had watched with interest as the marines on board were practicing just like the gunnery group. They would start on the lower deck and race to the rope ladders and climb to the narrow platforms just below the cross-spars near the top of the masts. They made it into a competition coming from both sides of the main deck and seeing who could reach the platforms first and get a shot off. The winner got a double serving of stew in Jubal's galley at noon.

The marines learned to balance themselves on the narrow platforms above the sails and to load and fire their muskets at about thirty-second intervals. John Paul liked the idea that they could fire close to a hundred musket balls onto the deck of any ship they were fighting each minute.

After a full day of sailing toward Nantucket, John Paul changed course to head for Muskeget Channel between Nantucket and Martha's Vineyard. From there it took about five days for the *Ranger* to sail from Nantucket Sound to Montauk Point on the tip of Long Island. They were sailing into a light headwind most of the way and it required them to tack back and forth in order to take advantage of what wind they had. They did not sight any British ships en-route, but did encounter two privateers and a French merchant that appeared to be headed toward New Haven, Connecticut. The plan for the French ship must have been to anchor out in Long Island Sound and unload the cargo into long boats at night. If they tried to enter the harbor at New Haven, they would have no luck at all getting past the blockade with the two man-of-war ships stationed there.

When the *Ranger* arrived in the bay at Montauk, John Paul was pleased to find one of John Brown's smaller ships anchored there, the one he used for mail, supplies, and communication. A long boat was sent over to the smaller ship to retrieve whatever might be there for the *Ranger*. John Paul was delighted to find two letters for him in the packet of mail, one from former Governor Stephen Hopkins of the Continental Congress Navy Committee, and the other from Aimee. He laid aside the letter from Aimee and opened the one from former Governor Hopkins.

Stephen Hopkins
Chairman of the Navy Committee
Continental Congress

Captain John Paul Jones
Care of the John Brown Shipyard Office
Providence, Rhode Island

Dear Captain Jones,

I know you received the communication about our official declaration of independence from Great Britain. Within that document, approved by Congress officially on July 4th, 1776, was the official name of our new country, The United States of America. All official documents, hereafter, will carry that name.

All ships of the U.S. Navy will be renamed to be consistent with our country's new name. Thus, the *Ranger* will now be called the *U.S.S. Ranger*, short for *United States Ship, Ranger*. Please make that change on all correspondence and, also, on the side of your ship.

After much study of the matter, our committee has decided that we need to raid British shipping on both sides of the Atlantic. We currently have approximately 1,500 ships working the coastline of the Colonies and doing a reasonable job of intercepting supply shipments meant for the British Army.

Earlier I mentioned to you the possibility that we would send you to northern France to ply your trade in the English Channel and the waters of Great Britain. Toward that end, we have talked to the envoy from France and they are amenable to that arrangement. You are the only captain we have assigned this responsibility so far. If you are successful, more will come and follow your lead. We recognize that you will not be able to get the merchandise taken from British prizes back to the Colonies. Thus, we authorize you to sell both ships and cargo in European ports and use the money for your enterprise there. It will serve as additional pay for your seamen as compensation for being so far from home.

Please use this letter as authorization to advance with dispatch to France to begin your new assignment.

Respectfully,

Stephen Hopkins

John Paul was elated that Chairman Hopkins had designated the *Ranger* to open conflict on the high seas in the English Channel and the waters around England, Ireland, and Scotland. Kirkbean, Scotland was John Paul's original home, the place he was born. He had not been back since he was a boy of thirteen. Surely, during his time there he would be able to visit his people in southwest Scotland.

His mind was flooded with thoughts, but his first thought was for Aimee and the children. He looked down at the unopened letter with Aimee's handwriting on the envelope. He broke the seal on the envelope, withdrew the letter, spread it on his table and began to read.

Captain John Paul Jones
In care of the *Ranger*

Dearest John Paul,

You are hardly out the door and I have need to talk to you. It seems there is never enough time to share everything that is in my heart. Your presence warms all of us and makes us a family. When you are gone it is as if a piece of our lives is missing.

The boys are fine, missing you every day, but growing and developing as they should. Our days are pretty routine with the necessities of life occupying most of the day but with ample time for play and studies. Daniel and Mary are both becoming experts at geography. We still use the big map John Brown's office gave us and they can identify every port where you might be. I found a big painting of a ship with three high masts and have hung it in the parlor where the children can see it every day. It cost as much as a new kitchen table, but its presence is a reminder of where their father is and what you are doing for our young country.

Please be assured that you are on our minds and in our hearts, as well as in our prayers every day. We are anxious for your return and life will move slowly forward until we see you again at our front door.

With love and respect

Aimee Adele Jones & the Children

Before John Paul had even finished the letter from Aimee he knew what he was going to do with the European assignment. He was taking Aimee and the children to France. They would find a place to live in one of the port cities in northern France and he would be able to see them on a regular basis.

It was one thing for him to be assigned to France for what would most assuredly be the duration of the war. It was quite another for him to be away from his boys and new wife for so long. He was anxious to cross Long Island Sound and to make his way up Narragansett Bay to *Providence*. But his plans had to be delayed as a storm had reached Montauk and his better judgement told him to hold fast in the bay until the stronger winds had passed. Aimee and the children were on his mind constantly. He thought about nothing else over the next two days as he left the *Ranger* anchored in Montauk Bay. He could not wait to retrieve them and to begin his trek to Europe.

Finally, it appeared the leading edge of the storm had passed, and John Paul called the men on deck for a conversation. He stood on the fantail to tell them of the letter from Stephen Hopkins and their new assignment.

"Gentlemen, we have been sitting here in Montauk Bay for almost three days letting the storm pass us by. All of that time you have been wondering where our responsibilities would take us next. Well, now I can share it with you. We have a new responsibility that is a first for any Continental Navy ship. We have been ordered to France." That comment drew an immediate reaction from the men. Watching their faces, John Paul thought that to some it must have seemed like a new adventure. To others, Europe must have seemed like the other side of the moon.

John Paul continued, "We are going to weigh anchor mid-day and head across Long Island Sound to the mouth of the Narragansett. We will hold up out of sight of land until the dead of night and then, when the tide moves in, we will ride it though the mouth of the bay and north to *Providence*."

John Paul expected a noisy reaction from the men that he was taking them to their home base and he was not disappointed. Most had family there and they needed time to talk with their people before leaving the Colonies for what might be several years.

"We will spend the next two weeks in *Providence* loading provisions for the six-week voyage to France," he said. "The *Cabot* was nearing full repair when we left last month, so we should be able to put together another flotilla to get us all past the man-of-war ships stationed at the mouth of the bay."

One of the men held up a hand to be recognized and asked, "Captain Jones, sir, what will happen to those of us who can't go with you to Europe?"

"It is a good question," responded John Paul. "I will write recommendations for any who must stay behind. Those recommendations will be held in the John Brown Shipyard office to be used with any future captain who may be looking for a good crew. When we dock in *Providence*, you will have three days to talk with your families and to get back to me. I will ask the first mate to compile a list of those who will be with us and those who cannot. We will then endeavor to find replacements for those we have lost.

"I should mention one more thing that has not been talked about," said John Paul. "The regulations we were given when we signed on with the new navy were pretty definite. Prize money was to be shared one half to the Continental government to help with the war effort and the other half to be shared with the officers and crew. Chairman Hopkins has told me that any prizes captured in and around British waters will be shared one hundred percent among the officers and crew."

That comment drew a great yell from the men. One of them shouted over the noise, "You can count me in. I'm going!"

When they quieted down, John Paul finished his talk. "Men, some of you have been with me for several years. You know we treat you fairly. Others of you are just getting to know me and the other officers. You have been together for just a short time, but you have the makings of a first-class crew. I want as many of you as can to come with us to France. Our presence in the English Channel will be a big surprise to the British. That is home waters for them and they are not used to interference there.

I anticipate we will do very well, especially in the first several months we are there. Chairman Hopkins promised that he would send several more continental ships if we are successful. I intend to be successful."

That drew yet another yell from the men. Then they slowly dispersed.

John Paul looked over at his sailing master and said, "Let's get the anchor up and set a course for Narragansett Bay. I intend to be in *Providence* by dawn tomorrow."

It was just past mid-night when the *Ranger* dropped anchor about ten miles out in Long Island Sound just south of the mouth of Narragansett Bay. The wind was light and out of the west and the rain came down in a steady drizzle. John Paul knew these were ideal conditions for sneaking the *Ranger* by the two man-of-war ships stationed at the mouth of the bay. He hoped it would hold for another three hours until the tide started pushing in toward the coast.

When the time came, they hoisted anchor and dropped the gray, gunny-sack sails. The ship began moving slowly toward the mouth of the bay. It was pitch dark and visibility was less than a half mile, perfect conditions to slip into the bay without being seen. John Paul sighted the whitecaps breaking on Whale Rock to his left as the helmsman steered the ship into the center of the channel. With the wind from the west-northwest and the tide taking them northward at about four knots, it was slow going up the bay. The trip took about three hours but soon they could see the rooftops of *Providence* off to their left and John Paul knew the main wharf was just a quarter mile farther.

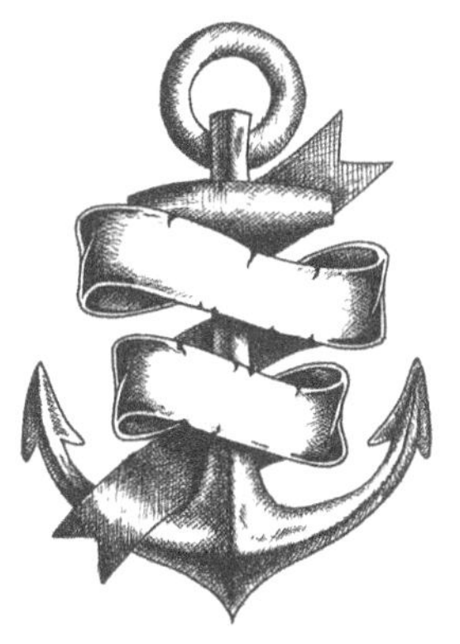

CHAPTER 17

BACK IN PROVIDENCE FOR
PREPARATIONS TO SAIL THE ATLANTIC

DECEMBER 12, 1777

It was about nine o'clock in the morning when John Paul pushed open the door at his two- story house on Planet Street. Aimee came to the door of the kitchen to see who was coming in and her face turned almost white. It two quick steps she was in his arms and he had lifted her up and was swinging her around. When they entered the kitchen all four of the children were seated at the table eating their breakfast.

Aimee cried, "Children, look who is home!"

Immediately there was a squeal from the children. Daniel was the first to get to him, almost tackling him to the floor. Then it was Mary, followed by Moses and little Elizabeth. Soon they were all sitting on the kitchen floor and laughing. Aimee went to the fireplace and began preparing another plate to put on the table for John Paul.

When quiet again prevailed, Aimee asked, "John Paul, what are you doing home? We didn't expect you for several weeks yet."

John Paul started to answer, but signaled her with his eyes that he wanted to wait a bit so the two of them could talk alone. He didn't want to bring up the subject of moving to France in front of the children until they had a chance to talk about it. She understood immediately and turned the conversation in another direction.

"Daniel, you should show your father the ship you made," said Aimee.

Immediately, Daniel jumped down from the table and ran toward the parlor. In a few seconds, he was standing next to John Paul with a two-mast ship he had constructed out of soft wood. It was fully laid out and painted. John Paul recognized that he had painted *Ranger* on the side of it and even the sails were the gray color of the sails that hung from the riggings of the *Ranger*.

"I did your ship, Father," said Daniel.

"Indeed you did, little man," said John Paul. "I am so proud of you."

It wasn't long before the breakfast dishes were empty. Aimee helped the smaller children down from the table and ushered the entire brood into the parlor where their lesson books and toys were.

She poured John Paul another cup of coffee and then gave him that look that said, *Now is the time, talk to me."*

John Paul smiled at her and said, "I have something overwhelming for you to consider. Chairman Hopkins has ordered the *Ranger* to France to disrupt shipping in the English Channel and around the British Isles. It is likely that we will be there until the war is over, whenever that may be."

Tears came up in her eyes. "Oh, John Paul, do you have to do it?" she asked. "You could be gone for years. The children need you. I need you."

"The overwhelming thing for you to consider is, how would you like to go live in France for a while?" John Paul searched her face to see her response.

Silence. She went totally speechless. She had been standing between the fireplace and the table and she pulled the closest chair out and sat down across from him.

"John Paul, how? When?" she asked.

"I think we have about two weeks before we must go. So, you have a few days to consider it and, if you want to go with me, you will have ten or twelve days to get ready," he replied.

"John Paul, we have four small children at home," she said. "I want to go wherever you are, but how will we ever get them ready for a trip on a ship? None of us have ever been on a ship, much less on the ocean."

That opened the floodgates, and there seemed to be no end of questions. What about the house? Will we sell it? Where will the children sleep on shipboard? Is there room for all of us in your cabin? How much can we take along?

"Hold on," said John Paul, laughing. "Give it time to sink in a bit. Let this rest. I need to go and see John Burroughs about the state of the *Cabot*. I am going to need him to help get us out of the bay when we leave in about two weeks."

John Paul left Aimee sitting at the kitchen table, frowning over her teacup, and was soon strolling down the street toward the Esek Hopkins house. When he arrived there, he found that John Burroughs and *Hannah* had moved back to their own home. It was just a couple blocks further, and he soon found himself on the front stoop knocking on the door.

Hannah opened the door, greeted him with a smile, and welcomed him inside. "John Paul, it is so good to see you again after just a few weeks. What are you doing home?"

"It is a long story," said John Paul. "Is John Burroughs home?"

"John," she called out. "It's John Paul!"

John Paul heard his friend's voice responding from another room and followed it down the hall. He found John Burroughs in the kitchen with a cup of coffee in front of him. His arm was still in a sling but in all other ways he looked like the old John Burroughs.

"How are you coming along, my friend?" asked John Paul.

"I'm on the mend," John Burroughs responded. "It won't be long now. The doctor says that as long as I don't lift the arm above shoulder height, the injured wing is usable. I think I am going to be ready about when the *Cabot* is ready to return to action. We have got to get back out there. We have been missing all the fun. Tell me what you have been doing and why you are back here after such a short trip. Is the *Ranger* all right?"

"She is fine," said John Paul. "We had a little chase from Admiral Howe and his man-of-war, but he couldn't catch us and we doubled back on him to Montauk Bay. A letter from Chairman Hopkins found me there, ordering me to France. We are going to see if we can disrupt British shipping in the English Channel."

"What an assignment, John Paul!" said John Burroughs. "When are you leaving?"

"Some of that depends on you," replied John Paul. "When do you think the *Cabot* will be ready and, more important, when will you be ready? I will need your help and the help of several others to get us past the sentries at the mouth of the bay. Hopefully, the flotilla tactic will work again."

"I think the ship needs only about another ten days, and I am ready now," said John Burroughs. "I didn't realize how shot up she was, but the shipyard has her seaworthy again. We just have to reset the cannons and get the provisions on board."

"I have given the crew three days to decide if they are going to France with us," said John Paul. "I think most will, but I will still have some recruiting to do."

"That is also true with the *Cabot*," said John Burroughs, nodding. "I lost most of my crew to you and others while my ship and I have been laid up. But this city is full of able seamen. I don't think it will take either of us long to form a crew that is ready to sail."

"I will leave you now, my friend," said John Paul. "I am so pleased you are healing well and are about ready to sail again. For a while there I thought I had lost you. This world, and my personal world, would not be the same without you."

"I'm tougher than I look. It will take more than a British *Glasgow* to take me out," John Burroughs said. "That is one ship I intend to meet again. I am not yet one hundred percent, but I will be before long. A couple of weeks of sea air will have me fit as a fiddle!"

Hannah walked John Paul to the door and stepped outside on the stoop with him.

"Is he really all right, *Hannah*?" asked John Paul.

"He thinks he is and that is half of the battle," she replied. "It has been a difficult journey to get to this point but the pain in his shoulder is much better now and he is straining at the leash to get back out there."

"I am pleased, *Hannah*," said John Paul. "He is my oldest and best friend. In the past couple of years, we have gone separate ways, but I miss him every day we are apart. I doubt we will ever sail together again but it gives me peace to know he is here and pleasure to see him whenever I can. I will be back tomorrow and each day until we are ready to sail."

"Bless you, John Paul," *Hannah* said. "He loves you like a brother."

She watched John Paul walk down the street and turn toward the shipyard. She thought to herself, *Neither he nor John Burroughs can stay away from a ship for very long.*

John Paul stopped at the shipyard office and checked the roster to see how many of his men had signed on for the assignment in France. The attendant there helped him post a notice for crew members. Altogether, he had forty-five crew members and another fifty marines who had left *Providence* Harbor with him less than two weeks ago. He hoped he did not lose very many who did not want to spend the duration of the war in France. But posting vacancies was necessary because he knew he would lose some men; he hoped not more than fifteen or twenty.

When John Paul returned from his rounds, he was pleased to find the children still occupied in the parlor. That meant Aimee would be in the kitchen working on the mid-day meal. She felt his presence as soon as he came into the kitchen. He walked up behind her and put his arms around her waist. She leaned back into him and sighed.

"What say, wife of mine? Do you want to spend the next couple of years in France?" he asked.

"Oh, John Paul. I want to do it. I want to be wherever you are," she replied. "But the children, can they make such a trip? What about their studies? We don't know the language! Where will we live? How will I shop for food?"

John Paul began to laugh. She turned around and playfully began to hit him on the chest. "Don't you laugh at my questions. This is serious. We have so many things we don't know and such a short time to get ready to go."

"Aimee, I face this every time I go off on a trip," John Paul said. "I am never sure where I will end up nor how long I will be gone. Moving to France is a big step, no doubt. But you aren't the first person to be faced with packing up and moving to another country. Almost everyone in the Colonies came here from someplace else and all faced the unknown of travel and new surroundings. They handled it and you can too. Shall I assume that all these questions and concerns mean you and the children are coming with me?"

"Oh, yes, John Paul," she responded. "We are coming. We don't know what we are getting into or where we will end up, but we are coming."

John Paul pulled her close and kissed her. He said, "I could take you upstairs right now."

"And I would go," she responded. "But, I have dinner almost ready and the children will be hungry any minute. So, upstairs will have to wait."

John Paul began to laugh and, shortly, Daniel and little Elizabeth were at the door and headed to their seats at the table.

The next night, John Paul called a meeting at Sabin's Tavern for ship's captains and owners as he had two weeks before. The meeting went very much as the earlier gathering. He explained that he needed to put together a flotilla to help get the *Cabot* and *Ranger* through the mouth of the Narragansett. Again, there were many men willing to help with the ruse. Several were ready to move merchandise down the coast or up to *Boston*, but others simply saw an opportunity to help the cause of independence with little risk to themselves or their ships.

The departure date was set for two weeks away. Weather would be a factor for the *Ranger* since they were headed across the ocean. John Paul did not want to take his family with four small children into an Atlantic storm. Unfortunately, he had no control over the weather. He had to take what came and deal with it.

Finally, the date came for the flotilla to form and sail down the bay. John Paul had marveled at the efficiency of Aimee as she prepared a bundle for each of the children and herself. She went with him several times to the *Ranger* so she could better think through everything from eating to sleeping arrangements. Each of the children had three blankets as bedding, two to lay on the floor of the captain's cabin and one to cover up with. She envisioned each of the sleeping blankets being rolled up and stacked in a corner when the children were up in the morning.

Jubal and Jim solved a part of the eating problem for them. Jim said he could deliver breakfast about mid-morning for the children. That would be after the men had eaten and before they began coming down to the ship's kitchen for the mid-day meal.

There was no mistaking the excitement in the children that a trip was coming, that they were going with their father on the *Ranger* all the way to somewhere called France. Aimee made a trip down to John Brown's office where they supplied her with a map of Europe, including where they intended to make their home in Brest, France. It was a small city on an inlet at the extreme northwest corner of France.

John Paul chose Brest because it was on a bay sheltered from the worst of the storms. Yet it gave easy access to British shipping routes both north and south, as well as into the English Channel. He could envision having cannons placed at the entry to the bay to keep any intruders out who came to hunt him down.

Finally, the day came when the *Ranger* was packed and every seaman was on board. Aimee herded her young charges onto the ship and down to the captain's cabin. Sailing time was set at 11 p.m. so they would make it to the mouth of the bay by around daybreak. Despite their excitement, the children were all asleep when the ship finally pulled away from the dock.

The flotilla was composed of fifteen ships led by the *Cabot* and the *Ranger*. John Paul had hoped for a few more, but fifteen was enough. John Burroughs and John Paul had talked earlier about their destinations when they left the bay. John Burroughs intended to go around Long Island and down the coast of the Colonies. John Paul intended to head straight east toward his eventual destination in France.

They reached the mouth of the bay in a light rain, all the better to hide their numbers as well as their direction. The two man-of-war ships began to give chase immediately but whether it was the gray gunny sack sails of the *Ranger* or the presence of the *Cabot* in the group, neither British ship followed the *Ranger*.

They sailed all of that morning toward Cape Cod with a slight trailing wind. Unfortunately, the storm picked up and as soon as they cleared the Vineyard Sound the waves were eight to ten feet high. The storm was obviously headed due east as they were, and they were facing the prospect of sailing all the way across the ocean in the midst of a storm. John Paul did not like the prospect of taking his family into the ocean under such conditions.

He told the sailing master to clear Nantucket Sound and then to chart a new course due north. His intent was to sail around Cape Cod and aim for Portsmouth on the Piscataquis River. He had been there for six weeks while the *Ranger* was made ready and he knew that port was not under a British blockade. He intended to hold up there and wait for fair weather.

John Paul went down to the captain's cabin to tell Aimee what was planned. He found her sea-sick, along with all four children. None had ever experienced anything like riding out an ocean storm in a ship.

"Oh, John Paul, I feel so bad. Does the floor ever stop moving?" moaned Aimee.

"It is lots better than this most of the time. We just hit a storm that has us tossing about a bit. I am turning us north to escape the storm and we are going to spend a couple of days in Portsmouth," said John Paul.

"But, John, does the floor ever stop moving?" she asked again.

"Actually, no," he responded. "But you get used to it."

"I don't think I will ever get used to this," said Aimee, looking distinctly green.

Shortly, John Paul found himself back on the bridge staring into the storm. He wondered if he had made a big mistake bringing his family on this trip.

The *Ranger* sailed out of the storm when it was about half-way around Cape Cod.

Considering the state of his family, John Paul thought it was still a good idea to seek shelter in the port of Portsmouth. He knew where they could stay and expected to be free of British threat while they were there.

The *Ranger* anchored in the bay at Portsmouth and John Paul gave directions to his sailing master and first mate. Then he helped his family into a water taxi and in a few minutes they were at the wharf.

Aimee spoke quietly to John Paul. "I never thought I would be so glad to stand on dry land. Oh, John Paul, it has been so miserable for the past three days."

"We will take a few days here and wait for fair weather," said John Paul. "The next time we head east, it will be much better. I promise."

The landlady at the rooming house where he had stayed when he was in Portsmouth before was glad to see him. That was especially true when he told her he wanted to rent the entire upstairs as well as to contract for meals for the five members of his family.

Aimee put the children to bed and then went to bed herself. John Paul walked down to the closest tavern, hoping to find some local talk that would give him insights regarding British operations in this region. Most of what he heard was good news. There had not been any man-of-war ships close by for weeks. Portsmouth seemed to be just enough out of the way to keep it safe from the kinds of conflicts experienced in *Boston*, *Providence*, and the rest of the Colonies.

John Paul made one more walk by the wharf and thought things looked fine on the *Ranger* from across the bay. He then made his way back to the rooming house and upstairs to the bedrooms. He checked in on each of the children and then looked in on Aimee. She was sleeping the sleep of exhaustion, mostly because she had been up for three days and nights with the children. He slipped into bed next to her.

The next morning, he was in bed by himself when he woke up. Aimee was already up getting the children dressed for the day. He took care of himself and met her on the stairs on the way down to the dining room. Even at that distance away they could smell breakfast cooking in the kitchen.

A few minutes later in the dining room, Aimee said, "I was sure I would never feel like eating anything again. But here I am eating some of everything. The children too. We must be past the sea sickness."

"I'm sorry it was so rough that first couple of days," said John Paul. "We were running from the British and didn't have much choice about where to run. We were in a light rain while we were in the bay, but the storm grew worse as we hit the open seas. It will be much better leaving from here than traveling a route farther south."

"Oh, John Paul, I'm feeling better now, but most of yesterday I was working out in my mind how to tell you to just take us home," Aimee confessed. "Today, I don't know what to think. If others have made this trip across, surely we can too. We would do most anything to be close to you. But being sick is no picnic. None of us feel normal today but perhaps tomorrow, all will be better."

"Right now, I am planning for us to be here for two days and then load up and head for the Azores, about two thirds of the way across the Atlantic," said John Paul. "They belong to Portugal and are neutral in all of the fighting that has been going on. We will hold up there and look for fair weather to make it the rest of the way to France."

"How far are the Azores, John Paul?" she asked

"It will take us about four weeks to get there if the breeze stays constant from the northwest, as it usually does this time of year," responded John Paul.

"Four weeks," she repeated weakly. "Oh, John Paul."

"It will all be better when we have calm seas and a stiff breeze at our back," John Paul assured her. "You may feel it some, but the worst is behind you. I will do my best not to get us into anything like the storm we experienced around Capet Cod. I promise."

The next night John Paul was surprised to hear the landlady calling up the stairs for him that he had a visitor. He pulled on his boots and went down the steps to the parlor and saw a familiar face, one that he had not seen since the night he and John Burroughs joined the Sons of *Liberty* dumping tea into *Boston* Harbor. It was Paul Revere.

"Captain Jones, I am pleased to have found you," the *Boston* silversmith said. "I have come on my fastest horse to Portsmouth to warn you that the British are getting ready to sail this way, hoping to trap you in Portsmouth Harbor."

"Are you sure?" asked John Paul. "How could they know we are here?"

"We don't know how they know, but they do," said Paul Revere. "Samuel Adams overheard a conversation in his tavern between the captains of two of their man-of-war ships. One of the captains was Admiral Howe, who evidently had you in his sights earlier and lost you. Evidently, he has been looking for you ever since."

"Do you know when they plan to sail?" asked John Paul.

"I don't, but it took me most of the afternoon and evening coming overland on horseback to get here, and they may be on the way here now," responded Paul Revere. "It can't be more than a three- or four-hour sail to arrive at the mouth of the Piscataquis River."

"Thank you, Paul. You have been a life saver. And thank Samuel and the Sons of *Liberty*," said John Paul sincerely.

John Paul climbed the stairs two at a time. Aimee saw the troubled look on his face when he entered their room. He said, "Paul Revere brought some bad news. A couple of British man-of-war ships are headed this way. We have to leave Portsmouth as soon as we can get the *Ranger* underway. I am going to the wharf and will gather the crew. You need to get the children dressed and ready. Jim will stay and help you. We will depart as soon as we have everyone on board. I will be back for you and the children in about an hour."

The meeting on the fantail a short while later included most of the leadership and many of the crew. John Paul looked over at the sailing master and asked, "Sir, is there any reason we can't depart as soon as we get the crew on board?"

"No sir, we have all of the provisions we need, and the ship is ready," he responded.

"Good," said John Paul. He turned his attention to the crew. "As you probably know by now, I received word about two hours ago that the British know of our location and two man-of-war ships are headed this way to capture us. One of those is captained by Admiral Howe, who chased us the last time we left *Providence*. We need to get out of this harbor before we are bottled up and can't leave." John Paul looked around the small fantail deck and asked no one in particular, "Are we ready to leave port and make four weeks' sail to the Azores?"

Several nodded their heads solemnly, but there was no vocal response.

"Then, everyone make ready. I will ask the first mate to let me know when we have a full crew on board. I intend to be gone within the hour, and sooner if we can. We are lucky to have a northeast wind at our back. It will fill our sails and get us up to speed very quickly. We will depart the wharf area with half sails, but as soon as we are clear we will drop full sails. It is my intent to reach the mouth of the Piscataquis at a full fifteen knots. If the British ships are lying just outside of the harbor, we may be able to push by them before they can get turned around to give chase. If they aren't there, we will be long gone before they arrive. Gentlemen, you are dismissed. Let's get the *Ranger* headed to France."

It was protocol to never exceed four knots when leaving a harbor area. There was often too much traffic of incoming and outgoing ships, and speed created danger. In this case, no one argued with the plan to pass the harbor entrance at whatever speed they could muster. The danger of getting caught by the British ships was much greater than that posed by any early morning incoming traffic.

John Paul was thankful for the strong breeze from the northwest that was filling the sails. Before dawn, the *Ranger* passed the mouth of the Piscataquis as planned, moving at a full fifteen knots. Everyone was vigilant, looking for the two British ships, but they were not there. Then John Paul looked south through his spyglass and scanned the sea for the high masts of the two man-of-war ships and, there on the horizon, he spotted just the tops of the sails. They evidently had left *Boston* harbor well before the break of day and rounded Halibut Point at least an hour ago. He couldn't tell how far south the ships were, but he thought it was at least fifteen miles. He knew that unless they had a look-out stationed at the very top of a mast, they couldn't see the *Ranger*. His ship would be long gone well before the British ships arrived at the mouth of the harbor.

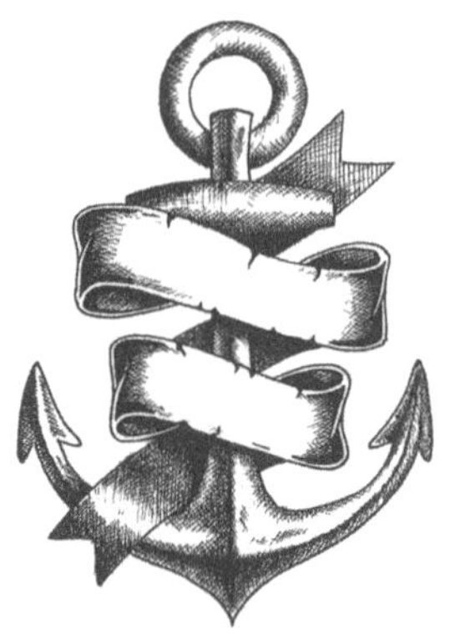

CHAPTER 18
SAILING THE ATLANTIC TO EUROPE
FEBRUARY 27, 1777

John Paul was feeling that fortune had smiled on his venture into French and English waters. The *Ranger* had given Admiral Howe the slip a second time. The winds blew briskly from the northeast, ideal for a course set for the Azores off the coast of northern Spain. The sun was high in the sky and there was not a cloud nor another ship in sight. Everything was going just as he had hoped.

He asked young Jim to go below and invite Aimee and the children up on deck for some fresh air. It was a few minutes before his family arrived on the main deck. Daniel appeared first at the top of the fantail ladder and ran the few feet across the deck to him. John Paul picked him up and together they looked out at the endless sea around them. Jim and Aimee helped the younger children up the ladder and, shortly, Aimee and little Elizabeth were standing next to him. He put Daniel down and picked up Moses, so he could see over the rail.

John Paul looked fondly down at Aimee and asked, "How are you and the children doing now?"

"It is better, John Paul," she replied. "But we are all still a bit unsteady on our feet. You promised it would be better and it is, but I am not sure we all aren't just a little ways from being sick again. Perhaps it will pass."

"We will be in the harbor at the Azores in about four weeks if the breeze filling our sails holds," said John Paul. "That will be our next opportunity to walk on dry land."

"We will make it," responded Aimee. "With prayer and patience, we will make it."

The words were positive, but the tone was anything but. John Paul smiled to himself, remembering the difficulty he had the first time he had been on shipboard almost sixteen years ago. He had felt like he was going to die, and hoped he would. As he had told Aimee, you get used to it. But no, the deck never stops moving.

Twice on the way to the Azores, John Paul sighted sails off in the distance, both times headed in the opposite direction toward the Colonies. At another time, he might have broken off from his course and sized up the ships to see whether or not they were worth taking as prizes. But his new assignment was clear. He had been ordered to English waters to disrupt trade and commerce around the British Islands and, especially, in the English Channel. The prospect of raiding ships with British flags close to their home base held great promise, and he was anxious to begin his new duty.

Four weeks had passed, and everyone was anticipating some shore time in the harbor town of the Azores. John Paul had a look-out placed in the crow's nest at the top of the highest mast with orders to call out when land was sighted.

Two more days passed with no word from the crow's nest, then came the familiar sound, "Land ho, land ho, dead ahead of the stern! We appear to be about fifteen miles out."

John Paul sent Jim down to the captain's cabin to tell Aimee, and shortly his family joined him on the stern of the ship.

Aimee said, "John Paul, will it be very long? I can't wait to touch my feet onto some solid ground!"

John Paul laughed. "It will be a bit more than an hour from right now. The chart says we will sight one island to the left and two to the right. We are to sail between them and will arrive at the port city of Angra do Heroismo. That is where we will dock for the night."

Aimee and John Paul took turns holding the children up so they could see the islands of the Azores where the ship was headed. He always loved standing on the stern of the ship and watching as the ship closed in on the harbor. He had absolute faith in the sailing master to slow the ship and maneuver it into the right location on a wharf or, if it was occupied, to drop anchor in the channel leading into the harbor.

This time the wharf was free, so the *Ranger* was maneuvered slowly until it made contact with the dock. He watched as the fore and aft lines were thrown to the attendants on shore and, shortly, they dropped the gangplank for free movement on and off the ship.

Aimee carried little Elizabeth and was the first to touch solid ground. The two older children followed and John Paul carried Moses down the gangplank. There was no mistaking the smile on Aimee's face. Four weeks on shipboard--and she had made it. Now she could breathe easy overnight before they had to climb back on ship for the last two weeks of their journey.

"Where will we stay tonight?" Aimee asked.

John Paul smiled. "We will be on shipboard tonight, but you can go back ashore in the morning. We will have some walking around time both now and all day tomorrow. We will not embark for the rest of our journey until after dark tomorrow night when the tide rolls in toward the mainland."

"All right, children," said Aimee, "let's go exploring. John Paul, can Jim go with us?"

"I think Jim has some duties with Jubal related to the mid-day meal for the men," said John Paul. "But he should be free by early afternoon. He can come and find you then."

His wife's stricken face made him think again. "Aimee, hold up for a few minutes until I get back," said John Paul. He disappeared up the gangplank. In a few minutes, he was back and in the company of two of the marines.

"I want to introduce you to William and James," he said. "They are going to go along to help you with the children. I would go myself, but I have some things I need to do with the harbor master."

Aimee looked closely at the two men. William was a big man, dressed in a blue jacket and carrying a musket. James was a slightly smaller version. Both looked very formidable. She thought to herself, *They may be going along to help with the children, but they look much more like body guards.* Aimee wondered what John Paul might be protecting her and the children from.

It was a bit after the mid-day meal when John Paul felt free enough to go into the town to find his family. They were sitting at a table outside a café a few streets up from the wharf. A shade made of sail cloth protected them from the bright sun.

As John Paul approached his family, Daniel yelled out, "Father is coming!"

Aimee stood up and hugged him. John Paul noticed that the two marines were at a nearby table with their muskets lying across their laps just out of sight.

"Well, I see you found a good place to eat," said John Paul. "What is tasty here?"

Aimee smiled and said, "Almost everything. Here, taste this."

She held up a morsel of seafood on a fork and he took a bite. Immediately he wished he hadn't. "Oh my, that is hot, hot, hot."

Aimee was laughing. "The fish is cod, but when I took my first bite I almost couldn't believe it. I asked the serving woman and she said they season it with something called 'piri piri.' It tastes like really hot chili peppers."

The serving woman appeared beside to the table. Aimee looked at John Paul. "Let me show you what I think I have learned. She looked up at the server and asked for "caldo verde." The woman nodded and went back into the café.

"What is it we just ordered?" asked John Paul.

"You are going to get some potato soup with chunks of sausage added for additional flavor. One of the marines suggested it to me. He has been here before. Then, for our sweet, we will order postel de mata," Aimee said. "The children have already had their soup and are now eating their postel de mata. That was also a suggestion of your marine. It appears to be a custard tart with some cinnamon sprinkled on top."

The soup arrived, and John Paul took a spoonful. He smiled. "This is pretty good—and not nearly so hot! As you said, it appears to be potato soup with some sausage for flavoring." As he continued to spoon the soup into his mouth, he asked, "How did your morning of wandering around go?"

"Oh, John Paul, it is such a quaint little village. We went into several shops just to look. I cautioned the children not to touch anything, but we did buy something. I guess when you break it, you own it. Moses picked up this little wagon and then dropped it. It lost a wheel. We now own a wheel-less wagon."

John Paul laughed, nudging Moses.

"One thing we learned for sure," said Aimee. "There are no English speakers here. We didn't find a shopkeeper who could speak more than a word or two of English. I am guessing that the British have steered clear of the Azores during the war years, first with Spain and then with France. This is a usual stopping place for both French and Spanish ships. I'm sure if I was speaking to them in French or Spanish many could respond to me."

John Paul finished the soup and took a bite of the postel de mata. "My, this is good," he said.

Aimee smiled. "I told you so. This gives me some faith that we can make it in a French town for a couple of years. I have been in this little town for just a couple of hours and I have already picked up enough Portuguese to order lunch. I am sure I can do that and better with a little time in France."

John Paul stood up. "I need to get back to the ship. Come back when the children get tired. We will be on board when it gets dark until the morning, then you can go wandering again."

"John Paul, a question," said Aimee. "Why the two marines? And, don't tell me it is to help with the children. What were you afraid of?"

"Aimee, this is unfamiliar ground for me as it is for you," he responded. "I think it is better to be safe than sorry. I did not know what you might run into here that would be unfamiliar and, perhaps, dangerous. When I chose your marine companions, I asked if any had been here before and found this one fellow who had come here many years ago. He said everything should be safe, but I felt better if you had a couple of men along who could deal with trouble if it came. We are too close to our destination to lose any of our family now. As I said, it is better to be safe than sorry."

Aimee nodded and with that John Paul headed back toward the ship. About an hour later Aimee and the children also returned to the ship. She put them down for a nap and then joined John Paul up on the fantail.

"This is such a beautiful place, John Paul," she said. "I hope Brest is just like this."

"I think it will be a lot like this, especially in the spring and summer," said John Paul. "I haven't been there either but those who have described it to me say it is about this size and protected on a small bay. One thing I can tell you is that the climate there is considerably cooler than here. The Azores sit in the midst of a southern flow of water up from the equator. The temperature here generally stays in the 60s and 70s all year round. Sometimes in the winter it gets down into the 50s. We don't have the benefit of that warm flow in Brest. It will get cold and wet in the winter and we will get some snow. It is close enough to the English Channel that it gets a lot of the channel weather, which is wet and windy."

"Oh, John Paul, I hope not too much," she replied. "Living in *Providence*, we got our share of cold weather and certainly deep snow and rainy weather. So, perhaps it will not be too different. Whatever it is, we will handle it."

The next day Aimee and the children again went exploring through the day in Angra do Heroismo. By the early evening they were all ready to get on with their journey. The *Ranger* made its way out of the harbor shortly after dusk and the sailing master set a course to the east-northeast. It was designed to take them to the coast of France just to the south of their destination at Brest. The plan was to follow the coast line up to the inlet that would take them into the small village of Brest.

They had covered four weeks of the six-week crossing of the Atlantic when they reached the Azores. As the days passed, John Paul felt very fortunate that the easterly wind held up and the *Ranger*'s sails were full almost constantly, day and night. They had not encountered bad weather, not even a light rain.

A look-out was stationed high in the crow's nest each day to watch for the sighting of land. Just when John Paul expected him to yell down his usual cry of "Land ho," he yelled instead, "Sail ho, sail ho." John Paul heard the sail master yell back, "Where about?"

The look-out yelled back, "Off the stern straight ahead. There are several sails traveling north together up the coast line."

John Paul climbed down from the fantail and walked the several steps over to the ladder that went up to the stern. He picked up his spyglass from the sail master and scanned the horizon. There were, indeed, several sails in the distance, perhaps fifteen miles away. Every time he looked there seemed to be more of them. Finally, he stopped counting at twenty. He also saw two man-of-war class ships, one in front and the other trailing behind. They were obviously escorting merchant ships from the Mediterranean north to England. John Paul's privateer instincts grabbed him and he wondered if he could cut out one or two of the merchant ships and claim them as prizes before either of the British ships realized what he was doing. The thought never left his mind as the *Ranger* drew closer and closer to the convoy.

John Paul had the sailing master turn almost due north and they followed the convoy about twelve miles to the west, just out of sight. When dusk arrived, they began to move closer to the cluster of ships. It was his hope to ease into the convoy without the trailing man-of-war realizing he was there or who he was.

When John Paul was working for John Brown, it had become a practice that all of his ships carried several flags from different countries. He had French, Spanish, and English flags stored below. Now he broke out his British flag, the Union Jack, and had it displayed from the aft mast as most of the other ships in the convoy were doing. Finally, in the dead of night, he could tell by the lights on the convoy ships that he was now in their flow. No one seemed to notice that he had joined the convoy.

John Paul's plan was to wait until just before dawn to sail in and cut out one of the most promising merchant ships. He thought his chances were pretty good to force an unarmed ship out of the convoy and to be gone before the trailing man-of-war realized what was happening.

His plan did not work. Just as he was ready to move forward toward the ship he had singled out, his look-out sighted the trailing man-of-war moving up on the outside of the convoy. The much larger ship was now close enough to monitor whatever the *Ranger* did, and to take action to safeguard the merchant ships. The prudent plan was to wait and bide his time, looking for another opportunity.

The opportunity never came. John Paul continued to sail as a part of the convoy for the next two days, constantly looking for another opportunity, but the trailing man-of-war seemed always close by and vigilant.

Finally, as they approached Belle-Ile and Port-Lewis, John Paul knew he had missed his opportunity. He eased his ship to the east side of the convoy, anticipating that when they pulled even with Ile-de-Sein he needed to be able to make a sharp turn to the east and into the inlet where Brest was located. By then dusk was approaching and the trailing man-of-war was well to the west of the convoy. When the *Ranger* made its course change to enter the inlet, few in the convoy even noticed.

Once inside the inlet, the waters were calm and they could see the lights of Brest just ahead and to the port side. He looked up at the mouth of the inlet, noticing it was very much as he had been told. If cannons could be placed on the east and west sides of the entry to the inlet, they would command the entrance. No ship could enter without facing a barrage of cannon fire. That would make Brest Harbor a very safe place for the *Ranger*.

The wharf was vacant, and it took less than twenty minutes to tie the big ship to the dock. They had been traveling for six weeks to reach this point and everyone was excited to be at their destination.

Aimee brought the children up on deck and approached John Paul. "Will we be going ashore tonight or wait until the morning?" she asked.

"I think it is best to wait for morning," replied John Paul. "I need to talk to the harbor master and I'm not sure where I would be taking you if we went ashore now. By tomorrow this time it is my plan to have you and the children in a place of your own, so you can begin getting accustomed to this new life. We will be staying in port for the next week getting the *Ranger* ready to go on patrol up in the channel. I should be able to help you and the children get settled before we leave."

"Oh, John Paul, I am so happy to be someplace, anyplace but on a ship out in the ocean," Aimee said. "This is going to be an educational experience for all of us: you, me, and the children."

John Paul looked fondly at his new wife for just a few seconds and thought to himself, *I am very glad I decided to bring my family along on this trip. She and the children are just too precious to leave behind.* With that thought on his mind, he walked down the gangplank in search of the harbor master.

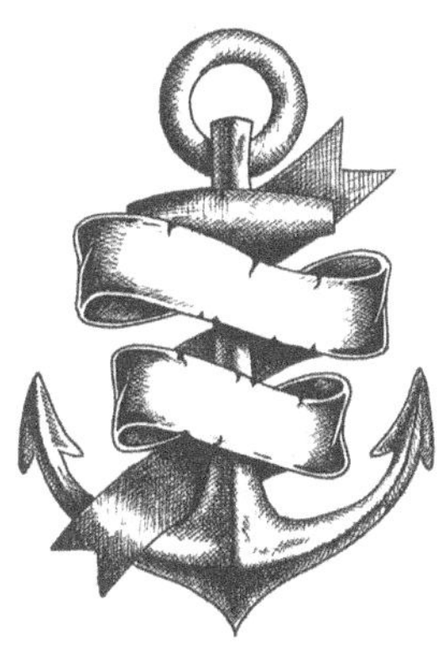

CHAPTER 19

FACING THE BRITISH IN THEIR HOME WATERS

APRIL 15, 1777

Within a few days of arriving, John Paul had his young family settled in a two-story house on the hillside above the city of Brest. Late that first week he was on the fantail of the ship when he noticed a group of three men who came to the gangplank and asked to be allowed to come aboard.

Mercifully, they had brought along an interpreter. When they were introduced to John Paul, he found himself in the presence of the mayor of the city and a representative of the French government, stationed in the province of Brittany. The conversation progressed slowly due to having to feed every sentence through the interpreter, who was not as fluent in English as he might have been.

John Paul learned that the officials had been told by King Louis's emissary in Paris that he was coming, and they welcomed him. They asked how they could be of help to him in his assignment in France and how long he anticipated staying.

John Paul told them he would be in Brest most likely until the end of the war between the Colonies and Great Britain. He talked with them about the entry to the inlet and the possibility of placing cannons there to command the entrance.

When he suggested his interest in placing cannons at the entrance to the inlet, there was much conversation back and forth in French between the three visitors that John Paul did not understand.

Finally, the interpreter told him that they would consider the matter. Their primary problem would be acquiring cannons and then soldiers capable of manning them. John Paul thought to himself, *Just give me a month and I will bring you enough cannons to equip both sides of the inlet entry. My marines can handle the cannons.* He didn't say what was on his mind, thinking it better to let them worry about his concern.

He also learned that there was another ship that was permanently stationed in Brest. It was out to sea now but should be back in a few days. It was privately owned and patrolled the waters off the Channel Islands north of Brest, about half a day's sail. It was known to bring back a prize from time to time. The mayor was anxious to know if the *Ranger* would be bringing back prizes to the city where cargos could be sold locally and ships refitted for sale as well. If that was the case, the mayor said, he was pleased to offer any help John Paul might need in order to be successful.

John Paul was pleased to tell him that he intended to raid British shipping in the English Channel and up north in the Irish Sea. His intent was to bring prizes back to Brest and, perhaps, other port cities along the coast of northern France. "Please tell the mayor that I am pleased with his offer of help," he told the interpreter. "My primary need right away is someone with English-speaking capability who can help my sailing master learn the waters north and into the English Channel."

That again led to much discussion in French among the three. Finally, the interpreter said they would consider the matter. Finding someone who knew the waters north into the English Channel was easy. Many were available to serve as local guides. They did not know of any who were fluent in the English language, however. They would have to do some searching for just the right seaman.

While John Paul was securing the *Ranger*'s berth and sharing his plans with the city leadership, Aimee and the children were learning of several things that were of interest to the family. There were two stores that sold foodstuffs not far from their house, and a weekly market in town. Neighbors told Aimee that Brest had a school. Daniel was now nine years old and Mary was eight. Moses was seven and Elizabeth was five. Aimee had been teaching the girls at home and intended to keep doing that for their time in France. None of the children could speak a word of French but her children seemed to be a curiosity on the street and several children from the area north of the city had come by the house. With access to a school that taught its lessons in French and many children to play with, she was sure her children would be bi-lingual very quickly. Daniel, especially, seemed to already be picking up the language.

Aimee, unfortunately, had not met any of her new neighbors, though she thought it would be just a matter of time. She had anticipated living in a small village, but Brest was anything but that. She wasn't sure of the population but thought it was almost as large as *Providence*, approaching 30,000 people. Also, like *Providence*, most of the population made their living from the sea. From her vantage point up on the hillside above the city, she could see the fishing boats moving in and out of the port. Most of the little boats were anchored out in the inlet. Early in the morning it looked very much like a flotilla of small boats heading out to sea. They began coming back in the late afternoon. By shortly after dusk she could count about eighty fishing boats anchored close to the harbor.

By the time a week had passed, John Paul was anxious to make his first venture into the English Channel. The mayor had sent word for him to come into the city to meet him at his office in the hotel de ville, or city hall. When he arrived, he was introduced to two men who had been identified as possible guides into the English Channel. Both were experienced seamen, and both had been prisoners of the English during the war that had ended just a few years before. They had been in a British jail for several years and had picked up enough English that, together, they could communicate directly with John Paul.

Both men returned to the ship with him. John Paul's sailing master was pleased to have some local help with charting his first trip north into the English Channel and both men seemed pleased to be employed by the

Americans. With this new help on board, John Paul felt ready to begin his European assignment.

He was a bit concerned about the sea floor and the safest routes north from the Brest inlet, so he waited until daylight to take the *Ranger* into the open seas. He intended to use this first voyage to map the area around the entrance to the inlet and to chart the Channel Islands north at the edge of the English Channel.

The sailing master took the *Ranger* out slowly, using only half of his sails. As he turned north from the inlet, he noted a small island off to his left. They were sailing in a cross-wind as the prevailing winds came west to east at this latitude. He kept the ship close to shore and when the *Ranger* reached a point just north of the Brest Inlet he turned east and followed the shoreline. Now headed east into the English Channel, John Paul felt a stronger breeze from the west. He fought the urge to drop all the sails and let the *Ranger* run with the wind. However, the primary purpose of this first voyage was to get familiar with the waters at the south edge of the Channel and he knew he needed to proceed with caution.

Shortly, he saw a small city on the coast just south of them. One of the French guides told him that was St. Malo. Just ahead, John Paul noted that the coast line turned due north. The sailing master guided them north into a cross-breeze and in about an hour they could see an island just ahead. The guide told them that was Jersey and was the first of the Channel Islands and there would be several more.

They had just passed Jersey when he heard the voice of the look-out, who was in the crow's nest above: "Sail ho, sail ho!" The sailing master called back, "Where about?"

The voice from the crow's nest called back, "Dead ahead off of the stern."

John Paul looked through his spyglass and saw what appeared to be a merchant ship anchored off one of the Channel Islands, the one called Guernsey. John Paul thought to himself, *This is too easy. We can't just by-pass such an obvious target.*

John Paul noted the English flag waving off the back mast of the merchant ship and ordered that the French flag be hoisted on the back of the *Ranger*. Great Britain and France were no longer at war, and a British merchant would expect to see a French ship in these waters and would not anticipate any hostilities.

John Paul directed the sailing master to raise all but two mid-mast sails and to move slowly toward the merchant ship. When he was almost even with the ship, he ordered the sails pulled up and the nose of the ship turned sharply toward the anchored ship. Within seconds they were close enough to throw their grappling hooks over the rail of the British ship. Following that action, the deck of the *Ranger* filled with marines and they began pulling the two ships together.

Any resistance John Paul might have expected did not materialize. Evidently, the captain and most of the crew were ashore in Guernsey. When his men were on board the merchant vessel, he counted only twelve Britishers to meet them.

John Paul asked for an inventory of the ship's cargo and was pleased to find that they were carrying mostly farm products and textiles. The merchant ship had no guns at all other than the small single shot that hung unused on the stern of the ship.

The twelve British seamen were put in a life boat and released to sail into port.

Within minutes, John Paul had placed his first mate in charge of the merchant ship and ordered it readied for sailing. He asked one of the two guides he had brought along to board the new ship to help the first mate navigate back toward Brest.

They loosened the grappling hooks and most of his men went back on board the *Ranger*. They waited for a few minutes and watched the merchant ship begin to sail toward the south. Within minutes it had dropped sails and was traveling well into the open seas.

John Paul asked the sailing master to set a course for the point north of Guernsey that bordered the southern waters of the English Channel. He did not intend to go farther on this trip. It was enough that he had seen the route north and taken his first prize here just northwest of France. He was sure the mayor of Brest would be overjoyed with the prospect of the new commerce that would be generated as they sold the cargo locally and auctioned off the ship to the highest bidder.

When the *Ranger* entered the inlet near Brest, John Paul saw the merchant ship already tied up at the wharf. The sailing master anchored the *Ranger* about a hundred yards out into the bay and they readied the long boats to take the men to shore for the night. As was their practice, they left about thirty men on board each night but that meant they had about fifty men to transport and, with only two longboats, they would need at least two trips to bring all of the men to the wharf.

When John Paul arrived at the wharf, he was not surprised to find the mayor waiting for him, with his interpreter. The interpreter said the mayor would be pleased to act as an agent for John Paul to sell the cargo and auction the ship -- for a price, of course. John Paul smiled to himself when the offer was made and, again, was not surprised. Everyone seemed to be anxious to share in the good fortune. John Paul and the mayor haggled over the price of his commission but, in the end, John Paul gave the mayor not as much as he wanted but enough to insure his good will and future support for his port activities.

Thinking ahead, John Paul realized this had all been too easy. Once word spread that there was an American ship in these waters, finding an easy merchant ship to "prize" would not be nearly as easy. He knew that if he became very successful -- which he intended to be -- the British would come looking for him. He needed to get those cannons up at the entrance of the inlet. He also wanted to check the depth of the water between the two points at the entry of the inlet. His ship needed fifteen feet of draft clearance, but he knew that a man-of-war needed about twenty-two feet. It was his plan to drop rocks into the entry to insure that a man-of-war could not enter the bay. He made a mental note to start that process tomorrow. It was a good job for the marines he had brought along for hand-to-hand fighting when boarding enemy ships was necessary. Major Whitlow, the commanding officer of the marine unit, could handle that additional project with his men.

Aimee was pleased to find her husband at the front door about mid-afternoon. The children were in the front room of the house and he sat down on the floor with them, which immediately attracted the two smaller children to climb all over him.

Daniel was full of tales of the children who lived close by and little Elizabeth was quiet as usual, listening to the other children chatter on about things they had been doing. Aimee stood by the door and smiled at his indulgence with their children.

He had been there only a few minutes when he and Aimee heard a knock at the door. The man who had come to find him spoke only broken English, but John Paul was able to make out that the mayor wanted him to come back down to the wharf.

He smiled at Aimee and said, "I'll be back as soon as I can. Don't wait supper for me."

As he walked down the hill, he realized that the other ship the mayor had told him about had come into port.

There was a reception committee waiting for him at the wharf. It included the captain of the other ship, the King's government official he had met earlier, the mayor, and the translator.

The conversation went slowly back and forth through the translator, but the substance of their discussion was the concern of the other captain for the purpose of the *Ranger* in the port of Brest and in these waters.

John Paul told him that his new country had an agreement with the French government for him to be here. When that comment was translated, the King's official nodded his head in support of his statement.

John Paul did not hide the fact that his purpose was to disrupt shipping in the English Channel and that he anticipated bringing a number of prizes back to Brest. When John Paul mentioned the prizes, he detected a slight smile on the face of the mayor, who had quickly learned the meaning of this English word.

But with each translated comment, the captain was becoming more and more agitated. It was obvious that he was not happy to have John Paul and the *Ranger* there.

John Paul did his best to assure the other captain that the two of them could share the waters of the inlet and the wharf and that both could find accommodations in Brest for the seamen.

That did not seem to placate the captain at all. John Paul finally asked him just what his major concerns were.

When that question was translated for him, the captain began to be speak in a very animated way, gesturing with his arms to emphasize his loud words. John Paul waited patiently for him to finish, wondering how the translator would ever remember all that he had said.

Finally, the captain paused to take a breath and the translator began to speak in his very best broken English. It seemed that the captain was sure that the British would know shortly that John Paul was there and send several of their largest man-of-war ships to find him. If they located him in the Brest Inlet, it was likely that both ships would find themselves at the bottom of the ocean. The captain did not want to get caught up in someone else's war, and he certainly did not want to run the risk of losing his ship. He stated emphatically that he was here first, and he did not want the *Ranger* to use this port.

When it was John Paul's turn to speak, he told the captain of his plan to place cannons on the north and south sides of the entrance to the Inlet to safeguard the port. He assured the men of his commitment to anchor his ship in Brest Inlet just as the French and Continental governments had agreed. In short, he wasn't leaving, though he was willing to make whatever concessions to the captain that might be necessary for him to feel comfortable with the *Ranger*'s presence in Brest.

When John Paul left the group of men, they were still talking. He had stated his position and there was no need for him to continue to be a part of the discussion.

When he returned home, he told Aimee what had transpired. True to her nature, she asked, "John Paul, do you think the British will come here looking for the *Ranger?*

"I think it is possible," John Paul replied. "Once we begin to make our presence known they will most likely come looking for us. This is French soil, though, and the possibility that they would come into the Brest Inlet and set up shop waiting for us to come back is not likely. If they chase us up in the Channel, we won't lead them home. We are going to have to be careful for the first several months we are here. Our salvation on the high seas will be our ability to know the Channel better than they do and being able to maneuver our ship better than they can handle theirs. We do have to remember that this is their turf. We are the strangers here."

THE PROVIDENCE GAZETTE

PROVIDENCE, Rhode Island, October 1, 1777--There is bad news from the western theater of the war. The British have retaken Fort Ticonderoga near the Adirondack Mountains in northern New York. It was the farthest northern fort in New York state and controlled access to the Hudson River.

The Battle of Brandywine, Pennsylvania was a British victory. The British drove the Continental Army toward Philadelphia, forcing Congress to flee inland to Lancaster.

The Battle of Saratoga was a victory for the patriots and may be a major turning point in the war. More than 5,700 British soldiers were captured. Benedict Arnold is the hero of Saratoga.

The big news is that France has joined the war effort against Great Britain. Their fleet and several thousand soldiers are headed to the U.S. to provide support.

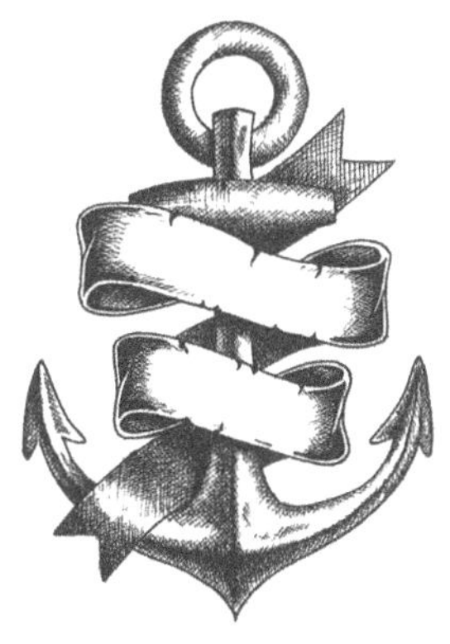

CHAPTER 20

WHITEHAVEN AND THE DRAKE

OCTOBER 12, 1777

The *Ranger* had been operating in English waters for almost six months and the hunting for British merchant ships had been good. Actually, the hunting had been better than good. Captain John Paul Jones and his crew had taken sixteen prizes. The mayor of Brest was overjoyed with the new commerce in his little port city, and the *Ranger* crew had prospered significantly since coming to France in the early spring. John Paul, especially, had become a rich man with bank deposits in a local bank as well as one in Paris.

The excursions out of the French port were shorter than they would have been if the ship was operating in American waters. The sailing distance into the English Channel from the Brest Inlet was relatively short, and the number of prizes available were many. It was not unusual for the *Ranger* to sail out early in the week and to be back in port by the weekend with yet another prize.

Having Aimee and the children in Brest was a special comfort for John Paul. Although he had been married for several years to Keziah, he had never been home in *Providence* for any extended period of time. Living with a wife and, especially, living with children, enriched his life significantly. The family adjusted well to living in France. The children learned to speak French fluently and there were many other children to play with. Aimee, while not as proficient in French as the children, hired a tutor and worked hard on her new language.

As the months passed, John Paul became more and more concerned about the probability that the British would come looking for the *Ranger*. He had set the cannons at the entrance of the inlet as a precaution and stationed six marines on each side to man the cannons should that become necessary. Rocks had been placed under water so that entry into the bay was limited to ships the size of the *Ranger* or smaller. So far, no British ships had appeared, but John Paul sensed that their arrival was inevitable.

To stave off being discovered for as long as possible, John Paul varied his route into the English Channel and back home every time the *Ranger* left the safety of the inlet. Sometimes they would hug the French coast and travel several days east past Calais and Dunkerque before turning north into the Channel. Other times they would cross over the Channel due north past Falmouth and Lizard Point and head up into the Irish Sea. His sailing master had become very familiar with the English Channel and the seas around the British Isles.

Just as they varied their route in and out of their port, they also varied where they took their prizes once they were captured. Sometimes they took them to Antwerp in Belgium or Boulogne on the northern coast of France. Twice they even took them all the way to Amsterdam in the Netherlands. The port cities were all very pleased to have the additional business. The many ports of call for the *Ranger* served to confuse the British about the location of their home port.

By the month of October, the waters around the British Isles were well into early winter and not only were the waves formidable but the salt water could be bitter cold. It was not unusual to find ice on the decks in the morning when the crew came up from their lower deck. The most popular thing on the menu in Jubal's galley was hot coffee.

John Paul thought early October would be about as late as they could raid anywhere north around the Channel Isles and resolved to make one more trip up into the Irish Sea before closing down for the winter.

He had not been back to his homeland in Scotland since he left there at the age of thirteen. His father had been a gardener in Kirkcudbright on the southern coast of Scotland. His family dissolved when his father was let go from his job by the Earl of Selkirk. Being the oldest boy in the family, John Paul went looking for work and found it in Whitehaven. He became a cabin boy on the *Friendship*, a merchant ship based in Whitehaven off the Solway Firth, a small port city in extreme northern England. The word "firth" in the Scottish dialect meant a large bay. So, Whitehaven was located on the Solway Bay on the border between England and Scotland.

John Paul did not anticipate finding any merchant ships in the northern part of the Irish Sea that time of year. Most of the merchant ships traveled between Plymouth, Portsmouth, and London along the southern coast of England. By this time of year no one was anxious to brave the cold winds and unpredictable seas of the more northern climes.

Instead, John Paul had in mind a different venture, one that did not make his crew very happy with him. He wanted to return to his home town of Kirkcudbright, to the manor house of the Earl of Selkirk who had so unceremoniously dismembered his family more than a decade ago. He wanted to kidnap the earl and offer him back to the English for ransom. The ransom he envisioned was not money but, instead, the freedom of several hundred Americans who had been taken off American ships and now languished in English jails. Needless to say, the crew of the *Ranger* was in it for the prizes and the income produced when the cargos and ships were sold. They could not see how they could prosper by kidnaping the Earl of Selkirk.

But John Paul persevered, and they sailed north until they were in the Solway Firth, anchored just off shore below Kirkcudbright. Taking two long boats, they sailed in under cover of darkness and found the shore abandoned. They walked without incident to the manor house of the Earl and knocked on the door. A servant opened the door and revealed that the Earl had been called away and would not return to Kirkcudbright for several days. John Paul and his men entered the house, took several items of silver, and retreated to the boats they had stowed on the beach. Once back on shipboard, John Paul had time to regroup and decide what they might do next that would strike a blow for their fledgling country.

Remembering his time in Whitehaven, he resolved to anchor the ship in Luce Bay for the next day and to enter the port of Whitehaven the next night. John Paul remembered the cannons placed at the entry of the port that had given him the idea to safeguard his own inlet at Brest. He knew that if he could capture and disable the cannon placements, the *Ranger* could enter the port waters and lay waste to the many ships that were usually anchored there.

John Paul was mindful of the history that no foreign country had invaded England since the Normans in 1066, more than seven hundred years before. He wanted the people of Whitehaven to not only experience invasion but for it to be memorable enough that they would not soon forget the name of John Paul Jones. The message to the leadership in London would be that their port cities were not exempt from harassment. He knew such an incident would renew the resolution of the admiralty in London to find his hiding place, but he thought the risk was worth it to instill fear in the population in England that an intruder was in their midst.

Following the pattern of the night before, they anchored the *Ranger* just outside the port of Whitehaven and went ashore in long boats. They approached the gun placements on the south side of the port, rendered the sentries unconscious, and proceeded to put nails in the firing mechanism of the cannons so they would be useless if anyone attempted to use them. No alarm had been sounded and the men of the *Ranger* moved across the port entry to the north side and repeated the process.

John Paul then signaled the men waiting just outside the port that they were free to enter, and they proceeded to row their long boats into the harbor. They set fire to one of the larger boats and then retreated back to the entry of the port. They were supposed to set fire to several of the boats anchored there and cut them loose, so they would drift into other boats and spread the fire, but that did not happen. The leader of the strike force told John Paul later that the men on the ship they had set fire to had begun to sound the alarm and they thought it best to retreat, hoping that the damage they had done would spread to other ships.

The major effect John Paul had hoped for did not materialize. They had neutralized two sets of cannons and set fire to one ship. But there was no prize to sell, no great victory to boast about, certainly not the major effect he had hoped for. Still, the outrage of the people in Whitehaven reached the leadership in London and spread through the newspapers of the cities throughout England. The Whitehaven raid had the desired effect on the people of England. It created panic.

John Paul ordered the *Ranger* southward, intending to arrive back at the Brest Inlet in a few days. He arrived at the Isle of Man in the middle of the Irish Sea and sighted the *Hussar*, a British gun boat that was smaller and had fewer guns that the *Ranger*. He resolved to take the British ship as a prize and ordered the *Hussar* to "come about" to be boarded. Instead, the *Hussar* attempted to run, but not before John Paul ordered a broadside into the British ship.

The *Ranger* and the *Hussar* played cat and mouse along the shore of the Isle of Man with the *Hussar* using its smaller size as an advantage, moving in and out of the shore waters where the *Ranger* could not go. Finally, the British ship disappeared and could not be found.

Disappointed, John Paul quickly realized that as soon as the *Hussar* reached a British port, his cover was blown and the British man-of-war ships would know where to find him. He stayed in open seas and headed farther south, keeping a sharp look-out for tall sails in the distance. He sighted two smaller British ships, captured their captains and crews, and sank the two ships primarily to keep them from reappearing in a British port where they could report the whereabouts of the *Ranger*.

From the crew of the two British ships, he learned that a British sloop-of-war, the *Drake*, with twenty guns, lay at anchor a few miles away at Carrickfergus Harbor, just at the edge of Belfast Bay in Northern Ireland. He reasoned that if he couldn't capture an English earl or burn English ships sitting at anchor late at night in port, at least he could take a British sloop-of-war. He ordered the anchor lifted and made for Belfast Bay. He arrived in the late afternoon and decided to wait until nightfall to engage the British ship.

It was approaching midnight when the *Ranger* entered the harbor where the *Drake* was anchored. The plan was to approach the British ship from the stern away from her cannons, to drop anchor at her front and attach her with grappling lines, then swarm over her top deck with marines. John Paul expected that they could take the *Drake* in short order with a part of her company on shore and the others sleeping.

Plans often do not go as outlined. However, to say the plan to take the *Drake* went afoul was very much an understatement. The *Ranger's* first mate was to drop the anchor on John Paul's signal just in front of the stern of the *Drake* with the grappling hooks pulling the two ships together and the marines ready to board her with guns and cutlasses in hand.

Unfortunately, the first mate did not drop the anchor on John Paul's signal. In fact, before the *Ranger* was stopped, it was a full hundred feet beyond the British ship. There was no chance to use the grappling hooks. Their chance at surprise was gone before the plan had a chance at success.

John Paul, instead of trying to make good of a pending disaster, ordered the sailing master to simply sail on. They turned the *Ranger* toward the port entry and sailed quietly away. No one on the *Drake* seemed to know of their presence. No alarms were sounded. Two ships had passed in the night and no one was the wiser. As distressed as he was that they had not taken the *Drake*, John Paul had to smile that the sentries on the sloop were such sound sleepers.

John Paul took the *Ranger* out of Belfast Bay and sailed north around the edge of Island Magee and into Larne Lough, an inlet just north of Belfast Bay. He was not about to leave the possibility of such a rich prize as the *Drake*. He knew that no foreign ship had ever taken a British war ship and he intended to be the first.

By mid-afternoon the next day, the *Ranger* had made its way back to the entry of the harbor at Carrickfergus, where the *Drake* still rode peacefully at anchor. John Paul ordered the high sails to be raised and tied and he let the *Ranger* drift slowly into the harbor, until she was just a few hundred yards from the *Drake*. The British sloop had sighted them when they came into the harbor. The crew began unfurling her sails, making ready to come out and challenge the intruder.

John Paul ordered the helmsman to keep the stern facing the British ship. He could see a British officer peering through a spyglass, and he did not want the officer to see the *Ranger's* broadside or count her gun ports.

The *Drake*, now with her sails catching the wind, was moving slowly out of the harbor. John Paul ordered his helmsman to follow suit. He wanted the *Drake* to be out of the harbor in the open seas where he could have more room to maneuver. When they were both outside the harbor, Jones hauled out the Stars and Stripes and the British ship ran up the red ensign of the Royal Navy. The two ships were roughly evenly matched. *Ranger* carried eighteen guns, all six-pounders. *Drake* carried twenty guns, all four-pounders, but she had almost fifty percent more men on board, about one hundred fifty to the *Ranger's* one hundred ten.

John Paul knew that any ship of the British Navy would have a well-disciplined crew and they would be well drilled. He did not trust the capability of his own crew. They were untested in ship-to-ship combat and most had never been in a sea battle before. He wished his men could have drilled them in gunnery with real ammunition, but powder was in such short supply that such practice consisted of simply running the guns in and out, not actually firing them.

John Paul needed to outsmart his opponent, to get an edge and keep it. He knew he could not afford to let the *Drake* get too close, or the superior British forces could board *Ranger* and take her with superior numbers. He did want to keep the British ship just close enough, where his greater firepower could slowly grind down the enemy ship. John Paul ordered the platforms up the masts filled with marine sharpshooters who could keep a steady fire of musket balls raining down on the enemy quarterdeck where the officers stood.

The sun was setting and the light fading. The moment had come to strike. He ordered the helmsman to steer straight across the *Drake's* bow. When they were even with the stern of the *Drake*, John Paul yelled, "FIRE!" and the *Ranger's* broadside sent a volley of grapeshot straight down the *Drake's* exposed deck, sending splinters flying and drawing first blood.

Now *Ranger* was vulnerable. It would take more than a minute to reload the cannons and fire again. As she slipped past the British ship, her stern was exposed. John Paul took advantage of the smoke hanging over the deck from the broadside and ordered the helmsman to spin the wheel and swing the *Ranger* around so the two ships were parallel, broadside to broadside, perhaps fifty yards apart. Before the *Ranger*'s cannons were ready to fire again the *Drake* took advantage of the lull. The British ship fired and the sound of the *Drake*'s broadside was deafening.

The quarterdeck where John Paul was standing with the other officers was a very exposed place when the enemy is hurling hundreds of pounds of metal from close range. By gentlemanly custom, officers did not duck or flinch. Jones stood there, stock-still, doing his best to ignore the iron that was flying everywhere. He could hear the yells of the wounded. One of the junior officers standing close to him was hit in the head and dropped dead. A marine fell from the high mast where he had been shot by a musket ball. He landed on the deck just below them.

For more than an hour, the two ships exchanged cannon fire every couple of minutes. Through the smoke, John Paul could see that the *Ranger*'s shots were beginning to have a serious effect. The *Drake*'s sails were riddled with holes and no longer drawing wind. The ship's foremast had been broken and hung down toward the deck. Her sails and rigging were cut to pieces.

The *Drake*'s captain had been badly injured, shot in the head by a musket ball fired by a sharpshooter from the high mast. The first officer was dead. With both officers incapacitated and unable to maneuver the ship, the *Drake*'s sailing master took the bullhorn and yelled, "Quarter, quarter!" signaling surrender. After just over an hour, the battle was over.

John Paul sent a boat load of marines over to take possession of his prize and to shackle the prisoners. The toll of dead and wounded on both sides was significant. The *Ranger* had lost thirty men, both dead and wounded, while the *Drake*'s total exceeded fifty.

John Paul sent his carpenter to the *Drake* to assess the damage. He needed both ships to be seaworthy so he could travel back to port to show off his prize.

Word of the defeat of the *Drake* moved quickly through Ireland, over to England and all the way to London where the Admiralty came immediately under attack from King George and Parliament. They dispatched two man-of-war ships to find the American intruder, as well as a thirty-six-gun frigate, the *Thetis*. A few days later, the *Boston*, a thirty-two-gun frigate that had been captured earlier from the Americans, was also sent out searching for the elusive *Ranger*.

Newspapers all over England reported about the American ship that burned British ships in their harbors and took one of their gun boats on the high seas. The previously invulnerable British Navy seemed like anything but in light of the success of Captain John Paul Jones and the *Ranger*.

As it turned out, the British Navy was searching in the wrong place for the *Ranger* and the captured *Drake*. When both ships were ready to brave the open seas again, John Paul took advantage of a southerly wind and sailed out of Belfast Bay to the north. They sailed around the north edge of Ireland and down the western coast, and then across the open sea to the northern tip of France. It was more than a week before they entered the inlet at Brest. Shortly after their arrival, there was a major celebration in the little port city. They were glad to have the *Ranger* back in port, but they were doubly glad to have the *Drake* and its cargo to sell.

The *Ranger* had been gone from port for just twenty-eight days and during that time the ship and its crew had sunk two smaller ships, invaded the southern coast of Scotland, burned a ship in the port city of Whitehaven, and taken a British sloop-of-war as a prize. True, the venture into the northern Irish Sea did not match the ambitions of Captain John Paul Jones, but there is no doubting the effect his raids had on the imagination of the British people. Many were beginning to have doubts about the cost of repressing the American rebellion.

Reports in the British newspapers about the exploits of Captain Jones and the *Ranger* went on for several weeks. One London newspaper wrote, "When such ravages are committed all along the coast, by one small privateer, what blame must it reflect on the First Lord of the Admiralty?" The British Navy had been the dominant force on the oceans for one hundred years. The one thing the people of England had always been sure of was that they were safe from attack by sea. Suddenly, their security was gone. To have one foreign ship land on British soil not once but twice in a day was just too much.

The legend of Captain John Paul Jones, already growing in the fledgling United States, now was running rampant in the British Isles. Who was this upstart who could attack British soil at will and disappear without a trace? Stories and poems were written about Jones, the invisible and invincible pirate. Mothers frightened their children with the bare mention of his name. In 18th century British history and, indeed, in British folklore, John Paul Jones had taken his place alongside the legends of Blackbeard the Pirate and Captain Kidd.

THE PROVIDENCE GAZETTE

PROVIDENCE, Rhode Island, May 1, 1778--France has formally recognized the independence of the former thirteen Colonies and promised to send aid. This is a major breakthrough and is attributed to the efforts of our ambassadors to France, John Adams and Benjamin Franklin.

Prussian Baron von Steuben arrives to assist General Washington in training the Continental Army at Valley Forge. By the end of the winter, the army is a much more cohesive and disciplined fighting force.

The British continue to hold New York and are using it as their center of operations to hold the middle of the country. They are dominant in New York and New Jersey and are a constant threat up the Hudson toward Canada.

The British have captured Savannah, Georgia. This is the first major defeat for American troops in the south. Attacking Savannah is the first major thrust of the British toward the south and brings into question the security of Charleston and its vital harbor.

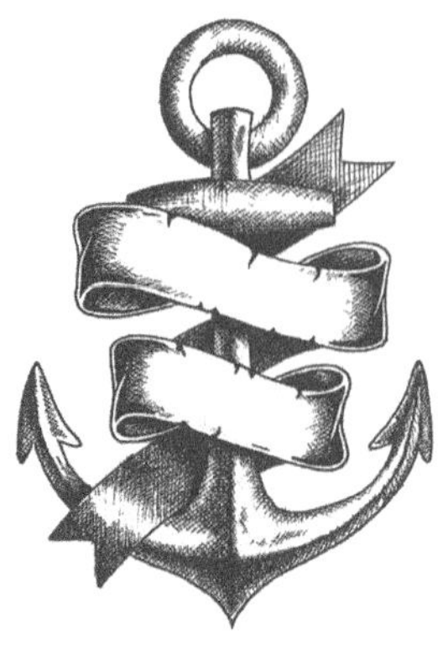

CHAPTER 21

BENJAMIN FRANKLIN AND JOHN ADAMS COME TO VISIT

MAY 1, 1778

John Paul received a letter in February 1778 telling him to expect a visit from Benjamin Franklin and John Adams, American Ambassadors to France. The word was that they would come as soon as the weather broke in the early spring. As the weather grew warmer, Captain Jones and the *Ranger* stayed close to home in Brest, not knowing exactly when the eminent visitors might arrive. Now, at long last, word came that they would leave Paris on the 26th of April with an expected arrival on May 1st.

John Paul met with the mayor of Brest twice in anticipation of the ambassadors' arrival. It wasn't often that dignitaries from Paris visited Brest. In fact, no one could remember that small sea coast city ever being visited by a representative of a foreign government. Right on time, about mid-day on the first of May, the two ambassadors arrived by private coach just up the street north of the wharf where the *Ranger* was docked.

John Paul had been looking for them from his ship and strode down the gangplank from the *Ranger* to greet them. He had met both men briefly when he visited Congress in Philadelphia back in 1775 at the time he received his commission in the Continental Navy. He knew both men by reputation, but prior to this visit he had not had a private conversation with either.

The mayor of Brest arrived just a few minutes later to provide the official welcome to the guests and show them to their accommodations at Brest's finest hotel. The upstairs rooms had been carefully prepared in anticipation of their visit, the curtains at the windows washed and fresh flowers on the tables. The plan for their three days in Brest included a major banquet in their honor with most of the city leaders in attendance.

For his part, John Paul wanted to give the ambassadors a tour of the *Ranger* and, perhaps, take them on a short cruise out into the Atlantic. He also anticipated talking with them late into the night to share his experiences in battling the British in the English Channel.

Mindful of the reputations of the two ambassadors, he had arranged a man to serve as valet to meet every need of Mr. Adams. He did the same with Mr. Franklin except the person chosen to serve as "valet" was female. Mr. Franklin had a well-known reputation as a ladies' man and loved the company of the female gender. The lady chosen was one of the widowed gentry who lived in a manor house up the hill behind John Paul's more modest house. She was instructed to see that Mr. Franklin's was well taken care of and to serve as hostess for him at the banquet. John Paul knew her to be a very attractive lady and she seemed most willing to be included in the festivities.

The banquet was a major celebration with entertainment provided by a traveling troupe of performers brought in from Le Mans in Sarthe Parish. The mayor delivered a speech celebrating the relationship between France and its new ally, the United States of America, as well as that of his city with Captain Jones and the American Navy. He said glowing things about the contributions of the two visitors, mentioning the many inventions of Mr. Franklin and the writings of Mr. Adams. However, his greatest accolades were reserved for Captain John Paul Jones, who had brought such prosperity to his city. All in all, it was a proper speech delivered in his very best French, understood by everyone present including his guests of honor, both of whom were fluent in French. John Paul, in contrast, was still struggling with his French and had to be told later of the gracious words of their host.

The day after the banquet, the last day of the visit by the U.S. ambassadors, Mr. Franklin asked for some time to speak privately with John Paul. "I have a little surprise for you," he confided.

They met in the courtyard near the city hall. When they were alone, Ambassador Franklin spoke in a low voice. "The French government has been working on a new ship for you, one that has sixty-four guns instead of the thirty-four you have on the *Ranger*," he said, looking over his half-glasses. "It should be faster and more maneuverable than the *Ranger* and will have more cannons and other armaments."

John Paul was almost speechless. Finally, he would have a ship capable of standing toe-to-toe with most English ships of the line. With the *Ranger*, he could take most merchant ships and was capable of an even fight with gunships like the *Drake*. He had learned not to engage any merchant ships with an English man-of-war close by. He knew he would have to run rather than to fight if caught in such a confrontation. That would all change with this new ship.

"I'm not sure what to say, Ambassador Franklin," John Paul said. "To what do I owe such an honor?"

Mr. Franklin laughed and said, "The French think you must have hung the moon. All the success you have had bringing prizes to their ports and propping up their local economies all along the coast has them thinking you are some kind of international hero. I'm sure you know that they have been fighting the British on and off for the past hundred years. In all that time, they have always been at a disadvantage on the high seas. To find someone who can humble the British fleet even a little is cause for a major celebration."

"When do you think the ship will arrive?" asked John Paul.

"I was expecting it before now. Our contact with the French government in Paris told me before we left for Brest that the ship was almost ready to sail. The work on it was being done in Le Havre, about half way up the

French coast in the channel, and that is no more than at three or four day sail from Brest," responded Franklin.

"Ambassador Franklin, I am overwhelmed," said John Paul. "To know that we have such firepower available will be great news to my men on the *Ranger*. They are fighters by nature and have no been happy with our having to run every time we see a man-of-war in the distance."

"John Adams and I will be staying one more night in your fair city and we should be on our way back to Paris by first light," said Franklin. "I want you to know that we have enjoyed our sojourn out of Paris and into the countryside and we have especially enjoyed the hospitality here in Brest. I would appreciate your sharing my sentiments with the mayor if I don't see him before we leave."

"With your permission, I will join you for breakfast before you leave in the morning," said John Paul. "I wouldn't want you to leave without saying a proper goodbye."

"You will have to come early," said Franklin. "I am not given to getting up before the chickens, but Adams is an early bird and says we need to be on the road by eight o'clock or so."

"I will meet you at the hotel by seven," said John Paul.

John Paul could hardly wait to get home to tell Aimee of his good fortune. She seemed almost as happy as he had been when Ambassador Franklin told him of the new ship.

John Paul was still at the kitchen table and wasn't halfway through his cup of tea when young Jim ran in. He was breathless with excitement.

"Captain Jones, sir," he said. "There are ships coming into the bay and they aren't British or French!"

"What flags are they flying?" Jones asked.

"I could not see a flag," Jim responded. "There are three of them and two are *Ranger* class. The third is smaller."

John Paul stood up and gave Aimee a quick peck on the cheek. "We will be back shortly," he said.

John Paul and Jim headed down the hill toward the water's edge. By the time they arrived, there were several people waiting at the wharf to see who had come into port. Among them were Benjamin Franklin and John Adams, as well as the mayor. As they watched, each of the three ships hoisted the Stars and Stripes.

Ambassador Franklin leaned over the John Paul and said, "I'm sorry. I was so caught up in the news that the French were sending you a new ship that I kept forgetting to tell you that the Navy Committee was sending you the other ships they had promised earlier. It is just coincidence that they have arrived during our visit here."

The names of the ships were clearly visible. The two larger ships were the *Alliance* and the *Pallas*. The smaller one was the *Vengeance*. John Paul was mentally counting the cannon turrets on the ships. The *Alliance* had eighteen visible, which meant they carried thirty-six cannons. The *Pallas* had sixteen visible, and the *Vengeance* only six. Altogether, John Paul calculated that his little fleet had the firepower of more than one hundred thirty cannons or, together, more than equal to most of the man-of-war ships sailing under the British flag.

The three ships anchored across the channel of the bay and three long boats were launched from the wharf to act as water taxis. Soon John Paul was watching the men disembark from the three ships down the rope ladders into the long boats as he made his mental calculations. Then he saw something that erased the calculations from his mind. There on the deck of the *Pallas*, looking down at the men climbing down to the long boat, was a familiar figure. Could it be? He was a good two hundred yards from the ship but the figure he saw was taller than the others standing and waiting their turn to climb down the rope ladder. He had on a blue coat and captain's hat that were very familiar.

He felt his heart leap in his chest. Either that was John Burroughs Hopkins, or it was someone who looked and moved so much like him that he had a twin.

John Paul asked Ambassador Franklin, "Sir, can you tell me who the captains of the three ships are?"

Franklin smiled and said, "I don't know the captain of the *Vengeance*, but the *Alliance's* captain is a Frenchman, Pierre Landais, and the captain of the *Pallas* is…" At that point Franklin stopped for just a few seconds before he finished his sentence. Smiling broadly, he said, "Captain John Burroughs Hopkins."

Having been a part of the discussion on commissioning officers of the Continental Navy, Benjamin Franklin well knew of the relationship between Captains John Paul Jones and John Burroughs Hopkins.

With Ambassador Franklin's statement, John Paul felt a flood of emotion rush over him. He had not seen his good friend since he had to leave him in his sick bed two years ago following his injury on the *Abigale*. He had gotten no word of him after that and had feared he might never see him again. Such feelings are usual during a time of war when communications are so hard. Yet here he was. He had come with the small fleet to join John Paul in harassing British shipping in the English Channel.

John Paul hurried down the steps from the street to the wharf with his eyes riveted on the long boat coming in from the *Pallas*. The closer it got the better he could see the smile on the face of John Burroughs Hopkins. He could hardly wait for the long boat to dock and the men to climb onto the wharf. John Burroughs was the last one to leave the boat, but he met the open arms of John Paul there at the top of the ladder.

It was a very long bear hug between the two old friends. When they broke apart words from both came rushing out.

Then, John Burroughs raised his hand to stop the flood of words. "I have some things I need to attend to, and then we can talk. We have some serious catching-up to do."

John Paul backed away and watched his friend walk over to Captain Pierre Landais and salute him. Captain Landais returned the salute and they talked for just a few minutes. By this action John Paul realized that Captain Landais had been placed in charge of this small flotilla.

John Burroughs left that short discussion and climbed the steps to street level where several of his men were waiting for him. Captain

Landais walked over to John Paul, came to attention and saluted. John Paul returned his salute.

"Captain Jones," Landais said in perfect but heavily accented English, "my orders were to deliver these ships to you and to stand by for your orders."

"I am very glad to see you," responded John Paul. "I trust it was an uneventful trip across and that your ships are in good shape and ready for the serious business we are involved in here."

"Yes sir," Landais said. "We had fair weather most of the way and the ships are not only in good shape, but the seamen are well drilled and ready for whatever action you assign."

"Good," replied John Paul. "You get your men situated and we will have a captains' meeting in the morning to give you the lay of the land or, rather, of the sea."

With that comment, John Paul turned to the mayor, who had just arrived at the wharf, and asked, "Sir, can I make use of one of your meeting rooms at the city hall in the morning at around nine o'clock?"

The mayor nodded and replied, "I will arrange it. Captain Jones, can you tell me how long we can expect these new ships to be with us here in Brest?"

John Paul said, "I'm not sure, Mr. Mayor. Their assignment is open-ended, like mine. I suspect they will be here until the end of the war."

The reason for the smile on the mayor's face was unmistakable. More ships and more men meant more prosperity for his city, and for him, personally.

John Paul stayed on the street above the wharf for several minutes. Then, he turned to Jim, who had been standing at his elbow. "Jim, go back to the house and tell your mother that we will be having a guest for dinner tonight," he said.

Jim smiled and said, "Can I tell who it is, or should we save that as a surprise?"

"You go ahead and tell your mother that John Burroughs is coming home with me," said John Paul, grinning. "We will offer him a bed, but I don't think he will take it. He will, no doubt, want to stay in town closer to his men."

It was an hour later when the two old friends entered the front door of the house that John Paul and Aimee called home. The children were in the parlor and all came to the door to see who was visiting them. Daniel remembered John Burroughs immediately and ran to him.

"My, what a big boy you have become," said John Burroughs as he picked Daniel up and swung him around. "You are going to make a sea captain like your pa for sure."

John Paul said, "I can see that your shoulder is healed now. Daniel is a pretty good sized boy now and picking him up like that would take a healthy shoulder."

"You are right, John Paul. I hardly feel it anymore," said John Burroughs.

John Burroughs set Daniel down, took Aimee's hand and gave it a light kiss on the back as was the custom of the time. When they parted he asked, "And, who are these young ladies?"

Aimee responded, "These are my girls. "This is Mary, and this is Elizabeth."

The little girls curtseyed, as Aimee had taught them. Mary reached her hand out like Aimee had done earlier while little Elizabeth hid behind her mother's skirts. John Burroughs laughed. He took Mary's hand and with all the flair of a French dandy, and kissed the back of it. She pulled away immediately, embarrassed, while John Burroughs smiled at little Elizabeth and said, "You are a little shy now, but it won't take you long to warm up to me."

Moses was still standing in the doorway, not sure what to do, when John Burroughs reached over and picked him up. The expression on his face said that he was not sure just how he should respond to being hoisted up into the stranger's arms. John Burroughs put him down before things began to go wrong and little Moses retreated to join Mary, holding on to Aimee's skirt.

"How about some tea?" said Aimee.

"A good idea," responded John Paul.

The children went back to playing in the parlor while John Paul, Aimee, John Burroughs, and Jim retreated to the big table in the kitchen. In a few moments, they all had cups of tea and a plate of pastries in front of them and the two friends began to talk.

John Burroughs could not help but look closely at Jim. He said, "Jim-boy, you have grown like a weed. When I last saw you, you were but a waif. Look at you now. Are you fifteen or sixteen now?"

"I'm fifteen but I will be sixteen in a few months," responded Jim, adding proudly, "I am almost five feet ten inches tall."

"I thought you might have grown a foot since I last saw you but perhaps it is only four or five inches," said John Burroughs, laughing.

"Tell me about your father, Esek," John Paul asked. "Is he well?"

"He is fine, though not very happy with the function of the Navy," responded John Burroughs.

"Trying to harness several hundred pirates had to be an impossible job," said John Paul.

"Well, that isn't all. The privateers are indeed incorrigible and not at all receptive to anyone telling them what to do," said John Burroughs. "The plan to go and come into the ports in flotillas to thwart the man-of-war ships the British have stationed there has worked pretty well. But despite being told to stay away from the strongest British ships, several have decided that they can exchange broadsides with them. I know of no case where that has worked out well. We have lost a number of our strongest privateers to what you can only identify as over-confidence or, perhaps more accurately, over-ambition."

"I am not sure we could have expected anything else," said John Paul.

"To their credit, we are doing pretty well raiding British supply ships," John Burroughs said. "I would be surprised if we didn't have almost as many cannons, muskets, and powder marked 'Made in England' as General Howe and the British Army have."

"I'm glad we are being at least somewhat successful with the original plan to cut off British supplies, whatever the headaches they create for our leadership," said John Paul.

John Burroughs continued, "As much a mixed blessing as the privateers are, they aren't the only problem. Some members of the Continental Congress and even one member of the Navy Committee have continually lobbied for us to try to break the British blockade by attacking the British man-of-war ships stationed at the mouths of our harbors. Every time my father goes to meet with the Navy Committee, he is subjected to constant criticism. Twice he has offered his resignation. We have very few experienced sailors in the Congress and they just don't understand that none of the ships they built for us have half enough cannons to face off with a man-of-war."

"That is also true here," said John Paul. "I have had really good luck catching merchant ships in the Channel and up in the Irish Sea. But every time we sight the sails of a high-master, we have to turn tail and run. We may be able to out-maneuver them and, in many cases, out-run them, but we don't have the fire power to exchange broadsides with them. At least that has been the case up to now. That may be changing over the next few months."

"What do you mean?" asked John Burroughs.

John Paul replied, "Ambassador Franklin told me this morning that the French are retrofitting a new ship for me that will have twice the fire power of the *Ranger*. If that turns out to be true, we may not have to run as often in the future as we have in the past."

Following a delicious supper prepared by Aimee, the discussion of the two old friends went on well into the night. Aimee and the children had long since gone to bed when John Burroughs indicated it was time for him to retire as well. He and John Paul walked down the hill together to a tavern near the wharf that let comfortable rooms. John Paul left his friend there and retraced his steps up the hill.

THE PROVIDENCE GAZETTE

PROVIDENCE, Rhode Island, May 1, 1778--France has formally recognized the independence of the former thirteen colonies and promised to send aid. This is a major breakthrough and is attributed to the efforts of our ambassadors to France, John Adams and Benjamin Franklin.

Prussian Baron von Steuben arrives to assist General Washington in training the Continental Army at Valley Forge. By the end of the winter, the army is a much more cohesive and disciplined fighting force.

The British continue to hold New York and are using it as their center of operations to hold the middle of the country. They are dominant in New York and New Jersey and are a constant threat up the Hudson toward Canada.

The British have captured Savannah, Georgia. This is the first major defeat for American troops in the south. Attacking Savannah is the first major thrust of the British toward the south and brings into question the security of Charleston and its vital harbor.

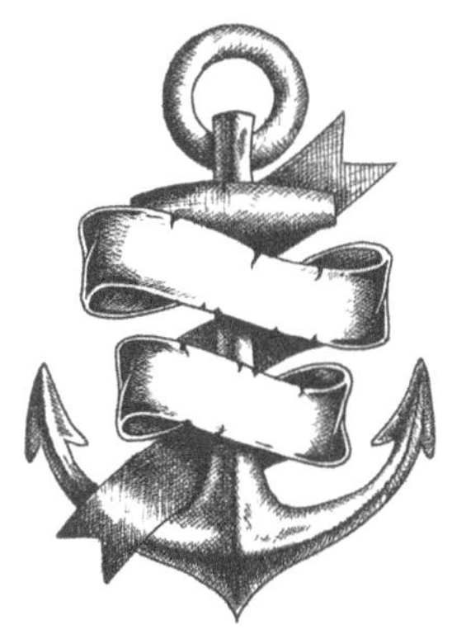

CHAPTER 22
THE BONHOMME RICHARD
MAY 6, 1778

Before he had gone to bed the night before, John Paul had given some thought to what he should wear to bid farewell to his ambassador guests the next morning and what would be most impressive to his new fleet captains at their nine o'clock meeting. He had several uniforms he used on shipboard as subterfuge when raiding British shipping. The all-white uniform made him look like a French ship's captain. The gray uniform with the red trim was his least favorite but it was copied after what was standard wardrobe for the captain of a Spanish ship. With either of those uniforms and a French or Spanish flag flying, it was hard to identify the *Ranger* as a U.S. Navy ship.

The standard captain's uniform he liked most had off-white pants with a blue jacket with gold trim. His hat was blue and tri-cornered, with gold and red trim. That is what he was wearing when he greeted the two ambassadors at breakfast the next morning.

Because of his long talk with John Burroughs, he had gotten to bed very late. He had been in bed less than four hours when he felt Aimee shaking him. Yet, as he anticipated meeting with Ambassadors Franklin and Adams, he did not feel at all tired. Instead, he felt an odd excitement. This was going to be a very important day.

He greeted the ambassadors at the bottom of the steps as they came down from their rooms at the hotel. He had chosen a table close to the fireplace and the only other people in the room that early were the three men who had come with the ambassadors from Paris, the coach driver and two guards. Before long these three finished their breakfast and left the room to prepare for their departure.

John Paul and the two ambassadors were provided a cup of hot tea when they sat down and, shortly, a maid delivered a basket of warm breads, jam and butter. There was little talking around the table as the food disappeared and when the men were almost finished three steaming bowls of oatmeal arrived. Each man added liberal amounts of butter to his bowl.

John Paul was the first to finish eating and he took advantage of the lull in conversation to address John Adams. "Mr. Adams, everyone knows of your writings and your contribution to the leadership of the Sons of *Liberty* in *Boston*. Many say that the separatist movement began in your law offices there in Massachusetts. Without your leadership, there would have been no effort to gain independence from Great Britain. The new United States owes you a great debt of gratitude. From a personal perspective, I very much appreciate your coming to Brest to visit me and the seamen of the *Ranger*. You do us great honor by your presence."

"I thank you for your kind words, Captain Jones," Adams replied gravely. "We are here because of the great contribution you have made to the cause of independence. Without brave men like you and your seamen, we would still be firmly under the heel of British authority."

"And you, Mr. Franklin," said Jones. "You are already known all over the world as an inventor as well as a statesman and a writer. Had there never been a fight for independence, you will still have your place in the history books. Few have made such a contribution to both mankind and their country."

"Oh, Captain Jones, you flatter me," said Benjamin Franklin, eyes twinkling behind his glasses.

"That is not my purpose, sir. From a personal perspective, your bringing word of the new ship that is to arrive shortly is an answer to prayer," said John Paul. "Our efforts in the English Channel have been mostly focused on smaller merchant ships. When we sighted a high-master in the distance, we had to turn and run. We did not dare risk fighting most of the British ships of the line. Now with this new ship with sixty-four cannons we will be much better able to defend ourselves. If we add that to the additional three ships the Navy Committee just sent, we will be able to stand toe-to-toe with most of the British Navy."

"That, sir, is the intent," said Mr. Adams.

"I have been thinking most of the night of what we might name the ship being prepared for us. I thought we needed a name that would commemorate both the French support of our mission and the cause of liberty. I think I have the right name. If you agree, we will call the new ship the *Bonhomme Richard*. 'Bonhomme' is a French word that means 'to carry on in one's own way.' '*Richard*' is a reference to Mr. Franklin's publication, *Poor Richard's Almanac*, which has helped shape the thinking of Americans regarding our relationship with Great Britain for thirty years."

"Captain Jones, I would be most flattered to have the ship named the *Bonhomme Richard*. I think the French would like it and I know I do," said Franklin. Glancing at his friend, he added, "I know Mr. Adams agrees."

"Right you are, Ben. Christening the ship the *Bonhomme Richard* seems just right," said John Adams.

Ambassador Franklin reached over, took John Paul's hand, and said, "As much as I hate to break up this gathering, I think Mr. Adams and I need to be on our way back to Paris. They say a trip of a thousand miles begins with a single step and I think it is time we take that step."

Within a few minutes the two ambassadors and John Paul were standing in front of the hotel where the driver had brought the coach. The customary handshakes and bows were shared and the two visitors climbed aboard. The driver spanked the horses and John Paul watched until the coach was out of sight.

It was still about thirty minutes until the meeting of the ship captains and John Paul walked slowly down the street toward city hall. He had just enough time to get his thoughts together before the meeting.

The room set aside for their gathering was small but adequate and John Burroughs arrived shortly after John Paul. "How were your accommodations?" John Paul asked.

"They were just fine. I slept like a baby," John Burroughs responded. There was no mistaking the warmth each felt with again being together.

Captain Briggs of the *Vengeance* joined them a few minutes later.

The group talked casually while awaiting the arrival of Captain Pierre Landais. Soon it was fifteen minutes past the appointed meeting time and still Captain Landais had not arrived. John Paul was about to postpone the meeting when he heard footsteps. The door opened and Captain Landais appeared. Without a word of explanation or apology, he took his seat at the table. John Paul began the meeting.

The meeting lasted for a solid two hours. There was much to talk about. The focus was on the English Channel, the Irish Sea, and the hazards of both wind and currents. This would be the first of several meetings of the captains. There would be other meetings that would include the sailing masters and others who needed the opportunity to learn from the experience of the *Ranger* seamen.

After John Paul concluded the meeting, he asked Captain Landais to stay for a few minutes. "Captain Landais," he said. "I would appreciate knowing why you were late for our meeting this morning."

Captain Landais stood up and took a couple of steps toward the door, then turned around and came back to the table. He leaned down over the table, putting his dark face close to John Paul's.

"Captain Jones, I am a captain in the service of the Continental Navy," he said. "I am not to be ordered around like a cabin boy. I don't like nine o'clock meetings. I don't like meetings at all. You did not consult with me about having this meeting. After participating in it I can say with authority that there is nothing you said to us this morning that was of much value. You may as well know that I don't have much respect for you. I know of your background running slaves and pirating up and down the coast in past years. Since you have been in the navy you have done nothing but grandstand for publicity. I have no understanding of why you were put in charge of this mission."

By this point John Paul was doing all he could to control his temper. He said, "You sir, are being insubordinate. This is my command and you will comply with my orders or you can be sent home on the next ship that has room for you as a prisoner in the hold."

Landais stepped away from the table and turned his back. When he turned around, he had his sword out and was pointing it toward John Paul. John Paul was immediately on his feet and lifted his own sword out of its sheath. Time seemed to stand still and neither man moved toward the other.

Just at that point the door opened, and John Burroughs stuck his head in. Seeing the two standing across the room pointing their swords at each other, he walked in and stood between them.

"Would anyone care to tell me what is going on here?" he asked.

Captain Landais said, "Oh, nothing much. I was just showing Captain Jones my sword."

Both men put their swords back into their sheaths but neither said another word. Instead, John Burroughs said, "Good, I thought for a moment I was witnessing some hostilities between the two of you."

Captain Landais said, "I will take my leave, gentlemen."

He stepped by John Burroughs and left the room. John Paul looked at his friend and said, "It was good you came in when you did. I was thinking I was going to have to run him through."

"Well," said John Burroughs, "I don't think that is the way to begin a relationship. It is good I came in."

Both laughed and sat down at the now vacant table. John Paul took out a handkerchief and mopped his brow. "What is wrong with that man?" he asked.

"I suspect he is upset because, after being in charge of his own ship and free to do as he pleased, he is now under your direction," said John Burroughs. "He said some things back in *Providence* before we headed for France that indicated he was not happy with this assignment. He was especially unhappy that you were going to be in charge. I suspect he would not have said these things if he had known of our prior relationship. Captain Landais is French and has been loaned to us by the French government. He is not happy with coming home to his own country and having to move down to second in command to a 'Yank.'"

"I hate to let a new relationship get off on the wrong foot," said John Paul. "But I do not intend to let him disobey my orders. The first time he defies me in public will be his last in this command."

"Let's talk about something more important," said John Burroughs. "While we were in our meeting, your new ship came in and from across the bay it looks to be a beauty."

"Everything is happening at once," said John Paul, jumping to his feet. "First, you and the others arrive from *Providence*, then the ambassadors finish their visit and leave, and now the *Bonhomme Richard* arrives. Let's go see it!"

As soon as they were out of the city hall, John Paul could see the new ship anchored across the bay from the wharf. Even from this distance it looked twice the size of the *Ranger*. John Paul liked having the gun turrets disguised so that the ship would look like a merchant ship until it got very close. That was not the case with the *Bonhomme Richard*. The gun turrets were clearly visible. The sails were down but John Paul could see that there were three masts, and each had three layers of riggings for holding sails. Without the sails up, it was easy to see that there were no platforms up high for marine sharpshooters to attack the deck hands of another ship. That would need to be remedied, he thought.

The two friends climbed down the rope ladder and stepped into one of the long boats that remained tied up to the wharf. It was a short ride out to the new ship. John Paul asked the man running the water taxi to wait on them for the return trip.

Once on board, John Paul was immediately impressed with the newness of the ship. It wasn't brand new since it had been retrofitted from a large merchant ship, but in virtually every direction he looked he saw new wood, new riggings, new sails—and it was so big! The sixty-four guns were on two levels, with sixteen to a level and thirty-two on each side.

John Burroughs leaned against the side rail and issued a low whistle. "This is some ship, John Paul," he said.

"There are some things I will want to do to it, but it will give us the firepower we have been lacking," John Paul responded.

It took almost an hour for the tour of the entire ship. They covered the lower deck galley, the gun turrets, the storage area for powder and the other implements of war. Finally, on the top deck again, John Paul went up to the poop deck and found the sailing master there.

"How does she sail?" he asked.

The sailing master responded, "Mighty fair, Captain, sir. We haven't really tried her out but coming from Abbeville to here she was easy to handle."

"How about her speed?" asked John Paul.

"She moves easily before the wind, but we did not test her top speed," he said. "I think she will top out at about sixteen knots when we get her trimmed proper."

"Is her hull clean?" asked John Paul.

"Yes sir, clean as a whistle," responded the sailing master. I have been with her since they took her into dry dock. They cleaned her hull first thing."

"What is her draft?" John Paul asked.

"She will draw about eighteen feet," the sailing master responded.

"It is a good thing you came in during high tide," said John Paul. "The entry will only take a little more than fifteen feet. If the tide had been out, you would have been dragging the bottom."

"I used the depth line coming in and we cleared the bottom by a couple of feet," said the sailing master. "Should I get her out of here before the tide goes out to keep her from being trapped?"

"No," John Paul responded. "We want to do some work on her, so we need her in close. We will have to be careful when we take her out and bring her back in."

In a few moments, the two friends were back in the long boat and they sat patiently as they glided easily toward the wharf. Once back on land John Paul stood for a short moment staring back across the bay at his new ship. Then he gave in to the overwhelming desire to get home and tell Aimee about his day and, mostly, about his new ship.

John Paul bade his friend good-bye and headed up the hill. Soon he was joined by young Jim who wanted to hear all about the new ship. He was full of questions which John Paul did his best to answer. Mostly, John Paul's mind was so full of the new possibilities of their mission here in France and things he needed to get done before they ventured out of the Brest Inlet again. The new ship would make searching for British merchant ships on the English Channel a very different experience.

From time to time, his confrontation with Captain Landais found its way into this consciousness. What would he do with a captain who was in obvious rebellion against his leadership? That would take some thought and a great deal of tact.

THE PROVIDENCE GAZETTE

PROVIDENCE, Rhode Island, August 1, 1778. The British have withdrawn from Philadelphia. This eases the pressure on the U.S. Congress which has been meeting in Lancaster, PA since the British occupied Philadelphia in the spring.

The U.S. Army under General George Washington has left Valley Forge in pursuit of the British who are withdrawing toward New York.

The U.S. Army has met the British at Monmouth, New Jersey and they have won a great victory. This is first major victory since The Battle of Princeton in January.

The war in the west, under the leadership of General George Rogers Clark, is going well. Our armies recently captured Kaskaskia, Cahokia, and Fort Sackville at Vincennes.

An effort was made to attack the British stronghold at Newport, Rhode Island but it failed due to poor coordination between the French and the U.S. Army troops.

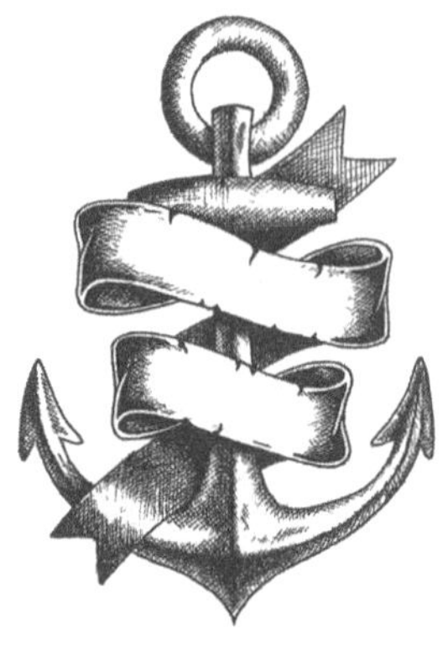

CHAPTER 23

ONCE MORE INTO THE ENGLISH CHANNEL

AUGUST 10, 1778

Captain Jones had given much thought time to the attitude of Captain Landais of the *Alliance* but decided to tolerate the French captain's attitude of defiance. In the second meeting he outlined his plan to add platforms for the marines to stand on just below the top spars on the masts of each of the ships. That addition had worked well for him on the *Ranger* and he wanted that advantage for each of the new ships.

He was aware during the meeting that Captain Landais was being uncharacteristically silent, but his facial expression spoke volumes. When the meeting was over he asked him to stay for some private discussion. As the others left, Captain Landais remained in his seat at the table.

John Burroughs came over to John Paul and asked, "Would you like for me to stay?"

"No, thank you," John Paul responded. "I think we will be fine."

When the room had cleared he turned to Captain Landais and asked, "You were very quiet during the meeting. Is there something you would like to say to me?"

Captain Landais looked hard at John Paul and responded, "Building platforms up above the sails is an idea designed to get us all killed. The British and French have always kept muskets away from the sails. Don't you know that a musket spits fire when you pull the trigger? One spark onto a sail can send the entire ship up in flames."

"I know it is a risk," replied John Paul. "Every ship we have is at a disadvantage when we face off with a British ship of the line. They have more cannons that we have, and they have a more experienced and disciplined crew. Yet, I'm not sure I would have won a battle since I have been in British waters without the marines scattering musket balls on the decks of the prizes we have taken. The sharp shooters give us an advantage against the British. When we take out their officers and helmsmen, it is like cutting off the head of the snake. They are dead in the water for our taking."

"That sounds good, but I am not about to risk my ship and my crew to a careless marine who sets my ship on fire," Landais responded.

"Captain Landais," said John Paul. "I have already ordered that the platforms be built on the Aliance, just like I have on the *Vengeance* and the *Pallas*. You will have forty to fifty marines on the *Alliance*. You will have to decide how best to use them. As for the other ships, we will all be drilling our marines on getting into position to command the top decks of every ship we come in contact with."

When the meeting was over John Paul sat for a while alone at the big table. He could feel the agitation in his blood. Captain Landais was easy to dislike. He was also an experienced sea captain. So far, he had been negative on everything John Paul had presented, but at least he was holding his tongue in front of the others. John Paul was determined to find something positive that his French captain could contribute that would be of benefit to the small fleet. He might feel an urge to discipline him and send him back to America but he really hadn't done anything wrong…yet.

Refitting the three ships for marine sharp shooters up among the sails was going slower than expected and John Paul decided to make one more run up into the English Channel as a solo while the work was on-going. The *Bonhomme Richard* was under construction like the other three ships, so John Paul decided to take the *Ranger* out one more time before turning it over to its next captain and crew.

It felt good to feel the sea moving under the keel again. The *Ranger* sailed through the entry to the inlet just as the sun came up behind the ship. The wind was light but in his face, coming directly from the west. The sailing master had tacked the ship back and forth three times to take advantage of the wind before the *Ranger* was able to turn north just inside Ushant Island. They sailed for about two hours before sighting Finisterre Point at the extreme west edge of the English Channel. When he cleared the far west edge of the point and turned east he could feel the wind begin to catch the sails and the ship began to move forward at an increasing pace.

By now the ship was in full sun and he could see St.-Poi-de-Leon off to the starboard side of the ship. Guernsey and the other Channel Islands would soon be in sight. His plan was to stay close to the French coast and to sail all the way up to the port of Boulogne at the east edge of the Channel before turning back.

By the third day of sailing, the watch had sighted Boulogne off the starboard side and the sailing master wasted no time turning north to begin trolling back to the east. Turning north slowed the ship and required re-rigging the fore and aft sails. With every turn of the rudder the sailing master was shouting instructions to the sailors manning the sails.

By the afternoon of the fifth day the *Ranger* was sailing into a direct head wind as they made their way back west. Making any progress at all required tacking back and forth, first north, then south. The look-out in the crow's nest had sighted no sails.

Late in the afternoon that day, a light rain began to fall and, if that wasn't enough to contend with, just at dusk John Paul could see a heavy fog coming in. It was obvious that no sighting would occur in the weather that was approaching. Rather than continue to fight the wind and having to tack back and forth blind in the fog, John Paul chose to drop anchor and roll up the sails. Considering the depth of the Channel, he knew he would not catch anything with his anchor that would hold them fast, but the added weight and depth would help keep the *Ranger* from moving too far from their present position. He knew there were no islands or sandbars in the middle of the Channel so there was no place to run aground. He felt safe just drifting there.

Except for the crow's next watch, he sent everyone below decks for supper and soon followed them. All were in bed for the night and John Paul was sleeping soundly when he felt someone touch his shoulder and say his name.

"Captain Jones," the voice said. It was Jim. "You need to come up on deck right away. We have big trouble all around us."

John Paul pulled on his pants and boots and followed Jim up to the main deck. He could see immediately what the problem was. The fog was still heavy around the ship but everywhere he looked he could see lights. Looking closer he could make out the vague outline of ships, big ships. The *Ranger* had drifted into a fleet of man-of-war ships, probably sent out by the British Admiralty to find him. John Paul knew he had but one course of action and it would require every crew member to do his job flawlessly. It would also require a goodly amount of Yankee luck.

"Jim," he whispered. "Go to the men's quarters and get the men headed to their battle stations. Tell them, not a word."

Jim was gone to the lower deck as John Paul climbed up to the bridge. He approached the helmsman and whispered, "Can you see your way clear to turn us around?"

The helmsman had not noticed the fleet of man-of-war ships until Jim had pointed them out to him. He had pure panic on his face. John Paul grabbed his arm.

"Get ahold of yourself, man," he said in as low a voice as he could muster and still make himself understood. "If we get out of this mess it will be because of your skills in manipulating a ship in almost no wind. We need to turn this ship around before any of the Britishers know we are here."

With mention of his skills, the helmsman's pride took hold and he seemed to take heart. John Paul could see the determination flooding his face. The seamen were already spilling out of the gangways onto the deck. Many were climbing the rope ladders to their places along the spars at the top of the masts.

John Paul knew that one slip, such as making contact with one of the British ships or even getting close enough to them that they could be identified as not a part of their flotilla, would mean disaster.

The helmsman motioned Captain Jones over to him and whispered, "Sir, the best way for us to get out of this mess is to back the ship up away from the two ships that are on either side of us. To do that I need the two sails from the main mast dropped into place."

John Paul saw immediately what the helmsman had in mind. He was going to drop the sails to allow them to catch what wind was stirring on the back side of the sails and to let the ship back up into the fog. Once there was enough distance between the *Ranger* and the two man-of-war ships on either side of them, he would push the rudder full right or left to cause the ship to turn. Once turned they would drop the rest of the sails and disappear into the fog in front of the flotilla of British ships.

John Paul gave the signal to the men who had taken their places up the main sail, and the sails were dropped. When they were secured he could see the wind filling them from the back side and felt the *Ranger* begin to move.

Unfortunately, when the sails dropped they made the characteristic sound that comes with making a ship ready to get underway. When John Paul heard that sound he also heard voices from the ships on both sides of them. They had heard the sails drop. They were trying to make them out in the fog. The *Ranger* only needed a few more seconds and they would be clear.

John Paul was holding his breath that Jim's vigilance was going to give the edge they needed to get the *Ranger* turned, the rest of their sails dropped, and the ship headed off into the fog before anyone knew they were there or at least knew who they were.

He watched as the helmsman manipulated the wheel, a little this way and then a little that way. The challenge he faced was to allow the ship to move backward without moving to either side. Ships were not made to sail backwards. The maneuver the helmsman was taking the ship through was not one that was practiced nor one most would have had any experience with. Still, as John Paul watched he felt the ship moving backward and saw the lights of the two ships on either side of them fading into the fog.

John Paul was thankful that he had a veteran crew who had been with him for several months. As soon as they arrived on deck, they knew the jeopardy they were in and knew also that silence was their best weapon right now. Captain Jones was giving orders strictly with hand signals from the bridge. The crew was in place and alert to every movement of their captain's hand. They climbed the rope ladders up the two main masts and waited for the captain's hand signal. When it came, the sails would drop as one and began immediately to catch the wind. It wasn't a strong wind but being the first ship to drop sails and catch the wind would give them several seconds head start should any of the man-of-war ships realize who they were and want to give chase.

Finally, the ship began to turn, and seconds passed as the *Ranger* swung to the left, slowed to a stop, and then continued turning. When the ship was almost turned around, the helmsman nodded to Captain Jones and he gave the hand signal. When he did the sound of the rest of the sails dropping was enough to bring additional voices from the two ships closest to them. John Paul smiled to himself. They were already too late to catch the *Ranger*. He felt the wind catch the sails and the ship began to move on the water. Within seconds they were away into the fog. With their gray sails it was likely that the lookouts on the British ships would never catch sight of them again.

It was several hours later when the sun burned off the fog and they had enough visibility to see land in the distance. They made their way south to the French coast and sailed into the port at Boulogne. Once inside the port John Paul walked over to the rail and sat down. It seemed the first time he had taken a deep breath since Jim had touched his shoulder several hours before.

John Paul thought about Jim and wondered what sixth sense had alerted him that something was wrong and brought him up on the deck to the chilling sight of two man-of-war ships anchored within feet of their position. He wanted to pat Jim on the back, promote him, praise him, pay him, give him something big and worthy. Jim had saved the ship, saved having an entire crew end up in a British jail and, most likely, saved John Paul from the end of a rope.

He knew Jim was down in the galley with Jubal working up a meal for the men. John Paul fought the urge to go down where he was and thank him face to face, to make sure all the men knew that it was his vigilance that saved the ship and all aboard. Instead, he sat down at the desk in his quarters and wrote out a proclamation to honor Jim.

Later that day, when he had all the men assembled on the deck, he told them of Jim's role in saving them all. They joined together in a "Hip, Hip, Hooray" for the young man. When they finished, John Paul issued his proclamation. He asked the sailing master to read it to the crew.

PROCLAMATION

Know ye all that Jim Shelton is a hero of the Ranger. The Ranger has had many heroes during the time we have been sailing together but none more important than this young man. The Ranger has always sailed with a first and second mate on board. Henceforth, there shall be a third mate and his name is Jim Shelton. Further, any prize taken on our way back to our home port will result in a bounty of one-half pound from each seaman that will be given to Jim Shelton for his yeoman service to this ship's company and saving us all from a British jail, or worse.

Jim was obviously embarrassed by all of the accolades. His face was red under his yellow hair and he kept shaking his head, sure they were making way too much over his contribution. John Paul knew they weren't.

Jim was much on John Paul's mind over the next few days. He thought of his own service on various ships going back a decade and more. He had started as a cabin boy at the age of thirteen, happy to get enough to eat each day. Jim had started just a few months younger. Now, Jim was sixteen. He had worked in the early days for the surgeons when they were in battle. Then he moved up to powder boy, supplying the gunnery people what they needed to keep the cannons firing. He was the swimmer they trusted earlier when they needed to give Admiral Howe and his man-of-war the slip. On this fateful night, he seemed to sense trouble was afoot and went up on deck to see if something was amiss.

John Paul asked Jim what it was that prompted him to go on deck.

Jim said, "Sir, as I lay in my bunk, I was used to hearing the waves hitting the side of the ship but that night there was a second sound as well. It sounded more like an echo of the waves hitting the ship, fainter and not at all in rhythm with the sounds I was used to hearing. I wasn't sure what it was but knew it was different and not as it should be. I came to the deck not knowing what was wrong but when I walked over to the rail the sound of the waves told me where to look. The lantern lights on the closest man-of-war could be picked out in the fog. When I looked closer I could see the shape of the British ship looming above the *Ranger*."

Even the helmsman did not see the man-of-war ships that surrounded them in the fog, but Jim did. He sensed their presence and could sound the alarm before the *Ranger* was discovered, silent though it needed to be. John Paul thought, *That boy was going to make a great sea captain. Oh yes, a great sea captain.*

The trip back west on the English Channel toward Brest was without threat from the British. They did find two British merchant ships that made worthy prizes to take back with them. They took both without firing a shot, put a new crew on them and set the officers and crews afloat in two long boats. They had experienced other trips that were more profitable and some that were less so. It was good to go home with something to show for their efforts.

When they were back home the highlight would not be sharing the prize money, though young Jim was now a major beneficiary of the bounty. The highlight would be John Paul telling Aimee what Jim had done and the response of the men to his vigilance. The look of pride on her face would, by far, be the greatest reward he would ever have, even if he lived to be one hundred years old.

THE PROVIDENCE GAZETTE

PROVIDENCE, Rhode Island, April 3, 1779—The war continues to go bad in the south. The British have captured Augusta, Georgia.

The British also have captured and burned Portsmouth and Norfolk, Virginia.

On a positive note, General George Rogers Clark defeated the British at Vincennes, Indiana.

Spain has entered the war as an ally of France. They continue to provide supplies to the U.S. but have offered no troops or ships thus far. This may prove to be significant as the war continues.

General George Washington's army has been wintering in Middlebrook, New Jersey. Conditions have been harsh but the troops are again on the march.

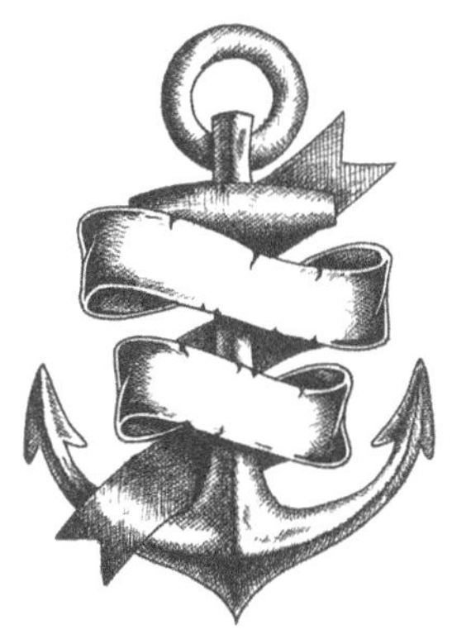

CHAPTER 24

THE BRITISH ARE COMING

MAY 1, 1779

Dawn was just breaking over the bay when John Paul sat up in bed. Aimee was still asleep beside him, but he was hearing something in the distance that made him come wide awake in just a few seconds. It was cannon fire.

He was into his pants and boots and down the steps to the front door in seconds. Standing a few steps down the walkway, he could see almost the full expanse of the bay. In the distance, down near the entrance of the inlet, he could see the smoke of cannon fire. Some of the sounds he was hearing were familiar. He knew the sounds made by the cannons he had placed at the entrance of the inlet shortly after he had taken up residence in Brest. The other sounds were, obviously, coming from ships just outside the inlet entrance. When he arrived in Brest he thought it was just a matter of time before the British came looking for him. Evidently, today was the day.

He hurried back inside and slipped on his blue uniform coat, which was hanging on a hook in the hall. Jim had come down the stairs fully dressed and ready to go and Aimee emerged from the kitchen holding two mugs of hot tea and a chunk of bread for each of them. There was no time for breakfast, but the tea and bread would hold them for now.

"Jim," said John Paul. "You run ahead and ring the bell. We need every man-jack of all four crews headed for their ships."

The bell was the warning system that told everyone in the village that trouble was coming. In earlier years, pirate ships had come into Brest Harbor and raided the village. The British also had come a time or two with their man-of-war ships that carried more than one hundred cannons.

John Paul soon was standing on the wharf and, one by one, the other three captains arrived. There was no reason to question who was at the entry to the bay. The British were there and by the sounds of the cannons, there were at least four of them and maybe more.

Captain Landais was the last to arrive and as he joined the others, John Paul launched into the battle plan. "When you get underway," he said. "I want you to form a battle line following the *Ranger*. We will move back and forth across the entry just inside the bay. Our target will be the closest ship. With all cannons aimed at just one ship, we should be able to disable it pretty quickly. When it moves or disappears under the waves, we will focus on the next closest target."

"What if several of the man-of-war ships come straight at us and breaks our line?" asked Landais sarcastically. "What will happen to your plan then?"

It was all John Paul could do to keep from hitting him in the mouth. He asked a good question, but the tone of his voice spoke volumes. Landais had heard the order but didn't care for it. He knew in a face-to-face battle with four or five man-of-war British ships their little fleet didn't stand a chance.

John Paul turned to Captain Landais and responded in an even voice. "You asked a good question, Captain Landais. We are in no danger of having one of those bigger ships enter our bay and break our line. They can do whatever they want out in the open seas, even blockade us where we can't get out. But when we came to Brest we did two things to protect our bay. We put cannons on the points both north and south. It gives us a stable setting from which to harass anyone attempting to enter Brest Bay without invitation. Those cannons not only protect us, but they can give us warning as they have this morning."

Captain Landais nodded. "And the other?"

"As a second precaution," continued John Paul, "we hauled rocks from the shoreline out into the entry of the inlet. We built up the floor of the entry until the clearance was just enough for our ships and smaller merchant ships to enter. It is not deep enough for any man-of-war to get through the entry into the bay. Their draft is too deep. If they try to enter, they will scrape the bottom out of their ships. I'm sure their sailing master knows that from their lead line. They need twenty-two feet of clearance to pass through, but our entry only gives them a half twain, about fifteen feet."

By this point, Captain Landais had taken off his hat and was bowing toward John Paul with each sentence. "I can see you have taken precautions to protect us, Captain Jones," he said, still with an unmistakable twinge of sarcasm. "It will be a pleasure to follow you into battle."

John Paul acknowledged the Frenchman with a curt nod and turned to look into the faces of his other two captains. He continued, "We can defend our bay both from our ships and from the points on either side of the entry. We may take cannon fire from them, but we can return better than we get. Our four ships in a line of battle can broadside with more than seventy cannons and when we turn about we can give them seventy more. We have clearance inside the entry to move back and forth freely. They are not sure how much room they have below the waterline and must be careful. The more careful they are the more stable and that means an easier target. At the same time, we will be moving on the water and thus they will have a moving target."

It took almost thirty minutes to get the four ships underway. In the meantime, the sounds of battle near the entry of the inlet continued. John Paul thought to himself that all the British were doing was exhausting their ammunition. They couldn't reach his ships from there and it was going to be very difficult to do much damage to the shore batteries. Cannons on ship board were always moving with the waves. Having accuracy with their cannons depended on being close enough that they could see the officers and crew on the other vessel. They needed to fire at point blank range. By contrast, a shore battery was stable. They could fire at a target, adjust the loft and aim of the cannon, and fire again. Accuracy was much better. A ship on the high seas was at a great disadvantage.

The four Continental Navy ships moved toward the entry to the harbor in a line with the *Alliance* following the *Ranger* and the *Pallas* between the *Alliance* and the *Vengeance*. John Paul knew this alignment would give him the best chance of doing the most damage to the small flotilla of man-of-war ships sitting just outside the entry to the bay.

As they moved closer to the entry, they could see that there were five man-of-war ships in the waters outside the entry of the bay. Two were clustered on each side of the entry firing at the shore batteries. The fifth ship was sitting silent back in the distance, probably commanded by one admiral or another from the British Navy. He was, no doubt, watching the action and planning his next move.

The wind was in their face as they approached the entry. If they had been sailing out to face the man-of-war fleet, ship to ship, having the wind in their face would have been a great disadvantage. However, they had no intention of moving across the entry of the bay. To make headway they needed to tack back and forth, and that process started as soon as they were close to the entry. Their progress north and south would not be fast, but it would put the British at a disadvantage as they tried to keep their cannons aimed toward four moving targets. In the meantime, the U.S. ships were able to fire their cannons in a broadside over and over, sending hundreds of cannon balls flying across the deck and into the hulls of the larger ships. The three larger American ships focused on the hulls and decks of the bigger British ships, while the *Vengeance* used its smaller caliber cannons and several deck guns on the sails of the closest man-of-war.

The battle raged back and forth for three hours and, finally, the British ships withdrew to join the one distant ship. By this time, they were badly battered, with sails hanging and many casualties.

John Paul ordered his first mate to signal his three ships to withdraw to the center of the bay. What would the five British ships do, knowing they couldn't enter the bay and that they were being battered not only by the four smaller Continental Navy ships as well as the very accurate shore batteries?

John Paul thought he knew what their next tactic would be. All gunships, British or American, carried large numbers of marines on board for boarding and hand-to-hand fighting. John Paul had always used his marines as sharp shooters firing from the top of the masts onto the deck of the ships he had targeted. Those tactics were of little value in this type of sea battle. Their muskets could not shoot accurately from this distance.

The British did not use their marines as sharp shooters. They stayed mostly below decks out of harm's way. But if the British could get them on shore, they could come up behind the shore batteries and neutralize the cannons on the north and south points. Then, they could move inland and attack the city of Brest. John Paul thought it likely that putting the marines on shore would be their next tactic and the time to do that most effectively was at night when they could launch their long boats without being seen.

When the five British man-of-war ships had withdrawn beyond cannon range, John Paul resolved to do the same thing. His first mate used the bullhorn to call for a meeting in the middle of the bay for the four captains. John Paul watched from the bridge as three long boats brought the captains to the *Ranger*.

When all were together on the bridge, John Paul asked, "They have withdrawn to lick their wounds and plan their next strategy. Do any of you have thoughts on what that might be?"

John Burroughs spoke first. "They have been hunting for you for months, so it is not likely they will withdraw and go home. They can't get at us through the entry of the inlet, so they might just be satisfied to blockade our bay and keep us away from their shipping."

The other two captains nodded their heads at John Burroughs's comments. Captain Landais added, "If they do blockade us, we are pretty well done. We can't leave the safety of the bay and face off with them with any hope of success."

John Paul looked at the three faces, waiting for any other comment. None was coming.

"I think they will send a landing party and try to attack us at our base in Brest," John Paul said. "We have about one hundred and eighty marines on board our ships and they are of little use to us in this kind of battle. The British have about twice that many marines on board those five man-of-war ships. Like ours, they are just sitting in the hold playing dominos while all of this is going on. If we watch closely I think we will see them leave to the north, one ship at a time, and return several hours later. There is a small inlet just north of us where they could muster their marines. A half day's march south would put them on the hill above Brest."

"That would make a lot of sense," John Burroughs replied.

"That may not be their plan, but I think we should get our marines on land and plan for an invasion from the north," said John Paul. "I believe they are planning a surprise party for us, but I think we can put together a welcoming reception for them that will spoil their party."

John Paul turned to young Jim, who had been listening to the discussion with great interest and said, "Jim, ask Major Whitlow to come to the bridge. I think you will find him in the hold with his men."

Jim disappeared, and John Paul turned back to the captains. "Gentlemen, let's start with the *Vengeance* and see if we can get our marines from each of the ships ashore in Brest without the British figuring out what we are doing. Captain Briggs, once you get your marines unloaded, come back to this location as soon as you can. We don't want to tip them off that we are on to their little scheme."

When Major Whitlow arrived on the bridge, John Paul took him down to the captain's cabin where he had maps that would be of use in a discussion of strategy. While John Paul and Major Whitlow were talking, the three captains returned to their ships and had similar discussions with their marines.

It took about two hours for the ships to unload their marines at the wharf in Brest and return to the middle of the bay. John Paul watched through his spyglass from the bridge as the marines moved slowly up the hill above Brest, well out of sight of the British ships. It took about twenty minutes for the last marine to disappear over the hill. They were moving with purpose. Fighting men are always anxious to get into the fray and detest being left below decks while the action is going on above them. Quickly briefed by Major Whitlow, they now had a mission and a purpose.

John Paul fought the urge to go with them. He had briefed Major Whitlow on what the best outcome for the mission would be and hoped the wily veteran military man could make it happen. He knew that if he went along he would itch to take command when the fighting started, and Major Whitlow was far more experienced in land operations.

John Paul kept a wary eye on the man-of-war ships and soon realized the tactic was just as he predicted. One would leave for a while and then return to be followed by the next. He counted in his mind the number of marines each British ship would carry, and the total came to more than four hundred. That would be double the number of marines he had just watched disappear over the hill just north of Brest. His troops would be badly outnumbered. But Major Whitlow told him that he and several of his officers had gone hunting in the area just north of Brest several times. They knew the lay of the land. He assured John Paul that familiarity with the terrain and the element of surprise would even the odds significantly.

Jim, as usual, was not far from John Paul. He was leaning on the rail just behind the helmsman. John Paul looked toward the young man and their eyes met. He waved him over.

"Jim, I have a job for you," John Paul said. "I need you to go into Brest and bring the mayor back with you. Take the dinghy and be back with him as soon as you can."

Jim, pleased to have something of importance to do, said, "Yes sir, Captain Jones. I will be gone and back before you know it."

John Paul watched young Jim as he rowed the small boat toward shore. The *Ranger* was about five hundred yards off-shore and once Jim reached shore he still had about a half mile to walk to get to Brest. One could hope the mayor would be in his office but, if not, Jim would need to hunt for him.

It seemed like a very long time before John Paul saw young Jim and the mayor in the dinghy coming directly from the wharf toward the *Ranger*. It took about twenty minutes for the long boat to arrive alongside and John Paul went to the rail above the rope ladder to welcome the mayor.

When the two men were back on the bridge, John Paul turned to his first mate who spoke passable French and began to outline for the mayor what was happening. The conversation moved slowly through the translator but John Paul did his best to assure him that the town had nothing to fear from the five British ships. They couldn't get through the entry. However, John Paul stood by and watched the Mayor's expression change as the translator shared the captain's suspicions that more than four hundred British marines had landed just north of the city and would head south under cover of darkness.

"What will we do?" the Mayor responded. "Should we tell the people to leave the city for their own safety? What about the elderly and the children? I was afraid of this when you brought the *Ranger* to Brest. Now, with these other three ships, it is just worse."

The mayor began to speak very rapidly and the translator was struggling to keep up.

"It was only a matter of time before the British figured out where you were and sent their man-of-war fleet after you. Now we are caught in a crossfire between the Americans and the British. What will we do?" the Mayor delivered the last sentence almost in a whisper.

John Paul did his best not to smile while the mayor expressed his disfavor with the situation. The city of Brest had benefited significantly from the presence of the presence of the *Ranger*. In fact, the mayor himself had become a wealthy man because of the arrival of British merchant ships and their rich cargos.

"Mr. Mayor," said John Paul. "We have already sent our marines to intercept the British we believe have landed north of us. My primary concern is two-fold. First, if our effort to hold the British off fails, what is the best thing to do for the people. Second, if we succeed, it is likely that we will have a significant number of prisoners we need to take care of. We can handle the security of that, but we need a place to hold them and they will need food and water as well as medical services."

The mayor considered what John Paul had said and then responded. "Captain Jones, I will call my council together to see what can be done to help. However, this is a problem you and your people have created, and you need to take care of it."

"Mr. Mayor," John Paul replied. "This problem belongs to all of us. You talk to your council and I will be interested in their response. You need to do it now. If all goes as planned, we will have prisoners on site as early as tomorrow night. Some of them will be injured and all of them will need food and water as well as shelter. You need to do whatever you can to help."

After the mayor had left the bridge to be ferried back to shore by young Jim, John Paul instructed his carpenter to bring up the spare sails and to contact the other ships to do the same. John Paul said, "If we end up bringing a large number of prisoners back to Brest, we need to be able to build tents to house them. The spare sails will provide a start in solving that problem."

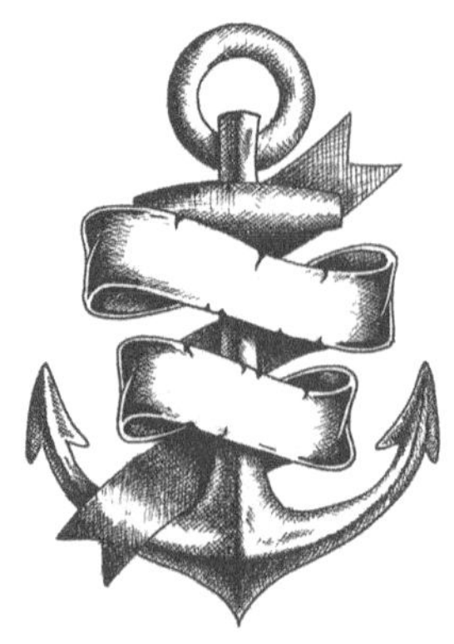

CHAPTER 25

THE TRAP

MAY 3, 1779

Time moved slowly for the officers and crew aboard the four American ships in the bay at Brest. John Paul thought and rethought his strategy. The look-outs kept watch on the British ships about a mile outside the entry to the inlet. Like the American ships, they remained clustered together. Night came and went and still they watched. There was no word from the marines John Paul had sent off on a mission to confront a force twice their number. If things went wrong, it could turn out to be a suicide mission.

The day went slowly with no movement of the British ships and no word from Major Whitlow and the marines. John Paul went over his options again and again. Having committed his marines to this land mission, he had few options left. If the British marines won the day in a battle with Major Whitlow and his marines, the British would be over the hill above the town and resistance would be futile. Surrender would take no more than an hour or two. His ships were momentarily safe in the bay but with the town in British hands and the entry to the inlet blocked they could starve them out in a couple of weeks.

The tension was almost to a breaking point on the ships. John Paul decided to send someone ashore to take a horse over the hill to make contact with Major Whitlow. Jim was the logical choice. If the news was bad, at the very least Jim would have a chance to escape the British on horseback to the east. He couldn't stand the thought of the boy being in a British jail. If the news was good, he could bring it back much faster on horseback.

It took them just a few minutes to get the small lifeboat over the rail and into the water. Jim climbed down the rope ladder into the boat. Just as he was ready to cast off, Jubal leaned over the rail and dropped down a sack of what John Paul was sure would be some food in case Jim was not able to return to the ship. John Paul watched as Jim rowed the boat ashore, landing just west of the town as he had before. John Paul watched him through the spyglass as he disappeared into the town.

It seemed like way too long before John Paul saw movement north of the town. A quick look through the spyglass told the story. It was Jim, on horseback, riding toward the crest of the hill. When he was out of sight John Paul lowered the glass and walked over to the rail. He sat down for what seemed like the first time all day.

Afternoon moved slowly into dusk and into darkest night. John Paul went to his cabin and tried to get some sleep. His body was exhausted, but his mind was racing. If Jim brought back good news he was sure what his next steps would be. If not, everything would be in chaos. The other captains would be looking for direction from him, a new plan, something that would, at the very least, provide escape for the seamen of their small fleet. Perhaps they could wait until the dead of night and try to run the blockade. Maybe one or two of them would make it through. The chances were not good but just maybe. If not, perhaps they could beach their ships on the south side of the bay and make their way overland to Quimper, the next port south. They could torch the ships to keep them out of British hands. At least they would avoid languishing in a British jail. If he lost four American ships in such a trap it was not likely he would ever get another command.

He tried hard to keep thoughts of Aimee and the children out of his mind but they kept creeping in. There seemed to be no other solution than to bring all of the families of the seamen on board and take them south with the ships if they had to run for it. Many of the seamen had the same problem he had with family on shore. Though very few had brought family from the states, dozens had married since they had come to Brest. His family and the others were a serious problem. At best, getting the families on board and then overland to Quimper would be a serious problem. At worst, they might be caught on land heading south by the British marines and be forced to fight in the open.

The more he thought, the more he realized there were no good choice other than a victory for the marines, even despite the odds against them. Everything rode on this contingent of one hundred and eighty men winning a battle against twice that many well-drilled and disciplined British troops. No matter how he tried, sleep was not likely to come.

After a restless few hours, John Paul was up before dawn the next morning. With the first rays of the sun he was looking at the ridge above the town through his spyglass. Nothing. Jubal brought him a cup of strong tea and some bread and butter and he sat on the rail at the back of the bridge. He was about half way through his mug of tea when he sensed movement on the ridge. He picked up his spyglass and walked over to the starboard rail. He scanned the ridgetop and saw men there and, shortly, more men. They were not dressed in the uniform of the American marines. It was, obviously, a large number of British soldiers. They had failed. His men had been defeated and the British were moving down the ridge toward Brest. His heart sank. Now what? Now what, indeed.

He scanned over to the far left of the group with his spyglass. There he saw several men in the familiar American marine uniforms. Then, he saw someone on horseback. It was Jim. He looked back at the men to the far left and could make out that they were carrying muskets. He scanned back to the first group he had seen, and though he strained his one eye through the spyglass, he could see no weapons.

A feeling of complete relief swept over him, leaving him feeling almost weak at the knees. They had won! Somehow, by some miracle, they had won. The men he had first seen were prisoners. He felt himself almost collapse against the rail. He was looking at a growing mass of humanity coming over the ridge but at the far right and left there were familiar uniforms. The British men in the middle were being brought back to Brest as prisoners of the Continental Navy! He looked one more time, hoping to see Major Whitlow and his standard three-cornered hat, but he wasn't to be seen. John Paul couldn't wait to pin a medal on his chest. What a victory! What a turn of events!

Before he could think about it, he had climbed the ladder down to the main deck and ordered a dinghy over the side. Then, he was down the rope ladder and into the boat. It was the first time he had rowed a boat in quite a while but he had not forgotten how. He headed for the wharf but couldn't resist the urge to look over his shoulder every few minutes to see the men still coming over the ridge above the city. They kept coming and coming, by the hundreds. He made a mental calculation and came up with one hundred and eighty of his marines and another four hundred or so of the British. There were a total of almost six hundred men. Mercifully, his group had the muskets and the British were walking empty-handed.

When he landed the dinghy at the wharf he tied it up and climbed up to street level. He walked quickly toward the hillside just to the west of the city where the throng of marines, both American and British, were headed. From the distance he could see Major Whitlow at the front of the contingent of marines on the western edge of the mass of men. Major Whitlow held up his hand to stop the men and using his hands as sign language he sat them all down in the high grass.

By then John Paul was moving across in front of the group of prisoners. He was dressed in his captain's uniform with its gold braid, a three-cornered hat similar to that of Major Whitlow on his head. It was obvious to the prisoners that he was someone important.

When he approached Major Whitlow, the marine leader turned and came to attention. His salute was sharp and returned by Captain Jones. Then Jones put out his hand and a smile spread across his face.

"I canna wait to hear ye story," said John Paul in his best Scottish accent. He was very much aware that he was within hearing distance of a number of the British prisoners and for some reason of which he wasn't yet sure, he wanted them to know he was a Scot.

Suddenly, John Paul had a hundred unanswered questions. "How did you manage to capture these British marines? Where are your wounded?"

Right then young Jim rode up on his horse, slid out of the saddle and came to stand next to John Paul. John Paul grabbed him and pulled him to him in a quick hug.

"You were a sight for sore eyes when you crested that hill on your horse. Seeing you in the distance through the spyglass was the first I knew that we were not being invaded by four hundred Britishers," he said.

Jim smiled and said, "Captain Jones, sir, there was nothing for me to do except follow along. When I found Major Whitlow they already had the prisoners in tow."

John Paul turned back to Major Whitlow. "So, Major Whitlow," he said. "How did you make this victory occur, and with no injuries?"

Major Whitlow came back to attention and began to report very much in a military manner.

Before Major Whitlow hardly got a word out, John Paul put his hands up and said. "Please be at ease, sir. I want every detail and if you persist in standing at attention you may be there for a very long time. Just tell me what happened."

"Well sir," he started. "As you know, we have been here in Brest for several months. Several of our officers are avid hunters and we have hunted the hills north of Brest at least once a week. We know the lay of the land up there pretty well. There is a long ravine about half way between here and the north shore with two high ridges on either side. I figured that the British marines would have to come through that ravine on the way south toward Brest and that was the place to set a trap. It helped that they were moving south in the dead of night."

"So, how did you spring the trap?" said John Paul.

"Sir, we took a chapter out of the Bible," he replied. "You will find the story in the book of Judges. We gave every other man a torch which meant that we had about ninety torches spaced along the two ridges. I took a contingent of twenty men and we placed ourselves at the south end of the ravine. When the British were all in the ravine and the first group were beginning to climb the hill at the south end, we stepped out from our hiding place and lit several torches in front of them. That was the signal for the torches on the ridges to be lit and for all of the men on the ridges to yell and make noise."

"So, they were looking up at what must have looked like a thousand soldiers ready to rain fire and brimstone down on them," laughed John Paul.

"You are right, sir," Major Whitlow responded, smiling. "We could see the fear in their faces. I yelled loud enough for all of them to hear, 'Drop your weapons or prepare to die where you stand.' The only sound we heard was the sound of muskets and pistols hitting the ground. We then marched them up the hill out of the ravine with our men on both sides of them and the rest was just an exercise in walking south until we hit the ridge north of Brest."

That was a story that John Paul would enjoy telling Benjamin Franklin and the other leaders of the revolution back in his new country.

"Major Whitlow, have you been able to assess how much in the way of provisions they have with them?" John Paul asked.

"Not very much, sir," he responded. I think they were traveling light, expecting to be able to find enough food in Brest to hold them for quite some time."

"I was afraid of that," John Paul said. "We have just enough for ourselves and I don't know how we are going to take care of four hundred prisoners of war."

John Paul felt the presence of young Jim at his elbow. Jim leaned in and whispered, "Sir, the man-of-war ships were provisioned to handle both the seamen and the marines they had on board. Perhaps you can negotiate food and water enough for these soldiers from their own ships."

John Paul smiled immediately at a good idea. He said, "That, Jim, is a capital idea. That is not the only thing I intend to negotiate for with them."

"Major Whitlow, may I address your prisoners?" asked John Paul.

"Certainly sir," he responded. "These are your prisoners, not mine."

John Paul walked over to the prisoners who were sitting in a large group in the tall grass. He took just a minute and looked over the group and realized there was quiet anticipation to hear what their future might hold.

John Paul spoke in his loudest voice. "Men, my name is John Paul Jones. I am captain of the *Ranger* and the leader of this small fleet of Continental Navy ships. I suspect many of you have heard of me in past months as we have traveled the length and breadth of the waters around the British Isles. "

There was a murmur from the men and many nodded toward him.

John Paul continued. "You are our prisoners and I must confess having you here is a surprise to us all. We are not prepared to feed and house four hundred additional men here at Brest. We know your ships just outside our inlet have food and provisions for you and we are going to go to them and ask that those provisions be provided for you. In the meantime, I suggest that anything you brought with you in the way of water or food be conserved until we can begin to bring your necessities from the ships. If your commanders refuse to help us, you may get very hungry here."

John Paul stopped for a moment and looked over the men again. "Some of you are already thinking about escaping from us. I would caution you that you are on French soil. As you know, Great Britain and France have been at war on and off for a hundred years. You are at war right now with the French. Any direction you run will put you in jeopardy from the French, many of whom have lost loved ones in battles with the British in past years. You will not find many friendly faces here in France. You are safer right here with us where we can trade you for American prisoners of war, than you are trying to run and hide in this part of France."

John Paul stopped for another few seconds and then said, "Do you have any questions for me?"

One man stood up and raised both hands to be recognized. John Paul nodded toward him.

He asked, "Sir, we are out here in the open with no shelter. Unless I am mistaken, there is a storm coming in. Where will you take us to get us out of the weather?"

"It is a good question," John Paul replied. "We are bringing our spare sails in from the four ships and will provide you with the necessities to make tents. We will count on you to make your own shelters with the material and tools we provide.

Another man stood. John Paul recognized him.

"Sir, if I am not impertinent to ask, is that a Scottish accent I am hearing when you speak?"

John Paul smiled to himself. He had hoped they had picked it up, had heard Scotland in his voice as he spoke to them. "It is indeed a Scottish accent. I am a Scot, born and raised in Kirkcudbright. I traveled to the Colonies on a British ship when I was thirteen and have been a proud colonist and servant of the King until these hostilities. I am mindful of the fact that the English have always looked down on their neighbors to the north in Scotland. But, as was the case with William Wallace, Rob Roy McGregor, and Robert the Bruce of history, from time to time a Scot will come along who can take the measure of any Englishman. Consider this one of those times."

When John Paul walked away from the prisoners he suppressed a smile. This group would soon be back in England, but they would not soon forget the ease with which they were captured nor the Scot who held them. The farther away he walked, the more he suppressed an all-out laugh. Finally, he was out of earshot and could laugh out loud. He couldn't wait to tell the story to Aimee.

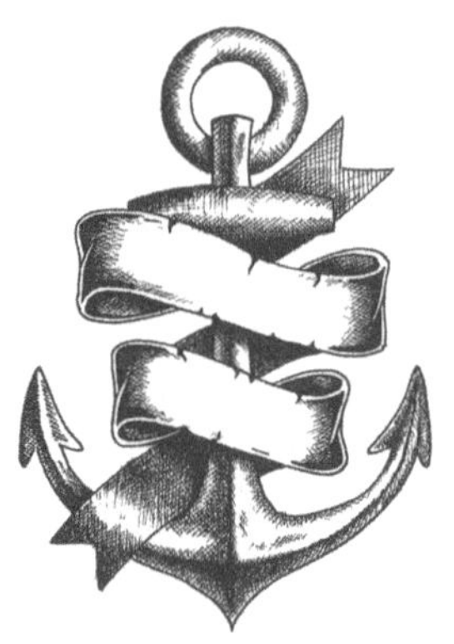

CHAPTER 26
NEGOTIATION
MAY 7, 1779

When John Paul returned to the *Ranger*, he asked that a long boat be made ready to take him, under a flag of truce, to visit the leader of the man-of-war fleet that sat just outside of their inlet.

He knew this was not a time for approaching them with hat-in-hand. He held all the important cards in this poker game. He had their four hundred marines and they couldn't very well go back to England without them. He was also safe within his inlet and they couldn't get to him in their ships and they had few, if any, men left who could invade. The more he thought about it the more he knew he was going to enjoy this face-to-face visit with which ever admiral the British had sent to find him.

John Paul knew that the lookouts for the British man-of-war ships had followed his progress ever since he left the *Ranger*. He was now approaching the flag ship of the five-ship fleet. His long boat flew a white flag and he had little fear that the white flag would not be honored. As much as they might like to capture him, leaving their marines in captivity was way more than they could tolerate and would result in severe measures from the British Admiralty.

John Paul knew that where the British prisoners were being held was out of sight of the five British ships, so he wasn't sure that the leadership knew that their men had been captured. With that in mind, he had brought along the marine officer in charge of the invasion force to be sure there was no mistake.

When John Paul climbed over the rail of the largest of the British ships, they were ready for him. He looked at a full contingent of seamen, marines, and British officers all decked out in their best uniforms and standing at attention. They were making their best effort to intimidate him. It didn't work. He held all the cards for this transaction and he would not be inclined to negotiate. He knew exactly what he wanted from them and he knew he had the collateral to get it.

He heard the murmur from the British seamen as the British marine officer John Paul had brought along climbed over the rail onto the deck and joined him. They recognized immediately who he was, yet the British officers seemed to ignore his presence.

"Captain Jones, I presume," said the ship's captain.

"Yes sir," replied Jones. "To whom do I have the honor of addressing?"

"I am Admiral Howe. I think we have met before, though only at a distance," he responded stiffly.

"I am sure you are right. You chased me halfway across Nantucket Sound once. I think you also tried to catch me at Portsmouth. So, here we meet again."

"Yes, this time I think I have you bottled up where you can't get away," said Admiral Howe.

"Perhaps, sir, but perhaps not. Time will tell," said John Paul.

"It is your white flag, so you called this little tete-a-tete. Why are we meeting?" Admiral Howe asked.

"Well, sir, I am guessing that you have realized that we have captured the contingent of marines you sent to raid Brest," Jones said.

His comment generated a murmur among the men and, immediately, one of the men closest to Admiral Howe leaned over to him and whispered in his ear.

"Yes, we are aware," he replied. "I see you have one of our officers with you. Have you come to bring him back to purchase your freedom from the inlet?"

"Not at all," replied John Paul. "We have your men and we intend to keep them. However, we do have a problem you can help us solve."

"Pray tell, what is that?" Admiral Howe responded.

"We did not anticipate having four hundred visitors to take care of, so we have your men but we do not have the necessary food or water to provide for their sustenance," said John Paul.

"How is that our problem, Captain Jones?" asked Admiral Howe.

"Well, of course, it isn't," said John Paul. "That is, unless you want to prevent them from starving to death."

Again there was a murmur from the seamen who lined the far side rail.

John Paul let his comment hang in the air for a few seconds before he continued.

"Admiral Howe, we have your men but we don't want them. We do not have the proper provisions for keeping prisoners at Brest or anywhere else in France. If we keep them for any length of time at all, we will have to disperse them to French jails all across the northern area of France. I am sure once in French jails they will not see the light of day again until this war that seems to go on forever is long over. You know about French jails and you know the French have no love for the British. The chances of any of these men seeing British soil again is very small."

That comment finally generated a series of whispered conversations among the British officers. When they finished, Admiral Howe turned back to John Paul.

"Captain Jones," he said, "we would ask your indulgence for a few minutes while I confer with my officers. We will leave this deck and return very shortly."

John Paul did his best to suppress a smile and watched as the admiral and five of his officers left the deck, presumably to the captain's cabin.

While they were gone, John Paul looked over the man-of-war with his educated eye. He had been on a man-of-war before several years ago and things had not changed. This ship was on the cutting edge of the latest in marine technology. He was at once envious. He knew he would never captain such a ship. Just the size of it was overwhelming, with its one hundred and thirty cannons and three masts with three sails each placed just so to catch the wind and not inhibit other sails further back on the ship. No wonder a man-of-war could move over the water at sixteen knots and higher, despite the fact that it was twice the size of any ship in the Continental Navy.

His thoughts were disturbed by the return of the admiral and his officers.

Admiral Howe again spoke to John Paul. "Captain Jones, you have indicated that you don't want to keep the men as prisoners of your country here on French soil. Do you have thoughts on how we can take them off your hands?"

"Admiral Howe," he said, "your government and mine have held prisoner exchanges from time to time. I propose that we exchange these prisoners for our soldiers that you hold in your camps in Portsmouth, Plymouth, Liverpool, and Weymouth. They have been in England now since early in the war and surely you are tired of feeding them by now."

Again, there were whispers back and forth between the officers that clustered around Admiral Howe.

When the whispers quieted, Admiral Howe said, "You are right, Captain Jones, we have several prisoner-of-war camps and many of your soldiers have been there for several years. However, such an exchange would require the approval of the Admiralty in London."

John Paul thought for a few seconds and responded, "Then, I suggest you move as quickly as possible to get approval. We will hold your men until you receive word from London. Tell your Admiralty that we know your men are highly trained and are very valuable to the Crown. Our men are mostly farmers and shop keepers and not trained soldiers. We are pleased to trade one of your men for two of ours."

"Captain Jones," Admiral Howe replied, "I'm sure you know that your demands are highly inappropriate. Our Admiralty will never approve such a demand."

"Perhaps not, Admiral Howe," John Paul responded. "But, never-the-less, those are our terms and they will not change."

Admiral Howe considered the words from the American captain, then said, "It will take us at least a week to sail to London and, if this transaction is approved, which I doubt, another two weeks to sail back to the closest ports, Plymouth and Portsmouth, to pick up the prisoners and come back across the Channel. Now, is there anything else we should discuss?"

"There is the matter of the food and water I mentioned earlier," said John Paul. "I am sure you are right that we will be keeping your men at least for a month and maybe longer. We are not equipped to take care of them and will need your help to have them in any shape to give back to you when the proposed exchange occurs."

"Captain Jones, we are interested in the welfare of our men and will supply you with whatever provisions we can spare," said Admiral Howe. "How do you propose we handle the transfer?"

John Paul thought to himself, This is going even better than I had hoped. He took a couple of steps toward Admiral Howe and said, "Admiral Howe, that is, indeed, a good decision. We are not interested in causing the deaths of any of your men. I think the easiest way to handle getting the provisions to where they need to go is for you to use the long boats you have on board your ships to transport the goods to the south point just below the gun placement. We can help you unload the goods there and then transport them by wagon back to Brest."

Once again the admiral at his officers and after receiving several nods, he again addressed John Paul.

"Captain Jones, we will begin loading the boats as soon as you leave us," he said.

There was a movement of the officers clustered around Admiral Howe indicating that the meeting was over. John Paul, however, did not move. After a few seconds Admiral Howe noted that Jones was still standing in the middle of the deck facing the cluster of officers.

"Is there something else, Captain Jones?" he asked.

"Yes," John Paul replied. "If the Admiralty approves our exchange we both know what to do to make that work for the good of your men. If it doesn't, we will be expecting an invasion by both sea and land from England. We shall spend our time over the next month preparing for such an invasion. A part of that preparation will be to contact our allies in Paris to send troops to Brest in anticipation of the British invading French soil. Suggest to your Admiralty that they consider well their response to our proposal. We will not be caught unaware."

No more words were exchanged between Admiral Howe and Captain Jones. As the British marine captain marine captain climbed over the rail and to the rope ladder that led down the side of the ship to the long boat, John Paul took one more, long look at the deck and the rigging of the man-of-war. Seamen standing close could see the look of admiration on his face and the shake of his head. Then he was gone over the side.

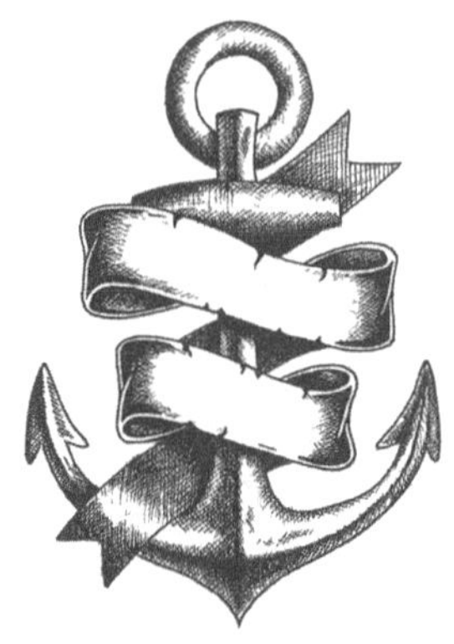

CHAPTER 27
NEW CHALLENGES

MAY 10, 1779

The four weeks that followed the confrontation with Admiral Howe on his flag ship moved slowly. The look-out on the *Ranger* had reported the absence of one of the British ships the morning after John Paul's meeting, presumably to consult with the Admiralty about the proposed prisoner exchange. There was nothing else for them to do but wait.

Under the supervision of Major Whitlow and his men, the British prisoners took the spare sails from the four ships along with wood from the mill in Brest and built tents. It was good that it was summer and, though temperatures could vary in Brest so close to the English Channel, it was tolerable in the tents. It rained the next night, just as the British prisoner who talked with John Paul had predicted. Mercifully, several of the tents were up by then and the men were protected from the inclement weather.

By the time the long boats from the British ships began to arrive at the point below the cannon placements carrying food and water, wagons from Brest were lined up on the road behind the point to carry the goods back to the city. Major Whitlow took charge of handling the food and his men were working both in the city and on guard duty at the prisoner camp.

John Paul sent a report of what had transpired to Benjamin Franklin in Paris with the request that French troops be sent to Brest in case the British decided to invade instead of exchanging prisoners-of-war.

John Paul used the month after the meeting with Admiral Howe to transfer his crew to the *Bonhomme Richard* which had been under renovation almost since its arrival. He also sent the *Ranger* across the Atlantic to report what had happened at Brest and to ask for three ships to transport the eight hundred former prisoners of war back home. Getting the *Ranger* out of the inlet required some additional negotiation with Admiral Howe. John Paul had to give his word that the *Ranger* would not return to British waters. It left under a white flag and turned south immediately down the French coast to take advantage of the prevailing winds and the quickest route home.

John Paul knew that many of the prisoners would be in bad physical shape and in his letter to Stepnen Hopkins and Comodore Esek Hopkins he requested that each of the ships be fully provisioned for three hundred men and that surgeons be sent on each of the ships.

John Paul also knew that it would take the *Ranger* about five weeks to make the trip down the French coast, out to the Azores, across the Atlantic to the Caribbean, and up the American coast. He anticipated their finding Stephen Hopkins, chairman of the Continental Navy Committee, or Commodore Hopkins in Philadelphia. Then, they would have to find enough ships to accommodate eight hundred men, provision them, and head them back across the Atlantic. That whole process would take at least ten weeks and maybe twelve. The small American fleet was not going to be sailing the English Channel this summer looking for prizes. Instead, they were going to be taking care of prisoners-of-war and preparing for an invasion that might or might not come.

John Paul had delegated the responsibilities for taking care of the prisoners to Major Whitlow and the *Bonhomme Richard* was now fully equip and ready for action. He had the luxury of spending most of his day time hours with John Burroughs. Before long it was like old times.

Most days they were either on shipboard or up on the ridge above the city supervising the breastworks they were building to defend the city in case the anticipated invasion materialized. They had stationed sentries along the coast north of them to report any British ship sightings.

In the evenings the two friends would retreat to his home up on the hillside, play with the children, and eat supper together with Aimee. In the early evenings he would walk John Burroughs back down the hill to the city and then return to sit in the parlor with Aimee until bedtime.

Several times he and John Burroughs would find Aimee at one or another of the stores in Brest shopping for groceries or looking for clothes for the children. With four children all growing more rapidly than seemed possible fitting them with clothes was a major issue. It was good that Aimee was good with a sewing needle.

About mid-morning four weeks and a few days after the confrontation with Admiral Howe, the look-out on the *Bonhomme Richard* reported that a long boat was approaching the entry of the inlet with a white flag displayed.

John Paul stood at the rail to meet the messenger from Admiral Howe. The messenger felt no need to climb the rope ladder to report to John Paul. He yelled up to the American captain from his seat in the long boat. It was as he had hoped: The message from Admiral Howe was that the Admiralty had accepted their bargain and ships would arrive within two weeks carrying eight hundred American prisoners-of-war.

John Paul was pleased to receive that report but he sent word to Major Whitlow, who was with his troops guarding the British prisoners, to be vigilant with the sentries they had sent north to keep watch along the coast for the possible invasion that had him worried. He knew that the Admiral could be attempting to lull him to sleep with his report of prisoners due a couple of weeks away. He would love to be able to trust the British, but he didn't.

In the meantime, he had been expecting that French troops would arrive any day in anticipation of the possible invasion. Finally, a letter arrived by courier stating that four hundred French troops had been sent his way with orders to stay in Rennes, about half-way between Paris and

Brest. The message said that should the British, in fact, invade John Paul should send word immediately and they would come the rest of the way to Brest.

John Paul couldn't help but smile. A forced march from Rennes would take about three days. He knew that if the British did invade, it would be with overwhelming numbers and the French evidently were counting on him to hold them off with his one hundred and eighty marines. By the time the French reinforcements arrived almost any British force that came would already have overrun his marines and would have taken Brest and control of the bay.

He had learned in his earlier confrontations with Captain Landais, the French national loaned to the Continental Navy, not to count on the French for anything. Still, all he could do was shake his head and smile. Their country was about to be invaded by the British and all they could spare was four hundred men.

The summer of 1779 passed uneventfully as John Paul and the small American fleet waited for the next development in their stand-off with the British. Either the American prisoners-of-war would arrive and an exchange would be made, or the British army would appear in the seas above the peninsula just north of Brest.

It was early July when three British ships arrived just outside the entry to the Brest Inlet, bringing the number of British ships there to eight. The look-out's excited voice told the entire ship that there were more British ships in their waters. Within an hour a longboat was launched from the lead man-of-war, bearing a white flag. John Paul sent one of his own long boats to meet it and before long his first mate returned to report that the eight hundred American prisoners were on board and ready for transfer.

John Paul sent word to Captain Whitlow to begin moving the British prisoners toward the south point where the exchange would take place. Two hours later, long boats were launched from the British ships carrying the first American prisoners west toward the mouth of the inlet. At the same time, John Paul sent a long boat from each of the American ships in the bay out to the point to help with the exchange. When each of the British long boats emptied it was refilled with British prisoners. Even with ten long boats moving back and forth, it still took about three hours for the prisoner exchange to take place.

When the last American prisoner was ashore, a loud yell went up from the men, both the prisoners and the American marines who had brought the British prisoners to the point.

John Paul arrived at the exchange site just as the last of the American prisoners waded in from the long boats, and he joined in their jubilation. He thought to himself later that he would never forget the sound of more than one thousand voices all yelling at the same time. While the tumult was going on, John Paul took the opportunity to look over the prisoners. He was appalled at their appearance. Most were without shoes and were shirtless. All had gaunt faces as if they had not eaten well in months. That, in fact, turned out to be the case. Reports from the prisoners were that they normally had one meal a day in the prison camp but when they went on board for the trip to France, there was no food for them at all during the five-day transit. Water was made available for them in barrels placed in the hold of the ships. Nine men had died during the trip. Their bodies were thrown over the rail of the ships into the Channel.

By contrast, the British prisoners had been fed well and they looked hale and hearty as they left the make-shift camp just west of Brest to walk to the exchange site below the south point.

John Paul sent Jim back to the city to ask the mayor to send as many locals as possible to help with the prisoners. They needed medical help as well as food and water. By nightfall they would need blankets. Also, with twice as many men to care for, the sail cloth tents were not large enough to accommodate the additional men.

By the time the U.S. prisoners arrived at the POW camp the town's people had already begun setting up to provide food and water for the newly freed men. Most of the men did not even sit down but, instead, went straight to the makeshift tables and began their first meal in almost a week. John Paul watched chaos reign as the men ate everything in sight except the tables and plates. About the time everyone had eaten their fill, a loud roar grew from the men gathered at the eastern edge of the rag-tag group of former prisoners. It spread until it was too loud for John Paul to hear a response when he asked what had brought on this uproar.

Two wagons entered the gathering and proceeded to the edge of the largest tent. They carried barrels of wine, beer and rum, complete with tankards. The men, now on their feet, were making their way toward the wagons as quickly as their weakened condition would allow. Fearing chaos, Major Whitlow took a musket from one of the men close by and fired it into the air. Immediately, the rush to the wagons stopped.

"There will be enough for everyone," he yelled. "Take your time and enjoy this gift from the city of Brest." With that action, the movement toward the wagons, relentless as it was, slowed and became much more orderly.

That first night about half of the men slept out in the elements. The tents, created for four hundred men were just too small for twice that many. By the next morning John Paul and his captains had resolved to take about two hundred of the sickest men on board the ships to give them shelter and food. Another two hundred were accommodated in Brest staying in the homes of willing families.

Word was sent out to the surrounding towns asking for donations of food, water, clothing, shoes, and virtually everything needed to accommodate eight hundred men who had been deprived of the necessities of life for several years.

Taking care of the men became the top priority of John Paul and his fleet, but it wasn't his primary concern. He worried about when the ships from the Colonies would arrive to take them home. He asked Major Whitlow to inventory the supplies that arrived from the surrounding towns and to anticipate what their needs would be until the ships arrived.

John Paul calculated in his mind how long it would take for the *Ranger* to sail down the coast of France and Spain to catch the western flow of the wind off the coast of Africa, to sail across the Atlantic and up to Philadelphia. He was sure ships would be sent to take the former prisoners off his hands. He was not sure how long it would take. His best estimate was around three and a half months. At best, that would bring the relief ships to port in Brest around the middle of August.

Major Whitlow's evaluation of food and supplies for the men was that they could make it to around the first of August before their food supplies ran out. Just as bad, the weather along the English Channel would begin to turn cold and wet by the first of September. If the ships did not arrive by mid-August, they would have another four hundred men who needed shelter since the make-shift tents would not serve as adequate shelter from the blowing rain and cold of the region that came with the fall of the year.

John Paul's fears proved to be unfounded. A small fleet of ships arrived just outside of the Brest Inlet at the end of the first week of August. The look-out in the crow's nest of the *Bonhomme Richard* reported five ships in the fleet. John Paul immediately sent out a long boat to share information with the leader of the rescue ships, telling them about the depth of the entry and suggesting that if they needed more than about fifteen feet in depth they should stay outside of the inlet.

While this was going on, John Paul surveyed the five ships, several of which he recognized. In the group were the *Alfred, Hornet*, and *Cabot*. All three had been with them on their first raid at Nassau at the beginning of the war. The latter had been John Burroughs Hopkins's ship that was almost destroyed in the confrontation at Montack Bay a few years back. The two other ships, the *Columbus* and the *Machias Liberty*, he had not seen before. None were larger than the *Bonhomme Richard*. So, all could enter the bay without problems sailing over the underwater rock wall that had been their protection from the British fleet.

As soon as all the ships were in the bay and somewhat protected from the ocean, which was getting more storm-tossed by the day, John Paul called a meeting of the captains at the city hall in Brest.

When all had gathered John Paul sat down at the end of the large table in the room and addressed the group. "Gentlemen, I cannot tell you how pleased we are to see you. It has been a long summer and your presence here to take our guests home is a most welcome occasion," John Paul said. "I'm not sure you could hear the yells from the men in the camp when your ships were sighted but we certainly heard it both on shipboard and in the city of Brest."

There were nods and smiles all around.

"We have managed food and water for our guests, but they have been on short rations for the past week because we were running low on supplies," John Paul continued. "We did not know when you would arrive."

Captain Ruble of the *Alfred* spoke up. "Chairman Hopkins gave us new orders as soon as the *Ranger* arrived. We made plans to head east right away." Three of our ships were in port in the Chesapeake at the time but we had to wait for the *Columbus* and the *Liberty* to arrive. In the meantime, we gathered provisions for the voyage. We knew time was very important because of the potential of storms on the Atlantic."

"You are right about that," said John Paul. "For that reason, we have to get you out of here as soon as possible. You will have the wind with you down the coast of France and Spain and should catch the westerly flow at the Canary Islands before heading across the Atlantic. I would suggest that you plan to spend a few days in the Canaries before heading west. You will find a good port there at Las Palmas. It is almost hurricane season and you should be able to get word on developing storms off the coast of Africa in port there. If storms are developing, you should stay in port. The Canaries are a very nice place to spend a couple of weeks. If not, the men will be anxious to get home and I would suggest you make sail as soon as you are clear to the Caribbean."

John Paul looked around the table and asked, "Do you have questions for me?"

"Yes sir, Captain Jones, if I may," said Captain Williams of the *Hornet*. "We came loaded with provisions and the room for men on at least two of our ships are extremely limited. Mine is one and the other is the *Cabot*." We will have to be very careful with the distribution of men on the five ships, with the largest group assigned to the *Columbus* and the *Alfred*. They may need to take some of the provisions we have in our hold for any extra men assigned."

"Of course, you are right," replied John Paul. "I will ask Major Whitlow who heads up our marines to evaluate each of the ships to see how the men should be distributed. Is there anything else?"

Hearing nothing else from the captains, John Paul adjourned the meeting but asked the captains of the three ships in his small fleet to stay for a few minutes.

When the room had cleared out, he said, "Gentlemen, as soon as we can get these rescue ships back on the ocean we have an immediate task before us." Everyone was looking at John Paul expectantly, wondering what other duties were being assigned to them.

"We have to move our home base from Brest, and the sooner the better," said John Paul. I want each of you to give some thought as to where we should move. I think it is only a matter of time before the British Army and Navy will be back with a major force to shut us into our sanctuary and capture us. This time we may not be so lucky. I would expect them to bring smaller ships that can enter the inlet. Earlier, we surprised and captured their men when they tried to come at us by land. The next time I expect them to bring a much larger force and they won't be surprised in the dead of night as they were this time."

"What are you thinking, Captain Jones?" asked Captain Briggs of the *Vengeance*.

"I am not sure. Perhaps the easiest and safest move is to retreat down the west coast of France and find a home farther away from the English Channel," John Paul responded. "However, we have developed good relationships on the northern coast of France and could even consider Rotterdam in the Netherlands. Give it some thought, and we will talk about this when we meet again after we get the rescue ships headed toward home."

As they were leaving, John Burroughs approached him. "John Paul, we have run into an interesting problem regarding the men we are taking care of in the tents west of Brest," he said. "Several of the men you captured with the British soldiers hid when you sent the troops back to the British ships. They are still here with our prisoners. What do you want done with them?"

John paused for a few seconds before responding. "How many of them are there?"

"I think the number is at least fifteen or so. I can check to be exact," he replied.

"Bring them to me," said John Paul.

While he waited for John Burroughs to return with the men, John Paul went across to the tavern and sat alone at a table with a tankard of ale. He was lost in his thoughts when young Jim found him there.

"Captain Hopkins is back with the British men, Captain Jones," he said.

When John Paul stood in front of the former prisoners in the city hall, he walked around looking at the men. All looked to be in pretty good shape considering the uncertainty they had lived with over the past several weeks.

Finally, John Paul asked, "Why are you still here?"

One man stood to face him. "Captain Jones," he said, "the men here asked me to speak for them. We want to go to America."

With that comment several of the men voiced their approval of what their spokesman had said. John Paul noted that all eyes were on him. None of the men had their heads down, looking at the floor as he might have expected. They were following his every move. They were very much aware that their future was riding on what he said and what he would do with them when this meeting was over.

John Paul pointed to a rather large man toward the back of the group. "Tell me about yourself and why you want to go to America," he said.

The man stood up and responded, "Most of us joined the British Navy from prison cells, your excellency. I, for one, was a debtor who couldn't pay my debts. I was doing just fine in my business, a general store, when the Crown decided to take my goods without paying me for them. I had to forfeit on several obligations. One of the men I owed money to called the law, and I ended up in prison. They sentenced me to stay there until I could pay. But how could I pay what I owed if I couldn't work and the Crown took what it wanted and left me with nothing? My choice was to join the marines or to stay in jail. I had no desire to do either but I had no choice. In England I will never be free and even if I am, who is to keep the Crown from coming and taking everything from me again? I want to go to America to be free again."

Several of the other men were nodding their heads before he finished. John Paul pointed at another man and asked him to tell about himself and why he wanted to go to America.

The man stood and told of having a farm that bordered the lands of a lord. That lord wanted his land and went to the King and asked that the land be added to his grant. "When the King agreed to do it, I was left with nothing," he said. "I protested, and they put me in jail. My children were given to other families to raise and my wife was given to another. I want to start over in America."

One by one, the stories told by the men were similar.

Finally, John Paul looked at John Burroughs and said, "I see no reason why these men shouldn't be included as a part of the prisoner exchange and taken to America. Arrange with Major Whitlow for them to have whatever they need and to be given equal treatment with our men."

"I will talk with Major Whitlow and it will be as you say," said John Burroughs. "I do envision some difficulty for these men when they get to our country. They have no connections there, no family, no jobs, and no familiarity with the country. They are coming like the Pilgrims did over a hundred years ago, but without their friends and family around them to provide support."

John Paul pondered those words for a few minutes and then responded. "John Burroughs, ask someone skilled in writing, may I ask you to prepare a letter of introduction to Stephen Hopkins, chairman of the Continental Navy Committee, for each of these men. Say in the letter who they are and ask Chairman Hopkins to do whatever is necessary to smooth the way for them in the weeks and months after they arrive in the Colonies. They will need jobs and a place to stay until they get on their feet in their new home. Prepare the letters for my signature."

A week later, the rescue ships were gone, and it was time for the captains to meet again.

"Gentlemen, we are now clear of our obligation to our prisoners-of-war and it is time to consider where we are going to move our home base," John Paul said. "Do you have thoughts for consideration?"

Two hands went up immediately. Captain Briggs of the Vengence said, "I think your original idea of moving further down the coast of France is a good one. We have several possible choices such as Quimper and Lorient, but I think the best choice is Vannes."

Captain Landais of the *Alliance* was immediately on his feet. "I think captain Briggs is right that those places are possible for us. However, I think that Le Havre up on the northern coast of France is the best choice for us. It gives us easy access to the English Channel and has an inlet as large as Brest Bay. We have been there several times with prizes and they love us there."

"Le Havre does have good possibilities for us," said Captain Briggs. "But, as easy as our access would be for getting into the English Channel, that is how easy it would be for the British Navy to find us there. Vannes is farther away, and it would take an additional half day to get into the Channel, but it is not only safer in terms of their finding us, it is also easier to defend because of the narrowness of the entry into the bay there. A British man-of-war would never make it past our shore batteries if they were placed on the north and south points there."

"I think both of you have done your homework on these suggestions," said John Paul. "My inclination is to move farther down the French coast away from the Channel. But much depends on the willingness of the city leadership of Le Havre or Vannes to accept us. It shouldn't take more than a week for us to investigate both cities and see how they would react to our coming. So, I am sending Captain Hopkins up to Le Havre to look over the inlet there and to meet with the city leadership. Captain Briggs, would you go down to Vannes and talk to the people there? We will await the return of both captains with their report on the viability of our moving our home base to one or the other of those cities. If we get rejected at both we will look further. Gentlemen, move with dispatch. We do not have much time before we can expect the British to return in force."

Within a week, Captains Briggs and Hopkins had returned with reports on what they saw at the two prospective sites for their new home base. Both were adequate for their needs, and offered positive opportunities. In short, either would work. It was left up to John Paul to make the final decision. In the end he opted for Vannes, further down the coast of France. The major advantage over Le Havre was the reception received by Captain Briggs by the mayor of Vannes. They had heard of the major contribution that the small fleet under Captain John Paul Jones had made to the commerce in the region, primarily enjoyed by the city of Brest and the surrounding area. They envisioned the same boom in business for their area if the Americans came to their small port. At the same time, being further removed from the English Channel, they felt more insulated from the prospect of a British attack.

John Paul talked with the captains about communicating with their men about the move. He said that, of course, they would need to tell the men who had been staying in a variety of different locations in Brest for the past two years. They couldn't just leave one morning and not return that night. Instead, he told the captains to caution the men about telling the people of Brest where they were going. He felt sure that if the people knew they were just south at Vannes, the British would learn about it before too much time had passed.

It was not a surprise that Captain Landais was at his door shortly after the captain's meeting about their proposed move. The look on his face spoke volumes. He was unhappy and not likely to be placated by anything John Paul might say.

"You are making a big mistake with moving us to Vannes," said Captain Landais. "It does not offer us the possibilities of Le Havre."

"I'm sorry you feel that way, captain," responded John Paul.

"I recommended Le Havre. It is home country for me and I know it well, "Landais said. "I am the Frenchman here. I know my country better than any of the others. You should listen to me when I recommend something to you that relates to French soil."

"I do understand what you are saying and certainly took that into consideration when I made my decision," said John Paul. "The final bit of information that swayed me to choose Vannes was the relative safety of distance from the British and the geography of the entry to the inlet there. It will be much easier to defend if the British find us again. They may be able to blockade us at Vannes but there is no way they can land an army and take us by land as they might at both Brest and Le Havre."

"You, sir, will live to regret this decision," said Captain Landais angrily.

With those words he turned and walked out, slamming the door behind him. John Paul had learned to take the words of the French captain as so much bluster. He had said things in the past that questioned both the authority and the wisdom of John Paul. He hoped the flare-up would get it out of his system and the man would simply comply with his captain's directives as he had done in the past. John Paul did his best to put it out of his mind.

The meeting with the mayor was exactly as he had anticipated. As was usual John Paul used a translator in his conversation with the mayor. He objected to their leaving. Not only did the city lose the prospect of additional economic stimulus from prizes brought home by the Americans but he, personally, stood to lose a considerable amount of income that had accrued because of his acting as an agent for the sale of merchandise from the prizes. Twice the mayor asked where they were going but John Paul declined to give him that information. In the end, the mayor left the room in a huff, but before John Paul could leave the chair he was sitting in, the mayor was back.

The translator had left the room so the mayor and John Paul were left to converse in broken French. As much as John Paul could make out the mayor came back with a very different attitude. He said, "Captain Jones, I'm afraid I have let my emotions rule my manners. Before you came, we were a sleepy little hamlet and with your going we may well return to our previous state. That isn't all bad. I want you to know that you're coming here was the best thing that could have happened to us. Our relationship has been mutually beneficial, and we are pleased you chose us. Wherever you go, we wish you well. Be assured that we will remember you and your men fondly." At least, that is what he hoped the mayor said.

John Paul stood and replied, "Mister Mayor." With that word he came to attention and saluted the surprised mayor. He then said, "We too shall miss your hospitality. Your people have bent over backwards to accommodate us. We shall not forget you or the warm feeling we have for your city and your people." John Paul wasn't sure the mayor had understood what he had said but he knew he would not mistake the salute. Whether he understood or not, the mayor smiled, bowed deeply, then turned and left.

Through the afternoon there seemed to be a long list of details that John Paul had to take care of. He sent Jim home to help Aimee prepare for the move. There were some tears from the children as they said goodbye to the friends they had made in the neighborhood and at the school. They were sorry to leave but there was also the excitement of again being on the move. John Paul was careful not to tell the children where they were going so as not to reveal their new location at Vannes. Secrecy was a vital part of maintaining their safety and, despite their desire to know, he did not tell them. Before dawn the next morning the small American fleet had left the bay and headed south for Vannes.

THE PROVIDENCE GAZETTE

PROVIDENCE, Rhode Island, September 1, 1779. The U.S. Army under the leadership of General George Washington is preparing to return to winter quarters at Morristown, New Jersey.

The war has now dragged on for four years and our soldiers are growing restless with the continual pressures of both deprivation and fighting.

By contrast, the war at sea continues to move forward successfully. Reports of various successes come almost weekly. Captain John Paul Jones continues to have great success in the waters around the British Isles.

Congress has authorized John Adams to negotiate peace with Great Britain. He has moved from his location in Paris to London under the protection of the Crown to see if common ground can be found for a peaceful resolution to the disagreements between the British government and the U.S. Congress.

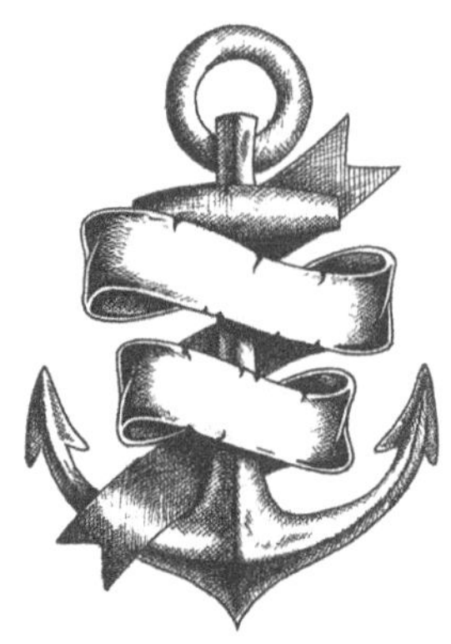

CHAPTER 28
ONCE MORE INTO THE BREECH
SEPTEMBER 10, 1779

The experience of moving into Vannes was very much like the one when the small fleet arrived at Brest. John Paul set about creating the gun placements at the north and south points above the entry to the inlet. He sent his sailing master out to see what might need to be done to block British man-of-war ships from entering the bay and was pleased to find that the entry would need no underwater wall to limit the passage of the larger ships. It stood naturally at around sixteen feet, a full six feet less than necessary to admit a man-of-war.

The gun placements on the points would be more effective than those they had created to command the entry at Brest. The mouth of the bay was much smaller so cannons on either side could command the entire entry. That meant that a ship of any size attempting to enter the inlet could be caught in a crossfire.

John Paul and Aimee went shopping for a new home in Vannes. It wasn't long before they found a good location just at the edge of the small city. Aimee and the children had mastered French so relating to their new surroundings was much easier than the transition into Brest. They knew there was a school for the children and, though the shopping district was smaller than they were used to, it was adequate for their needs. It wasn't long before things on the home front were back to normal.

With Aimee and the children taken care of and satisfied with their preparations to protect themselves from attack, John Paul began to turn his attention to their reason for being in France in the first place. He wanted to make one more trip into the English Channel before the fall weather made such a venture impossible.

He talked at length with the other captains about what their best possibilities were for a last venture into the English Channel. Finally, a plan took shape. They decided to take the small fleet north up the French coast into the Channel and sail east along the northern coast of France until they reached Calais. They would then turn back west and sail down the middle of the Channel within sight of the British coast. There were four ships in their fleet and it was his plan to send two ships after any British merchant ship they sighted. The goal was to intimidate any prospective prize to the point where the target would give up without a fight.

It took about a week to ready the small fleet for the last trip of the year. When the ships and crews were ready, they exited their new surroundings and headed into the Atlantic. Unlike their home base in Brest, they couldn't leave the inlet and just turn north into the English Channel. They had to sail southwest toward Belle-Ile, passing Quiberon Island to their north, before they could turn northwest toward the English Channel. Winds, as usual, were in their face when they turned north which forced them to have to tack back and forth to make progress. It took them a full day of sailing before they reached the southwest edge of the English Channel. When they turned east around the point north of Brest, John Paul breathed a sigh of relief as he watched the sails fill with the strong winds coming out of the west.

From that point on progress was fast. They moved along the northern coast of France at about sixteen knots and passed the Channel Islands, Jersey and Guernsey, on the starboard side. Within a half day John Paul could see Le Havre to the south. He had a moment of emotion when he saw the entrance to the Le Havre bay in the distance, remembering the confrontation he had had with Captain Landais over whether they should move their base there. Landais had been right in one part of his argument:

If they were based in Le Havre, they would have had much quicker access to the English Channel than from Vannes. It had taken them a full three days to get this far and they still had two days to go before they reached Calais. But John Burroughs's estimation when he went to look over the bay at Le Havre was that it would be easier for the British fleet to find them there. He also knew that the bay at :e Havre would be more problematical to defend than the bay at Vannes, which had a smaller entry. That, in the end, is what had persuaded John Paul to choose Vannes.

His plan was to sail to Calais, anchor overnight just off the coast in the Channel, and to turn back west into the Channel the next morning. If there were merchant ships about, he anticipated they would be moving between the British ports of Dover, Portsmouth, and Plymouth on the morning tide. Sailing west, the winds would force slow going but the same was true with the merchant ships. Their small fleet would have better luck capturing ships headed west than those sailing with the wind toward London.

It was late in the day on September 19th when the sailing master pulled up the sails and dropped anchor just off the coast of France near Calais. John Paul looked off the fantail at the other three ships in his small fleet. The *Bonhomme Richard* was significantly larger than the other three ships. But, together, they would be a commanding force as viewed by any merchant ship they decided to target. They might even be a match for a man-of-war if they could work together in a face-off with one of those lions of the sea. Their cannons together were a match for the fire power of most of the ships in the British fleet. Individually, if confronted by a man-of-war, they would need to get the wind behind them and run for the French coast. Together, they could stand and fight. It was a good feeling, one that John Paul had not had since he began fighting this war in the waters around the British Isles.

When dawn broke John Paul ordered the signal flags up, which indicated to the other ships a movement back westward down the middle of the Channel. They began their slow and laborious effort to sail into the wind, which was strong out of the west in their faces. After several efforts to tack back and forth, the sailing master appeared at John Paul's side. His report was not good.

"Captain Jones, sir," he said, "we knew that traveling west down the Channel was going to be a slow process with the prevailing winds hitting us in the face, but they are stronger than usual for this time in the morning and that does not bode well for later in the day when they usually pick up. I think it is likely that by mid-afternoon we will be losing ground to the wind with every tack."

"What do you suggest?" asked John Paul.

"We may want to anchor here for a day or two and wait for better winds," he said. "Another option is to forget sailing back down the Channel into the wind and go north around the eastern coast of England. We would be sailing with the prevailing winds coming from our portside but with England to our west it would knock off most of the strength of the wind. It may not be what you planned, but we could circle England and Scotland and come back down through the Irish Sea. The winds up north will be colder but our previous experiences there are that they are not as sharp as they are through the Channel."

John Paul ordered the ships to weigh anchor and draw up their sails. His plan was to see if he could wait out the winds and begin sailing west the next day. They waited all day and into the night. The winds persisted and even grew stronger in the afternoon, thought they seemed to ease a bit as the sun set.

The next morning, he awoke to even stronger winds than the day before. It was as if old Neptune was deciding his course for him. He couldn't sail back down the English Channel so the only route open to him was up the eastern coast of England, just at the edge of the North Sea.

It was the morning of September 20th when he decided to take the northern route. He knew it would be much colder going north and instead of being in the Channel for five or six days as he had planned, he was now deciding to extend their last excursion of the year well into the month of October. Considering the normal weather in the North Sea and the English Channel in October, he knew he was taking a risk. Still, it was not a greater risk than sitting in the middle of the English Channel less than a half day's sail from London. The British had their primary base for their man-of-war fleet just west of London at Queenbourgh. If they discovered the Americans' presence here and sent ships to intercept them, John Paul's fleet had no place to run except into the wind through the English Channel. That risk of discovery in this location was much greater than the weather problems he might face in the North Sea or coming back south through the Irish Sea.

John Paul ordered the signal flags to relay their change of plans. He turned the *Bonhomme Richard* east and watched the winds fill the sails as he headed toward the east exit from the English Channel. He noted with pleasure that the other three ships seemed to understand his signal flags and followed the *Bonhomme Richard* back past Calais and along the coast of the Netherlands toward Rotterdam.

When they neared the city of Flushing on the northern coast of the Netherlands, they turned due north into the North Sea. He felt safe in the open sea but kept a look-out in the crow's nest with orders to report the top of any sail he sighted in any direction.

By the second day they were well north of London and John Paul was feeling much safer than earlier. They had not sighted any merchant ships, but he anticipated it would be just a matter of time. They were in a major shipping lane headed into London and he felt it was unlikely he would meet any opposition this far north that his small fleet couldn't handle.

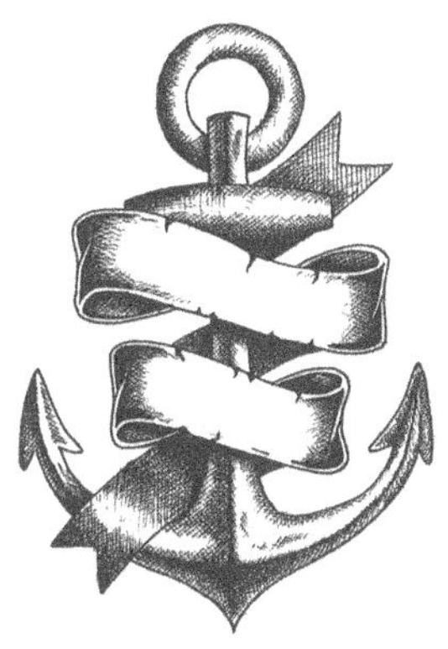

CHAPTER 29

THE BONHOMME RICHARD AND THE SERAPIS

"THE GREATEST SEA BATTLE IN AMERICAN HISTORY"

SEPTEMBER 23, 1779

The British ship *Serapis* was about ten miles to the starboard side when it was sighted by John Paul Jones, Captain of the Continental Navy ship *Bonhomme Richard*. It was mid-afternoon on September 23, 1779. A soft wind was blowing from the southwest and the tide was coming in toward Flamborough Head on England's east coast. The two ships had sighted each other at almost the same time and both changed course to move closer to assess the relative fire power of the other. With the light wind blowing from the southwest, it would take the two ships almost four hours to meet face-to-face there at the edge of the North Sea.

Looking through his spyglass, Jones saw a convoy of more than seventy merchant ships in the distance that the British warship was protecting. He could only speculate about the cargoes they were carrying, but imagined ship-building materials, commodities such as tea and coffee, and textiles that had made Scandinavian countries famous. *Serapis* approached the *Bonhomme Richard* with confidence. After all, it was a man-of-war ship built for battle. It was bigger, stronger, and faster than the *Richard*, which was a converted merchant ship, re-fitted by the French for the Continental Navy barely a year ago.

Three years into the war for independence, no Continental Navy ship had ever captured a British man-of-war. In fact, the Navy Committee of the Continental Congress and the admiral of the fledgling navy had directed captains to stay away from direct confrontation with the larger and stronger British ships. John Paul Jones was not one to worry about orders from his land-based leadership. They did not know of the challenges faced day-to-day by the ships of the American navy, nor of their capability. Jones saw an opportunity to make history and ordered his men to prepare for battle.

By late afternoon, about an hour before the two ships would come together, the upper deck of the *Bonhomme Richard* was cleared for action: bulkheads, chairs, tables, bunks, any objects that were portable and wooden, were stowed in the hold. Anything loose enough to fly around when a cannon ball exploded was taken below to reduce the possibility of injury to men who would be on the deck manning the sails and the rudder. Sand was sprinkled on the decks to keep them from becoming slick with blood. On the lower decks, below the cannons, the carpenters who served also as surgeons put out containers to hold amputated arms and legs should such become necessary.

Marines who were along for the fight when the ships were joined and the fighting became hand-to-hand combat were below decks until called into action. They were clustered at the gangways leading to the upper deck, both to be ready to join the fight and to keep sailors who were needed on deck to handle the sails from disappearing to the safety of the lower decks.

As *Serapis* approached, a second, smaller ship that had previously been hidden from sight emerged from the other side of the man-of-war. It was the *Duchess of Scarborough*. Jones recognized it as a sloop-of-war. The *Serapis* was a heavy frigate, one of the man-of-war class that usually carried sixty or more cannons. The sloop might carry just sixteen cannons. Yet Jones was not alone either. The *Bonhomme Richard* was the leader of the small fleet of four ships and it carried forty cannons; the *Alliance*, thirty-six cannons; the *Pallas*, thirty-two cannons; and the *Vengeance*, twelve.

Compared to the two British ships, Captain Jones knew he had more fire power. The four American ships could encircle the larger British ship and hammer away at her from all sides, or they could run along in line of battle, discharging broadside after broadside before the enemy could reload.

The flags they used as the communication device between ships were ready to be hoisted on the fantail's short mast, just below the country flag. As was his custom when sailing in British waters, John Paul was flying the British flag from the smaller aft mast. Below the country flag, different colored flags carried different messages. The *Bonhomme Richard* now hoisted three flags, two blue and one that was blue-and-yellow. To an experienced navy captain that meant "Form a line of battle."

Jones could envision history in the making. It was as if he had been sailing the oceans for the past decade just for this moment in time. He climbed to the fantail of his ship and looked back at the three ships that were following. To his dismay, he realized they were not responding to the orders of his flags.

The other captains either couldn't see his flags or they were just ignoring his commands. He watched as the *Alliance* turned to starboard and moved away. Captain Landais, as usual, seemed to have ideas of his own and apparently had decided not to support John Paul in his confrontation with a man-of-war. The *Pallas*, under Captain John Burroughs Hopkins, sailed slowly forward without changing course. The smallest of the ships, the *Vengeance*, hung back.

At just that moment, the larger British warship swung open her gun ports and showed her teeth. She was a two-decker with a full contingent of heavy cannons, at least sixty of them on the side of the ship they could see. They were ready for combat.

In his mind, John Paul knew the *Bonhomme Richard* was on its own. He had two choices: turn and run or stand and fight. Jones was furious, yet his face was an impassive mask. He would have Landais's head when this was over. By now he was accustomed to gross insubordination. The French captain had disagreed with him on almost every order he had given since he joined the American fleet at Brest. Early on, Jones had almost come to sword's points with him. Despite the fury he felt, he had no time to think about Landais now. If he was on his own, he would make the best of it. Dealing with Landais would come later.

Jones channeled his emotions into the battle to come. Major Whitlow was standing by on the bridge awaiting his orders for the marines. "Major Whitlow," he said, "order your sharpshooters to the masts."

Major Whitlow was gone almost before he finished speaking. Within a few seconds he heard the movement of men from the entry to the hold and marines began to climb up the rope ladders to the platforms next to the top spars of the two main masts.

John Paul ordered his helmsman to bring his ship about so that he was headed directly toward the front of the *Serapis* where the only gun was a small swivel single shot. He wanted to avoid a broadside from the larger frigate. They moved ever closer to conflict, ever closer to victory or death, ever closer to history.

Had they been on a pleasure cruise they would not have missed the full moon just coming up over the horizon. The early evening wind was slight and in their favor and the water was still, almost glassy.

He turned to his first mate and, in a much softer voice than one might have expected, said, "Sir, order the drummers to beat to quarters." The first mate moved quickly over to the edge of the bridge and shouted down the order to the drummers who had taken their place on the main deck just below the bridge. They immediately began to beat their drums.

Shortly, men emerged from below decks and ran to battle stations. Sailors climbed the two main masts to be ready at a moment's notice to change the sails to gain every advantage the wind could provide. The marines took their places on deck, most lying down next to the side rails where they could not be seen by the sailors on the British ship.

John Paul looked up at the riggings and then down at the men on deck below him. He knew that many of them would be dead before nightfall. Others would be injured and suffering below decks where the surgeons worked. He had no time to lament what was to come, he had a battle to fight and it was coming at him faster than he thought possible in such a light wind.

In the distance, Jones could see the merchant vessels putting up sails and turning toward the shallower waters of the shoreline where larger vessels couldn't follow. Jones turned his attention back to the Serapis, which was looming ever closer to his port side.

The battle plan had been drilled into the men and he was sure each officer knew exactly what to do. The *Richard* had six eighteen-pounders that were on the lower deck. Their target was the hull of the Serapis. He had twenty-eight twelve-pounders, fourteen on each side. They were to fire directly into the enemy's rigging to disable her. On the quarterdeck, he had six nine-pounders which were also to be aimed at the sails and rigging. He knew to win the battle he had to slow down the larger ship which was, nevertheless, more maneuverable than his refitted merchantman.

Much of the refitting of the *Bonhomme Richard* when the ship arrived at Brest had been in preparation for just such a situation. Just as he had done with the *Ranger*, Jones had built a platform high up in the rigging where his marksmen could stand and fire down on the seamen on the deck of the Serapis. Major Whitlow had split up the marines between the rigging above decks and the poop deck, which was built higher than the deck of the Serapis. If the *Serapis* put men in the riggings above decks, they were to be the first targets of the marines. He did not want to lose his men to their muskets before he could board the enemy ship.

By then, John Paul had become resolved that he would be in this fight alone against two British ships, but a movement behind him and off to his left caught his eye. It was the *Pallas*, which had maneuvered to confront the *Duchess of Scarborough*. He felt an immediate rush of emotion. He never doubted he could count on his friend, John Burroughs Hopkins, captain of the *Pallas*. Now, John Paul could put his full focus on the Serapis.

For the first time, John Paul heard the voice of Captain Pearson of the Serapis. He was on the bullhorn. He said, "This is His Majesty's ship, Serapis. What ship is that?" John Paul waited as long as possible before responding, edging closer to the rail with his own bullhorn. He handed it to his sailing master, instructing him to reply, "The *Princess Royal.*" The *Princess Royal* was a British East Indies merchantman that was about the same size as the *Bonhomme Richard.* A few seconds passed, but the ruse did not work at all. They knew the *Richard* wasn't the *Princess Royal.* He saw the gun ports lift and knew the *Serapis* was going to turn her starboard side to him and position for a broadside.

Captain Jones ordered his false British colors taken down and his newly minted stars and stripes run up the aft mast. At just that instant, a nervous marine from up on the *Bonhomme Richard's* rigging fired his musket. It sounded like a thunder clap. Instantly, both ships erupted, firing their broadsides at once.

More than forty cannons and scores of small arms fired at nearly the same instant. The air was filled with the sounds of splintered wood and the cries of the wounded. Smoke was everywhere so much that John Paul no longer had a clear view of the deck of the Serapis. They were at very close quarters and almost every shot hit its target.

One of *Bonhomme Richard's* eighteen-pounders exploded in a blinding flash. It tore a hole in the side of the ship just above the waterline. On the lower deck where the cannons were positioned, men lay dead. Those who weren't dead were badly burned. The eighteen-pounders were utterly useless. Without his eighteen-pounders, John Paul knew that the only chance he had was to get close to the *Serapis* and board her. His strategy from that point on was to ram the *Serapis* and to use his grappling hooks to pull them together so he could send his marines across to the enemy ship.

Most of the men on board the *Bonhomme Richard* had been with John Paul on the *Ranger*, some as far back as the *Katy*. All were experienced hand-to-hand fighters and well trained in boarding tactics. Jones ordered the helmsman to maneuver his crippled ship directly toward the Serapis. The sailing master of the *Serapis* realized the *Richard's* strategy too late and could not get the British ship away. The two ships came together and their riggings became entangled. John Paul's crew had its grappling hooks ready threw them across to the deck of the British ship. They held, locking the warring ships together.

Teams of men pulled on the ropes attached to the grappling hooks to pull the two ships closer together. When they were close enough, the gangplanks were extended to allow the marines to board the Serapis. The British seamen were ready for them lining up near the rail on the other side of the deck. As the *Richard's* marines crossed onto the deck of the Serapis, they were met with volley fire which drove them back across the gangplanks. They gathered and charged again before the *Serapis* marines could reload and the two fighting units tumbled into hand-to-hand fighting on the main deck of the British ship. From this point on fighting was with knives, cutlasses, and an occasional pistol. Men rolled on the deck in mortal combat. As soon as one was dispatched, another took his place.

Just at this point, the *Alliance* under Captain Landais pulled up close to the two entangled ships and fired at both, doing more damage to the *Richard* than the Serapis. Locked together as they were, neither ship could use her cannons on the other, but the cannon balls from the *Alliance* did considerable damage. Jones lost two of his officers to the broadside and the hull of the *Richard* was fractured on the starboard side by the *Alliance* cannonballs. Furious, Jones signaled Captain Landais to stop firing, but the *Alliance's* cannons continued to hammer away for several minutes before she sailed away.

For the next thirty minutes the fighting was all hand-to-hand on the deck of the Serapis. The *Richard's* sharp shooters were focused on the bridge of the British ship where the officers were stationed. One by one they picked off the leadership of the Serapis. It appeared that the battle was swinging to the Americans when John Paul saw the *Alliance* again approaching from the port side.

When she was alongside the *Richard,* she fired another broadside into both ships. It flashed into John Paul's consciousness that Captain Landais was trying to sink the *Bonhomme Richard.* The *Alliance* fired another broadside into the starboard side of the *Richard* . John Paul could feel the jolt of the cannon balls landing on the side of the *Richard* and marveled that the ship could still be afloat after such devastation. The *Alliance* pulled away to a safe distance from the battle that continued man-to-man on the deck of the Serapis.

Despite the heavy damage to both ships, the men fought on into the night. Twice during the battle, Captain Pearson of the *Serapis* called out to Captain Jones, asking if he was ready to strike his colors. It was during the second of these exchanges that Jones responded defiantly, "I will not strike my colors, I have not yet begun to fight!" The fight went on until almost midnight.

Finally, one of the officers of the *Serapis* struck the British flag. His captain and several of the officers were either dead or badly injured. Most of their fighting men were wounded and he was sure his ship was damaged so badly it was doubtful it could make it back to port.

Six fighting ships were still afloat there in the North Sea off the east coast of England when the sounds of battle went quiet. The decks of both ships were on fire and, by firelight, all could see the Stars and Strips flying over both the *Serapis* and the *Richard*. Jones and the *Bonhomme Richard* had achieved an improbable victory over one of England's finest warships.

John Paul felt the elation of victory but his heart sank as he looked at the devastation all around him. The bodies of the dead and dying littered the deck of the *Bonhomme Richard* and from what he could see it was even worse on the main deck of the Serapis. He looked across the main deck and saw a familiar figure coming toward him. He had to look twice to be sure but it was young Jim. His face was black with soot and his shirt was in tatters. He had been below decks working as a powder boy to help keep the cannons firing.

"Are you all right, Captain Jones," he asked.

John Paul leaned back against the rail, suddenly overcome by weariness. He hardly recognized his own voice when he responded to Jim. "I'm O.K., just having trouble breathing with all this smoke. Jim, we have to get these fires out," he said. "The *Serapis* has struck her colors. We need every able bodied man to fight the fires."

"I'll take care of it," Jim responded. He turned and surveyed the deck for men who could take on that task. Everyone he saw were either wounded or collapsed on the deck from exhaustion. Jim couldn't tell who was injured and who was not.

Jim saw one of the drums that had been used to "beat to quarters," before the fighting began. He picked it up and, with one of the drumsticks he found on the deck, he began to beat on it. He hoped that whoever heard the sound would come toward it. He was not disappointed. Several men appeared, some from below decks on the *Richard* and others from the Serapis.

"The fires, men, the fires," he yelled. "We have to get he fires out."

The men moved quickly to douse the flames, using buckets kept along the rails with ropes attached to dip water from over the side of the ship. The buckets were the extent of the firefighting equipment on the ship but they did their job. Soon the fires on the *Richard* were out and men moved across the gangplanks to the *Serapis* to douse the fires there as well.

Finally, it was over. The fighting had stopped, the fires were out, and both ships were still afloat. John Paul was back on his feet and he climbed up the ladder to the bridge. The *Richard* was listing badly to the port side. And water was pouring in where the *Alliance* had opened her hull with the broadsides.

Celebrating a victory would have to wait. Both ships were badly damaged and they had to make the best of an impossible situation. A quick walk around told John Paul what he suspected. The *Richard* was worse off than the Serapis.

Jones transferred his command to the wounded British ship and sent his sailing master and boatswain back to attempt to salvage the *Bonhomme Richard*. Three crews of men worked diligently for two days trying to repair the badly damaged ship. Unfortunately, she was too far gone. She sank lower and lower in the water as the crew watched from the deck of the Serapis. On the third day, they watched their flag ship sink into the depths of the North Sea.

Captain John Paul Jones and his crew sailed slowly into the wind toward a friendly port in the Netherlands. The sailing master and the carpenter spent much of the next week making emergency repairs to the *Serapis* to keep it afloat. They had all the members of their small fleet as well as the two British prizes, the *Serapis* and The *Duchess of Scarborough*, with them when they made the port at Texel, north of Amsterdam. Then, it was time to celebrate.

THE PROVIDENCE GAZETTE

PROVIDENCE, Rhode Island, October 15, 1779. Word has just come to us of two great victories in Europe.

Captain John Paul Jones and the marines assigned to his fleet of four ships captured four hundred British troops who were attempting to attack the U.S. home base in France. The British troops were exchanged for eight hundred American POWs. Those former British prisoners are even now on board U.S. ships and headed home across the Atlantic.

The Bonhomme Richard, the ship given to the U.S. by France for use by Captain John Paul Jones, met a British man-of-war, the Separis, in one on one combat in the North Sea off of the British coast. The U.S. ship won a great victory.

The Bonhomme Richard eventually sank due to heavy damage but Captain Jones and his crew brought two prizes, the Separis and the Duchess of Scarbrough, to port in the Netherlands.

Captain John Paul Jones, long known for his seamanship and daring is nearing legendary status in the United States where his exploits against the British have been chronicled in the news media over and over in past years.

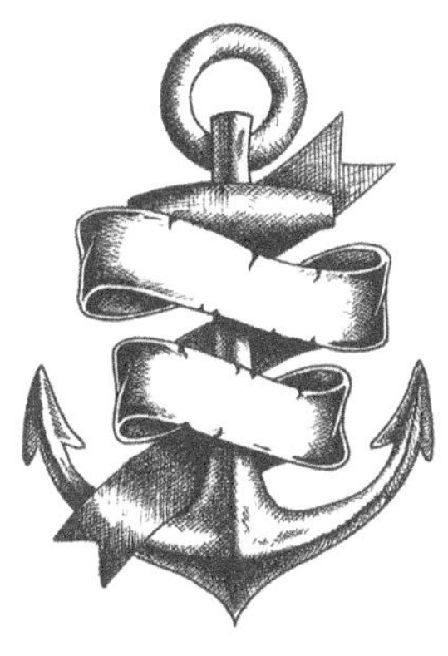

CHAPTER 30

EPILOGUE

SEPTEMBER, 1783

The Revolutionary War was officially declared by the Continental Congress in 1776 with publication of the Declaration of Independence. However, it actually began with the incident of The *Boston* Massacre (1770). It continued with The *Gaspee* Affair (1772), and the *Boston* Tea Party, (1773). By 1775 hostilities had broken out around *Boston*, and the Massachusetts Militia was in open conflict with British troops stationed throughout that colony. Many of the noteworthy battles preserved by history, such as the Battle of Bunker Hill (June, 1775) and the battles of Lexington and Concord (April, 1775) were fought before war was officially declared.

With the declaration of war, the Continental Congress, in reality, had little hope of victory over what was acknowledged to be the strongest military force in the world, the British Army and Navy. Great Britain had kept its army on colonial shores for decades and it constituted a well-organized and well-drilled machine. Having fought wars in Europe with both France and Spain over the preceding century, the British soldiers and sailors were well-equipped and seasoned. The British Navy had dominated the oceans for almost two hundred years, from the time of the Spanish

Armada in 1588. How could the thirteen Colonies mount an army or a navy capable of facing such a foe?

George Washington, ever the realist, acknowledged early in the conflict that his best strategy was, "to sink Britain under the disgrace and expense of slogging through to victory." Simply surviving against the vaunted British military was a brilliant feat involving countless small, and large-scale, operations to keep the enemy off balance, under strain and demoralized. In the end, it could be said that the Continental Army and Navy won by not losing.

Several of the Colonies had militia units in the 1770s which could be nationalized and placed under the leadership of General Washington. However, with the navy the Continental Congress was starting from absolute zero. They had no navy and no money to create one. Certainly, they did not have the capability to create a navy that could stand and fight the British man-of-war class ships that could carry more than one hundred cannons and marine units on board for hand-to-hand fighting.

The war for independence from Great Britain continued for another four years following the great victory of the *Bonhomme Richard* over the Serapis. Much could be written about what transpired in both the land and sea wars that raged both in the American and in British waters in Europe. However, this story is about the beginnings of the U.S. Navy. By the end of 1779, the Americans had begun to establish dominance over the oceans by sheer numbers, both along the coast of the U.S. and in the English Channel.

The Continental Congress commissioned seven ships in 1775 and an additional six in 1776. It was hampered by a limited taxing authority, and the money needed to build and support ships simply was not available. All the officially commissioned ships were smaller, capable of raiding merchant and supply ships but not of facing man-of-war class ships that dominated the British Navy.

No one knows how many privateer ships were committed to the conflict, but the port of *Providence*, Rhode Island alone launched sixty-five privateer ships between April and November of 1776. One cannot take the statistics from one county in the Colonies and generalize it to the entire population; however, in Essex County just thirty miles north of *Boston*, more than one hundred privateers were registered. A close estimate of the number of total ships involved in the conflict at the end of the war in 1783 would include twenty-seven ships commissioned by the Continental Congress and more than two thousand privateers. The bulk of these were sailing the waters along the coast of the Colonies and into the Caribbean. However, a number were sent to Europe to raid the waters around the British Isles. Thus, most of the Continental Navy was made up of privateers, or so they were called by the American government. The British still referred to them as pirates.

The profound effect of the combined official and privateer navy on the war was undeniable. While no official statistics were kept on the total number of British ships sunk or captured during the war, the commissioned ships reported 198 British prizes. The unofficial listing of ships captured and sold as prizes or refitted for Continental Navy purposes by the privateers numbered more than 2,300.

No such number of lost ships is listed among the documents of Great Britain during the period of history between 1775 and 1783. However, London newspapers were full of war reports. One article reported that 565 British ships were lost from January to December in 1779. Another said that "Insurance rates on shipments across the Channel have skyrocketed with unverified sightings of privateers infesting waters from Ireland to Spain." A third indicated that British businessmen were ready to throw in the towel, urging the King to negotiate, "an accommodation with the colonists upon commercial principles."

Additionally, newspapers mocked "the clerks of the Admiralty" for their rosy war reports. They highlighted demeaning incidents such as military transports surrendering to privateers armed with wooden guns, and a Royal Navy frigate accidentally discharging a celebratory holiday volley into an adjacent troop ship.

All reports from the Colonies were not positive either. It will never be known how many seamen lost their lives sailing on privateer ships. An indication of loses may be projected, however, by statistics out of the coastal towns of Essex County, thirty miles north of *Boston*. Newbury Port listed twenty-two vessels destroyed and a thousand men dead. Nearby

Salem lost almost a third of its fifty-four registered privateers. Gloucester lost all twenty-four of theirs. Two-thirds of Beverly men between the ages of eighteen and sixty were taken captive off privateer vessels by the British. A third of the women in Marblehead were widowed, and more than a fourth of the children were fatherless. The postwar populations of adult males in that one county at the end of the war was roughly half what it had been before the war. Hundreds of tax abatements were granted to families whose breadwinners were listed as "missing at sea," "taken and sick," "died abroad," "in the hands of the British," or "long absent, and assumed to be lost."

The beginning of the U.S. Navy and, in fact, the Revolutionary War is a story of success against impossible odds and what has come to be called "Yankee ingenuity." Above all, it is a story of the indomitable spirit of every person to be free and to be willing to make the ultimate sacrifice to achieve that freedom for themselves and others. For that noble reason, thousands lost their lives in the war for independence from Great Britain. They were fighting for their independence and, ultimately, for freedom. There is no greater motivation.

THE PROVIDENCE GAZETTE

PROVIDENCE, Rhode Island, September 30, 1783. A frontier militia force captured a loyalist force of more than 1,000 at Kings Mountain, North Carolina. (October, 1780.)

The Battle of Cowpens in South Carolina was a decisive victory for the United States. (January, 1781)

The French fleet met the British in the seas off of Yorktown, VA and were victorious. Additional French troops arrived to support General Washington and the U.S. Army. (September, 1781)

In the most decisive battle of the revolution, Cornwallis and his 8000 British troops surrendered at Yorktown. (October, 1781)

The House of Commons voted against waging further war in America: Officials are empowered to seek peace negotiations. (February, 1782)

The Netherlands has recognized the independence of the United States. (April, 1782)

A skirmish in South Carolina was the last wartime engagement on the Eastern Seaboard. (August, 1782)

A committee was appointed by the U.S. Congress to enter peace negotiations with the British. The committee is made up of John Jay, Benjamin Franklin, John Adams, Thomas Jefferson, and Henry Laurens. (August, 1782)

A preliminary peace treaty was signed in Paris. (November, 1782)

Great Britain officially declared an end to hostilities in America. (February, 1783)

The main part of the Continental Army and Navy have disbanded. (June, 1783)

All British troops are out of the United States. (November, 1783)

The Treaty of Paris was signed, formally ending the war. The treaty is ratified by Congress. (January 1784)

THE HISTORY BEHIND
PIRATES, PRIVATEERS AND THE U.S. NAVY

Pirates, Privateers, and the U.S. Navy is a fiction-based-on-fact story about what would eventually become the U.S. Navy at the start of the Revolutionary War. The causes of the Revolutionary War began when the British created the Navigation Acts in the 1600s. Over the years, the Navigation Acts created more and more restrictive trade policies for the Colonies. As the thirteen Colonies entered the 1770s, those policies would not allow trade with France, Spain, or any European country other than Great Britain. Even importation of such commodities as sugar and molasses from the Caribbean were restricted. In the opinion of many, those policies were strangling business and commerce in the Colonies from Rhode Island to Georgia.

The overriding ambition of the Continental Congress when it began meeting in 1774 was to keep the Colonies out of war with Great Britain. As the mid-1770s, arrived it became obvious that war could not be avoided. Open hostilities began as early as 1769 with the *Boston* Massacre, followed by The *Gaspee* Affair in 1772 and the *Boston* Tea Party in 1773, and they did not end until 1783, fourteen years later.

When open warfare finally broke out in 1775, the Continental Congress faced an almost impossible dilemma. They had no authority to form an army or navy, no taxing authority, and no centralized government to direct the activities of the thirteen Colonies.

Here is some historical background that will enrich your understanding of the book.

CONCERNS OF THE CONTINENTAL CONGRESS HEADED INTO THE WAR

When the First Continental Congress met in Philadelphia in the fall of 1774, its intent was to meet for a month or two to deal with the issues of the Navigation Acts. Instead, the members were still meeting more than a year later. At the beginning there were no planned discussions among the membership regarding breaking away from the British Empire. Most judged themselves to be loyal subjects of the King. That began to change in the spring of 1775.

A few firebrands in the Congress, including John Adams, Benjamin Franklin, and John Hancock, had begun to visualize a free country in North America. Most, however, were not at all disposed to consider such a thing. As the weeks and months passed it became more and more obvious that the differences between the Colonies and Great Britain could not be resolved peacefully and more radical action was necessary. Still, despite open warfare going on around *Boston*, many held onto the notion that peace with their mother nation was the only sane route. They did not have an army or navy and they did not have the money or the authority to raise either. Fighting a war with Great Britain seemed an impossibility.

Though many of the Colonies had militias formed under the direction of state legislatures and governors, there was no unified command. In the minds of many, the creation of a navy was simply not feasible. Even if the Colonies could face off with the powerful British Army, there was no possibility at all of challenging the domination of the British on the oceans.

GUNS: MUSKETS AND RIFLES IN THE REVOLUTIONARY WAR

The standard gun carried by American frontiersmen in the mid-1700s was a musket. It fired one round pellet at a time with approximately thirty seconds required to reload to fire a second time. The round pellet left the muzzle of the barrel like a knuckle-ball and the possibility of hitting a target at fifty yards was no better than one in three. It could move to the right, left, or down as much as twenty inches. For that reason, what was called "the Napoleon Formation," was used in battles. Troops would mass side by side, march toward each other until they were about fifty yards apart, and then fire their muskets in tandem. That tactic was designed to get multiple lead balls flying at the enemy so that if you didn't hit what you were aiming at, perhaps the person on your right or left would. Napoleon Bonaparte had perfected this tactic in France and it was thought to be the only practical approach to dealing with the inaccuracies of the musket.

Rifles had been experimented with in the early 1700s by putting grooves, called rifling, in the barrel of a musket that stabilized the bullet when it left the muzzle of the musket. Rifling increased the accuracy of the weapon considerably, but by the beginning of the Revolutionary War the rifle still was not in wide use.

During the Revolutionary War, a few of British soldiers were equipped with rifles. They became the sharpshooters of the British Army. However, the colonists did not have such weapons and it was another ninety years, around the time of the U.S. Civil War, when such weaponry began to become universal.

TRAVEL BACK AND FORTH ACROSS THE ATLANTIC

References were made several times in the book to trips made back and forth across the Atlantic. A trip from *Boston* or *Providence* in America to France generally took approximately five weeks. Traveling directly from France to America, however, might take as much as two and half to three months. The difference in timing was caused by the prevailing winds in the north Atlantic, which were west to east.

By contrast, a more efficient route from east to west across the Atlantic was to travel down the coast of France and Spain to the northern coast of Africa. There, the prevailing winds were east to west.

The winds north of the equator run in a circular path as per the drawing below. It was possible to travel from *Providence*, Rhode Island to France, down the coast of Europe to northern Africa, across the ocean to the Caribbean, up the coast of the U.S. back to Rhode Island, and always have the wind at your back.

When Christopher *Columbus* made his trip to the new world, he was using the southern winds that took him to the Caribbean. The Pilgrims, in contrast, did not know the pattern of the winds in the northern Atlantic and thus ended up with a full three-month journey from Plymouth, England to Massachusetts, sailing straight into the wind virtually the entire time.

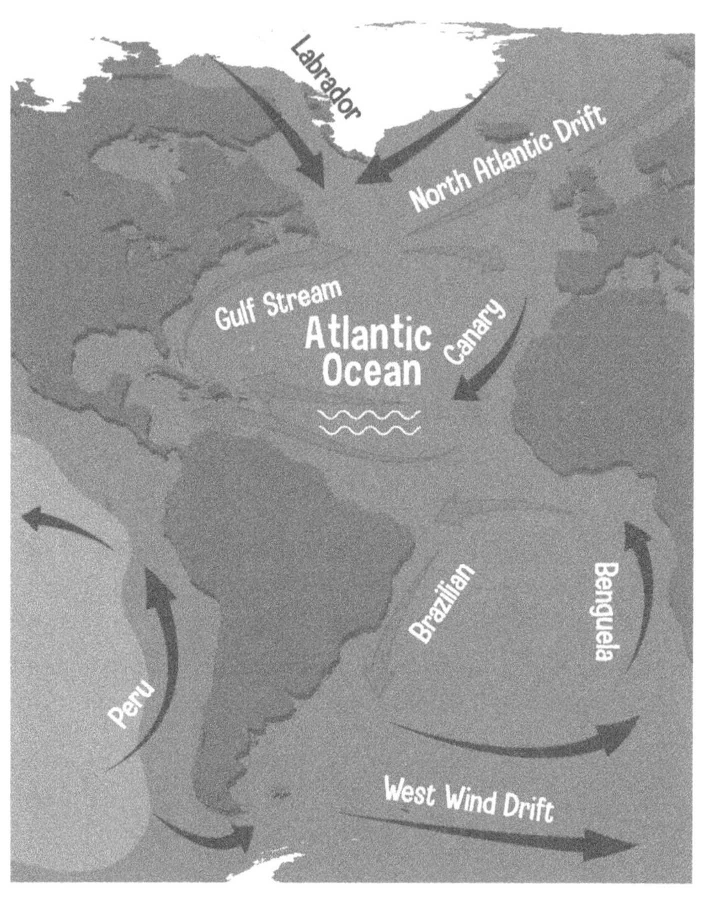

Labrador
North Atlantic Drift
Gulf Stream
Atlantic Ocean
Canary
Brazilian
Benguela
Peru
West Wind Drift

TWO HUNDRED YEARS OF BRITISH SEA POWER FROM 1580 TO 1780

Several countries dominated the oceans from 1400 to 1580. Portugal was the first to venture out around the globe. Vasco da Gama discovered a sea route to India and Ferdinand Magellan circumnavigated the globe. Spain followed the Portuguese in dominance, and names like Hernan Cortes, Juan Ponce de Leon, Hernando de Soto, and Francisco de Coronado became synonymous with exploration and conquest.

When Henry VIII became King of England in 1509, he realized that the safety and security of his small island country was dependent on having a strong navy. Other countries were larger than England and could put more soldiers on the battlefield but if he could control the English Channel with sea power he would always be secure. This lesson was not lost on his daughter, Queen Elizabeth I, who continued to invest in ships and exploration during her forty-four-year reign that began in 1558.

England and Spain were sea power rivals until the advent of the Spanish Armada in 1588. Spain sent an armada of 135 ships north into the English Channel with a plan to transport the Spanish Army, then the most powerful in Europe, from the Netherlands to invade England. An out-numbered fleet of British ships met them in the Channel and with superior seamanship left the armada decimated. That ended Spain's plans for conquering England and it left England as the dominant power on the oceans. With that dominance, England created the British Empire over the next centuries, which eventually stretched all around the globe. At one time, it was accurately said that the sun never set on the British Empire.

At the beginning of the American Revolution, England still had the most dominant navy in the world. The American Colonies challenged them with nothing but gall and Yankee ingenuity. At the end of the war in 1783, the United States still did not have a navy that could challenge England but as someone said at the time, "*Hornet*s are dangerous not because one could sting you but because, despite their size, they attack by the hundreds."

THE BENEFITS OF USING PRIVATEERS FOR COUNTERING BRITISH STRENGTH ON THE OCEANS

Perhaps no decision of the Continental Congress was more successful or had more far-reaching effects than that of deciding to include privateers in the effort to neutralize the effects of the all-powerful British Navy.

The primary issue in winning the land war was how best to cut off the supply lines of the British Army in the Colonies. The second most important issue was finding the necessary supplies to support General Washington and his troops as they fought the land war against the strongest army in the world. The answer to both questions was to incorporate the pirates/privateers into the fledgling Continental Navy. By the time the revolution began, privateers had been roaming the oceans for a hundred years. Incorporating them into legitimate navy efforts to cut supply lines and bring the confiscated materials to General Washington for use by his troops was a stroke of genius. That genius could be credited to the Navy Committee of the Congress under the leadership of Stephen Hopkins of Rhode Island.

Many heard the laudatory comments about Washington and his troops following the victory at Yorktown that effectively ended the war. Few, however, heard Washington thank the French for the seven thousand troops that accompanied his army during the siege of Yorktown nor his appreciation of the cannons, powder, and other war materials he used on the British during that battle. He later said that more than half of the instruments of war he used during the last years of the war could have had a "Made in England" tag. All were supplied by the privateers who had continually raided British supply ships from 1775 through the end of the war in 1783.

PRISONERS-OF-WAR OF THE BRITISH AND THE COLONIES

Prisoners of war are a major concern in any war. That was especially so in the Revolutionary War. It was a time when germs were not yet known, when cleanliness was not valued, when doctors still practiced in the backs of barber shops and when surgeons on ships doubled as carpenters. Because of issues related to sanitation, lack of clean drinking water, and lack of food, more soldiers actually died in prisoner of war camps than on the battlefield.

Early in the war, the British had POW camps in England near the port cities of Plymouth, Portsmouth, Brighton, and Weymouth. As the war progressed it was too costly and time- consuming for them to take prisoners to England so they created POW camps in New Brunswick and Nova Scotia. By the time the war entered the 1780s they had prisons on ships in most American harbors. Overcrowding and impossible conditions made being housed on one of the prison ships almost a death sentence.

The Americans had POW camps as well, at least one in each of the Colonies. Conditions were little better in those camps than in those run by the British.

RESOLUTION OF THE SITUATION WITH THE FRENCH CAPTAIN FOLLOWING THE BATTLE BETWEEN THE *BONHOMME RICHARD* AND THE *SERAPIS*

In the story of the battle between the *Bonhomme Richard* and the Serapis, it was hard to miss the rank insubordination of Captain Pierre Landais of the *Alliance*. He had clashed with his commanding officer several times before that crucial battle. When the battle started he was directed to form a battle line, which he refused to do. When the battle was underway and the two ships were joined, he brought his ship up and fired broadsides at both the *Serapis* and the *Bonhomme Richard*, killing men on the *Richard* and heavily damaging it in the process. Observers stated that it was obvious Captain Landais was trying to sink the *Richard*. He probably caused more damage on the American ship than the Serapis. In the end the *Bonhomme Richard* was lost.

Following that battle, ten days passed before the *Serapis* limped into port in the Netherlands. On the day following, Captain Jones wrote letters of condemnation regarding the behavior of Captain Landais to both the Continental Navy leadership in America and Ambassador Benjamin Franklin in Paris.

Both later acknowledged the insubordination of Captain Landais. However, Ambassador Franklin had just negotiated a major new agreement with the French that would provide both troops and ships to help with the war effort. He was not pleased with the prospect of court marshalling the only ship's captain loaned by the French to the Americans for the war effort.

Captain Landais left France and returned the *Alliance* to the Colonies, continuing to serve in one capacity or another through the rest of the war. He retired from the navy in the United States and lived out his days there. He never paid for his indiscretions in any visible way.

One footnote of irony related to the fact that when the navy was dissolved in 1883 the last ship still registered as a U.S. Navy ship was the *Alliance*. They finally put her up for auction. She brought $26,000 into the treasury of the U.S. in 1884.

WHAT WAS THE FUTUE OF THE U.S. NAVY FOLLOWING THE REVOLUTINARY WAR?

After such a successful start, it would be satisfying to say that the navy continued to provide necessary service to the country until today. However, that is not the case. When the war was over and General Washington recommended that the army be disbanded, Congress also disbanded the navy. Thus, the country did not have a navy again until the War of 1812 some thirty years later.

Many of the seamen went back to merchant transport and others returned to their practice of piracy on the high seas. Captains of ships like John Burroughs Hopkins and John Paul Jones continued to serve on ships as the following sections detail.

WHAT HAPPENED TO JOHN PAUL JONES FOLLOWING THE REVOLUTIONARY WAR?

John Paul Jones was a wealthy man at the end of the Revolutionary War. Yet, as was obvious during his service to the Colonies, he was not motivated by money. He was well known, nearly legendary, in both the new United States and Europe. When the Continental Navy was disbanded he was still in France. The French government offered him a commission in the French Navy with the rank of Rear Admiral, a status he coveted but never received in the Continental Navy. He took it and served in the French Navy from 1783 to 1785.

In 1785, he was offered a commission in the Russian Navy with the rank of admiral and placed in charge of developing this navy. He served in Russia for seven years until being felled by a serious fever. He was brought back to Paris for medical attention and died there at the age of 48. In the early 20th century, his body was brought back to the U.S. and he is buried on the grounds of the U.S. Naval Academy in Annapolis, Maryland.

There is no mention of Aimee, John Paul's second wife, or any of his children in subsequent history. Before he died, John Paul Jones wrote a last will which left all of his belongings, money, and holdings to his two sisters in Scotland and their children. It is likely that his second wife, Aimee, and his two sons, Daniel and Moses, preceded him in death sometime between 1779 and 1795. If that were not the case, it is hard to imagine that one or all would not have been mentioned in his will.

In the fictional will at the beginning of this book there were bequests for all three of Aimee's children. However, that was not the case in the John Paul Jones will that is recorded in history. Alas, none of Aimee's children existed in history. All were fictional characters. History tells us that John Paul had two sons with his first wife, Keziah. His second wife is mentioned in history as well, but she did not bring any children to this new marriage. Jim, the cabin boy, was introduced into the story to create a link between John Paul and Aimee which resulted in the second marriage of both. An inventive writer might have brought the two together in the market where he met Keziah. But creating this new relationship through young Jim seemed more colorful and interesting and it fit well into the rest of the story.

WHAT HAPPENED AFTER THE WAR TO THE THREE HOPKINS MEN WHO WERE KEY FIGURES IN THE ESTABLISHMENT OF THE CONTINENTAL NAVY?

Stephen, Esek, and John Burroughs Hopkins all survived the war and continued to make contributions to the newly formed United States for several years following the war.

Stephen Hopkins had served as governor of Rhode Island, and then chief justice of the Supreme Court of Rhode Island prior to becoming a member of the Continental Congress. He was a signer of the Declaration of Independence and was one of the most respected members of that first Congress. John Adams wrote in his memoirs about Stephen Hopkins "… that he had wit, humor, anecdotes, and knowledge of science and letters. He had read Greek, Roman, and British history and could quote poets Pope, Thompson, and Milton." Stephen Hopkins died shortly after the war ended in 1785 at the age of 78.

Esek Hopkins had been captain of a ship for many years before the war and in 1775 he became commander of all military forces in Rhode Island. When the Continental Navy was formed, the Continental Congress appointed him commander in chief, or commodore. He was the architect of the first great success of the navy when he guided his small fleet to Nassau and took several shiploads of much-needed war material and supplies from a British supply depot. These were carried back to General George Washington. Following the war, he returned to Rhode Island where he was much appreciated. He served for several years as an Rhode Island state assemblyman. He died in 1803 at the age of 83.

John Burroughs Hopkins, who maintained a presence throughout the book, was a captain in the Continental Navy from its beginning. When the war was over, he became involved in scientific studies for the U.S. government. One such study was measuring the size of the planet Venus and another was studying the size of our solar system. Evidently, these studies were done on shipboard in the middle of the Atlantic where there was no light pollution. He was written up several times in the *Providence Journal* for his contributions to furthering the scientific knowledge of that time. He died in 1796 at the age of 54.

WHAT HAPPENED TO BENEDICT ARNOLD, THE COLONIAL GENERAL WHO BECAME A TRAITOR TO THE CAUSE OF FREEDOM FROM GREAT BRITAIN?

Perhaps the greatest shock and disappointment to General George Washington during the war came with the revelation in 1780 that General Benedict Arnold was a traitor. He had been one of the most trusted generals in the Continental Army and had won great victories in both Connecticut and upstate New York. General Washington gave him command of the garrison at West Point, New York and the responsibility to control the Hudson River. General Washington judged the Hudson to be the most vulnerable path to New York City and holding the river was the key to keeping the British from splitting New England from the rest of the Colonies. General Arnold conspired to give West Point and control of the Hudson to the British and the plot was discovered. Arnold escaped to Canada, accepted a commission in the British army and fought against his former country through the rest of the war. At the conclusion of the war Arnold lived out his years in England. His name has become synonymous with the word "traitor," in the history of the United States.

GEORGE WASHINGTON'S VISIT TO CONGRESS FOLLOWING THE WAR

When the war was over in 1883, General George Washington visited Congress to officially resign his commission. During his time in front of that august body, he had a number of things to say that were noteworthy.

General Washington recommended that Congress dissolve the army and the navy. He was not a proponent of having a standing military. He further recommended that each state have a militia that could be called up if the country should again be threatened with war.

Washington believed it was possible that the British might again attack the U.S. from their base in Canada, just a short boat ride up the Hudson River. While he didn't say it during this meeting with Congress, he later recommended that a law be passed that required every man over the age of eighteen to own a musket. It was his belief that if an attack came every man needed to be armed and ready to help defend the country. Congress did not follow his recommendation on this issue. However, Washington's feelings on this subject probably influenced the thinking of George Mason when he wrote the first ten Amendments to the Constitution, including the Second Amendment that speaks to gun ownership. That amendment was approved by Congress shortly after Washington became president.

A VISIT TO THE NEWSEUM IN WASHINGTON, D.C.

During a recent trip to Washington, D.C., this writer paid a visit to the Newseum. It is the only museum dedicated to free expression and the five freedoms of the First Amendment: religion, speech, press, assembly, and petition. The displays use newspapers from across the country to tell the story of our nation from before the Revolutionary War to today. The visit came during the time when I was writing this book. Because of my research, you will understand that I was most interested in the display of newspapers that related to the Revolutionary War. I found that display on the second floor.

An entire wall was devoted to the conduct of the war from the Battle of Bunker Hill all the way through to the capture of Yorktown. The newspapers displayed along the wall gave a blow-by-blow description of every land battle, ever victory, and every defeat. Even the wall above the newspapers had paintings that depicted many of the highlights of the war.

What was missing, however, was any mention at all of sea battles. There was no presentation of the contributions of the Continental Navy, nothing about the battle of the *Bonhomme Richard* and the Serapis, nothing at all about Captain John Paul Jones, the so-called father of the U.S. Navy. A follow-up call was made to the Newseum to be sure the history of the U.S. Navy is not there and this writer didn't just miss it on his visit to that museum. They said that, "Indeed, they were not included. The navy battles might have just been left on the cutting room floor. You can't include everything."

Why no mention of the contributions of the privateers, of the Navy Committee of the Continental Congress, of the thousands who died fighting the overpowering British Navy? Why not, indeed? That question is worth asking on my next visit there or, perhaps, on the visits of readers of this book. The history of the U.S. Navy is rich with bravery, dedication, commitment, and sacrifice. It deserves a place in every museum where it is appropriate.

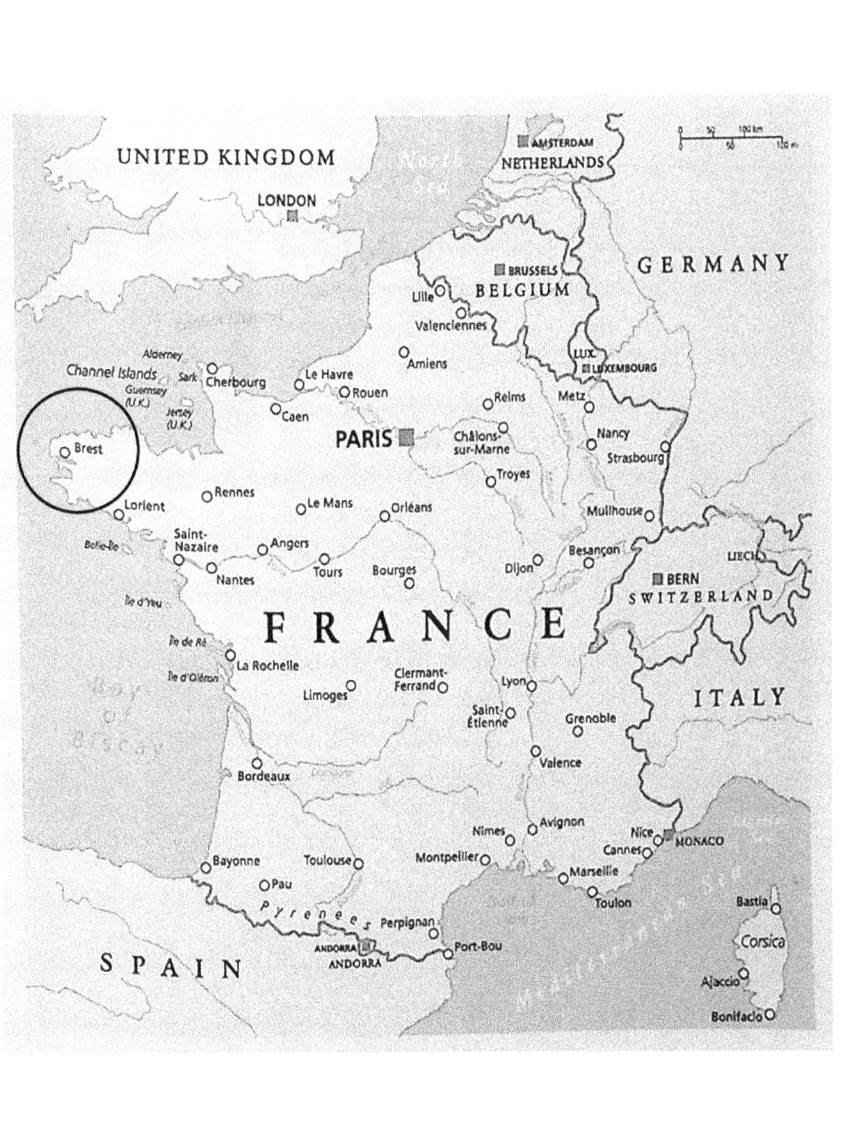

UNITED KINGDOM
NORTH SEA
LONDON
AMSTERDAM
NETHERLANDS
BRUSSELS
BELGIUM
GERMANY
Lille
Valenciennes
LUX.
LUXEMBOURG
Amiens
Alderney
Channel Islands
Sark
Cherbourg
Le Havre
Rouen
Reims
Metz
Guernsey
(U.K.)
Jersey
(U.K.)
Caen
PARIS
Châlons-
sur-Marne
Nancy
Strasbourg
Brest
Troyes
Mulhouse
Rennes
Le Mans
Orléans
Lorient
Besançon
LIECH.
Belle-Île
Saint-
Nazaire
Angers
Dijon
BERN
Nantes
Tours
Bourges
SWITZERLAND
Île d'Yeu
FRANCE
Île de Ré
La Rochelle
Île d'Oléron
Limoges
Clermont-
Ferrand
Lyon
ITALY
Bay
of
Biscay
Saint-
Étienne
Grenoble
Valence
Bordeaux
Nîmes
Avignon
Nice
MONACO
Bayonne
Toulouse
Montpellier
Cannes
Marseille
Bastia
Pau
Toulon
Pyrenees
Perpignan
Corsica
SPAIN
ANDORRA
ANDORRA
Port-Bou
Mediterranean Sea
Ajaccio
Bonifacio
0   50   100 km
0   50   100 mi

ABOUT THE AUTHOR

Born in Missouri and a long-time resident of South Carolina, Dr. Mark L. Hopkins is a mid-westerner by birth and a southerner by choice. He holds three degrees from Missouri universities. He taught history for several years and is past president of four colleges, one each in the states of Iowa, Illinois, South Carolina, and California. Dr. Hopkins writes a weekly column that is syndicated by GateHouse Media and is regularly published across thirty-seven states and more than five hundred newspapers. Dr. Hopkins's wife, Ruth, is a professional artist. They have three grown children and six grandchildren.

Writing this book was a labor of love for Dr. Hopkins. As one can tell from the history of the birth of the U.S. Navy, the Hopkins family played a role almost from the first with Stephen Hopkins chairing the first Navy Committee of the Continental Congress and Esek Hopkins being the first commodore of the naval forces. The 20th and 21st century Hopkins family also contributed to U.S. Naval history with an uncle, a brother, and nephew all serving during both war and peacetime.

Dr. Hopkins is semi-retired in South Carolina. He continues to write on a daily basis and often speaks to civic clubs and seniors' groups. Dr. Hopkins can be reached by E-mail at Marklhopkins@yahoo.com .